Patrick Neate lives and works in London, often at the same time. His first novel *Musungu Jim and the Great Chief Tuloko*, is also published by Penguin.

Twelve Bar Blues

PATRICK NEATE

VIKING

VIKING

Published by the Penguin Group
Penguin Books Ltd, 80 Strand, London WC2R 0RL, England
Penguin Putnam Inc., 375 Hudson Street, New York, New York 10014, USA
Penguin Books Australia Ltd, Ringwood, Victoria, Australia
Penguin Books Canada Ltd, 10 Alcorn Avenue, Toronto, Ontario, Canada M4V 3B2
Penguin Books India (P) Ltd, 11 Community Centre, Panchsheel Park, New Delhi – 110 017, India
Penguin Books (NZ) Ltd, Cnr Rosedale and Airborne Roads, Albany, Auckland, New Zealand
Penguin Books (South Africa) (Pty) Ltd, 24 Sturdee Avenue, Rosebank 2196 South Africa

Penguin Books Ltd, Registered Offices: 80 Strand, London WC2R 0RL, England

www.penguin.com

First published 2001
4

Filmset in Monotype Dante 12/14.75pt

Printed in Great Britain by Clays Ltd, St Ives plc

A CIP catalogue record for this book is available from the British Library

ISBN 0–670–887919

For Grandy, who told me all thirty-four stories.

Acknowledgements

I am gratefully indebted to the material of several writers, musicians and prostitutes which inspired and informed *Twelve Bar Blues*, in particular Louis Armstrong, Papa Celestin, Mervyn Cooke, Elizabeth, Harmony, Billie Holiday, Jodie, David Lan, Jess Mowry, Toni Morrison, Michael Ondaatje, Rakim, John Reader, Lewis Taylor and Huw Thomas. A special acknowledgement is due to Laurence Bergreen for his remarkable biography of Louis Armstrong.

Thanks too to Mum and Dad, Polly, Vince, Mills, Jane, Caroline, Christah Kalulu, Guru Bain, Tin Rowley, Count Drewfus, Frenchie, Miss M, Ils Da Phat Serb and, most of all, KZ for their low-end theory of love, support and criticism.

Twelve bar blues: the most common harmonic progression in all jazz; it comprises twelve bars based on tonic (I), dominant (V) and subdominant (IV) harmonies, organized in the simple pattern: I–I–I–I–IV–IV–I–I–V–V–I–I.

Contents

BOOK TWO: Dissonance

Prelude: Because stories are forgotten

(Maponda, Zambawi, Africa. 1790)

Some four generations after a great chief called Tuloko first led his people north to settle on the flood plains of the place they named the Land of the Moon, two boys grew up side by side in Maponda, a satellite village of the Zimindo kingdom of Tuloko's descendants. Their names were Zike (pronounced 'Zee-kay', a word that means 'sacrificial gift' in modern Zamba) and Mutela (a name whose meaning has long been lost to the past). They were born just two days apart and the celebrations of their births in the village of Maponda overlapped, so that their fathers were doubly drunk and their mothers received double the advice from the *makadzi* who spoke with their gums and packed dung on to their faces to protect their skin from the sun. Mutela was born to Musape, the most powerful *zakulu* in the whole of the Land of the Moon. Zike was Taurai the farmer's son. Taurai was known for little other than his capacity to sleep for days at a time.

Since the two boys were born the same sex at the same time in the same place, they shared at least as many destinies as they kept to themselves. With few other children in the village, one such destiny was that they grew up as best friends. They swam together in the water hole and picked leeches off each other from the places that were hard to reach. They shot *boka* birds from the treetops with makeshift slings. They engaged in vicious stone fights with the troops of baboons that lived in the hills to the west of the village. Sometimes, Zike allowed Mutela to use him as a guinea pig on which to practise his magic. He knew this was safe because his friend was yet to suffer the *zakulu* illness that would confirm his status as a witchdoctor.

'When I open my eyes,' Mutela would say, 'you will have become a *zveko* ant.' Or, 'I have given you the gift of flight, Zike! Spread your arms and touch the clouds!' Then, when Zike remained an earthbound little boy, Mutela would become very frustrated and blame him for his lack of cooperation. But Zike didn't mind. He just laughed.

As a child, the times that Zike liked best were the evenings, when all the chores of the day were completed and he and Mutela could lie back by the water hole and watch Father Sun disappear behind the western hills. Then Zike would sing with a voice as soothing as running water; both songs that his mother had taught him and other wordless songs that he made up on the spot. Sometimes Mutela would join in but he was cursed with a voice like an angry jackal's and he knew it. But he didn't mind. He just closed his eyes and bathed in his friend's melodies.

As Zike got older and his voice strengthened, the people of Maponda came to listen to him sing. 'Zike,' the *mboko* would say, 'your singing is a blessing on our village.'

By the time the two boys were thirteen years old, Musape was beginning to worry about Mutela. If his son did not experience the *zakulu* illness soon, he would never follow in his footsteps.

However, unbeknownst to Musape, Mutela had already begun to find the *zakulu* skills coming to him day by day. Although he was yet to suffer the *zakulu* illness, he could perform successful curses, minor healings and make a butterfly hatch from its chrysalis with a twitch of his will. Mutela told no one about his new-found talents. Not even his best friend. Where previously he had been all too keen to practise his unsuccessful magic, now that it came to him so easily he found it both embarrassing and a little scary. Perhaps if Musape had known of his son's special gifts from the outset, he would have been able to teach him about their responsible use. But that is not what happened.

Soon Zike's reputation as a singer spread way beyond the boundaries of Maponda village and people came from far and wide to listen to him. Sometimes *mbira* players and drummers would join in and the party would carry on late into the night. On one occasion Musekiwa, the chief of Zimindo himself, came to find out what all the fuss was about. That evening Zike sang better than ever before. Because he sang not to the chief but to his daughter, Vacheke, who had accompanied him. She was a slim girl of about Zike's age with eyes like an eclipse of the moon and her bare breasts were perfectly rounded in the spring of puberty. She wore a head-dress of sea shells that must have been imported from many miles away and, as she listened to Zike sing, the corners of her mouth flickered delightfully and she bowed her head in an effort to retain her composure.

When Zike had finished singing and the assembled crowd had dispersed and the night was returned to the music of the crickets, he told Mutela that his stomach felt twisted and sick.

'That is because you are in love, my friend,' Mutela said quietly.

'Don't be so ridiculous!'

'You are in love with Vacheke,' Mutela said. 'And so am I.'

After that Vacheke came to listen to Zike every night. She sat opposite him on the far side of the water hole and their eyes met above the dark pool, floating on the breath of his melodies. But they never spoke because they did not know how to have such intimate conversations. As they stared at one another, Mutela watched the pair of them and the smallest seed of jealousy fell into his fertile heart. Within a day, this seed had sprouted roots and within a week the roots gripped his heart so tightly that he felt he could hardly breathe.

One morning, before Father Sun had stirred, Mutela went to his friend's kraal and stole his favourite staff, a thick branch of baobab wood that Zike had lovingly carved into a sturdy shaft. Mutela took the staff to the water hole and he drew a circle in the dust and he embedded the staff up to its middle. Then he found a sharp flint and cut a notch into the wood, one handspan from its top, and he said the ritual words that only the *zakulu* know (for they learn them in their dreams). Mutela returned the staff to Zike's kraal before the family woke up.

That night the people gathered early to hear Zike sing. They jostled on the banks of the water hole to get the best view but they made room for Vacheke because she was the chief of Zimindo's daughter. Zike stood at the water's edge and he could see the stars of the sky reflected in Vacheke's eyes reflected in the rippling water. She is the whole world to me, he thought.

He drew a deep breath. He planned to sing the beautiful love song that his mother had taught him when he nursed at her breast. But the first note caught in the back of his throat and emerged from his lips as a strangulated whine. Zike's face heated in shame. He tried to correct the note but his voice would not obey him, for Mutela's spell was working its magic. The crowd began to laugh. Zike's panicked eyes stared at Vacheke but her head was bowed and her hands covered her face. Zike felt a fearful sorrow well in his chest and the bitter taste of bile rise in his throat. He turned and ran into the night, the catcalls of the people chasing him on his way.

As Zike's audience dispersed, Mutela saw his chance to comfort the distraught Vacheke. He held her hand as he walked her back to Zimindo and, on the way, he spoke to her in the magical language of the *zakulu* (though Vacheke never knew it). By the time they reached the *musasa* tree that looked like a young man's face, Vacheke was under Mutela's spell and her lips rose to meet his as he bid her goodnight. Mutela returned to Maponda with a step as light as the air. He felt no guilt for what he had done because he was too young to understand such things. What does a *zakulu* do, Mutela thought, if not control another man's fate?

The next morning Mutela slept until Father Sun was high in the sky. But Zike was up with the cock. He went to see Musape, Mutela's father, and he told him what had happened the previous night. Musape reached out his hand and held Zike by the throat. His brow furrowed and he shook his head and kissed his teeth expressively.

'You have been cursed, Zike,' he said. 'A powerful curse that will be difficult to expel.'

'But can you cure me, *zakulu*?' Zike asked, his voice like dry sand.

'The only cure is time. But I will pray to the moon to intercede with Father Sun to speed your recovery.'

Zike left Musape's kraal with a heart as turbid as a rainy-season sky and his confusion only grew when, that night, he saw his best friend walk hand in hand with his beloved Vacheke. But Zike's blood was clean and he accepted his destiny with the grace of a *boka* bird in flight. He spoke to Mutela and Vacheke. 'My friends,' he said, 'I wish you well with your love, for surely fate has spoken to us all.' Mutela nodded but he said nothing. Vacheke bowed her head and her eyes filled, for Zike had never addressed her before and now he did so with a voice that grated like two flints. Zike returned to his own kraal and nobody in the village of Maponda saw him for many days.

Some two weeks later, to the relief of his father, Mutela finally fell prey to the *zakulu* illness and his suffering was worse than any Musape had seen. Where most would-be *zakulu* suffered for no more than a week, Mutela ran a fever for almost a month and slipped in and out of delirium like a *shangu* spider that guards its sandstone lair. For a while, Musape was worried that his son might die.

Mutela was so sick that his curse over Zike soon evaporated and his magical hold over Vacheke was broken. But Zike did not notice his freedom because he feared for the boy he thought of as his friend. And Vacheke did not notice her freedom because she feared for the boy she thought of as her love. On one occasion, Zike and Vacheke met at Mutela's bedside and greeted one another mournfully. In spite of himself, Zike looked at Vacheke and he felt that he wanted to sing. In spite of herself, Vacheke heard Zike speak and she thought that his voice had recaptured its former glory. But Zike did not sing and Vacheke said nothing.

One morning, Mutela's fever finally lifted and the village of

Maponda breathed a sigh of relief. Musape washed his son's face and pressed water to his lips and he could barely contain his joy. As for Mutela, he was as weak as a new-born calf and his mood was sombre (for he had learned many of the skills of the *zakulu* in the nightmares of his delirium). But he knew what he wanted to do.

'It is good to have you back, Mutela,' Musape said.

'Dad,' Mutela began slowly, 'I have suffered the illness that marks me as a *zakulu* and an adult. So now I want to marry as soon as possible.'

Musape smiled proudly. 'Of course you do, my son. And who is your chosen bride?'

'Vacheke.'

Musape's face darkened and he bit his lower lip so hard that a droplet of blood welled up on his teeth. He pressed his hands together until the joints cracked and he shook his head like a dog drying itself.

'Vacheke?' Musape said at last. 'You cannot marry Vacheke. For she is the daughter of the chief and now you are a *zakulu*. It is the law of Tuloko himself that the chief's line and the *zakulu* can never marry; for the chief is responsible for the people and the *zakulu* is responsible for the chief.'

Mutela stared mutely at his father and then pressed his face into his hands. He felt as empty as a carcass gutted by a hungry jackal and he bitterly cursed his fate. Though Mutela was now a *zakulu* and supposedly an arbiter of these things, he could see no justice in such a destiny.

That night Mutela rose from his sickbed for the first time and he sat with Vacheke and Zike on the bank of the water hole and they watched the nervous bushbuck take their evening drink. Mutela explained what his father had said with a voice as barren as the grain store in a time of famine. Zike, whose heart was pure, touched his friend on the shoulder and murmured sympathetically. Vacheke bowed her head, for she did not want her face to betray her relief.

For a while, the three of them sat in silence; the two boys scared the bush buck away tossing pebbles into the water hole and Vacheke plaited grass on her lap. Then, without thinking, Zike began to sing and, before he knew it, his voice had recaptured all its old strength and tone. He sang a wordless melancholy tune that filled the air with what might have been and Mutela hung his head. Eventually Mutela looked up to find Vacheke staring at Zike with misty eyes that needed no words, her chest heaving perceptibly with quickened breath. Quietly Mutela got to his feet and left the two of them alone. He walked away and he did not look back but he knew what he was not seeing; partly because he was a *zakulu* with the gift of sight, mostly because he was a jealous lover with all the wretched knowledge that comes with such emotion.

Zike and Vacheke were to be married a month later. At first Vacheke's father, the chief, objected to the match, for Zike was no more than the son of Maponda's most idle farmer. But he changed his mind when he heard Zike sing once again because it was the kind of voice that brooked no argument.

Zike told Mutela of the marriage with a heavy conscience. But his friend clapped him on the shoulder and smiled grimly, for Mutela knew that all the jealousy and bitterness in the world – even all the magic! – could not change the laws of Tuloko. And if he could not marry Vacheke himself, then surely the happiness of his friend was the next best thing. Surely.

The night before the wedding, Zike drank the traditional *kachasu* beer and retired to his bed early, as was customary. But his mind was full of the future and it took him a long time to calm his thoughts. When he finally fell asleep, his dreams were as disturbing as they were vivid. He dreamed that Mutela stood before him in his sleeping hut. It was definitely Mutela but his face was unrecognizable – twisted like the roots of an ancient baobab tree – and he stood as tall as an *nzou*. Zike sat up and stared at his friend. He tried to ask him what was happening but nothing came out of his mouth. Mutela was speaking silently too, his lips moving with unknown words. The next thing Zike knew, he was staring down at himself where he slept. He could see Mutela too, looking up at him, his expression caught in a grotesque leer. Suddenly the wind was rushing in Zike's ears and his eyes began to water and his ears were full of a curious beating sound. He rubbed his eyes with his knuckles and found himself nestled in the feathers of an enormous eagle. He looked downwards and he could see nothing but clouds. He looked behind himself and he saw Vacheke's face disappearing in the distance. Zike screamed and the eagle turned its head and fixed him with one eye. Then it dipped one wing and Zike felt himself slipping and slipping. Desperately he clung to the feathers as his legs dangled into nothingness. But the eagle rolled and Zike lost his grip and he fell.

When Zike's disappearance was discovered the next morning, Vacheke was inconsolable. Her father suggested that Zike had perhaps run away. But Vacheke knew that Zike would never have done such a thing and she ran to see Mutela. She found the young *zakulu* sitting silently by the water hole. His cheeks were streaked with tears although Vacheke misunderstood their source.

'Oh Mutela!' Vacheke pleaded. 'You are a *zakulu* and only you can help me. Where is our beloved Zike gone? Surely you can return him to me.'

'He is not coming back,' Mutela said quietly.

'How do you know? How can you be sure?'

'I know,' Mutela said. 'I can be sure.'

In the weeks following Zike's disappearance, Vacheke would not eat and the weight dropped from her face and breasts and hips. But her father did not worry too much, for there were plenty of eligible young men and, in any case, for all his gifts as a singer, Zike was hardly an ideal prospect. In fact, the chief of Zimindo never fully accepted the scale of his daughter's loss and when, some months later, Vacheke was found floating in the water hole outside the village of Maponda, he consoled himself that such a tragic accident was surely a sign of Father Sun's own wishes. Mutela carried out the burial rituals and the chief thanked him with a gift of cattle and Mutela nodded his gratitude and smiled without teeth.

Two years later, upon the death of Musape, Mutela succeeded his father as the senior *zakulu* in the area and he soon married a young girl named Nakayi, who was as timid as a child. Every night Mutela beat his new wife in a vain attempt to alleviate his guilt until, one day, he could not control himself and he pummelled her face so hard and so long that she was left as blind as darkness. Mutela preferred her like that as she could no longer look at him (let alone inside him). Thereafter their marriage was relatively stable and Nakayi bore him six children and Mutela beat them too.

Mutela wished for death every day. But he outlived Nakayi and, upon her death, his eyes also failed in one of those ironic twists of destiny that ensured he had nobody to lead him to the toilet by the arm. The *zakulu* lived well past sixty and, in fact, even death brought him none of the peace he craved.

As for Zike, he woke up on the morning of his wedding with a coarse feather tickling his cheek. He sat up abruptly and found himself in a shallow, man-shaped depression in an unknown land. His nose was full of a smell that seemed both fetid and fresh all at once. His ears were filled with a sound that swelled and died like a distant storm. These were the smells and sounds of the sea, though Zike did not know them because the Land of the Moon had no sea.

Zike's head was throbbing and his mind raced. He thought back to the previous night. He remembered going to bed, he remembered his dreams – the fall, the eagle, Mutela's face as he stood over him. He thought of Vacheke in the traditional adornment of marriage and he buried his head in his arms and he wept bitterly. Zike knew in his mind what Mutela had done. But his heart did not want to accept it.

After maybe two hours, when the heat of the day began to build, Zike gingerly lifted himself to his feet and surveyed the landscape. To his surprise, he saw a band of around twenty men coming towards him. They were armed with spears and their genitals were covered with cloth and their feet were bound in animal skin. Instinctively Zike felt nervous but he approached the men with a broad smile, traditional greeting and clapping. As Zike spoke, the men looked at one another with blank faces. Then the group parted and Zike found himself face to face with the most extraordinary man he had ever seen. If, indeed, he was a man at all.

This creature's body was fully covered in a strange costume unlike anything Zike knew, smooth and soft and adorned with all kinds of shining ornaments. In his hand, he – for it was a 'he' – held a device of heavy black metal, hollowed at the tip and curved to the shape of his palm. His skin was the colour of a plucked bird and it flaked and peeled at his forehead. His hair, though largely hidden beneath a simple hat, was like wet straw. Zike had heard talk of such men from far to the east and west of the Land of the Moon but he had always assumed they were the stuff of myth.

Perhaps I am already dead, he thought. And he voiced this aloud to the white man. 'I'm dead,' he said. 'That's right, isn't it? I'm dead.'

But the white man didn't understand what he was saying and he simply raised his eyebrows in surprise. 'He'll do,' he said – though Zike didn't know it – and, before he realized what was happening, he was bound at the wrists and dragged to the very edge of Africa.

Mutela's magic was more powerful than even he knew. It carried Zike to the outskirts of the Angolan settlement of Luanda, where he was found by James Harris, the Dorset-born first mate of the American ship the *George*, and his band of native slavers.

From Luanda, Zike was transferred to the barracoon at Lamarinas Bay where he was kept for two weeks, chained in a group of thirty or so men in a makeshift prison with a ceiling so low that they could not stand straight. On 24 April 1804, he was loaded on to the *George* with 500 other slaves and the next day they set sail; first for Jamaica and then on to New Orleans. The Atlantic was unkind and the journey took almost four weeks. More than 150 slaves died on the crossing. Some from hunger, some from sickness, but most from injuries sustained because their chains stopped them holding balance on the tossing sea. Others were killed merely because they were unfortunate enough to be chained to a number of corpses as the dead were cast into the *George*'s wake.

Zike, however, survived. He did not want to survive, his will to live was quite broken and, as others fought for scraps of food like animals, he was happy to starve. But fate is a notoriously untrustworthy god who is worshipped only by fools and, from some perspectives, it was the random hand of fate that kept Zike alive. Where other slaves were traumatized by their experience of hell in the *George*'s hold, Zike's mind was strong with the abandon that accompanies despair. Zike was not scared to go hungry. He was not scared by the pressure sores that erupted all over his body, nor by the ever-present stench of death; not even by the inhumanity of his captors. Zike had no interest in life. Consequently, he lived.

He was sold in the New Orleans slave market at the beginning of June 1804 for the sum of $115. He was bought by Langford Frederick from Jackson Hill, Mount Marter, the owner of one of the largest cotton plantations in the whole of Louisiana. Frederick renamed his purchase Ezekiel Black, corrupting the boy's 'savage' name and adding his wife's maiden title. Some two years later, a fellow slave, Elizabeth Langford (originally a Cormantine from the Gold Coast) fell pregnant by Ezekiel Black and the two were married. On their wedding night Zike told his new wife the story of Mutela and Vacheke and he made her promise that this story would be passed on to their children and grandchildren. This was not because Zike wanted revenge – such a thought was far from his mind – but he knew that there was a debt to be repaid by Mutela's descendants to his own.

'I no longer know who I am,' Zike explained. 'Mutela took that from me.'

There was also a degree of prescience in Zike's insistence to Elizabeth, for two days later he was found dead in a cotton field, his eyes peacefully closed.

Langford Frederick looked at his dead property, cursed his misfortune at such a duff purchase and proclaimed that the boy must have had a weak heart. But Elizabeth knew that Zike's heart was not weak but broken.

In fact Elizabeth never kept her promise to Zike. A widow after just two days of marriage, she felt little responsibility for Zike's past. Besides, she had barely known Zike at all, only well enough to discover that she was not his love. So the story of Zike, Mutela and Vacheke was lost to history – only preserved in the imprecise metaphors of a folk song in the Land of the Moon – and the debt went unpaid for the best part of two centuries. But fate is a perverse trickster with no sense of timing. Catch his eye and you can bet he'll reel you in like a fish on a line. Even after 200 years.

BOOK ONE

Polyphony: the simultaneous combination of more than one melodic line.

I: *One kind of black*

(Mount Marter, Louisiana, USA. 1899)
Lick Holden was christened Fortis James. His momma Kayenne called him that because he was her eighth child and it was a strong-sounding name. Damn! He was going to have to be strong, all right.

There wasn't much in the way of celebration surrounding Lick's birth. This was partly because he was Kayenne's eighth; partly because he was a breech birth and he almost killed his momma; and partly because his papa had bunked six months before. Mostly, though, it was because Fortis James 'Lick' Holden was born in the Cooltown district of Mount Marter just as the twentieth century was coming up for air; and a new birth was a blessing to no one, least of all the child.

Some ten years later, when Lick first blew his horn in the funeral parades that snaked their way down Canal Street through Cooltown, he watched the way the sombre mood of such events soon evaporated into a festival of dancing and ragtime or jass (as the music was called back then – or 'jasm', both shortenings of 'orgasm'). Lick loved to watch the fine ladies swing their hips and stomp to those African beats. But he couldn't help but wonder if the whole scenario was somehow disrespectful. He asked Momma Lucy (his grandmother) about this and she told him, 'Fortis! You gots to celebrate a life somehow!' But Lick didn't buy Momma Lucy's explanation any. The way he saw it, the funeral parades were not celebrating a life so much as its passing. And that was the truth of life and death for a negro in Cooltown.

Momma Lucy was there when Lick was born. She held her daughter's hands and stuffed her mouth with rags to bite on. She knotted the umbilicus and slapped the life into Lick until he screamed loud enough to make the wooden walls shake.

'The boy sho' got some lungs, Kayenne,' Momma Lucy said and she held Lick under the armpits and examined his features, wiping the mucus from his nose and eyes.

Black babies are born in a variety of shades from pink to tan. But Lick was born dark with full lips, a spread nose and a proud African forehead.

'The poor boy's been born a six-out-seven negro!' Momma Lucy exclaimed and she cackled like a witch.

Momma Lucy popped a bottle of dime hooch and swigged deep. Then she poured some down her daughter's throat until it spilled over her chin. Then she emptied the remainder over Kayenne's rupture and Kayenne dug her nails into her mother's arm until she drew blood. So Lick was born to the sound of screaming: his own, Kayenne's and Momma Lucy's. But Lick screamed the loudest.

In later years the first sound Lick could remember was not screaming but singing. Kayenne sat him on the outside staircase of their ramshackle apartment when she aired the two rooms, and he looked out over Canal Street as his six older sisters did the laundry in the gutter bowl below. They scrubbed the clothes until their nails bled, with bit soap collected by a neighbour from the white folk she worked for. And they sang away their troubles with voices as sweet as molasses.

'When the devil comes to take me to hell,
Make sure you cry to Gabriel,
Don't let the devil take my sister down,
She been in hell in old Cooltown.'

Lick loved to hear his sisters sing. Because he knew nothing of the devil or hell or Gabriel and Cooltown was his world.

One time when Lick was around nine months old and he'd just learned the use of his limbs, he crawled to the edge of the staircase and looked down on his sisters at work. He liked the way their picky heads bobbed and their necks dipped as they scrubbed and sang. They reminded him of the scrawny chickens that pecked the dust out back. But the sounds they made were a whole lot prettier. Lick leaned out from the staircase to try and get a better look but his little body wasn't up to much balancing. With a sudden scared shriek, he fell from the staircase the full four yards to the street below and landed head first in the gutter bowl with a splash.

Kayenne heard the shriek and she came whooping from the apartment like a banshee, two-timing the stairs with her skirt hitched at the waist. But she reached the street to find her second daughter, Tomasina, clutching Lick to her chest. Lick sneezed a couple of times and he certainly caught a little chill but he wasn't hurt bad. That didn't stop Kayenne giving all her daughters a wupping like the accident was somehow their fault.

When they heard the commotion, a lot of the Canal Street neighbours gathered round to watch the free entertainment. The men laughed at the thought of little Fortis Holden being an expert diver like the white good-time boys who leaped from the steamers into the depths of the Mississippi and they retold the story to passers-by and they nudged each other with their elbows and sucked on their cigarettes like they were scared they might escape. The women pulled their shawls tight around their shoulders and muttered to one another. Some said that it was 'surely a blessing'. Others looked at Kayenne and whispered that such fortune had the smell of witchcraft. But Big Annie – acknowledged as the expert on all matters of religion and juju by virtue of her husband's working for the white minister – soon set matters straight.

'T'ain't no hoodoo,' she said. 'An' t'ain't no religion neider. Jus' good luck, plain an' simple. Kayenne, that boy of yours sho' lucky to be alive.'

When Big Annie said this, the other women nodded in agreement and Kayenne nodded too. But she looked at her sniffling son with his rack of ribs and bloated hungry belly and she couldn't be sure how lucky he really was.

Truth is, Lick would surely have starved before he walked if it hadn't been for Kayenne's eldest daughter. She was named Lucy after her grandmother but Lick never knew her as nothing but Cheese.

Cheese was fifteen years old when Lick was born and she'd just become a mother herself, though all too briefly. Cheese had been raped by one of Kayenne's many sweethearts (though Kayenne never knew it) and she gave birth to a little boy she called Jesus (after the immaculate conception she'd invented in her head). But Jesus never had much desire for life and he breathed for just two days with a rattle in his chest like a purring cat. Then the purring stopped.

Of course Cheese was distraught when she found that Jesus had died next to her while she slept and she clung to the corpse for a further two days. And, since her own time was due, Kayenne didn't notice the silent little bundle until the smell became unavoidable.

So Kayenne sent for Momma Lucy and Momma Lucy took her granddaughter and the body of her great-grandson to Big Annie for a blessing because there was no point bothering the minister for a baby who'd barely tasted the bitterness of life. Momma Lucy promised Cheese that Jesus would receive a good Christian burial and sent the young girl home to her sisters. Then Momma Lucy and Big Annie weighted the corpse down with two stones and sent it to the bottom of the Mississippi. Because that was best for everyone.

The next day Lick was born.

Of course Cheese couldn't accept that baby Jesus was dead. And because Cheese couldn't accept it, her body couldn't accept it neither. And the young girl's breasts were swollen fit to bust. Now Kayenne, whose teats were raggedy from years of chewing and her body tired to the point of death, couldn't see no point in good breast milk going to waste. So Cheese was nursing from day one – not just Lick but her sisters too. And her heavy pubescent breasts produced milk aplenty, so that she could suckle the whole family from dawn till dusk without running dry.

Every time Kayenne received a visitor, they would find Cheese in the corner rocker feeding one child or another. Usually Lick. On one occasion Paddle Jones, a steam man who was sweet on Kayenne, swung by for the first time in months. He saw the way Lick hung on to Cheese's titty and the look of bored resignation on the young girl's face.

'Damn!' Paddle Jones said. 'That girl got enough milk over for cheese!'

And the name stuck.

Cheese nursed her siblings (and even her mother sometimes, truth be told) for three years. There was never enough food for the family to eat – maybe a pot of red-bean stew that had to last two days – but, when things got desperate and little Lick was crying with the hunger, Cheese would take out a fecund breast and blink her pretty eyes. Over time – though Kayenne never noticed, certainly never acknowledged it – Cheese began to fade away. Her face pinched and her womanly hips contracted and her pretty eyes blinked ever slower like a cow's. Two days before Lick's third birthday, Cheese died in her sleep. When Kayenne looked at her daughter's corpse, she barely recognized her, for there was nothing of little Lucy (named for her grandmother) left to see.

Though Lick Holden was not quite three when his eldest sister died, he never forgot her. Years later, when rich young white men bought him a drink in some Cooltown honkytonk or other and asked him how he hit that top C, Lick would look at them and say: 'S'cos I fed on powerful stuff as a shooter. Sho' made my lungs powerful strong.'

'What were you eating?' the white men asked earnestly.

'Cheese,' Lick said. And he peeled his biggest smile and the white men figured this was some strange kind of nigger humour.

Although there were eight kids in Kayenne's household (seven after Cheese died, six when Falling Down fell down one too many times) and they called one another brother and sister, only Cheese and Tomasina (Sina for short) were full siblings. Otherwise the relationships were as mix and match as a patchwork quilt.

Cheese and Sina were the daughters of Razor Harry, the two-bit Canal Street pimp with crooked teeth and mastery of the blade. Though she hadn't seen him since just after Sina was born, Kayenne still called him 'my husband' and she always expected him to show up some day with his short temper and his razor blade. Kayenne figured that she loved Harry as much as she knew how to love any man. And she had the scars to prove it.

The next three children were of unknown fathers, the offspring of the tricks Kayenne turned to put food on the table. Though she often tried to figure their background from the depth of their complexion.

With Falling Down, Kayenne's other son, there was no doubting that his father was pure white. Not that this information narrowed it down any, since white good-time boys were a dime a dozen in Cooltown back then. Sometimes in her darkest moments Kayenne wondered if Falling Down's mixed parentage was somehow to blame because there was no doubting that the boy was, as Momma Lucy put it, 'an egg or two shy for market'.

When Falling Down slept, Momma Lucy said it was like 'looking 'pon the face of God hisself' because nobody could deny the little boy was the most beautiful child in the whole of Cooltown. His skin was as lush as toffee, his limbs had the length and grace of a willow sapling and the soft curls on his head twisted upwards as if they were reaching for the heavens. But when Falling Down woke up each morning he broke his mother's heart. He opened his eyes and they were deep black, as lifeless as a stagnant pond, and his voice, when it came, was the voice of a slurring drunk which nobody but Kayenne could understand.

Worst of all, Falling Down couldn't walk without falling down. He would stutter a few steps with all the coordination of a new-born foal before lurching violently to the left (always the left) and collapsing on his side. And when Falling Down fell down, there was no way he could right himself without assistance and he would lie thrashing in the dust or on the floor or in the gutter like an upturned stag beetle.

One evening Kayenne sent Falling Down out to buy a piece of coal or two from the cart in Canal Street. Generally she didn't have to worry because she could rely on a good neighbour to pick her son off the ground. But this time, when Falling Down collapsed, he fell right on a jagged rock that embedded itself in his left temple. At first no one took no notice. They walked by saying, 'No mind. It's jus' Falling Down and I'll right him soon's I bought my scrap of coal.' Then Lil' Annie (Big Annie's daughter) saw that Falling Down's legs weren't thrashing no more and his dead eyes were truly dead. And there was all kind of commotion as the men carried Falling Down's body back to Kayenne.

There was a good turn-out at the funeral; partly because Cooltown liked nothing better than a funeral and partly because Falling Down was a popular kid whose tragedy let people see the best in themselves and the worst in their situation. But when the minister gave his address and started talking about a boy named 'Jacob', nobody knew who he was talking about except Kayenne.

Jacob was thirteen when he fell down that last time.

Next in line after Falling Down came Sister, who never got a proper naming, and Ruby Lee. These two deep-black girls couldn't have been more than ten months apart in age and, the way Lick remembered it, they did nothing all day but fight like alley cats. But, despite their mutual loathing, they both went the same way in the end; turning tricks from the age of twelve and addicted to opium and alcohol before they even started the bleeding.

After Ruby Lee, there was a three-year gap to Corissa, a fragile-looking little girl who clung to her mother's ankles like a freshwater mollusc. Sometimes when Kayenne brought a trick back late at night, Corissa would leap from the bed and fasten herself to her mother despite the man's attentions. Sometimes the trick wouldn't notice or mind, especially if he was dizzy drunk, and on occasion Corissa even made it into her mother's bed, weeping into the hard mattress as all manner of gruntings and groanings filled the claustrophobic space beneath the blanket. Sometimes, however, the trick would lose his temper with the clinging little girl and he would smack her with the flat of his hand or throw her across the room and into the wall. White men were the worst for this, like the presence of childhood was a marker of their guilt. But Corissa never cried out because she was a whole lot tougher than she looked.

In later years, when Lick saw a young whore with a fat lip or bloody nose and those tearless, plaintive eyes, he would shake his head and say, 'That girl got a touch of Corissa about her.'

Corissa's father was Squint-Eye Jack, a low-life thug from Story-ville in New Orleans. He was also the man who'd raped Cheese (though no one, besides the two of them, knew it). A long time later, Squint got his comeuppance when he was lynched by a mob of good-time boys for unwittingly looking at a white lady in the wrong kind of way. After the birth and death of Jesus, Cheese had prayed for such a revenge so hard that she felt sure she was heading for hell. But, when it came, it was too late for her to see.

Just a year older than Lick, the last sister of Kayenne's household was Sylvie, though she wasn't actually Lick's blood sister at all. Sylvie was the daughter of Marlin, Kayenne's own stepsister. Marlin had died in childbirth, so Kayenne took little Sylvie into her house-hold because she couldn't leave her blood on the street and, as Momma Lucy said, 'Seven don't starve no worse than six.'

Now Marlin was the half-caste daughter of Momma Lucy and a white trader from up North – Chicago or some place. And Sylvie was the offspring of Marlin and some plantation boy who'd headed into Cooltown to lose his virginity on his eighteenth birthday. So that made Sylvie what was known down South as a 'quadroon'; a negro girl with no more than one quarter of black inside her.

Some twenty years later, Sylvie looked up the word 'quadroon' in a dictionary and the closest word she could find was 'quatrain'. And Sylvie couldn't believe the definition staring back at her: 'A stanza of four lines, usually with alternate rhymes.' So Sylvie and Lick penned a song called 'Quatrain Blues' that gave equal weight to Lick's prowess on the horn and the sentiments of Sylvie's uncertain status.

'My grandma was a negro,
My grandpappy, he was white,
My pappy was a white man too,
No shakes that I's so light.'

And when Sylvie sang it, she invested the words with such feeling that no one could have doubted her meaning. And when Lick's horn blew over the top of the chorus, some said that women would be staring at that cornet to try and figure where the wailing baby was hiding. Louis Armstrong heard 'Quatrain Blues', third or fourth hand, down in New Orleans around 1922 and plagiarized the melody long after for one of the jazz standards he composed with his second wife Lil. But no man could remember which song it was and, if Sylvie ever heard it and thought she could, she was never saying. Besides, such 'liftin'' was commonplace at that time – from negro spirituals to church songs – and nobody paid it no mind.

To look at Sylvie as a little girl, you would have never known she was a negro at all. With her thick black curls, pretty aquiline nose and hazel eyes, she could easily have passed for an Italian or a Jew. And, as she grew up in Kayenne's household, Sylvie was soon aware of her difference from her brothers and sisters. A light complexion was a prized commodity in Cooltown, as valuable as near anything but food or a paying job, and Sylvie was proud of her good fortune. When she walked down Canal Street to beg an offcut or a drop of lamp oil, she would raise her chin above the horizontal and swing her arms by her side as she'd seen the white ladies do. She sat demurely on the rough church benches and rested her chin coyly on her shoulder. As her siblings wolfed their food as though they feared it might jump from their bowl, Sylvie nibbled a dough ball like it was an Oriental delicacy and sieved her water through her teeth like fine wine.

In between bouts of impatience, Momma Lucy looked at her granddaughter and couldn't help but laugh.

'Sylvie!' she exclaimed. 'You look down your nose at us po' negroes like you's the Queen of Sheba herself!'

After the passing of Cheese and Falling Down, Sina and Sister and Ruby Lee and Corissa found this an excellent image to hang on to. Because Sylvie would tilt her neck and look down the length of her precisely sculpted nose in a way that none of her flat-nosed sisters could hope to do. And they hated her for it.

If Sylvie had little but contempt for her sisters, her relationship with Lick was of an altogether different nature. Sylvie liked nothing better than to boss Lick around and, as she strutted down Canal Street, Lick would toddle behind her like, she thought, 'my negro servant'. Lick was surely devoted to Sylvie. But, if anything, he was devoted to the blackness he saw inside her. Because, for all her 'airin' and gracin'' (as Lick liked to call it), she sometimes couldn't help but show her nigger heart. During a funeral, more than any of her sisters, Sylvie would lose herself in the insistent rhythms of the jass. When the parade reached the jetty at the end of Canal Street and dusky Old Hannah washed the Mississippi in golden light and the prostitutes got low down and dirty and the men got drunk, there was little Sylvie, eight years old, in the middle of the heaving bodies. She would set her legs a yard apart and bend them at the knee, she would ride her skirt over her thighs and grind her child's hips with her head thrown back and her eyes tight shut and her curls tossing from side to side until Kayenne caught up with her and dragged her home by the ear. And the next day Sylvie would sit on the steps outside the apartment, resentfully nursing the welts from Kayenne's strap, and she sang her sorrow for Cooltown to hear and her eight-year-old voice would rise from her groin with the throaty rasp of sexual abandon and the Canal Street prostitutes would come to their balconies and their ribs rose and fell on the tides of Sylvie's song. And Lick sat unseen on the top step and his breathing came quickly and he crossed his legs and squeezed them together.

So Kayenne's household was a patchwork quilt, all right. Patches were removed and patches were added but they were stitched together with a strong thread that could mostly stand the strain. Sometimes, when Kayenne lined her kids up for inspection before the Sunday service, she would look them up and down and her tired face would crease into an indefatigable smile.

'Sho' my kids like every colour of the rainbow,' Kayenne liked to say.

When Kayenne said this, none of the brothers and sisters said a word. But Lick for one knew that his mother had it all wrong, even if he couldn't express his reasoning at the time. Different shades they may have been – Cheese, Sina, Falling Down, Sister, Ruby Lee, Corissa, Sylvie and Lick – but there was no doubting they were still all black.

I: *Lick and Naps and all kinds of trouble*

(Mount Marter, Louisiana, USA. 1907)

There were three types of trouble you could get into as a negro kid in Cooltown and by the time he was eight years old, Fortis James 'Lick' Holden had tasted them all like an infant tongue-dipping moonshine without the swallow.

The worst type of trouble was with white folk. It was worst because whatever you'd done, you could be sure that the punishment would exceed the crime. Lick knew of kids who'd been beaten senseless for mimicking an accent or cakewalking behind a white lady; and he'd received a stinging slap or two himself for no more than a misplaced glance at a fine-looking gentleman or for leaving his ice cart outside the wrong shop front. And, of course, Kayenne had surely told Lick the story of Squint-Eye Jack who'd been lynched down in Storyville for the sins of his lazy eye.

After white-folk trouble, the next worst type for a negro kid was trouble with your own kind, which had a whole chanciness to it that could make it more scary still. Say you stole a sweet orange from a fruit man's wagon just because you couldn't bear the fresh smell that tickled your nose like ambrosia and say the fruit man caught you at it. Well! You surely had some quick figuring to do because the fruit man might pat you on the head and say, 'Shooter! You know you just got to aks me.' Or he might pull his razor and slice your face so bad your own Momma wouldn't know you. See, it was just how Momma Lucy used to tell it: 'Desperation has a craziness all of its own.'

All the kids in Cooltown agreed, therefore, that the third type of trouble was the best. And that was trouble with the law. Law officers stood on every corner of Cooltown – at least until sundown anyhow

– and they liked nothing better than to pick up a little nigger for all manner of misdemeanours. The law officers were all white, of course. But they rarely had the time or inclination to administer a beating (save for repeat thieves) and they could generally be relied upon for no more than a stern lecture using words like "jucation' and "spect'.

Back then, when he wasn't hang-dogging after Sylvie (who wasn't no blood relation), Lick spent most of his time with his best friend Naps, Big Annie's youngest son. Naps was a small wiry kid with a wicked streak that ran through him like a vein in a cliff face. He had a terrible daring about him and the devil's smile that made grown men giggle like babies. His real name was Isaiah but this name was lost on account of the boy's ability to sleep just about any place, from the cradle of a tree branch to the roof of his family's apartment (any time his momma was on the war path). At first he was called 'Oddnaps'. Later just 'Naps'.

Naps got Lick into all manner of trouble. But mostly it was law trouble, the best type. On one occasion, when they'd been ejected from the balcony of Brown Sugar's low-rent honkytonk for the umpteenth time and received their umpteenth lecture from two of Cooltown's finest, Naps explained it to Lick like this: 'You get in trouble with white folks and you may's well fall down a hole so deep you can't even see the sunshine. Now with negroes, be like gettin' stuck in swamp mud right up to your waist. But law trouble? That's no worse than splashin' through a puddle, Fortis boy. No worse than splashin' through a puddle.'

With hindsight, therefore, Lick was kind of glad that, when big trouble followed his eighth birthday, it was the law type. But, at the time, he didn't feel so lucky. It was Naps's fault. It was always Naps's fault. And it happened like this.

Lick was seven years old when he took his first job to support Kayenne's shrinking household. Sina had long since left to marry an itinerant preacher and, the last Kayenne had heard, she'd made it all the way up to Chicago. Sister and Ruby Lee were still in and out of the apartment. But they spent most of their time in Brown Sugar's, turning tricks and spending the chump change on opium and alcohol. As for Corissa, Kayenne hoped she'd soon grow up and find herself a good husband. But there wasn't too much in the way of 'husband material' to be found in Cooltown and the way Corissa reacted to men – with a nervous tick and a lost tongue – suggested that, even aged eleven, she was destined to, at best, prostitution and, at worst, a spinster's life. Meantime, she looked after the apartment and the fading soul of Kayenne who now spent most days sitting in the corner rocker and watching the shadows for the ghosts of her past that came at night. What with Sylvie being Kayenne's favourite – though she wasn't even her blood daughter! – and above any kind of working, that left little Lick to earn what money he could.

It was Momma Lucy who found Lick a job with Old Man Stekel, the Jew who owned a general store in the Jones district of Mount Marter, right where it bordered Cooltown. Stekel was just about typical of Mount Marter's poor white folk, caught between a rock and a hard place. As a Jew, the richer whites considered him 'jus' one step above a nigger' and they would shop in his store only as a last resort. The negroes, on the other hand, distrusted Stekel as a white man who was sure to con them out of their hard-earned nickels and dimes. And, besides, they couldn't afford much of what he sold anyhow.

So Old Man Stekel had two principal ways of scraping a living. First, he opened his store on Sundays when the good Christians were in church or with their families and he could furnish shame-faced whites and blacks alike with an ounce of butter or tobacco. Second, he sold ice to the Cooltown honkytonks to freshen their liquor and to any negro kid with the terrible thirst and a penny to spare. And this was where Lick fitted in. Because Stekel was too old and too scared to be pushing an ice cart down Canal Street when Old Hannah hid her face from a devilish night in Cooltown.

Every evening, about seven o'clock, Lick would run the ten

minutes to Jones to collect the ice cart and he'd be greeted at the neatly swept shop front by Old Man Stekel himself or, sometimes, his son Dov (with hair so curly and lips so fat that Lick was sure he had some black in him). The negro kids skitted Lick from the first day for his association with a man who'd 'killed the Lord Jesus hisself'. But that didn't bother Lick any because Stekel was always good to him, paying what he could afford and feeding him a good Jewish meal of chicken and flat bread any time there was some to spare. And, for his part, Stekel always regarded Lick with a mixture of admiration and concern: admiration for the way the seven-year-old managed to shift the hefty weight of the full ice cart and concern that he might be stopped by a gang of white good-time boys before he even reached Cooltown (white boys for whom a good time got no better than the chance to 'teach a nigger kid a lesson').

Lick soon knew the routine of his job as well as he knew the expressions on his sister Sylvie's face. He would start at the north end of Canal Street (right by Kayenne's apartment) and work his way down the long line of honkytonks: Brown Sugar's, Tonk's, Toothless Bessie's, Black Cobb's. At some of these places, they actually employed doormen – terrifying giants with scarred faces and gentle hands – who would come to the cart and tuck an enormous ice block under each arm. But, mostly, fetching the ice was the job of the most junior whores, who laboured with a block between them and then cussed each other if they dropped it in the dust. Often, outside Brown Sugar's, it was Sister and Ruby Lee who were sent out to fetch the ice and if they'd smoked enough pipes of opium or gage they wouldn't even know their own brother.

Lick used to say, 'They's flyin' so high, they be lookin' down on the angels.' But it didn't bother him any because that was Cooltown all over and it was Lick's world.

When he'd reached the end of Canal Street, the second part of his job began. He would turn the cart round, take out whatever ice was left in the compartment and parade back the way he came, singing out his ice at the top of his voice. Even at the age of seven,

Lick's voice had that rasping tone that seemed to bounce off the buildings and carry for a mile or more.

Lick sang all kinds of foolishness: 'Iced sasparilla! It's a real belly filler!' Or, 'Come buy your ice! It sure tastes nice! Cures pox and lice! Taste it once you'll want it twice!'

Then Lick would take out the heavy sharpened metal spatula that Old Man Stekel called a 'doohickey' and he'd scrape away at the top block of ice until he had a nice pile of fragments. Next he took a sheet of waxed paper from the stack on the back of the cart and rolled it expertly into a cone. He scooped the ice to the brim of the cone and upturned a splash of sasparilla over the top just in time for his first customer.

The shooters came running for a taste of the ice – negro kids of prostitutes, pimps and preachers; because there weren't no other kind of kids in Cooltown – and their faces lit up as they brandished their dirty pennies. And their eyes watered happily when the cold hit the back of their throats.

'A penny a lick!' Lick would shout. 'A penny a lick! No penny, no lick!'

More than half a century later, white jazz junkies (or 'mouldy figs') who called themselves 'purists' wrote their histories of New Orleans jazz, lifted mostly from the slanted recollections of men like Louis Armstrong, Joe 'King' Oliver and 'Jelly Roll' Morton. And they felt obliged to make mention of the mythical Lick Holden and his golden horn, though they knew little of his life. So they faithfully retold a story that Louis Armstrong noted down in one of his many notebooks: how Holden's name came from the fact that 'he blew that horn a real Lick'. But the fact is that Lick lost the name Fortis years earlier on Canal Street as he sold his sasparilla ice to the crowds of eager kids.

'A penny a lick!' Lick would shout. 'A penny a lick! No penny, no lick!'

Truth be told, Lick loved his job for Old Man Stekel and even the kids who skitted him only did so out of jealousy. In the first place

Lick was earning money and in the second place he'd gained a certain notoriety as 'Lick the Ice Boy'. But, best of all, when the steady flow of customers trickled and dried around 11 p.m., Lick and Naps could gorge themselves on sasparilla ice and sneak through the windows or on to the balconies of the honkytonks and listen to the Cooltown musicians play the ragtime, blues and jazz so loud and so hard that their hearts would soon be leaping to keep up.

Lick sucked in the atmosphere of those Cooltown tonks like it was the freshest air he'd ever tasted. His eyes feasted on the black men who cakewalked so pretty (just like the 'airin' and gracin' white folk up in Jones or Sinclair) and the white good-time boys who paid double for their hooch though they didn't even know it and the prostitutes who shook their tushes so low they looked like they were buffing the floorboards. But it was Naps who described it best. Because Naps had a way with words that Lick loved to hear.

'The drummer's like a skeeter in the rains, so excited by all that flesh on show. The piano fingers like them river bugs that start to dance when the wind skims the surface. The bass is like a cart nag that can only walk so slow and the sax is like the trunk of a hephelant in Africa that's blowing its nose for all the animals to hear.'

'What about the horn?' Lick asked. 'Tell me, Naps! What about the horn?'

'The horn, Lick boy? That's your pappy's doody! An' you see the face of the cornet player? That's what your pappy look like when he was makin' you with your momma.'

And Lick sulked when Naps mentioned his pappy. Because Naps knew all too well that Lick had no idea who his pappy could be.

Hidden at the back of the Cooltown honkytonks, Lick and Naps heard all the first great musicians that the twentieth century had to offer. No wonder it fired their blood so! It wasn't just the Cooltown natives neither but some of the famous band leaders who'd made the twenty-mile journey from Storyville, New Orleans, to experience what became known as the 'Cooltown buzz'. And there was no horn man greater and none more famous than Storyville's

Charles 'Buddy' Bolden, the man with a steamer's lungs, steel lips and a tone so syrup sweet that he could make any ballroom, honkytonk or whole damn street smell of sex and good times. Lick only got to hear Buddy Bolden play one time – God knows what year it was but history puts it around 1907 (when Bolden was on the run from New Orleans and the complications of his love life) – and he vowed that night that he would learn to play the horn. It was also the night that Lick got in big law trouble, the best kind of the three.

Generally the doormen, pimps and prostitutes weren't bothered any by the presence of Lick and Naps, not unless there were law officers on the prowl. But when it came to Toothless Bessie's, the biggest honkytonk in Cooltown, it was a whole different story on account of an enormous light-skinned doorman by the name of Evans (or 'Good' as he was universally known). There was no reasoning behind it. It was simply that Good had taken a dislike to Lick and he was damned sure that no shooter was going to make a fool out of him. So he ejected Lick and Naps from the honkytonk on such a regular basis that his presence in Canal Street began to hang over Lick like the sword of Damocles itself. And Lick soon concluded that a visit to that particular honkytonk just wasn't worth the sore behind and the mouthful of dust. But the night Buddy Bolden came to Cooltown to play Toothless Bessie's? Well! Even just turned eight, Lick wasn't going to miss an opportunity like that.

The two boys stowed the ice cart down an alley and snuck through a window without too much bother. They knew that Good would be keeping his eyes open, both inside and out, but they hid themselves behind a table of rowdy steam men and they figured they were invisible enough. When Bolden's band took the stage, there was no sign of the great man himself. And the band slipped into some easy ragtime that moved the dancers' feet but left Lick wishing for something more. Suddenly, when they'd been playing half an hour or so, the band were drowned out by a cornet so loud Lick would have sworn it was a steamer's horn but for the tone as clear as light through new glass. And then the great man appeared and the whole honkytonk rose to its feet in silent, deafened awe. Lick couldn't help himself. Despite Naps's tugging arm, he climbed on a chair to get a better view and whooped at the top of his voice to hear the cornet played so.

Next thing Lick knew, an enormous paw grabbed the scruff of his neck and lifted him clean off his feet. With his other hand, Good caught Naps by the throat and dragged the two boys to the door of Toothless Bessie's. Good cracked their heads together until their ears rang and their eyes streamed.

'I see you roun' this 'stablishment again an' I cut you so full of holes they be usin' you to strain beans!' Good shouted. And Lick and Naps would surely have taken a further beating but for a fight inside that took the doorman's attention.

They sat in the street for a moment or two until their heads cleared and they looked at one another sheepishly and they dabbed gingerly at the sore spots with fingers that came away bloody. Lick slowly lifted himself to his feet and said, 'I's goin' home, Naps. 'Cos my head feel like a choppin' block an' no mistake.'

But Naps and his wicked streak had no intention of letting Good Evans get away with such treatment.

'Lick boy!' he said. 'You be runnin' from that big ol' mulatto and you be runnin' every night.'

Naps had a plan to humiliate Good and, though Lick was uncertain about its merits, he went along with it anyhow. Because Naps had a way with words.

With Good momentarily distracted inside the honkytonk (pulling two steam men from a pimp after they'd set upon him for what might be termed a breach of trade description), Lick and Naps quickly located the ice cart. They pulled it from the alley and rested it at the foot of the stairs to the balcony that circled Toothless Bessie's. Next they tried to carry the whole cart up the steps. But, though it was now only a third full of ice water and slush, it was still too heavy to lift. At this point Lick was of a mind to give up but Naps unbolted the top basin from the cart and they just about managed to lug that up to the balcony as the freezing, viscous liquid sloshed over their bare feet and ankles. Naps giggled softly at the brilliance of his plan (though he'd given no thought to escape) while Lick pressed his face to the first-floor window, transfixed by the sight of the heaving dance floor and the blowing of the great Buddy Bolden and wishing he was still inside.

'Lick!' Naps hissed and Lick knew it was time. The two boys crept across the balcony and peered down at the top of Good's head as he ejected the two steam men with strong arms and stronger language. Naps could barely suppress his laughter as he and Lick dragged the heavy basin to the edge. They exchanged a silent nod and upturned the basin as best they could until the liquid splashed down on the unsuspecting Good.

The doorman's reaction was comical. At first he seemed not to notice the freezing slush that hailed on to the top of his head and down the back of his shirt and vest. Then his body suddenly jolted as if struck by lightning and he let rip a loud, snorting sound like a riled bull. Good covered his head with his arms and bent himself double so that the liquid pounded the middle of his back. He could surely have jumped out of the way. But it was as though he had resigned himself to the collapse of the sky itself or the ice had actually frozen him to the spot. And still he kept snorting, loud and long.

Up on the balcony, Naps was laughing uncontrollably as he raised one end of the basin high, determined not to waste a drop. Lick was laughing too. Until he heard the sound of metal scraping metal and he looked into the basin just in time to see the heavy doohickey fly off the edge of the balcony and down into the street. The sharpened implement dropped with the precision of a balanced sword and embedded itself neatly between Good's shoulder blades. Good's snorting suddenly stopped and he dropped to his knees as the last of the liquid rained down on him. Naps was laughing so hard that he couldn't see, so he kept right on laughing. But Lick saw the doohickey find its target, he saw the huge doorman fall and it was as though time stopped for a moment. Lick's eyes were suddenly blind and his limbs were numb and his ears were deaf to anything but the sound of Buddy Bolden's horn. And Lick seemed to hear that horn like it could be an escape route, a climbing, uneven path that led to some place else. Because the band's swung rhythms, driven by Bolden's soaring horn, hid what *was* behind the sounds of what was *not*.

Lucky for Lick and Naps that Good Evans didn't die (though he never walked no more after the surgeon botched the removal of the doohickey). Because they'd never have seen Cooltown again. Lucky that they landed in law trouble rather than the random retribution of Toothless Bessie's other doormen. Lucky too that they came up before Judge Augustus Pinckney in the Sinclair Juvenile Court. Because Pinckney was a liberal reformer and the two boys escaped with four years apiece at the Mount Marter Correctional School for Negro Boys (or the 'Double M', as it was known) on the outskirts of town. Lucky for Lick that he'd heard Buddy Bolden play on the night he was arrested and he'd found his calling at the age of eight. Because Naps had no such purpose and no such luck and his way with words led him to nothing but good pimping. And there was no such luck for Bolden neither. It can't have been more than a month after that night in Cooltown that Bolden was incarcerated in the insane asylum at Jackson, Louisiana, for beating on his mother-in-law. And, while Lick was released from the Double M four years later with a cornet in his hand, Bolden was locked up for a quarter of a century to his death in 1931. Because even the third kind of trouble was enough to finish the original jazzman. And there was no luck about it.

I: *Of Dogtooth Jones and the Knuckle Law*

(Mount Marter, Louisiana, USA. 1907)

The Mount Marter Correctional School for Negro Boys (ages eight to fourteen) was an imposing structure. Standing on Jackson's Hill, a mile or so outside town, it was painted bright white and, when the sun rose behind it, the windows looked as black as coal. To some of the new Double Ms who were led up the hill in the first light of morning (often with rope-bound wrists), the building looked like a gaping face that would gobble up their lives if they'd let it and the younger ones couldn't hold back their sobbing, not even to avoid the bored cuff of a thirsty law officer who looked forward to a cup of coffee.

In a previous lifetime, the Double M had been the homestead of the Frederick family, one of the largest cotton farms in all Louisiana. The Fredericks lost a whole lot of land in the civil war and most of them moved west and (contrarily) north around 1870, driven out by the new culture (or lack of it) of the Union troops that occupied nearby New Orleans. Only one offshoot of the family remained on a relatively small plantation outside Mount Marter and you can bet they were bitter, even by white-folk standards.

The ancestors of many of the boys in the Double M had been slaves in the Fredericks' cotton fields. So, for such boys, there was a certain irony in the circumstances of their confinement ('We the house niggers!' they used to say). Not that such a realization helped them any.

In 1885 the building and the surrounding few acres were reclaimed by the town of Mount Marter for their present use and the Double M soon acquired a fearsome reputation. Although it was staffed entirely by blacks, the governor was a white Yankee whose given name – Theodore Spinks – had long been lost to the grandiose sobriquet of 'the General'. Nobody knew what army the General had commanded and nobody was asking. Truth be told, the General had never seen a day's fighting in his life but he was a nasty, cowardly man, the kind who needs a title on which to hang his thin moral fibre.

The General ran the Double M on the principle of what he termed 'the two disciplines'. What this meant was that, while the school was organized with a military regularity by day, at night its only rules were imposed by the boys themselves and they called them the 'Knuckle Law'. The General's hypothesis was a simple one. At one level, he supposed the boys might learn from the imposition of formal discipline and apply it to their own lives. At another, he figured that, after dark, the boys would surely pick out any bad apples that had been missed during the daylight hours. In practice, the General's supposing was just shy of the mark, so that it was the bad apples who applied the Knuckle Law with all the cold violence of the daily regulations (although none of the adult squeamishness or fears of supposed legal restraint).

One consequence of 'the two disciplines' was the creation of two distinct tiers among the Double Ms; the 'Shooters' and the 'Knuckles'. The Shooters were mostly (but not exclusively) the younger boys, who managed to escape the worst of the calculated hardships of the daily regimen. Instead their purgatory came at night, when Old Hannah set gold over Mount Marter and the Knuckles came hooting and hollering through the echoing dormitories, ready to mete out random revenge for their place in the system.

The Knuckles, on the other hand, bore the brunt of the staff's taste for beatings and abuse. Certain teachers licked their lips at the sound of a switch chewing bare flesh or the sight of a boy gagging as his head was lifted from the trough and he spewed water from his lungs. Little wonder that the Knuckles had a good idea how to administer lessons of their own in the silence of the hoodoo hours.

The Double M housed some tough kids back then; tough kids who'd been sentenced for tough crimes on the tough streets of Cooltown. Just because there was no boy over the age of fourteen (since a fifteenth birthday for one of the long servers marked their transfer to the adult prison on the other side of town) doesn't mean there were no violent criminals among their number: little kids who'd tried to rob Brown Sugar's honkytonk with a zip gun; scarred kids who'd ribboned each other's face in a vicious razor fight; and haunted kids who'd murdered a bantam girl for the sake of their (and her) honour. And top of the tree was Dogtooth Jones, an impossibly bulky, wild-eyed thirteen-year-old. He'd only been in the Double M about a year but his story had been mythologized in the pages of the *Mount Chronicle* and he was already known as 'the main man' or 'the man with the plan' by the other Knuckles.

Dogtooth was inside for double murder and, even at thirteen, he was looking at his future through iron bars. Born in the harbour district of Cooltown, where Canal Street meets Kellerway, he was the only son of a young whore called Chutney and her bad-tempered pee-eye, who went by the name of Jones. Now Jones wasn't around too much when Dogtooth was growing up. But when he surfaced from the Canal Street scum every six months or so, Dogtooth would take an almighty wupping before being kicked to the curb for the fortnight of his father's visit. Chutney watched these beatings with tired eyes, buttoned jibs and a screaming heart. During these times, Dogtooth would steal dime hooch from the crates stacked behind the honkytonks and hole up in one of the harbour ware-houses. There he plotted his revenge and drank himself some courage.

Now the fact of the matter is that Dogtooth's story was no worse than most. The majority of Cooltown kids – especially whores' children – took to beatings like babies to a breast. But Dogtooth, who was growing bigger by the day, simply couldn't stand the viciousness of his pappy (who had breath to make your eyes water), the sheepish silence of his momma and the lonely nights in the warehouse, when the only sound to be heard was the witches on the wind.

One night Dogtooth drank himself so high that he almost fell down the ladder as he clambered from his warehouse hide-out. He found himself a nail and he found himself a plank and he banged the nail a half-inch into the plank with a broken brick. Then he made his way to Chutney's room on the corner of Kellerway. He opened the door quietly but there was no way Jones was going to hear him above the sound of his own groans. So Dogtooth hid himself in the shadows, as silent as death, and watched his parents squeeze the lemon.

Dogtooth must have stood in those shadows for the best part of two hours, waiting first for Jones to finish and then for the even breathing of sleep. He walked to the edge of the bed, his face as calm as deep water, and raised the plank above his head. Then he brought it down with a fearsome cry, embedding the nail deep in the nape of Jones's neck. Jones woke up and – though the devil's slaves were already beckoning him down below – he wrenched himself free of the nail with a sickening sucking sound and stumbled from the bed to the middle of the room, swaying gently, with a quizzical look upon his face, and his hand pressed to his neck as blood spat through his fingers. Then he fell to his knees and forward into hell.

Of course Chutney woke up too and Dogtooth was in no mood for forgiveness. So he beat her with the plank and his fists and any other object he could lay his hands on until his mother's face was unrecognizable. Then, as she lay there, wheezing, choking on her own teeth and blood, Dogtooth raped her, pushing his twelve-year-old self inside her as the final humiliation.

It was this horrific twist that caught the imagination of the *Mount Chronicle*. Murder was not so uncommon in Mount Marter and down in Cooltown negroes killed negroes with a regularity that sang the realities of hardship like a funeral chorus. But a boy raping his own mother? The white journalists with their okey-pokey opinions relished the opportunity to analyse the negro mind and explain what they'd always known. Black folk too shook their heads and tried to break it down for one another to make some kind of sense. But explanations didn't help any. As Momma Lucy said to Big Annie, 'We's all crackin'. That boy jus' gone bust.'

In the Double M the story was that Dogtooth Jones had invented the Knuckle Law himself. And, though the older boys knew that the law pre-dated Dogtooth's arrival, nobody was denying it. Because nobody crossed Dogtooth.

Apart from the exhibitions of his strength and bloodlust (enthusiastically inflated in the gossiping that followed them), Dogtooth never went to sleep. In the first place, this gave him an almost metaphysical quality that struck fear into the young minds of the Double Ms. In the second place, his insomnia made sleep a dangerous place to visit especially for the victimized Shooters – 'Ain't no nigger as dangerous as a sleepless nigger.' In the early hours, when even the other Knuckles were dreaming of better lives, Dogtooth could be seen prowling around the dormitories with the soft-stepping assurance of the devil himself. Every now and then, he would bend over a silent body as if jealous of its peace, and the shadow of his strange pendant could be seen against the moonlight of a window. It was this pendant that had earned him the name Dogtooth. Although nobody believed that it was canine at all. Rather a souvenir from his momma's own mouth.

The first rule of the Knuckle Law was a kind of rite of passage to which all the new arrivals were subjected. After the lights went out and the doors were locked and the staff of the Double M had returned to their wing, Dogtooth Jones would go to the washroom and retrieve an old bucket and the Double Ms would gather round – both Knuckles and Shooters alike – and they would chant 'Bucket! Bucket! Bucket!' Any new boys were then thrust into the centre of the heaving circle and Dogtooth and a few of his jigs would strip the boys with ruthless efficiency and hard knuckles as the crowd laughed and bayed. Next, the terrified boys were lined up, naked, and Dogtooth marched up and down in front of them like a sergeant major at inspection.

'Who goes first?' Dogtooth exclaimed. 'You negroes gonna piss in this here bucket like the bush niggers y'all are!'

One boy was then pulled from the line and ordered to wet the bucket. But, generally speaking, the boy would be so nervous and his bladder pinched so tight that he'd be lucky to squeeze a drop. Most times a new boy was more likely to shit himself than perform and the Double Ms would bay and curse until the goose-bumps rose all over his body. Then, with exaggerated formality, Dogtooth Jones would inspect the bucket and inspect the boy's doody before straightening himself up and signalling to the other Knuckles.

'I set this straight for you like Genesis,' he said (he always said that: 'straight for you like Genesis'). 'We gonna beat your Shooter ass until the bucket full!'

Then Dogtooth and his jigs would live up to his word, battering the new boys with ruthless violence, clubbing them with fists and knees and elbows, while the other Double Ms cheered them on (relieved as they were to live one night free of their own fear). Of course the bucket never filled. But that wasn't the point. The point was to satisfy Dogtooth's thirst for thuggery, and sometimes he was so thirsty that the new boys would be spitting teeth for an hour or more before Dogtooth called a halt. Then Dogtooth would lift the bucket over his head and dump its contents on whichever poor fool had particularly needled him (for whatever reason). And, as the child cried, he would say, 'Tears don't do you no good. But piss'll heal up them wounds good and proper. Any slave nigger tell you that.'

The night that Lick and Naps arrived at the Double M was a night of mixed fortune. They were unlucky that they were the only two new boys to arrive that day (so that they took the full force of the beatings). But they were lucky to find Dogtooth Jones in a more placid frame of mind than usual (he had not slept for three successive nights and, though his temper was short, he wasn't up to much in the way of fighting). Consequently, when Lick was led to the middle of the excitable circle of Double Ms and his bladder contracted and his doody shrank to the size of a peanut, he escaped with a relatively mild wupping, although, since Lick knew no different, this didn't comfort him any. And he soon curled himself into a ball on the cold floor and accepted the fierce blows of the Knuckles with the patience of despair until, eventually, he managed to lift himself to his knees and piss a little.

As for Naps, he took a beating too. But, with his cast-iron nerves, he pissed like a horse on a hot day. And when the Knuckles threw their punches, he decided to fight back, talking all the time. Because Naps had a way with words.

'Come on, you pissy fuckers!' he screamed. 'I fuck you up like the white man! I fuck you up good! I beat you so senseless they put your nigger ass in the 'sylum!'

Naps flailed his arms and thrashed his legs as the Knuckles desperately tried to pin the wiry Shooter to the floor. And, at one point, Naps even managed to catch Dogtooth Jones square in the chops with the flat of his forearm and the circling crowd of Double Ms were momentarily silenced by the sight of Dogtooth sprawling on his backside. Dogtooth rose with a roar and even this oversized kid looked a whole lot bigger than usual. He picked up the piss bucket – which, thanks to Naps's bladder was more than half full – and raised it above his head, sending all the Knuckles around Naps screaming for cover.

'Lil' Shooter gonna bath in piss!' Dogtooth shouted, his wild eyes flying in all directions.

'Fuck your momma!' spat Naps through snot and tears.

'Did that already!' Dogtooth said and his mouth twisted into a leer that had the younger Double Ms covering their eyes.

Suddenly, with one swift movement, Naps sprang to his knees and raised his fist in one sharp uppercut between Dogtooth's legs, slamming into the boy's pubescent nutsack with a ferocity that rode on a heady cocktail of fear and anger. Dogtooth's wild eyes seemed to pop from his head and for a second he tried to hold his balance. Then it was gone and, as his cheeks hollowed and his jibs gaped, he collapsed backwards and upturned the bucket so that piss splashed all over his face and shoulders.

There was an empty second, like the instant before a thunder clap, then the Double Ms erupted in laughter that roared with released feelings. And Naps got to his feet and soaked up the noise like a natural performer. He circled Dogtooth as the bigger boy clutched his groin and spluttered urine.

'I may be a Shooter!' Naps shouted. 'And that's why I ain't got no big cookies! But I *still* know how much that smarts!'

And the Double Ms laughed all the harder until Dogtooth dragged himself to his feet and his eyes silenced the crowd like lightning on a stormy night.

Of course the humiliation of Dogtooth Jones didn't hurt his reputation any (though, through the following months, the Shooters dried their pillow tears on the memory). Because Dogtooth was both too strong and too cunning to lose his authority over a little bucket of piss. But Naps's bravery on his first night in the Double M did ensure that he was immediately accepted as a Knuckle. While Lick had to live the sorry life of a Shooter. At least at first.

Consequently, Lick's first few months at the Double M were the worst of his life, lonely and painful in equal proportion. Until Naps got into a position of respect to protect his friend and – more particularly – Lick came to meet Professor Hoop and learn the subtleties of that brass sculpture called the cornet. However, while Lick got out of the Double M after four years with his destiny apparently playing its own tune beneath his nimble fingertips, for others fate was a pitfall; a perceived future that looked like one hell of a ride. So Lick lived through music (for all the good it did him). So Dogtooth Jones died in a razor scrap at the age of sixteen in the adult prison on the other side of town. And Naps? He died a grifter's death the wrong side of thirty, caught up in the numbers games of New York City. And all for the sake of a little bucket of piss.

I: *Three-out-four jazz, six-out-seven sister*

(Mount Marter, Louisiana, USA. 1908)

There's long been much dispute about the origins of jazz music among the mouldy figs. Why did the music develop as it did? And, more to the point, why did the music develop *where* it did, in the marching bands and honkytonks of New Orleans and the towns of the surrounding bayous? Many people see jazz as a product of the unique and rarefied atmosphere of New Orleans back then: a multicultural synthesis of negro, Cajun, Creole and even Yankee influences. There's surely some truth in that and there's surely a degree of cosiness in such a cosmopolitan solution. But jazz was first and foremost negro music with its roots in the slave trade and the blues that wailed out oppression like a clarion call from the God-part of your gut.

Others have played up jazz's foundations in the rhythms and blue notes of Africa, the beats whose intensity is only matched by their syncopation and the flattened sevenths of a chorus that sing like a lost language. They point to Louis Armstrong's tour of West Africa in 1956 when Satchelmouth blew his chops out in front of seventy chiefs at Gold Coast University, improvising 'Stomping at the Savoy' over the frenetic cross-rhythms of the tribal drummers.

Now nobody in their right mind would deny the link (as clear as daylight) between jazz and Africa. But that doesn't explain the Louisiana cradle any, for slavery was a ubiquitous part of the whole of the USA's Southern states and South America and the Caribbean too.

So jazz was the bastard child of a unique set of circumstances, born from the history of one race at the singularity where cultures clash. But it was also the child of its fathers: King Oliver on horn,

Sidney Bechet on clarinet, Kid Ory on trombone, Jelly Roll Morton on piano and Baby Dodds on drums (now there's a five-piece band to make your heart beat a mite faster!). And – though his name is lost to time – jazz was Lick Holden's baby too. Where 'history' paints its pictures of the past with broad dialectical brush strokes, 'fate' concentrates on the personalities that were surely put on this earth at a particular time in a particular place for a particular reason. So it's no great shakes that folk like to look at their lives with a sense of destiny and none more so than the black people, for whom history has produced a whole lot more questions than answers.

Perhaps it was fate, therefore, that put a cornet in Lick Holden's hands towards the end of fall in 1907. Or perhaps it was the end of the American-Spanish war in 1898 that swamped Louisiana with cheap second-hand brass instruments, discarded by the military bands. But mostly it was the Double M's own Professor Hoop. Because the strong arm of fate is a contrary son of a bitch that works hardest through an individual's own will.

For a Shooter in the Double M, time moved as slowly as Old Hannah on a dusty summer's afternoon. Days dragged by and exhausted the Shooters with the effort of keeping themselves to themselves, and nights crept up and enveloped them with the seemingly endless fear of Dogtooth Jones and the Knuckle Law. But, for the select few, the Professor presented an escape route, a chance to climb out of the day on a simple blues progression, to batter down the walls of the Double M with a robust chord, to shuffle past the staff as they were enchanted by the sounds of music. And this opportunity was as literal as it was metaphorical. For the one public face that the Double M showed to the world (and the General's pride and joy) was the school's marching band.

Lick had been suffering in the Double M for some three months before he even knew of the band's existence. Then, one chilly afternoon when the breeze seemed to carry the fallen leaves like a dreamer's hopes and Lick was on slop duty out by the old barns, he heard a sound that stock-stilled him in his tracks. It was a single horn introducing a melody that Lick knew all too well, a melody for Psalm 23 that he'd heard often enough in the church down in Cooltown. Lick drew breath and his chest swelled and his eyes were momentarily sour with tears. Though the tone was brittle and the fingering clumsy, the sound was strong and it transported the little boy back to a place he'd tried to blank from his mind for comfort's sake. Then the bass drum kicked in and the cymbals clashed and fragile clarinets joined the melody with voices like children.

Turning the corner of the last barn into the paddock that sloped down the back of Jackson's Hill, Lick came across the band, around twenty-five strong, ankle-deep in the coarse browning grass, playing their hearts out in a shaky rendition of the hymn. In front of them stood a tiny black man with a hunched back and a bald spot in a neat circle on the crown of his head. About sixty years old, he wore an immaculate three-piece suit about two sizes too big, a white shirt that frayed at the collar and a purple bow tie so wide that it touched his lapels. On the tip of his nose sat a delicate pair of half-moon spectacles and in his hand he held a pocket watch that he consulted from time to time. At first sight the man appeared to be motionless (excepting the occasional glance at the watch). But, as he looked on, Lick realized that every now and then the man would turn his head a fraction and jut his chin as the horns came in or the trombone cut. This was the man who took charge of the Double M's marching band under the grandiose title of Director of Music. His name was Gabriel Hoop, though everyone called him 'Professor' on account of his spectacles and his ability to read music from a page.

The hymn came to an abrupt halt on the strength of some unseen signal from the Professor. The little man didn't speak but he pushed his glasses back to the bridge of his nose and the band members began to fall out. The concentration of practice broken, the boys chattered and laughed as they returned their instruments to the barn next to which Lick stood. Some of the Shooters acknowledged Lick with a raised eyebrow or a flick of the head as they passed. But others – the older boys in particular – ignored his presence like he was an unwelcome intrusion. It didn't bother Lick a hoot in hell. He was dumbstruck by the possibilities of music and the curious little man at the centre of it all.

Soon the Double Ms were all heading back to the school and their conversations faded to a whisper. But still Lick stood watching the Professor, who hadn't moved a muscle, just stared off into the sky like he was tracking the flight of an invisible bird. Lick wanted to say something but he didn't know what to say. Although he was at three o'clock to the Professor, he was sure he'd been seen and he didn't want to take a scolding for hanging out where he shouldn't. The wind picked up and banged the door of the barn that housed the precious instruments. Lick's nose was running a little and he shivered and wiped it on his forearm. Slowly, the Professor turned his head until he was looking directly at Lick. His expression didn't move much but he raised his eyebrows in a 'so whatchasayin'?' kind of look. Swallowing his fears, Lick approached the little man because that's what he thought he should do.

'So what's your name, boy?' the Professor asked, tilting his head back to look at the sky once again. His voice was deep and quiet but his lips barely moved as he spoke. It was like the sound hummed from his chest.

'Lick, sir. Lick Holden, sir.'

The Professor nodded his head a little, like he was confirming what he already knew. 'You ever wonder why God put you 'pon this earth?'

Lick didn't know how to answer. He was only eight years old and fearful of tricks.

'You hear the question, Lick boy?' the Professor repeated.

'Yessir,' Lick replied. 'God put me 'pon this earth to care for Momma Lucy, Kayenne and my sisters.'

'Them's noble intentions for sho'.'

The Professor lapsed into silence and stared off into the sky. At first Lick followed his eyes and tried to figure out what transfixed him so. Then he turned and stared at the Professor himself. Though he gave the little man half a century's head start, he was almost as tall as him, so when the Professor suddenly turned his head they were immediately eyeball to eyeball. The Professor's glasses had a curious effect that took Lick by surprise, magnifying his eyes to look like two peeled eggs. Lick suddenly felt extra nervous.

'So what you after, Lick boy?'

Lick swallowed. 'I want to learn to play the horn.'

'Can you blow me a note?'

Lick didn't understand what the Professor meant and he glanced over his shoulder at the barn where the instruments were kept.

'No!' the Professor said, his voice bristling with irritation. 'Jus' whistle me up a note through your jibs.'

Lick bit his lower lip. He felt so shy that he wanted to cry. But he pursed his lips and blew and the delicate sound seemed to die at once on the breeze. The Professor sniffed a little and adjusted his bow tie and he walked right up to Lick until their noses were near touching.

'Give me a high note,' the Professor said without moving his lips. 'The highest and most beautifulest note you can.'

Again Lick blew, this time with his lips barely parted. As he whistled and the sound wavered unmelodically, the Professor moved behind him and circled his arms beneath his ribs. Then, with one swift action, the Professor squeezed Lick tight, straightening his spine and lifting his chest, and forced the note out higher and with a clarity that Lick associated with birdsong. For a moment Lick was astonished by the sound and sensation. But, as the air began to fade, his head felt light and airy and colourful patterns played in his eyes until the Professor let him go.

'You see?' the Professor said triumphantly as he caught his breath. 'Next week, Lick Holden. Come see me next week.'

And, with that, the Professor marched off and by the time Lick's sight cleared he was nowhere to be seen.

The next week Lick was on slop duty again. But he skipped it and followed one of the Shooters he'd recognized in the band as he made his way out back of the Double M for practice. The band members collected their instruments from the barn and lined up in the paddock awaiting the arrival of the Professor. Lick lined up too. Though he had no instrument, he puffed out his chest like a soldier on parade.

When the Professor appeared he marched straight to the front of the band and then paused for a moment. He looked directly at Lick.

'What you doin', boy?' the Professor asked irritably and Lick felt his face heat and fizz.

'I's here for practice.'

'An' what you gonna practise? You gonna whistle us a tune through them big negro chops of yours?'

Lick didn't know what to say. He heard some of the Double Ms sniggering behind him as he stumbled, head bowed, to the edge of the paddock. He sat beneath an old oak tree so that the shadows hid his face and he watched for a full hour as the band went through their repertoire of church music; his eyes wide and his mouth dry. By the time the Professor eventually dismissed the band, Lick's legs were stiff and his backside sore. But when the Professor called him over with a glance and a raised eyebrow, he sprang to his feet in an instant and ran towards the little man. Not least because the Professor held in his hand a cornet that he'd kept back from one of the older boys. Instinctively Lick reached for the instrument but the Professor's face flickered with disdain and he turned away.

'Come with me,' he said.

The Professor trudged so slowly down the back of Jackson's Hill that Lick (who felt he should walk behind) found himself tripping over the little man's heels. But not once did the Professor turn around or speak any.

It took about ten minutes to reach the stream at the bottom of the slope, opposite the steep climb of the next hill along. As far as Lick knew, it didn't have no name, though negroes from those parts had long called it 'Echo Hill'.

At the stream the Professor stopped. Lick could hear nothing but the gurgle of the running water and the occasional pop of a bubble as his bare feet sank a little into the soft ground.

The Professor spoke without turning.

'You know what it's like to hold a cornet, Lick boy?'

Lick thought for a moment. He remembered something he'd heard the men – pimps mostly – say back in Cooltown.

'It's like holding a woman,' he suggested.

The Professor span around suddenly and his eyes were wet and laughing.

'Who tell you that?'

'Squint-Eye Jack, I guess,' Lick said sheepishly. 'One of them pee-eyes, for sho'.'

The Professor smiled a gap-toothed, black-toothed smile.

'Don't you go believin' no man who sells you his woman,' he said and his hand stretched out and brushed Lick's ear. Lick started and backed away. He'd heard all kinds of stories of young boys out in the bayous. But no sooner had he shown this mark of affection than the Professor was looking up again, out over Echo Hill.

'To hold a cornet,' the Professor began, 'it's like holding God hisself in your hands. You know why? Let me tell you. 'Cos when God speaks, he speaks with the sound of the horn and if that ain't the truth then he can strike me down right here. So when you take up the horn, you talkin' God's language. You talkin' directly to God. You see what I'm sayin'?'

'For sho',' Lick replied. Though he didn't understand any.

'Here,' the Professor said. And he thrust the cornet into Lick's hands, his face so animated that it made Lick's heart jump in his chest. 'Now blow me a note.'

The cornet was heavier than Lick expected and the metal was cold and smooth like morning glass. Tentatively Lick's fingers curled around its intricate shape and he pressed the mouthpiece to his lips. He remembered something else the men in Cooltown used to say

– 'Imagine you takin' your woman's nipple in your mouth.' But that helped him none.

'Now blow me a note,' the Professor said again and Lick blew for all he was worth. He blew till his eyes popped and his cheeks puffed out with the strain. He blew till his lungs ached like he was running from the Knuckle Law. He blew till he saw the Professor doubled up in front of him with his fingers in his ears and his face caught somewhere between a wince and a smile.

'Enough!' the Professor said. 'That really all you gotta say to God, Lick boy?'

Thereafter Lick practised with the Professor every week. Just once a week at first. Then twice a week. Then with the band and twice a week as well. It took six months for Lick to join the band and another six before he was first cornet. But it was those times when Lick blew his horn at Echo Hill and the sound bounced back and washed him in its tone and the Professor nodded with satisfaction that were the most precious. Lick couldn't figure why the Professor wanted to help him so – he wasn't used to no adult treating him good – but he was lost in the possibilities of the music, the subtle recipes of craft and soul, of dexterity and emotion.

One time they were standing at the bottom of Echo Hill and two sisters on the brow had sat down with their baskets of fruit for a moment, captured by the clarity of Lick's playing. The Professor turned to Lick and the blink of his eyes told the boy to hold up a second; then he fixed him with a look so intent that Lick felt his stomach turn somersaults. Lick looked down at the little man – because that's what he had to do these days – and tried to keep his breathing steady.

'Let me tell you something, Lick boy,' the Professor said. 'You wanna blow the horn good, you play with four parts of the body. At the moment you play with jus' two: your head and your chops.'

'Sir . . .' Lick began. But the Professor wasn't finished.

'Now don't let that worry you none. 'Cos most of them horn players, whether they playin' hot music or hymns, don't be usin' no more than one part of the body at best! An' you already got two an' you not even ten years old!'

'Yessir,' Lick said. 'What parts I missin'?'

'Not for me to tell you that, Lick boy. You find that out for yourself in good time. In good time. You hear me?'

'What about Buddy Bolden, sir? How many parts he blow with?'

The Professor's face softened and the beginnings of a smile played on the corners of his mouth.

'Ol' Buddy?' he said. 'He play with three parts. Ol' Buddy never had much use for the head.'

Try as he might to put an exact finger on the science of it, the Professor couldn't explain Lick's gifts any better than that. It was just that when Lick lifted the instrument to his lips . . . Damn! Truth was, to call Lick's cornet 'an instrument' didn't make no sense. You may as well have called his arm 'an instrument' or his fingertips or his jibs. Because the first time Lick picked up a horn, the Professor knew that it was no less than an extension of his own self.

All in all, Lick was surely lucky to find music in the Double M (Big Annie had always said the child had fortune on his side) because without it he would have disappeared without trace like countless other boys, Shooters and Knuckles alike. Lick himself saw the cornet like a safety ring that hangs on the cabin of a Mississippi steamer, keeping him afloat while others gave up their tired fight and allowed themselves to drown in the misery of it all. Certainly Lick's life in the Double M didn't improve any just because he got used to the routine.

For starters, Lick was a Shooter. But his position was compromised by his skills on the horn and, particularly, his friendship with Naps. After Dogtooth Jones was transferred to the adult prison on the other side of town at the beginning of 1909, Naps succeeded him as the 'main man' and the 'man with the plan'. Naps was barely ten years old when he took over from Dogtooth and there was a whole number of bigger and older boys who would have jumped at the chance to enforce the Knuckle Law. But Naps had a way with words and he talked with a weight that punched harder than any teenage fist and no one dared cross him for fear of his tongue. With Naps as his friend, Lick was grudgingly left alone by the other Knuckles, but they weren't none too happy about it and they certainly weren't going to accept him as one of their own. As for the Shooters, they resented Lick's special status and would have nothing to do with him neither. So Lick was left with no one for company but Naps and his horn. And Naps, in his new position of power, was full of himself like a dog with the bitches in season. 'You better be good to me, Fortis,' Naps used to say. ''Cos I the main man an' you my own personal fuckin' nigger!'

When Naps said this, Lick would just nod and tap out on his thigh, practising his fingering for some number or other.

On top of the resentment of the Double Ms, Lick suffered at the hands of the staff too. They knew of Lick's lessons with Professor Hoop, and none of them was too keen on such special treatment. Consequently, Lick felt the stick of their bitterness on an all too regular basis, beaten around the back and face and covering his precious jibs with his hands. Though he was nothing but a Shooter, in the daylight hours he took more wuppings than most Knuckles.

But worst of all for Lick was when the family visits trickled and stopped. The Double M had one day a month set aside for family to come and visit the inmates (because that's what the boys were – inmates) and, for the first year of his incarceration, Lick expected Kayenne and Corissa and Sylvie as regular as clockwork. Sometimes Momma Lucy, even Sister and Ruby Lee, came too.

After about a year, Sylvie (the quadroon, light-skinned sister who wasn't no blood relation) dropped out of the equation. For the following few months Lick quizzed his mother as to what had happened to her. But Kayenne would tell him nothing about that and, truth be told, nothing about much else neither. For Kayenne was fading away, although Lick – with the selfishness of a child – barely noticed it was happening. A further year after that, there was one month when Lick received no visitors at all. Then another. The third month, shy Corissa turned up on her own and told Lick that Kayenne had got the sickness.

'She gonna be all right, though,' Lick said confidently. And Corissa didn't reply. But Lick didn't worry because Corissa was never one for talking.

In later years, Lick often wondered what he would've said to his mother if he'd known that he was never going to see her again. Not a whole lot, probably. There was so much that he wanted to say that amounted to so little. Sometimes Lick figured he could have simply said, 'We po' negroes, Momma.' And that would have been sufficient.

For the final two years of his sentence, Corissa's visits became less and less frequent. Not that it bothered Lick any. By the end, he was a hard-hearted, twelve-year-old young man who devoted all his energy to surviving the Double M, and any emotions were only played out to the sky on the crystal sound of his borrowed horn. But when, some three weeks before his release, word came that Kayenne was dead, Lick wept until he was physically sick.

Naps, who was now looking at a further two years' time for an overenthusiastic application of the Knuckle Law, held Lick's head as he vomited.

'Chuck it all up, Fortis boy!' Naps said. 'Get all that shit out yousself!'

But Lick looked at Naps and knew that he couldn't sick up the pain. Because the pain was not an illness inside, it was a part of his very own being. Just like his cornet.

Now Lick had played with the Double M's marching band at any number of funerals in the preceding two years. But he'd never expected to play at his own momma's. And when it came to the church service, conducted by Cooltown's black preacher, Lick played that same melody from Psalm 23 as dull as anyone had ever heard and the congregation looked at one another and spoke with their eyes. And Professor Hoop watched with a heart as heavy as lead.

Afterwards, Lick led the procession down Canal Street to the

Mississippi jetty. It was a steamy summer's evening, just sweating for a celebration. But still he couldn't play with no fire because his own soul was doused, fizzled out on the tide of injustice that had stolen his mother just weeks before he came home. Only when the band actually reached the jetty did Lick's playing expand. And, the way Lick saw it, it was his cornet (the part of himself reserved for such emotions) that took the decision.

When the band reached the jetty, there was a brief silence as they waited for the assembled crowd of church folk, prostitutes and pimps to catch up and Lick cleared his horn of spittle. Then, on the Professor's signal, he launched into a version of the old spiritual 'The Far Bank of the Jordan'.

Even as he hit that first note, Lick knew that something had changed. He must have played that number a thousand times before but it had never sounded like this! At first Lick himself wasn't sure whether it was good or bad. His horn had never been so rough and ready, so off-key, pained and raw. As he blew, he looked at the other members of the Double M marching band and none of them could join in; they all just stared at him, their faces contorted into all kinds of expressions. He looked too at the assembled mourners. But they weren't moving as you'd expect for the end of a funeral procession and their bottles were full in their hands. His eyes caught Big Annie in the middle of the crowd and her cheeks were streaming with tears. And there was old Momma Lucy, seated on an upturned fruit crate with her head buried in her skirts. His own two peepers began to salty-sting and he kept on playing for all his worth. He blew like every note was the voice of Kayenne herself. And the gaps between them? They were the gaps that Kayenne's death had left in the life of her family and friends. No wonder Big Annie and Momma Lucy cried so. Nobody had ever heard music played this way; surely not by a twelve-year-old boy.

Suddenly, as Lick launched into the second verse, the melody was joined by a single voice, as beautiful as any, corrupting the words for her own purpose.

'I see my momma,
On the far bank of the Jordan,
On the far bank of the Jordan,
I see,
I see my momma,
On the far bank of the Jordan,
My momma is a-callin'
To me.'

Through the pain of his tears, Lick made out a solitary woman
approaching from the end of Canal Street. He blinked back the sting
and stared at her as he blew. It was Sylvie, all right (the sister who
wasn't no blood relation), though Lick would have struggled to
recognize her but for her voice. It had been three years since he'd
last seen her and thirteen-year-old Sylvie had grown into a woman.
What's more, she'd grown into a white woman. Her hair was long
and dark and gently curled in that style that white women liked,
her skin was porcelain pale (long hidden from the sun) and her
clothes were just so fine. Lick's heart rattled against his ribs when
their eyes met.

She still sings like a six-out-seven negro, Lick thought.

'Sweet Jesus . . .'

Sylvie began the third verse and Lick held back with his cornet a
little, tracing Sylvie's melody with the expertise of years of practice
in front of Echo Hill.

'On the far bank of the Jordan,
On the far bank of the Jordan,
I see . . .'

Her voice was restrained and respectful and loose and angry all
at once.

'Sweet Jesus . . .'

56

Clean and dirty like a baby at birth.

'On the far bank of the Jordan,
Sweet Jesus is a-beckonin'
Me.'

Lick held the final note, pure as ice, for maybe twenty seconds before flattening it to sound as melancholy as the passing of childhood.

When the note faded, Lick was immediately surrounded by a bunch of people all clamouring to talk to him and to pat his back and pump his hand. They said things like, 'Fortis! You play that horn like the angel Gabriel hisself!' and, 'St Peter never gonna turn your momma down at the gates of heaven when you play like that!' and, 'It's a holy gift, Fortis! A holy gift!' Lick didn't listen to them. He struggled to get free and find Sylvie. But by the time he had disengaged himself, she was nowhere to be seen and Lick felt an emptiness inside him like his very heart had stopped beating from exhaustion.

The band struck up a simple ragtime and some folk began to dance. But Lick wasn't of a mind to play no more and he stumbled through the crowd to the edge of the jetty and stared over the quiet waters of the Mississippi that stretched as far as he could see into darkness.

'Lick boy!'

Lick span round and the Professor was standing in front of him, his eyelids flickering and his breathing heavy.

When did he get quite so small? Lick thought.

'Yessir?'

'Lick boy, you out the Double M in three weeks an' you takin' that cornet with you. From now on, that cornet is your own personal property. You see what I'm sayin'? 'Cos that cornet a part of who you are. No. That cornet the best part of you.'

'Yessir. Thank you.'

Teacher and pupil stared at one another and there was nothing more to be said between them and they both felt embarrassed, like the love of a father for his son approaching manhood (at twelve years old, for landsakes!).

'You playin' . . .' the Professor began. 'You blowin' that horn with three parts of your body now, Lick. Your head, your chops an' your heart. Your hear, Lick boy? You nearly the whole musician.'

'What's the fourth part?' Lick asked. Though he knew how the Professor would answer.

'Not for me to tell you that, Lick boy. You find that out for yourself soon enough. You hear me?'

'Yessir.'

In fact it was eight or nine years before Lick became a 'whole musician'. And it was eight or nine years too before he clapped eyes on Sylvie again. And those two facts were as surely connected as history and fate.

IV: *The chief, the* zakulu, *the monkey ears*

(Zimindo, Zambawi, Africa. 1998)
History stripped the Land of the Moon of its name and identity for more than a hundred years of colonialism before fate restored them both at independence with the help of the ancestors and a freedom fighter by the name of Zita Adini. During this century the boundaries of the land extended from the original Zimindo settlement – not just to the Great Lake in the west and to the eastern highlands (that are called 'The Mountains That Kissed the Sky'), but to the south too, where white people found copper ore in abundance, and to the temperate northern territories, where tobacco grew like weeds. And the native people soon coughed up the dust from the mines and the smoke from cheap cigarettes.

In this time, the Land of the Moon was called variously Eastern Rhodesia, Manikaland and Manyikaland before Zita Adini, an Oxford-educated eunuch, drove into Independence Square in a Soviet-made armoured car and announced to cheering crowds, 'This is Zambawi, the Land of the Moon!' Although, of course, this speech was made in Queenstown, the nation's capital, about 200 miles north of the flood plains of Zimindo, the original Land of the Moon, where the Great Chief Tuloko built his first village, and 190 miles north of Maponda, where a boy's love was kidnapped by his best friend's jealousy.

Two decades and one incestuous coup later, Tongo Kalulu, the chief of Zimindo, was sitting in the concrete block that was the centrepiece of his kraal. He was a tall, long-limbed, deep-chested man with proud eyes and a granite jaw. Of course he was. For Tongo was a direct descendant of Tuloko, a line that passed through Taurayi who threw a stone more accurately than any baboon, Musekiwa who cried for his drowned daughter and Tongo's own grandfather Shingayi, a hero of Adini's independence struggle. But Tongo didn't know his history and he didn't think about such things any more because he had reached that age when ideals have decamped without waiting for pragmatism to show up in their place.

After Zambawian independence, many traditional chiefs chose to enter mainstream politics as members of parliament. But Tongo had little interest in such business, preferring instead the lazy exercise of a chief's remaining 'traditional' authorities. Where as once a chief took tithes from his villagers, assigned settlements to newlyweds and accepted wives as ceremonial gifts, these days such powers were continually rescinded by Enoch Adini, the Oxford eunuch's son (born, in fact, on the day of the castration) and Zambawi's second president. So Tongo had little to do but attend the marriages of orphan brides, pass judgement over minor land issues and settle squabbles between local schools' football teams. Otherwise, he spent his time arguing with his wife, Kudzai. Generally these arguments concluded with her threatening to return to the city or him threatening to send her back there. Then Tongo would chew his fingers in frustration before rehashing the arguments with Musa, his *zakulu* and right-hand man, over a cold beer at a nearby bottle store or a pipe packed tight with *gar*, the local marijuana.

Although Tongo was an extremely popular chief, fair-minded and easy-going, anybody would have been astonished to discover the direct ancestral line that tied him, however loosely, to the Great Chief Tuloko. Because, other than his looks, Tongo showed no outward sign of the greatness in his genes. Indeed, in the eyes of his people, the closest he ever came to heroism was when he agreed to finance the purchase of a car battery before the 1994 World Cup finals which allowed the whole village (and others from miles around) to watch Nigeria's majestic defeats through a black-and-white TV snowstorm. But only Musa knew of Tongo's family tree and he wasn't telling anyone, least of all the chief himself. As a *zakulu*, Musa had various unusual wisdoms. One such wisdom was the unique knowledge of ancestry through dreams. Another was that there is little honour to be found in humbling the humble.

Tongo leaned back against the breeze-block wall and skinned himself a cigarette with a dexterity that belied his heavy hands and thick fingers. He often came to sit in this building because, although he had personally put hours of labour into its construction, it remained unused and Kudzai didn't like to come inside. How long had the concrete house been standing? He had begun it in the year that the rainy-season storms washed away Maponda dam and he remembered that he'd had to relay the foundations from scratch. How long ago was that? Five years at least. And now the building stood, whitewash peeling, in the middle of the mud-brick *rondevals* that circled the perimeter of his kraal, and Kudzai skirted around it like a child around a tomb. Because that's what it had become. A tomb to might-have-beens, to fate's clumsiest intervention, to unborn children. And now? Now it should have all been so different. But it wasn't. As far as Tongo could see, fate was like a falling mango when a shouted warning meant no more than an upward glance and a face full of ripe flesh.

Tongo had left Zimindo village when he was the 21-year-old chief apparent. He secured a place at Gokwe Teachers' College on the outskirts of Zambawi's second city, Lelani, and he studied African history and he went to the nightclubs and he discussed politics into the early hours over cups of black chicory. So he was not like the other locals. That's what he thought. He was an educated man, a man of the world, a thinker.

While the other villagers struggled over a child's picture book, Tongo read Marx and Hayek, Ngugi and Nyerere. Where the villagers prayed for good rains and good harvests, he knew what it was to desire an object (be it a pair of American jeans or a Japanese cassette player) like a soldier lusts for a whore's *pau pau*. Whereas the villagers married at seventeen to suitable brides with bony backsides and sandpaper skin, he learned 'real love' from Hollywood movies – tragic, ecstatic and immutable.

When Tongo had returned to the village at the age of twenty-four (upon the death of his father), he'd immediately passed all kinds of arbitrary local statutes. He forced the village grain sellers to form a union to negotiate with the state Grain Marketing Board for better prices. And the Grain Marketing Board stopped purchasing Zimindo's grain with immediate effect. He banned the whores from congregating outside the bottle store on a Saturday night and they prowled outside the mission church on Sunday mornings instead. He pronounced that Musa's funeral rituals (which involved consumption of vast quantities of overproof *kachasu*) were 'a classic case of false consciousness'. And the funerals continued but the new chief's invitations went single-mindedly and mysteriously astray.

So Tongo was surprised that nobody helped him build his concrete house; particularly when the villagers gathered in the teeming rain at the gate of his kraal and watched him struggle with a spade, knee-deep in slipping mud. At one point he fell forward, face down in the sludge, and he was sure he heard some stifled laughter over the rumbling thunder.

Within six months every one of Tongo's new laws was long forgotten.

Tongo had left Gokwe Teachers' College with numerous hates and two passions. He hated concepts that ended in '-ism' and '-ization': colonialism, nationalism, communism and capitalism; westernization, Africanization, nationalization and privatization. And he didn't notice the contradictions in his loathings because he'd learned just enough to confuse criticism with thought. On the other hand, he loved jazz music and Kudzai. And, while his hatreds soon seeped out of him on his return to village life, his loves (for the most part) remained.

Tongo loved jazz because of Kudzai. He'd met her at one of the infamous Gokwe parties that started with broad philosophical discussion and passed through raucous dancing before culminating in an almighty punch-up. Of course it wasn't every evening that ended in a fight, but it was generally agreed that this was the mark of a good night out.

They met over that drunkard Kamwile's cassette player (the only one on campus) at a Friday night shindig. A bunch of trainee teachers were sniping over the music; some wanted Zairean rhumba, others South African *d'gong*; others demanded the local *mbira* sounds. Tongo was hovering on the fringes. He didn't much care about the music but he recognized the sweet scent of a budding argument.

Everyone was too busy trying to hear their own voices above the din to notice Kudzai slip her tape into the deck and they only looked round when the smooth arc of Coltrane's sax leaped out of the speaker and over their heads. Then everybody stared at her, all right. But nobody said a word; partly because she was a stranger (and therefore deserved a certain brief respect) and partly because she said, 'It's American', a phrase that forced the young people to nod their heads with exaggerated sagacity and ignore the fact that Coltrane was hardly the most dance-floor-friendly music. It was also because Kudzai was just so extraordinary to look at.

Later the women agreed that she was definitely the plainest girl they had ever seen, while the men were forced to admit that she had 'a certain something' ('Sexy like an ugly fruit,' one said and the others nodded). But, at that first encounter, the whole group were silenced by her appearance.

She was short. But not short enough for comment. She was chubby. But only in that African way that makes men turn their heads. Her breasts were enormous and strained the knit of her pullover and her backside was peachy inside her jeans. But these attributes applied to most of the women in the room. She wore her hair natural, evenly cut about two inches from her scalp. Although all the other girls relaxed or braided or corn-rowed their styles, natural hair could hardly be described as unusual, could it? So what really set Kudzai apart were her features.

Her complexion was uneven, with dark circles around her eyes and lighter streaks from her cheeks to her mouth. Her eyes were small and slanted and carried an expression that mixed sweet and spicy, like *piri piri* bananas. Her nose was round and yellow-tinged, like a ripe Cape gooseberry. And her mouth was gargantuan and sexual and she smiled gummily, revealing sparkling white teeth and the occasional glimpse of a pointed pink tongue. But it was her ears that were most peculiar. They were large and slightly pointed like . . . like what?

Kudzai smiled nervously as the others stared. She didn't go to many parties and she wasn't used to being the centre of attention.

Suddenly Kamwile, the owner of the cassette player who was now almost too drunk to stay upright, whispered 'monkey ears' under his breath and those closest to him began to giggle. Emboldened by his success, Kamwile spoke louder. 'Monkey ears!' he exclaimed and the whole group stared at Kudzai and began to laugh, one by one.

It was such an accurate description. Kudzai's ears *were* exactly like a monkey's. It was one of those tip-of-the-tongue descriptions that leave you wondering how you failed to come up with it yourself; a description that, once heard, will stick like a spoiled child to its mother's skirts, that labels its victim more precisely than their name, that outlives its target with spiteful longevity ('Did you hear? Kudzai is dead.' 'Who's Kudzai?' 'You know the one. *Monkey* ears').

Kudzai's broad smile collapsed and her slanted eyes blinked and her round nose twitched a little. She self-consciously touched her left ear. But she realized what she was doing too late and the trainee teachers laughed all the harder.

Only Tongo wasn't laughing. Because, for some reason, he couldn't see it. All he could see was this peculiar, sexy girl who was surely about to cry and he rounded on Kamwile and shouted at the top of his voice, 'Shut up, penis nose!'

In retrospect, Tongo wished this had been a well-thought-out retort because then he would have been able to take pride in its brilliance. But in fact 'penis nose' was a fairly common Zamba insult and its accuracy was simply fate or chance or both (as if there is any difference). Because the nose of the cassette player's owner, fuelled by years of alcohol abuse, did bear remarkable resemblance to a penis. And no sooner were the words out of Tongo's mouth than the focus of the hilarity switched to poor Kamwile and Kudzai was able to slip out of the room with a thankful glance at her unwitting saviour. And Tongo followed her.

Their courtship was remarkably brief. Kudzai fell in love with Tongo for his prospects (as a rural chief), his good looks and, most of all, the naive passion that lit his face when he listened to her. When she played him her jazz cassettes, his brow furrowed and his eyes danced with concentration upon her intricate explanations of structure and rhythm and harmony. He even listened to her favourite Miles Davies and pretended to enjoy it. And when she said things like, 'You've got to listen to the notes they're *not* playing', Tongo kept to himself the opinion that he could easily do that in the silence of his own bedroom.

As for Tongo? He loved Kudzai for her city ways that seemed so sophisticated, for her pure heart that never held an unkind thought and her sexual gymnasticism that would have made even baboons howl in jealousy. But most of all he loved her for the music she gave him. She unpicked jazz for him, the chords and counterpoints and cross rhythms. And he just listened to that music which seemed so exotic (so *American*) and so African all at once. He imagined small combos in smoky bars in never-to-be-seen cities and he was sure that he would fit right in.

Tongo asked Kudzai to marry him one night while she pressed her head to his chest and listened to the strong thump of his heart. Kudzai laughed in delight and kissed him passionately and he felt her tongue on his molars. Then she pulled away and looked at him seriously.

'Just so long as you don't tell anybody about the monkey ears,' she said.

And Tongo replied, 'What monkey ears?'

Because he'd never seen the likeness himself.

Kudzai's father, a bass player in one of Queenstown's five-star-hotel bands, disapproved of the match. Chief or no chief, why would Kudzai choose to return to the *gwaasha* when he had spent the best part of thirty years trying to build a life in the city? Had she achieved her teaching qualification only for the purposes of finding a husband? No, she had not! Consequently, Tongo and Musa the *zakulu* (in the absence of Tongo's dad) spent many evenings in Queenstown persuading Kudzai's father of the benefits of the union. The negotiations took almost three months before Kudzai's father came round on the understanding of a sizeable *lobola* payment. Sometimes, now, Tongo wondered whether he'd been had.

At first the marriage was an unqualified success. Although the villagers described their new chief as '*chi pizva chi ngobe vakumade*' (literally: as vain as a blind warthog), they took to his wife like beetles to dung. Though Kudzai came from the city, the women were unthreatened by her exceptional plainness, while the men fantasized in private about her wet smile, the blink of those eyes and her ears that looked like . . . like what? And Kudzai enjoyed the experience of her new life in the *gwaasha*, the welcome of her neighbours, the fresh taste of morning and the sounds of Bird that rang out from the cassette player (a wedding gift from Musa the *zakulu*) over the calls of the *boka* birds, the lowing cattle and the screeching goats.

Now, some five years later, Tongo tugged so hard on his cigarette that his lungs felt like they might burst and he wondered if it as possible to pinpoint precisely when the marriage had begun to go wrong. But for the umpteenth time he was forced to conclude that it had been a gradual process.

People began to talk about a year into the marriage, when there was no sign of a chiefly successor. At first it was no more than idle chatter – why had Tongo built a fancy concrete house if he had no plans to procreate straight away? – but it soon degenerated into the kind of gossip that made the *makadzi* giggle behind their hands and shake their heads like sociable hippopotami.

'Perhaps Tongo's root does not thicken in the spring,' said one. 'Maybe he is cursed by the spirit of the cassava, a notoriously floppy tuber.'

'Or perhaps she is as barren as a mule,' offered another. But everybody shook their heads at this; for weren't her sizeable breasts and hips sure signs of fecundity?

'His father never had that problem,' said a wise old whore. 'He was up with the moon and even insisted on seeing the sunrise before he was ready to finish ploughing.'

Initially Tongo and Kudzai tried to ignore the talk because their sex was as athletic as any newlyweds could expect. But the constant carping was always going to take its toll in the end, especially since Kudzai's cycle remained as infuriatingly uninterruptable as a mother-in-law's nags. They tried everything they could to conceive: they asked Musa to intercede with Cousin Moon; they drank the tea he gave them that was made of chincherinchee pollen; Kudzai performed headstands before, during and after sex and, for one fortnight, she even tried to cork herself with a mango stone to give her husband's sperm every chance to find its target. But the harder they tried, the less they enjoyed their coitus and still pregnancy seemed as distant as the spirit of the *zveko* ant that lives forever on the horizon.

Then, one evening when the batteries in the cassette player had run dry and there was no Coltrane sax to sing of 'A Love Supreme' and Kudzai was so tired that her mood bristled and her thighs ached, she pressed her hands into Tongo's chest as he knelt above her and she whispered, 'Not tonight'. And he rolled off and he didn't say a word. The next day Kudzai tried to make it up to him and she indulged in all the sexual tricks that she had learned in puberty from her aunts. But Tongo's confidence was gone and he could not rise to the occasion and instead he prowled around the walls of their sleeping hut and berated his wife.

'It's true!' he raged. 'You are as barren as a mule, as dry as famine and as capacious as a whore. No wonder we have no children. It's like trying to fuck yesterday's porridge.'

'Tongo,' Kudzai soothed, 'calm down. We will have a baby when Father Sun sees fit. Our sex has always been as glorious as the dawn chorus and twice as noisy and it will be again. Look at it this way: with no children we have all the more time to practise.'

But Tongo wouldn't be pacified. He was furious, although, on later reflection, he wasn't quite sure why. And then he said it. And though he immediately regretted his words, he was too proud to take them back.

'Well!' he spat, 'I should take you back to the city and see if your family can sort you out. I should demand *lobola* to be repaid!'

Kudzai's face darkened and her slanted eyes shrank to two points. For this was a terrible insult.

'And I should go to the city,' she said. 'Tell them how you mistreat me. I should find a job in a school and teach all the children of Queenstown how Tongo, the chief of Zimindo, is as flaccid as a *jubu* tree's catkin!'

After this confrontation, it is unsurprising that the relationship degenerated still further. Tongo took to sitting in his concrete house that Kudzai refused to inhabit and he smoked many cigarettes and drank crates of bottled beer. For her part, Kudzai performed her wifely chores with methodical care and she tried to ensure she was asleep before her husband came to bed. They still had sex occasionally, when Tongo was drunk and insistent or when Kudzai yearned for that strong touch that she feared she might forget. But where once their lovemaking had been magnificent, it was now perfunctory, almost tiresome, like a hacking cough or a bored yawn.

It was with no little astonishment, therefore, that Tongo had greeted the news of his wife's pregnancy some six months before. She'd rolled over one morning and smiled at him winningly and gently caressed his cheek with her palm. She rested her head on an elbow and twisted one leg between his and he saw her eyes were dancing. Tongo breathed deeply and tasted her sweet scent that had once promised trust.

'What?' he asked, smiling too.

'Tongo,' she said, 'We're going to have a child. At last.'

Tongo's smile was fixed to his face like a scar. His heart leaped against his ribcage and his guts twisted like a vine around a passion tree as he tried to conjure the right words from his mouth. They had only made love once in the previous two months.

'Are you sure it's mine?' he said.

Six months later, therefore, Tongo found himself staring at the wall of the concrete block he'd built for his family, tugging on a home-made cigarette and waiting for the arrival of his best friend, right-hand man and *zakulu*, Musa. Since the announcement of his impending fatherhood, Tongo and Kudzai had barely spoken, let alone made love. And if this fact is understandable, it is also understandable that it did nothing but contribute to Tongo's sense of cuckoldry. In his confused state's Tongo tried to sing himself sane. But he could think of nothing but jazz standards that reminded him of Kudzai. So, in the end, he resorted to a traditional song his mother had sung him as a child and his insecure voice died against the peeling concrete walls.

'*Sikoko kuvizva sopi vadela, zvumisa vabe pi kupe zvade. Sikadzi kuzvizvi, kadzi dacheke, putela makadi nade.*' ('And the boy with the voice that rings over cool water sings words that nobody hears. And the girl wearing seashells, the noble chief's daughter, has drowned in a pool of her tears.')

What traditional claptrap! Tongo thought, irritably. Zamba myths and stories always seemed to be full of phrases like 'the pool of tears' and 'the puddle of grimaces' and 'the ditch of broken promises'. But what did these people know about the real world? He resolved to ask Musa. And where in the name of Tuloko was Musa?

Musa the *zakulu* was in fact no more than half a mile away, traipsing through the bush, cursing the sun for its enthusiasm and then arrowing remedial prayers at Cousin Moon to intercede apologetically with Father Sun for his rudeness. He was trying to roll a joint on the move but a combination of the dreadlocks that whipped about his face with every stride and the unusually moist *gar* made it almost impossible. Generally he would have sat down where he was and spent an idle hour or two bathing in the sweet smoke. But, even by his own standards (that were so lax as to barely be 'standards' at all), he was quite exceptionally late and he knew that Tongo would be getting frustrated and running out of songs to sing.

Musa always had trouble with timekeeping because, as a *zakulu*, he lived in so many different times all at once (especially in his dreams). How, for example, could you possibly be 'late' when visiting the future from the present? It was an impossible conundrum. But Tongo had little sympathy for Musa's troubles since, from his point of view, if you lived in all times at once, you should never be late at all.

Musa was particularly late today because, yet again, his dreams had kept him awake and consequently he struggled to get up from his sleeping mat. He was worried because dreams this vivid were always significant and always meant some great change in the present and probably in the past or future too. Every *zakulu* knew the distinction between 'now, then and when', or the distinction between conscious and unconscious; these things were no more than questions of perception. Divisions of time were just as ridiculous as the colonial *musungu*'s attempts to divide the Land of the Moon, as if it were any business of theirs. Self and other were no more separate than a handshake, and dreams and reality as united as two bodies in the height of passion. A *zakulu* was, therefore, the facilitator of unity. But at the moment Musa felt as alienated as any common man. He couldn't unpick the meaning of his dreams, and what use was a *zakulu* who didn't understand dreams?

Recently Musa had taken to using sex to exhaust him into dreamless slumber. But with no desire for marriage (and, more pertinently, no desire to pretend it was an option), this had increasingly meant indulging in prostitutes whose sexual prowess was matched only by the boredom in their expressions. And Musa knew of the perils of promiscuity (he had treated several such cases in his time) and he had eventually resolved to 'go it alone' (something he had not previously attempted since suffering the *zakulu* illness in puberty). It had been a long, agonizingly lonely and depressing night and, when Father Sun first peeped his head over the horizon, Musa passed out anyway and was haunted by exactly the same set of images that were as coherent in form as they were nebulous in message.

And so the *zakulu* had been inexcusably late for his morning appointment. What's more, the meeting at the 'Ngozi family kraal was just as irritating and long-winded as he'd feared.

Stella 'Ngozi, a flirtatious young creature with sleepy, been-to-bed eyes, was due to marry at the end of the month and her father, a traditional old fart by the name of Tefadzwa, was expressing concern about his daughter's 'honour'. Musa knew that this was a euphemism; that Tefadzwa was worried that she might bring shame to her family and risk the *lobola* payment by failing to bleed on the wedding night. But how was a father (or even a favourite auntie) to ask a daughter about the state of her hymen?

Musa hated these virgin restoration jobs. Personally, he found them as morally dubious as they were mentally taxing. But he couldn't convince Tefadzwa to look at things his way; especially as the old man insisted upon talking around the subject like a cautious mosquito whines around the candle flame.

'What makes you think,' Musa began slowly, 'that your daughter's honour is not . . . what can I say? . . . intact?'

Tefadzwa shook his head. 'I am sure her honour is sound, *zakulu*. For Stella is a good girl. But sometimes, these days, young girls face temptations and tradition is broken.'

'Broken?'

'Indeed. Tradition, that is.'

'And if it is broken . . . tradition, I mean . . . will that be such a terrible thing?'

'*Zakulu!*' the old man exclaimed. His voice was almost scolding. 'Tradition is what binds the two families and it cannot be broken before marriage. For it is in marriage that a woman's honour falls like a gate before a rampaging bull. What makes a man appreciate sunlight more than the drawing of a curtain? If the land ploughed itself, would a farmer appreciate its bounty? When the covered well is left open, all kinds of hooligans may urinate in the fresh water! When the *jubu* tree . . .'

Musa held up his hands in resignation before Tefadzwa could tie himself in any more metaphorical knots. He shrugged and he sighed and he said, 'I'll see what I can do,' before ducking quickly into the girls' sleeping hut.

Inside he found Stella sitting alone, which was a relief; no nosy *makadzi* to complicate the issue. The girl was just as pretty as he remembered, with her high forehead, full lips and those sleepy eyes. She was clapping in the traditional greeting and she looked very nervous. Musa smiled in what he hoped was a reassuring way. Because he hadn't been alone with her since . . . well . . . this was very embarrassing.

'So Stella,' he began breezily, 'how are you? And how is Tatenda?'

'We are fine thank you, *zakulu*.'

'And the wedding plans?'

'They are fine, thank you, *zakulu*.'

'And you and Tatenda. I am sure you have already . . . well . . . I'm sure you know what I am asking.'

The young girl looked away, as shy as a young bushbuck.

'No matter,' Musa continued. 'Let's get started.'

It was almost an hour before Musa emerged from the sleeping hut to the concerned questioning of the father of the bride. No, there was no problem, Musa placated. His daughter was as honourable as a prepubescent. Yes, a fresh chicken would be a kindness but a gift of money was quite out of the question.

Musa answered politely but he felt he had to get away. The concentration of his magic had given him the most blinding headache and now he was later than ever. Generally, restoring virginity – a simple, painless spell to Cousin Moon that guaranteed a drop of blood or two on the marital sheets – took no more than ten minutes, though he sometimes drew it out to twenty for appearance's sake. But today Cousin Moon had been particularly recalcitrant when it came to answering his requests for an audience. Perhaps, Musa reasoned, it was these vivid dreams he'd been having. Perhaps the moon was in no mood to discuss mundanities when there were greater portents approaching the horizon. Then again, maybe it was just too hypocritical to restore a virginity you have taken yourself.

The *zakulu* stalked out of Tefadzwa's kraal rubbing his head ruefully. He needed a joint.

It was mid-afternoon, therefore, before he arrived at Tongo's kraal and his headache had already faded in a puff of smoke. The heat of the sun, however, was still infuriatingly stubborn. He paused at the gate of the chief's homestead and mopped his brow on his sleeve and threw back the nest of dreadlocks from his face. There was something disjointed about his movements that gave them an (appropriate) hypnotic quality, as though his bones were a collection of spare parts loosely fastened with twine. When Musa tossed his head, it looked as though it might fly off at any moment. And his every stride resembled an argument between leg bones where the ankle is dragged reluctantly along by the strength of the thigh that would itself love to resist the power of the hip.

Musa leaned on the chief's fence and looked into the kraal. This was surely a melancholy place: that stupid concrete house (a monument to Tongo's former pomposity); the fattening chickens who never made a family meal; the silence that was broken only by the faint sounds of Tongo's tuneless singing. *Maiwe!* Surely it was nothing a kid or two wouldn't fix.

The *zakulu* found the chief, as expected, in the concrete block. Tongo looked up as he entered and tapped his watchless wrist. Musa shrugged and sat down next to him.

'So how are you, my friend?' Musa asked.

'What is the point of complaining?'

Musa nodded, fully aware that a torrent of complaint was sure to follow such a rhetorical question.

'We are not making love any more,' Tongo continued, barely pausing to draw breath. 'Since the pregnancy Kudzai looks at me like I'm something that crawled out of the toilet. Because of what I said.'

Musa sighed. 'As far as I remember, you barely made love before the pregnancy. You two were so celibate that you made the hermaphrodite *wedza* worms, notorious onanists all, look positively sociable.'

'But then we didn't make love because of anger. Now it is a sadness that weighs down upon us as heavily as a maize sack at harvest.'

'So why don't you apologize?'

Tongo looked at his friend sadly. His handsome, manly face suddenly looked childlike and pained. 'Because what if I'm right?' he said. 'What if the child is not mine? For three years we performed *gulu gulu* as though we were trying to repopulate an empty city on our own. And nothing. Then when our sex is relegated to a quarterly quickie she suddenly becomes pregnant. It doesn't make sense.'

'Don't be ridiculous, Tongo! Who do you think Kudzai slept with? One of the Chitembe brothers whose eyes are too close together? A born-again from St Oswald's mission who has to pray for forgiveness three months in advance? You're just feeling sorry for yourself, that's your trouble. Have you not heard the ancient Zamba saying? *"Ku toko chimbe: vaste, kukuku, gulu ni bondore. Tatemba vade topa ni chimbele kunzwa vazve peloto."* The language is a little archaic but it means something like, "There's only four things in life: eating, shitting, fucking and dying. And if you get the first three right, the fourth won't seem quite so depressing." Something like that. It seems to me, Tongo, my friend, that you need a good seeing-to. And if Kudzai can't deliver the *pau pau*, then you'd best find someone who can.'

The chief tried to protest but Musa held up one hand to silence him (concealing a yawn with the other).

'You don't want the marriage to be over before the baby is born,' he continued. 'Listen to me as your friend and your *zakulu*. Relationships are always triangular. Why else does the *musungu* so often confuse the words "monotony" and "monogamy"? Even a married man always desires another, whether she is a real person or a conjuring trick of his lustful imagination. And a woman? She has one relationship with her husband and another with the man she would like him to be.'

'And that's it?'

Musa nodded. 'That's it. Until a baby is born and then, in a ideal world, the child becomes the apex of the triangle.'

'So your solution to my marriage problems is that I poke someone else. Fantastic.'

Musa sniffed. His headache was beginning to return because poor sarcasm always gave him a headache and he was bored of listening to Tongo's moaning. Chief or not, *zakulu* or not, friend or not – it had been going on for too long. And didn't he have enough troubles of his own when those dreams kept him awake and other people's problems sent him to sleep? Besides, he wasn't suggesting infidelity. Rather he felt that Tongo should get off his morose backside and help himself.

'Let's go for a beer,' he suggested and he hauled himself to his feet. But Tongo showed no sign of moving.

'I should never have married her,' the chief complained. 'Everybody said so. Even her father didn't want me to marry her.'

'But you love her, my friend. And whether you like it or not, that's just the way it is.'

'And what's love worth in the marketplace?'

'That depends on the marketplace,' Musa said, edging towards the door.

At last Tongo stood up too.

'Even that drunkard Kamwile said I shouldn't marry her. He said that she had monkey ears. Although I don't see it myself.'

Musa paused in the doorway and looked back at his friend.

Monkey ears? He pictured Kudzai's face and he knew that he would never be able to see her again without packing up laughing. 'I think you'd best keep that quiet,' he said.

Outside there was nobody around. The children of the village were rounding up the cattle, the men were already drinking and the women were still busy in the fields (Kudzai with them, luckily for Musa). Tongo was deeply pensive and walking as slowly as a wildebeest with a death wish. But the *zakulu* strode away. He wasn't sure whether he could really smell the beer on the afternoon breeze or he just needed to change his shirt.

'Zakulu?' the chief said. 'Where is the pool of tears?'

'What pool of tears?' Musa replied, hurrying ahead.

'In the song.' Tongo began to sing. '*Sikoko kuvizva sopi vadela, zvumisa vabe pi kupe zvade. Sikadzi kuzvizvi, kadzi dacheke, putela makadi nade.*'

Musa stopped in his tracks and stared at his friend. The lyrics of the song clicked something in his head and he rubbed his knuckles into his eyes and tugged at his dreadlocks to make sure he was awake. Because the images from his dreams attacked him from all sides like jackals around a carcass: the boy with a voice that sang through time, the naked girl floating in a pool of sorrow, a baobab staff, a *zakulu* gone bad, an eagle . . . He shook his head violently from side to side and, when he had finished, he found Tongo looking at him curiously.

'I am sorry, my friend,' Musa said. 'But no beer for me today. I must go to bed and find out what in the name of Cousin Moon is going on.'

IV: *To pounce or not to pounce*

(Zimindo, Zambawi, Africa. 1998)
Most locals agreed that the American archaeologists' Land Rovers were the most exciting convoy to visit Zimindo since the revolutionary guerrillas had set up camp in the village some six years before (just prior to the coupsters' final push on the capital). This judgement was somewhat theoretical since, six years earlier, the villagers had unanimously fled to the bush before the soldiers' arrival in order to conceal their chickens and their daughters from the ruffians' rapacious appetites. So the only local who could have made a genuine comparison was Musa, as the *zakulu* had himself been at the head of the revolutionaries' advance. But when the archaeologists turned up he was coming to the end of five days of sleeping and the cough of the odd engine was never likely to disturb him.

For about a month, everyone had heard the rumours that a team of *musungu* were digging holes in the ground near where Maponda dam used to stand ten miles away. But a lot of people (who remembered the rumours about the witch who gave birth to a *chongololo*) didn't believe the story, while the rest thought anything was possible of a bunch of *musungu* and it was generally best to let them get on with it.

When the Land Rovers pulled up outside Mr Mapandawanda's store, the children swarmed around them begging for sweets or a bottle of Coke. But when the archaeologists descended, most of the younger kids ran screaming to their mothers since they'd never seen such a hairy (and scary) collection of men. Some of the archaeologists had such fulsome beards that it took a moment or two to discern their eyes. One man reflected later that 'The *musungu* were so hirsute I feared they might have put their heads on upside down,' and his drinking companions packed up laughing and snorted 'true enough' through their giggles.

But it was the young black woman who descended from the first vehicle that caused the most fuss. She was wearing a traditional *chitenge* and a Java-print headscarf and she was quite as pretty as a *jubu* tree's blossom. In the absence of the chief (who was presumably holed up in his concrete house, smoking cigarettes and moping about the state of his life), Tefadzwa 'Ngozi took it upon himself to greet her.

'*Mazvera se masisi,*' he began.

The young woman smiled and replied in an eccentric accent. '*Uribo bra!*' she said, which roughly translates as 'All right, baby!' And the women of the village wondered why a girl should dress for the most traditional funeral and then greet a respected elder like a whore.

Soon it became clear that the woman was a foreigner and she spoke little Zamba. But she was determined to try and the locals were determined that she should (it was bad enough that the *musungu* made no effort with the local language but a black woman?). Consequently, whenever she lapsed into English the men would engage her with blank stares and say things like 'me no speak well' in exaggerated houseboy voices while the women covered their giggles with their hands.

'I have come here from America,' she announced. 'I am insulting the chief.'

The men looked at her wryly. 'Join the club,' they said. And, 'Wait your turn.'

But Tefadzwa's wife caught her drift (because Zamba is an infuriatingly subtle language) and she said, 'She doesn't mean "insulting". She is confusing *chiseda* with *cheseda*. Give the girl a break.'

It was twenty minutes before the young woman received the directions she wanted because the locals were having such fun.

Tongo had of course heard the growl of the Land Rovers' engines and he was insatiably curious. But he felt that it was hardly decorous for the chief to go running like a stray mongrel at the first sounds of a hubbub. So he located his ceremonial sash instead and he moved two wicker chairs and the cassette player from his sleeping hut to the concrete house and he sat back and smoked a cigarette and he tried to look nonchalant. Where was Kudzai? For the sake of appearances, Tongo wanted his wife next to him. But she was working in the fields as usual, steering well clear of the arguments and tension. By rights, Musa should have been there too. But the *zakulu* was in the middle of some serious dreaming and Tongo knew better than to wake him.

Tongo smoked three cigarettes while he was waiting. Every now and then he went to the door of his house and he heard the sounds of nearby laughter and he tutted impatiently. Surely one of the locals would have the manners to bring the visitors to his kraal?

Eventually, Tongo heard the noise of an approaching throng and he straightened his sash and lit another cigarette, aiming at an appearance that was both dignified and unaffected. He took a deep breath and opened the door of his house. It seemed like the whole village was gathered outside and they cheered his emergence in a 'this'll-be-funny' kind of way. At their head stood a beautiful young woman in vibrant traditional costume, all vivid blues, natural greens and sunshine yellows. This was not what Tongo had been expecting. He furrowed his brow and asked 'Who died?' before he could think better of it. The attendant village collapsed in unrestrained laughter and the young woman looked utterly bewildered.

'She has come all the way from America,' one man called.

'To insult you,' added another.

'Be careful, chief,' warned a third. 'She's got a posse of beards behind her.'

The young woman approached, head bowed, clapping in the traditional way. But Tongo smiled reassuringly and offered her his hand saying, 'No need to bother with that.' He cast his gaze over the assembled crowd that was waiting expectantly for the next trigger to hilarity and he took a decision. 'You'd better come inside,' he said and he ushered the woman through the door before turning back to the villagers.

'OK. Show's over.'

The majority of the villagers began reluctantly to disperse but a group of elders got their heads together and approached the chief, Tefadzwa 'Ngozi to the fore.

'Tongo,' Tefadzwa began, 'we were wondering about the where-abouts of Kudzai.'

'She is working in the rape plots, which is surely where you should be. Why do you ask?'

'A beautiful young woman has come to your kraal alone, chief. And your wife is nowhere to be seen.'

'And?' Tongo asked. 'What's your point?' And the muscles of his face tightened because he understood the insinuation precisely.

Tefadzwa looked uncomfortable.

'A young woman is as an open gate to a jackal. She is like an exposed buttock to a mosquito. For does the *shamva* choose its direction? It does not. Whatever its intention, it flows where the current leads it, according to the lie of the land. And do the giraffes not warn the reedbuck when a pride is hunting? Of course they do. And when the cow follows the cattle thief through the gate, is it not still robbery? Of course it is.'

Tongo stared at the old man with as obtuse an expression as he could muster and Tefadzwa's wife, who was used to her husband's prevarications, kissed her eight remaining teeth and decided to take over.

'What we are saying, noble chief,' the woman began, lowering her chin respectfully. 'Is that people will talk.'

Tongo laughed. 'Let them talk,' he said flippantly.

'But if you would sanction the presence of a *kurimadzi* . . .' she continued.

'A chaperone! You're joking, aren't you? The trouble with you lot is you love sticking your noses into the sensitive spots like dogs on heat! You spend an hour baiting this poor American before you bring her to my kraal and now you can't bear to be cut out of the action. A *kurimadzi*? For goodness' sake!' Tongo paused. His self-righteousness almost rendered him speechless. 'I am a married man!' he exclaimed.

This, of course, was exactly the elders' point. But they saw the anger rising in Tongo's chest and they knew better than to argue with the chief, partly because of his position and partly because they liked him. Because Tongo was basically a good chap and there wasn't anything wrong with him that couldn't be explained by the unfortunate triple team of good looks, intellect and the chieftainship of a (very) small village. So they backed away slowly instead, nodding with an exaggerated formality that ensured he couldn't miss their disapproval and Tongo turned on his heel and entered his house, clucking like a peacock. If he had been entertaining any thoughts of a quick pounce, they had now been banished by a potent dose of the moral high grounds.

Inside, it took Tongo's eyes a moment or two to accustomize to the sombre light. But when they did and they settled on the young woman who was shifting awkwardly from foot to foot in the far corner, his indignation quickly faded and an uncomfortable and obtrusive lump rose in his throat until he felt like a python swallowing a stubbornly indigestible rodent. This American *was* sexy all right. She was tall and slim with clean features and gentle curves that suggested saucily beneath her clothes. She was everything, Tongo thought, that Kudzai was not.

The young woman approached him and this time it was she who extended her hand. '*Uribo bra!*' she announced and Tongo was somewhat taken aback.

'"Hi sweetheart" yourself,' he said. 'But wouldn't it be simpler if we spoke in English?'

Sweetheart? The young woman was confused by the chief's informal language. But she quickly gathered herself and said, 'My name is Olurunbunmi Durowoju; Bunmi for short. I am Professor of Ethnoarcheology at Northwestern University in Chicago.'

'Tongo Kalulu,' said Tongo shortly. 'Chief.'

For a moment the two stared at each other curiously. If some pauses are pregnant, heavy with unbirthed sentiments, then this one was simply obese; an unspoken conversation that was trapped beneath cross-cultural flab. At last Tongo said, 'Have a seat,' and the professor perched on one of the uncomfortable wicker chairs while Tongo lounged in the other.

She sat demurely with her lips pursed and her back straight, her thighs tightly closed and her hands resting on her knees. Tongo thought her coy demeanour was surely no more than an affectation. There was, he sensed, something about the way her long neck reached so elegantly for the upward turn of her chin, the way her nostrils flared involuntarily, the outline of her calf muscles that disappeared modestly beneath the swathes of her *chitenge*, something undeniably and deliberately erotic. Or perhaps, he reflected, his sexless lifestyle had taken more of a toll on his psyche than he'd realized.

'Olurunbunmi,' Tongo tried. '*Olurunbunmi*. Bunmi. Is that an American name?'

'Nigerian. Yoruba. It means "gift from the gods".'

'I thought you were American.'

'African-American. We're all African originally.'

Tongo shook his head. This woman spoke in riddles as knotty as any *zakulu*. She certainly sounded American with that clipped twang in her accent that suggested a funk soundtrack to her childhood. 'So you were born in Nigeria?'

Now Bunmi looked confused. 'No. I mean, I changed my name. Why would I keep a slave name?'

'Oh,' Tongo said seriously. 'I see. So your ancestors were Nigerian?'

'No. I don't know. They could've been. But I was christened

Coretta Pink. I tell you, "Pink"! Probably the name of some plantation owner.'

'Coretta Pink,' Tongo said, nodding. He liked the sound of it on his tongue, exotic and sweet-tasting. 'That's a pretty name.'

Bunmi began to shake her head. She was getting frustrated. This exchange was going nowhere fast. 'No,' she said. 'It isn't a name at all. More like a brand or a label that I don't want. If somebody calls me Coretta, I feel uncomfortable. Why should I want to live with a label I don't like?'

'Ah! I understand you, Bunmi!' Tongo said. 'Like "monkey ears".'

The bemused archaeologist stared at the smiling chief. 'Exactly,' she said, though she had no idea what he was talking about.

Bunmi felt her fingers ruck the material at her knees. The conversation wasn't going according to plan. She had dealt with chiefs all over Africa in her time, donning her traditional costume and fawning obsequiously before various combinations of ignorance, arrogance, lust and corruption. But this brief meeting suggested something disconcertingly inconsistent about Tongo that she found hard to explain. One comment seemed knowingly mocking while the next was idiotic in the extreme. His demeanour slipped continuously back and forth across the fine line between arrogance and slight retardation. He was undoubtedly a handsome man but his manner was occasionally as gauche as any adolescent's. And whereas he had initially (and obviously) undressed her with his eyes, he was now determinedly reclothing her. What's more, he seemed to be adding layers of woolly jumpers and unflattering baggy trackpants on the catwalk of his imagination.

Tongo lit another cigarette with a flourish and sauntered across to the cassette player. He dropped a tape into the deck and the sounds of Coltrane's 'Blue Train' filled the room. The chief assumed that he looked as sophisticated as he felt.

'Jazz,' Tongo said expressively. 'Do you like jazz?'

'Sure,' Bunmi said and she wondered why the chief was standing like that, leaning louchely against the concrete wall like a downtown pimp. 'Look. Perhaps we could get down to business.'

'To business?'

'Sure. I'm an archaeologist . . .'

'An archaeologist?'

'Exactly. We excavate . . . you know . . . dig up . . . artefacts . . . things . . . that have been buried a long time. Things that tell us how people used to live a long time ago.'

'Really?' Tongo said. It was a struggle not to laugh but he didn't want to interrupt because he was enjoying watching this curious American woman squirm. There was something titillatingly squirmy about her.

'Zimindo Province is a fascinating area. My theory is that the earliest Zamba settlements are located in this province. When your people migrated northwards into what is now Zambawi, I figure Zimindo was the first place they stopped. We've found artefacts in this area that date back almost 250 years; pottery, axe-heads, foundations. You ever heard the myth of the Great Chief Tuloko?'

'Tuloko?' Tongo mused ironically. 'I think so.'

He was mildly irritated with her condescending tone (had a black ever sounded so much like a *musungu*?) but engaged by the passion with which she spoke. It reminded him of the way Kudzai used to talk about music in the time when they still had conversations. His decision not to pounce had already been reversed, resurrected and repealed. Now, at the thought of his wife, it was reinstated once again.

'Well!' Bunmi said triumphantly. 'Whether he was a real chief or not' – Tongo raised his eyes to the ceiling and offered a quick prayer of forgiveness – 'there's no doubt that his first settlement was near here. It might even be below this village.'

'Really? Amazing,' Tongo said, sounding utterly unamazed. 'So what can I do for you, Mrs Professor?'

Bunmi stared at him and she drew a deep breath. Tongo noted the way her chest pressed against the material of her Java print top.

Her breasts were plausibly more voluminous than he had previously realized.

'Well,' she began, 'we've been working on a site nearby. Near where the dam used to stand. When the dam was washed away, it revealed all kinds of interesting deposits. But there is something in particular we've found . . .'

'An artefact?'

'A head-dress. Tongo . . . I'm sorry . . . Chief . . . Chief Tongo . . . it's quite a find! A *cozaka* shell ceremonial head-dress that most likely dates back 200 years. We're excited about it. *I'm* real excited about it. You see . . . I don't know what you know of African history . . .'

'Fill me in,' Tongo said. And he wondered if his attempted ironies were too subtle or Bunmi simply too thick-skinned.

'OK. It's always been assumed that, before the arrival of colonialism, the Zamba were fairly typical Bantu nomadic pastoralists; a simple society of farmers with limited bartered exchange between villages that wouldn't have looked a whole lot different to this one.'

'Simple society. Right. Got you.'

'But this discovery? This one head-dress turns that whole theory upside down. Because the *cozaka* shells must've been imported from as far away as Mozola. We're talking almost 2,000 miles!' Bunmi was getting overexcited and her voice tightened like an *mbira* string. 'And you know what else? The ecological record shows that the land between here and Mozola was nothing but tsetse plains. So you see what I'm saying; how was the journey made? And *cozaka* shells were part of a ritual Mozolan exchange cycle . . . you know . . . like money. So maybe Zimindo was involved in that secondary economy. I tell you, this shit's crazy!'

'Crazy shit,' Tongo said. 'So?'

'So? So this tells the world so much about pre-colonial Africa. Even now, too many Western archaeologists still see Africa as some primitive, cultureless kind of place but this explains to the world who the Zamba really are. It's about ethnic identity. It explains where you come from.'

The chief stared at the archaeologist. He could feel his heart pounding against his ribcage and his breath came short. Was this lust again? No. He was just infuriated by this patronizing young woman who had the cheek to be so damn sexy when he hadn't tasted *pau pau* for the best part of six months, two weeks and four days. Tongo tried to put another cigarette in his mouth but he found that the last was still alight and hanging from his bottom lip.

'Where we come from, eh?' he began slowly. He was speaking with exaggerated intonation even though he knew it was wasted on his guest. 'I see, Coretta. I'm sorry, *Bunmi*. So *you* can explain where *we* come from. Fascinating. It sounds like you've got it all worked out. What could you possibly want from me?'

The professor smiled at the chief just as sweetly as she could. She even deigned to peel her lips and give him a glimpse of her perfect teeth. Perhaps this wasn't going so badly. Perhaps this guy wasn't such a doofus after all. She produced a folded piece of paper and a ballpoint from somewhere about her person, an action that made Tongo's imagination boggle.

'I just need you to sign this. Export forms. It's a requirement of your government. We need your signature to take the head-dress back to the US for more accurate testing.'

'For more accurate testing?' Tongo said, sitting down. This was his chance.

'Exactly. To pinpoint the date.'

'Right. Why?'

'Like I said . . .'

'No. I mean, why do you want to take the head-dress? Or rather, why should I let you take it?' Bunmi was about to reply but Tongo wasn't going to be interrupted. He leaned forward with his elbows on his knees. The professor unconsciously sat back in her chair.

'You said that this head-dress explains where we come from. Well, Bunmi, as a graduate of African history myself, let me tell you something about us Zamba. I hope you won't take this the wrong way but we *know* where we come from. We were colonized for more than a century; we were called primitive, savages, *kaffirs* and *munts*; so do you think we would have survived without a powerful sense of history passed down through generations with the strength of a dominant gene? We have been through more changes than a *zvingwe* pupa and now that our nation has emerged as a beautiful butterfly, the West still wants to pin us to a corkboard in one of their museums with a sticky label underneath.

'And say, for the sake of argument, that we *didn't* know who we are. It's still none of your business. You say that you will explain our culture to the world? Well! We don't give a whore's knickers what you think. Frankly I sometimes wonder why you Americans aren't more concerned with your own screwed-up identity. But you know what? I know it's got nothing to do with me.'

Tongo paused and looked at Bunmi. She was impressed. How could she not be impressed by such an impassioned speech? I'm good, Tongo thought. I'm really good. Eloquence, intellect and charm in one six-foot slab of chief! Even if I've had to knot my *chongwe* for more than six months, I'm still *nice*!

'But without us you wouldn't even know about the head-dress,' Bunmi tried.

But Tongo knew she was beaten and he paused to allow the weightlessness of such a retort to float embarrassingly in front of the professor's face.

'So it's finders keepers, is it?' Tongo said quietly. 'Like Livingstone at Victoria Falls or Leopold in the Congo? I don't think so.'

'And that's your last word?'

'Well,' Tongo said, 'I'm sure we'll talk again.'

At that moment, Coltrane's music stopped like a clock. The chief stared at the professor and the professor stared at the chief and neither quite knew what the other was thinking. In fact, neither was entirely certain what they were thinking themselves. The professor couldn't tell whether the chief was hitting on her or insulting her. But she figured that it was quite possibly both, in that curiously masculine manner that allows a man to chuck you, fuck you and chuck you again in the space of an hour. Something like the way her father (a conservative preacher by the name of Isaiah Pink) had taken the belt to his child's backside and prayed for forgiveness between each stroke. And now, as then, she wasn't sure how to respond. Tongo definitely had a certain something: an aura, an exoticism, a dangerous spiciness. But she could have been describing the jambalaya that her dad used to make for special. And perhaps it was just her hormones talking after an unbathed month in the bush with nothing but beards for company.

As for the chief? He realized that the controversial anti-pouncing bill had been (finally?) overturned in his body's lower chamber. He *knew* he was hitting on her. But he didn't know why and he didn't know why he didn't know. And he wasn't sure he wanted to know anyway. Trouble was, every time he blinked he saw Kudzai staring back at him from his eyelids. And she wasn't wearing that disenchanted, depressed, uncertain expression of the last six months but the expression of the woman he'd married.

Tongo resolved not to blink again. That was easier than facing the face that was painted on the inside of his eyes.

So the chief and the professor stared at one another in silence because neither knew what to say next. And only one of them ever blinked.

Out in the rape fields, some two miles away from the village, Stella 'Ngozi was typically late for the day's harvesting and she was soon entertaining the women with her gossiping about her forthcoming marriage and the 'rumours' she'd heard of Musa the *zakulu* who had a sexual appetite worthy of a jack rabbit. At first Kudzai Kalulu paid no attention because, as the chief's wife, she was above such small talk. Besides, it took all her concentration and willpower to bend over six months' worth of pregnancy and heave out the crop by its roots. But when she heard Stella move on to the extraordinary arrival of a convoy of beards and the beautiful young woman who'd insisted upon an audience with the chief, she straightened her back and pricked up her ears that, she insisted, looked nothing like a monkey's. And you can bet the other women noted her reaction and they shook their heads as Kudzai hurried from the fields.

It took Kudzai the best part of forty minutes to make it back to her kraal. This was partly because she had a backache and her baby kept kicking like a natural footballer and partly because she kept stopping, uncertain of what she was doing and what she was going to say when she got there. Tongo was a good man, wasn't he? Not like the other chiefs she'd met who would sleep with a whore and then demand change from a packet of cigarettes. Sure he could be as lazy and vainglorious as a preening *shumba*, but he was hardly the adulterous type.

He doesn't have the balls, she thought. And then she cursed herself for the tactlessness in what she saw as the likely accuracy of such a critique. Besides, potent or otherwise, she knew that any man could be ruled by his chopper (it was as much a part of his identity as the trunk to the *nzou*) and she had to admit that recently she hadn't been giving his blade much of a greasing.

When she finally reached the homestead, she believed her worst fears were confirmed when she heard the sounds of Coltrane from the concrete building and any sympathy for Tongo quickly jumped ship. Listening to my tape on our wedding present in his stupid, stupid house! she thought ferociously. And she tortured herself for a minute or two by stalking around the borehole and conjuring all manner of sybaritic antics before her mind's eye. Her womb began to twitch painfully but she put it down to anger. And she only mustered the willpower to actually go and investigate when the music stopped and she could hear nothing else from inside.

Kudzai took a deep breath and steeled herself like a bee preparing to use her one and only sting. She pushed open the door and found her husband sitting opposite a hatefully beautiful young woman. The chief's wife tugged at her earlobes self-consciously.

At first, it didn't seem all that bad. She didn't see the twin-backed quadruped, the shunting *nyama*, the gossamer fountain, or any of the other terrors she'd half-expected. Instead, the two of them seemed to be engaged in one of those staring matches that children bet on with mangoes. And Tongo was clearly winning.

But when Tongo heard her come in, he span around and stood up quickly and he began to blink like a snake that's just discovered the joy of eyelids. And his expression said it all. She might as well have caught him with his *chongwe* in the mealie porridge.

'Kudzai!' Tongo exclaimed. 'Professor, this is my wife, Kudzai.'

Bunmi stood up but Kudzai wouldn't meet her eyes. Instead she said to her husband, *'E kuri kwe hoore?'*

Tongo was surprised. He had never seen his wife so angry (though, with her extraordinary features, it would have been unnoticeable to anyone without a diploma in Kudzaisms), let alone heard her speak so disrespectfully.

'Hoore?' the professor exclaimed. 'Did she just call me a prostitute?'

The chief giggled nervously. 'A prostitute?' he blustered. 'Ha! Did you hear that, Kudzai? A prostitute, eh? Talk about a diplomatic incident waiting to happen! No, no, no; *"Hoore"* is a term of affection, like "sister"'. He looked at his wife pleadingly. 'Isn't that right, sweetie?'

'Kuzvani Zamba?' Kudzai asked her husband.

'A little,' Bunmi said, answering for him.

Kudzai smiled viciously and approached the professor, clapping in the traditional manner. *'Uribo, ku pfanzvi, makanwe chiporo sisi dopo gudo?'*

The professor smiled and clapped too. *'Ndiribo! Makuribo, hoore?'*

Tongo looked on helplessly. He knew that this was getting way out of control, although the professor was none the wiser. His wife's left hand was rubbing her stomach ruefully and she winced a little. But her right hand clenched against her thigh and he was scared she might clap her rival. Because, as far as Kudzai was concerned, she had just asked Bunmi how it felt to be the 'limp-legged, cavern-fannied daughter of a baboon' and Bunmi had replied, 'Fine. How about you, harlot?'

The chief positioned himself between the two smiling women and put his hands on his wife's shoulders. Her small eyes were welling up and her pointed ears twitched a little as she sniffed through her gooseberry nose. How Tongo loved her at that moment! Which made it seem all the stranger to him that she could suspect him of infidelity (because men only ever know themselves as well as fat people know their feet). And besides, wasn't *he* the theoretical cuckold? It was peculiar how the fates chose to obtund a significance, even reverse its polarity, with one gesture of their fickle will.

'The professor and I are almost finished,' Tongo soothed. 'Go and put your feet up, my darling, and I'll be with you in a moment.'

Kudzai's eyes fell and, reluctantly, without looking at Bunmi, she stalked from the room. Tongo felt the full force of the anti-pounce lobby demonstrating in his brain's higher functions and he turned to the professor and he felt his mood bristle, because hadn't she caused this trouble?

'Is our business concluded?'

'I'm sorry, Tongo,' Bunmi said. 'Is there a problem?'

'No problem. But now I must attend to my wife.'

Bunmi nodded. She wasn't getting anywhere anyway. Her persuasions – for the chief's signature, of course – could wait for another time.

'You should come and visit the dig,' Bunmi suggested as she was escorted from the room.

'Yes. Of course. The dig. Most definitely,' Tongo replied. But his mind was already wandering elsewhere, particularly when he saw the group of village women bearing baskets of rape who were gathered at the fence of his kraal. And there was Stella 'Ngozi, of course, talking under her breath and waiting her moment, like the chief vulture perched in the tree above a kill.

The women watched curiously as Tongo showed Bunmi to the

gate and shook her hand mechanically and turned away without meeting their eyes. Bunmi greeted them with a smile as she passed and they muttered "*hoore*" under their breath and they were infuriated when her smile only widened and she nodded enthusiastically. Their attention turned to the chief's sleeping hut, however, when they heard a commotion from inside. They dug each other in the ribs and craned their necks (as though such effort might enable them to see right through the mud-brick walls). Suddenly Tongo appeared in the doorway and he was waving his hands like a crazy man and his expression was contorted in fear.

'Find the *zakulu*,' he shouted, his voice rasped and wavering. 'Find the *zakulu* now!'

The women looked at one another. 'But chief,' Stella said, 'he is in the magic sleep and he gave instruction that he wasn't to be woken for anything.'

'I don't care what Musa said,' Tongo screamed. 'Kudzai is dying. Bring the *zakulu* here now!'

Stella heard the pain in the chief's voice, saw the seriousness in his face and smelled the sickness on the breeze. She dropped her basket of rape to the ground and she set off as fast as she could.

When Stella 'Ngozi arrived at Musa's *kraal*, the *zakulu* was there in fact but elsewhere in every more important way. As she walked into his sleeping hut – a venue that brought back more than a few memories – and found him on his bedmat, the *zakulu* was standing on the tallest mountain of the Eastern Highlands (that kissed the sky) while an anthropomorphic eagle as big as a house pointed off into the distance with one enormous wing. Stella poked the *zakulu* violently in the ribs, something she'd wanted to do ever since her deflowering, but he was too busy listening to the eagle to stir. He just turned on his right side and began to snuffle gently while she berated him to wake up.

In Musa's dream story, the eagle was saying, 'He fell off just there. Can you see? Right at the edge of the world. There's a hole in the ground the shape of a handsome young songster.'

Musa squinted and strained his eyes and said, 'Oh yes, of course,' even though he couldn't see anything because there was no way even a *zakulu* could see all the way to Angola. He lied partly because he was exhausted and he was enjoying this pause in the breakneck adventures of his sleep and partly because he had no desire to irritate a house-sized bird who could have eaten him for whatever meal was now due.

How long had he been dreaming? Musa had lost track of time about two days previously because it was almost impossible to keep your body clock in order when you were buffeted between past, present and future like a *kabwe* chick in a circle of playful *shumba* cubs. He had seen stories unfold before his eyes that then screwed up into balls and tossed themselves into time's whirlwinds until they were lifted into the air. He saw a *musungu* he'd known from the coup six years before and he didn't recognize him. He saw faces he'd never met and he knew them like family. He witnessed the death of a beautiful young girl who was dressed like a queen in her nakedness. He heard the most exquisite voice strangle like water down a drain. He caught the birth of a baby who screamed like the trumpets on Kudzai's cassette player. He confronted two elegant *musungu* women with negro faces and he turned just in time to spot himself disappear into a peculiarly vaginal rabbit hole and his foot waggled in the air behind him and he noticed he was missing a toe.

The *zakulu* looked up at the mammoth eagle and he felt suddenly irritated. He knew that the knowledge of dreams was essentially symbolic in nature. But he sometimes wished that Cousin Moon, his ancestral cronies, Fate and his best friend, Choice, might humour him with a bit of straight-talking.

Occam's Razor, he thought. That's the trouble with these omniscients. They never grasp the principle that making the fewest possible assumptions is generally the best way to explain a thing.

'Why did you do it?' Musa asked the eagle.

'Do what?'

'Kidnap the boy.'

The eagle shrugged lazily and turned the question back on him: 'Why did you?'

Musa was taken aback. 'What have I done?' he asked.

'What *have* you done?'

'What do you mean?'

'What do *you* mean?'

Musa was about to continue this exchange but he thought better of it and gave up. For a terrifying, feathered monster, this eagle certainly did a fair impression of an irksome younger brother. Instead the *zakulu* took a deep breath and decided to enjoy the mountain air and work through the few things he knew for sure.

He knew he felt guilty. No. He *was* guilty. He didn't know why or when or what he'd done but he knew that he (or, more likely, one of his past selves) had done wrong and he was going to have to make up for it somehow. He knew that he had to make a journey. He wasn't sure of the destination yet but that wasn't too much to worry about. He was well aware that the longest journeys often finished at their beginning while a brief excursion could easily lead to the middle of nowhere. What else? The *zakulu* didn't *know*, but he was fairly sure, that the climax to his dreaming was close at hand. He had that sense that time was about to take shape, to unravel, to crystallize. He also knew, suddenly and much to his surprise, that someone – not the eagle at least – was slapping him repeatedly about the face.

Musa sat up with a start to find Stella 'Ngozi clutching her stinging palms under her armpits. He ran a finger across his tender cheeks and then put his hands on his head. When he felt his dreadlocks, he immediately knew he was no longer asleep because in his dreams Cousin Moon always insisted upon a haircut.

'Stella 'Ngozi!' he exclaimed. 'What do you think you're doing interrupting the *zakulu*'s magic sleep? Just when it was getting good too! Do not mess with me, Stella! For I can make your womb shrink to a peanut and Tatenda will look outside the marriage for fresh *pau pau*!'

At least that's what Musa thought he said. But after five days of the magic sleep, all that came out of his mouth was a gobbledegook concoction of back-to-front Zamba, belching and the arcane language of the ancestors.

Stella stared down at him, bewildered. But, having slapped her hands raw on the *zakulu*'s bristling face, she wasn't going to give up now. '*Zakulu*! It's Kudzai! The chief sent me here to wake you. He says that Kudzai is dying.'

Musa contemplated her blankly for a moment or two before shaking his head vigorously from side to side to try and jounce some sense back into it. He offered a quick prayer to Cousin Moon to beg forgiveness for the interruption and he allowed Stella to help him up (because five days' sleeping takes its toll on a man). He was somewhat surprised to find that he was naked and it took a good ten minutes to ease his stiff joints into some clothes and a further ten to count and double-check his toes before squeezing his feet into his boots.

'Let's go,' he said at last.

By the time the *zakulu* reached the chief's homestead, Tongo was going out of his mind with worry. The village women had ushered him out of the *rondeval* so that they could tend to Kudzai and he just paced back and forth between the doorway and the borehole, wringing his hands and scratching his head. His wife was going to die. He was convinced of it. And he kept asking himself the same unhelpful question, 'What have I done to deserve such a fate?' and, before his brain had time to offer the unhelpful answer, he asked himself the question again. What have I done to deserve such a fate?

The appearance of Musa, who was stumbling like a drunkard and slurring his words, offered Tongo little comfort. But the *zakulu* patted him on the shoulder and said, 'Don't worry, my friend. It is not Kudzai's time. Do you not think I would have heard something if she was about to join the ancestors in Tuloko's garden?'

Tongo had to suffer another hour of pacing, questioning and

cursing before Musa emerged from the sleeping hut with the most peculiar, pained expression on his face, as though the wind had changed and pinched his cheeks in a fixed and ghoulish grimace. Tongo immediately bombarded him with questions but the *zakulu* wouldn't say a word until he had led his friend out of earshot of the village women.

'What?' Tongo pleaded. 'Tell me, Musa. What is it?'

The witchdoctor performed facial gymnastics for a moment or two before his expression returned to something like normal. 'I tell you something, Tongo,' he said. 'I wish you hadn't told me about the monkey ears. It's hard to treat a patient when you're permanently on the precipice of hilarity.'

'Musa. Please. Tell me. Is Kudzai all right? Is my wife going to die?'

'To die? Of course not. She is bleeding from the womb but it is nothing that *garwe* soup and two weeks of bedrest won't fix. You're child is a feisty one, my friend; six months new and he's already trying to come out and see the sights! I tell you, it took quite some talking to persuade him he was better off where he was. In the end, I had to tell scare stories about snow and ice and freezing wind that sends your *choko* yelping for cover before he agreed to stay put. I think the poor kid thinks he's going to be born an Eskimo.'

Tongo barely heard Musa's words. He bent double in relief and sucked in the air like a *kapenta* diver taking a breath. 'Can I see her?' he asked.

'I don't think that's such a good idea.'

'Is she sleeping?'

'No, but I don't think she wants to see you right now.'

'What? Nonsense!' The chief scoffed and he brushed aside Musa's protestations and entered the sleeping hut. The *zakulu* sighed and shrugged his shoulders. It had been an odd day. Most odd. One moment he was confronted by the vagaries of a dream's shapeless magic, the next he was staring reality, mundane and morose, squarely in the face as his friend did his best to fuck up his marriage. And, in between, he'd witnessed the halfway house in the magical reality of creation. It was little wonder that distinctions didn't seem so important, for they were no more than man-made pontoons spanning a dry river.

Musa began to count out loud. And he was surprised to reach thirty-eight before the chief reappeared, stooped and crestfallen.

'What is it?' the *zakulu* asked. The question stemmed more from a morbid sense of the appropriate than any genuine interest. For he already knew the answer.

'Kudzai!' Tongo said bitterly. 'I don't know why I married her. Everyone said it was a mistake but I wouldn't listen.'

'You've changed your tune.'

'Changed my tune! Nonsense. I've been saying as much for months.'

'Not when you thought she was going to die.'

Tongo shrugged coldly. 'A fuss over nothing. Sun rising? Women are sick. Sun setting? Women are sick. Having babies? Women are sick. And who's to say it's my sprog anyway? I tell you I'm damned if I'm going to play daddy to another man's issue.'

Musa stared at his friend. His attitude was no less astonishing for being expected but Musa knew men too well. Sun rising? Men fucked up. Sun setting? Men fucked up. But having babies? Then they really fucked up with the unstoppable fatalism of felled trees. Men were as confused as hydrophobic hippos or philanthropic crocs or the *zvambwe* that nit-picks a lion's arse and then, at the sight of its teeth, clucks, 'Fly away? Me? I couldn't possibly!' He loved Tongo like a brother and, when he squinted, he could see the Great Chief Tuloko's heart beating nobly in his chest. But his friend certainly had a capacity for idiocy that did little service to his gender. The *zakulu* sighed heavily and rubbed his eyes with his knuckles. For didn't he have more important issues to consider like the meaning behind his magical dreams?

'I'm going on a journey, Tongo,' Musa said.

'A journey? You can't. I need you.'

'Sorry, my friend, but I have been told by Cousin Moon himself and when he tells you to jump, you just cross your fingers and pray you don't land in the toilet ditch.'

'Where are you going?'

'I don't know yet. I'll tell you when I get there.'

Tongo contemplated Musa quizzically for a second or two. He was vaguely intrigued but he knew that he wasn't going to get any answers. And besides, he was in that curiously male frame of mind that is utterly and hermetically solipsistic. So he just shrugged and said, 'I'm going to take your advice. I'm going to find some fresh *pau pau.*'

Musa nodded absent-mindedly. He remembered that he'd left his *gar* at his kraal and he needed a joint. 'Who did you have in mind?' he asked lazily. 'Remember, my friend: there's not much adult about adultery.'

'Didn't you say every relationship is triangular?'

'And so it is.'

'Well, until now I haven't been able to see the point (if you catch my drift). But I've met this tasty little piece and it feels right to me and none of my ancestors has a word to say against it. I tell you, she's got real spirit and a celestial backside to die for. Perhaps Kudzai was a mistake, *zakulu.* Perhaps it's time I faced up to that and sent her back to the city once and for all. Because what's a responsible chief to do? We can't have some bastard succeeding me as the chief of Zimindo.'

'I thought you loved Kudzai.'

'Love?' Tongo scoffed. 'I never realized you were such a pigeon-toed romantic, my friend. You? Musa the *zakulu* who can't remember the last place he left his *chongwe*? I ask you, what is "love" when compared to "fate"? Put those two one-eyed beasts in the wrestling pit and you know who'll come out on top. And that's how this feels, my friend; it feels like my destiny.'

The *zakulu* watched the chief, steady-eyed. He knew that arguing with self-justification was as pointless as trying to stop the wind by cursing. And when you threw destiny into the mix? There was nothing to fall back upon but traditional proverbs and aphorisms. Because that's what they were there for.

'The ancestors teach us that destiny is both the solace of the strong and the refuge of the weak.'

Tongo tutted. 'I know that!'

'But they also teach us,' Musa continued, improvising desperately, 'that destiny is sometimes no more than your penis in disguise.'

Tongo turned away from the *zakulu*. He didn't need to hear this horseshit because hadn't he made up his mind and blamed it upon fate? And he closed his eyes for a moment before blinking them wide open again at the sight of Kudzai's face staring back from his eyelids.

'You tell me you are going away, my friend,' he said quietly. 'Just give me your blessing.'

'You have my blessing,' Musa said. 'May Cousin Moon guide you so that your every action may bring honour to the Great Chief Tuloko.'

The chief gazed at the *zakulu* and his eyes were hard and impenetrable. 'Thanks for nothing,' Tongo said bitterly and he turned on his heel and stormed off towards his concrete house.

A moment or two later, Musa heard the sounds of Kudzai's cassettes and he sucked his teeth pensively. There was nothing more to be said, so he decided to head back to his own kraal because he needed to gather his thoughts, to smoke some *gar*, to beg Cousin Moon to look after his friend in his absence. And, most of all, he had to start packing.

I: *A man called Fate*

(Mount Marter, Lousiana, USA. 1912)
When Lick returned to Cooltown's Canal Street after four years in the Double M, he found that nothing had changed and everything too. There were still the same old honkytonks (though Toothless Bessie's had been renamed plain Bessie's on account of the madam's new dentistry) and the doormen still ejected steam men – steamed up on dime hooch – with strong arms and harsh language. But Lick knew none of the doormen no more. And none of the steam men neither. Kids played in the gutters – the same old games with string balls and tin cans – but Lick didn't know these shooters' names and he was right out of the pecking order.

Most of all, Lick noticed the difference in Kayenne's household, no more than a fossil of what was lost. Lick could just about remember the days (be they real or re-imagined) when the two-room apartment held Kayenne and her eight kids. But now Cheese and Falling Down were dead, and Ruby Lee too after her pee-eye cut her up outside the back of Brown Sugar's. Sina was in Chicago (as far as anyone knew) and Sister dealt with Ruby Lee's death flat on her back in the tonk, flying high on an opiate cloud. According to Corissa, Sylvie was long gone for the bright lights of New Orleans and nothing had been heard of her since. And, of course, Kayenne's corner rocker was now empty. Though sometimes, when he was alone, Lick would nudge it a little, just to hear the reassuring creaking of tired wood.

So that left just Corissa and Lick in the apartment and, small as it was, they rattled around like two dried beans in a cooking pot. Corissa didn't go out much or speak much or do much. She tended the house and cooked food when there was food to be cooked; but mostly she just lay on her dead mother's bed, clinging to its smell and haunted by the ghosts of the men who'd slept there.

Most days Momma Lucy came visiting. She had aged a whole lot during Lick's time in the Double M and now her eyes were failing and she couldn't climb the outside staircase without a good deal of huff and puff. But, in the sunset of her life, Momma Lucy wanted her family around her. What was left of them.

Although she spent a lot of time at the Canal Street household, generally speaking she didn't set foot in the apartment. 'There too many memories in that room for an old woman,' she used to say. 'Them give me the heebs.' Consequently, she preferred to sit outside the door on the top step – during the long heat stretch especially – fanning herself with a prayer book and listening to all the comings and goings. Momma Lucy was a well-known figure in Cooltown and folk would call up to her from the street below: 'Yo! Momma Lucy! How you's keepin'?' And she replied, 'I jus' fine. The Lord, he take care of his own.' Always the same answer, though she often couldn't tell whom she was addressing.

With Momma Lucy ever-present on that top step, the Canal Street shooters were soon playing a new game. They took it in turns to climb the staircase, just as silent as cats hunting birds, and they tried to touch Momma Lucy's skirts without being seen. 'Who dat?' Momma Lucy exclaimed when she felt the tug at her hem. 'You think I too old to wup you good?' But the shooter would be laughing and down the steps in an instant and Momma Lucy sighed and stayed right where she was.

The first time Lick caught a shooter playing this game – a young kid, couldn't have been more than six years old – he gave him a mighty hiding. But Lick wasn't there all the time and the game only stopped when Momma Lucy's sight grew so weak that the challenge of climbing the staircase unseen was no longer testing enough for laughs.

On his release from the Double M, Lick spent a long time doing nothing. For some two months, he didn't work or even pick up his horn. By day he just walked the streets of Cooltown, renewing old acquaintances and making new ones. In the evenings he took a meal from Big Annie who, though she had none to spare, felt a degree of obligation on account of Lick's friendship with Naps and her own with Kayenne (God rest her soul). At night, he hung around outside the tonks, listening to the music and scrounging the odd beer from the drunken cleeks. Lick couldn't muster the spirit for anything more.

He remembered the day Professor Hoop asked him why God had put him on the earth.

He had replied, 'God put me 'pon this earth to care for Momma Lucy, Kayenne and my sisters.'

But now his sisters – excepting the silent Corissa – were dead or so elsewhere as to make no odds and Kayenne was dead too and Momma Lucy was surely soon to follow the same way.

Momma Lucy tried all kinds of different tactics to snap Lick out of his depression. Sometimes she cussed him – 'Nobody never heard of no lazy negro!' – and sometimes she encouraged him (to find work, to blow his horn). But mostly she pressed him with her own religious convictions.

'Put your faith in Jesus, Lick boy!' she said. 'God give you the strength for this life, an' paradise when you cross that river to the next.'

But Lick didn't trust in God no more; not even the God that spoke through his cornet. 'I don't bother God none,' he said. 'So God don't bother me.'

When Momma Lucy heard this, her useless eyes filled with tears and after that she visited the church in Jones twice a week and prayed for Lick's soul.

Eventually Lick snapped out of his torpor. But it wasn't Momma Lucy's prayers or her chiding that did it. No. One night Lick returned home from a night at Brown Sugar's joint so late that Old Hannah was just beginning to peep over the horizon. He pushed the door open – real quiet so as not to wake Corissa – and the room was bathed in the pale light of the early morning sun. Corissa was lying on her momma's bed, fast asleep on her front with her thumb in her mouth, one leg out straight and the other tucked up to the side. Her position rucked her dress up over her thighs right to where her buttocks should have been. But that clear, acute light that only comes with the earliest rays showed that Corissa's legs were as skinny as two broomsticks. The tendons behind her knees were accentuated like tree roots above ground and her legs just went up and up until they met at the bottom of her back. She was so thin that Lick could barely believe she was alive at all and his heart skipped for a moment or two until he saw her lips murmur to the strangers she met in her dreams.

Skin an' bone, Lick thought. Skin an' bone! If she were a chicken she wouldn't even feed a hungry child!

Lick went to bed in the other room with heavy eyes and a heavy heart. But he couldn't sleep any. Because there was still one sister to care for and he'd forgotten all about that.

That morning, after Lick had been lying restless for no more than two hours, he got up and headed straight into Jones to Old Man Stekel's store. He hadn't been back there since his release from the Double M but the Jew greeted him with the *nachus* generally reserved for his own son. He put his hands on Lick's shoulders and then on the top of his head.

'Fortis Holden?' Stekel said. 'That you? Look what a big man you are these days. And how is your grandmother? I haven't seen Mrs Lucy for a long time.'

Old Man Stekel gave Lick a job on the spot, as an extra pair of hands for deliveries and to carry boxes of groceries out to the foul-smelling motor vehicles driven by fine-looking white gentlemen in fashionable caps, long coats and thick goggles. But, truth be told, Lick knew that Old Man Stekel and his son Dov could have managed the store just fine without him. There wasn't enough work for the three of them and Lick spent many an afternoon sharing a soda with Stekel and listening to the old man tell stories about his home town, far away in a place in Europe called Prague.

Once Lick asked Stekel if he ever considered going back there, going home. And when he asked that question, the old man fell silent and his expression gained a wistfulness that Lick liked to see.

'Let me tell you something, Fortis,' he said. 'A Jew has no home. For a Jew, home is where you work. Plain and simple. This is my home. This is where I work.'

'What about a negro?' Lick asked. 'I's wantin' to know where my home is too. Is it Africa?'

Stekel smiled and slowly shook his head.

'Is this my home?' Lick asked, pointing to the store. ''Cos this is where I's workin'.'

The old man spoke quietly: 'Fortis, I spent my whole life finding my home. Maybe you'll be lucky; maybe you'll find yours sooner than that. But I can't tell you where to look. It's not for me to say.'

Some years later, when Lick looked back at those painful months after his release from the Double M, he realized the debt he owed to Old Man Stekel. Of course by then Stekel was dead and gone but Lick knew that there was some sense of repayment just in the acknowledgement. And when he thought of the few men who'd had an influence on his childhood – Paddle Jones, Squint-Eye Jack, even Professor Hoop – Lick recognized that the old Jewish store keeper was the closest he'd known to a father.

After that first day of work back at the store, Old Man Stekel gave Lick a small package of food – corn cobs, beans and a piece of ham. Lick protested but Stekel waved him away. 'Fortis,' he said, 'when was the last time you had a proper meal in your house? I'm sure you can put this to good use.' And Lick couldn't argue with the truth of that any.

When Lick got home, Momma Lucy was sitting on the top step.

'Lick? That you?'

'S'me, Momma Lucy. I got a job.'

Momma Lucy's lips trembled with the ghost of a smile. 'You a good boy, Lick,' she said.

Inside, Lick found Corissa still lying on Kayenne's bed, like she hadn't moved a muscle all day. Her eyes were wide open and her breathing came wispy as fine cotton.

'Corissa,' Lick said, 'I got a job.'

Corissa didn't say even a word of acknowledgement. Lick sat on the edge of the bed and placed a hand on his sister's bony hip. 'I said I got a job. I brought home some food an' I needs you to make me somethin' to eat. You hear?' Still Corissa didn't move and Lick sighed deeply. 'Momma's dead an' she ain't comin' back. But I's alive an' I's hungry an' I needs you to make me somethin' to eat.'

Slowly, mechanically, Corissa swung her legs over the side of the bed. She stared directly into Lick's face with eyes so sad that Lick felt like she was a blackbird pecking at his soul. She didn't say anything, but she took the package of food from Lick's hands and set about preparing a meal. Lick watched her all the time and her movements were like an old woman's: slow and painful. She cooked up a stew, just like Kayenne used to make only not so good, and when it was ready Lick went to the door and called for Momma Lucy to come to the table.

But Momma Lucy said, 'There too many memories in that room for an old woman. Them give me the heebs.'

'Momma Lucy,' Lick said carefully. 'You know I ain't bein' disrespectful. But Kayenne and Cheese and Falling Down and Ruby Lee, they's all dead. But we's alive and we's hungry.'

And Momma Lucy looked at the fuzzy image of her grandson and she said, 'Give me a hand up, Lick boy, an' let's eat.'

Lick barely ate a scrap – partly because it didn't taste so good and partly because he was too busy watching Corissa. At first Corissa just picked at her food. Then she tried a whole mouthful and then she gobbled the whole lot down just like a hungry dog. She even ran a spoon around the cooking pot so as not to waste the remains of the gravy. And, as Lick watched her, she seemed to fatten a little before his eyes; her cheeks and jibs seemed to fill out and her shoulders squared. Lick smiled and, on an impulse, he went to the other room and retrieved his cornet from under the bed. While Corissa cleaned the dishes, Lick sat out on the steps and held his cornet in his lap and practised his fingering. He hadn't played for a long time and he wasn't sure he still had it in him. But eventually he lifted the horn to his lips and tried out a simple blues number he'd composed a couple of years before as he sat on the soft banks of the stream beneath Echo Hill.

The notes came awkwardly at first and there was rasp in his tone that sounded ugly to Lick's fine ear. But the rasp soon cleared and, by then, Lick was too lost in the music to notice anyway, playing with his heart and his head and his chops. Prostitutes and pimps who were heading to the Canal Street tonks paused beneath the steps to listen to Lick's music. And customers who'd already picked up their main squeeze for the evening looked into the young whores' eyes and wondered if they'd ever know what it was like to really love a woman. Some of them called up to Lick as he blew saying things like, 'Damn, boy! You play that horn real good!'

When Lick finished, he ruefully ran a finger over his lips. They were surely sore from lack of practice.

If I'm gonna play the horn right, he thought, I got to look after my jibs and that's the truth.

He wondered if there was any pig fat left in the pan that he could use to soften his mouth and he turned to call in to Corissa. But she was already standing, quiet as a mouse, in the doorway. Lick smiled. For some reason he was a little embarrassed.

'What the name of that song?' Corissa asked. Lick realized that he hadn't heard her speak for days. Weeks maybe.

'The Double M Blues.'

'You goin' out tonight?' Corissa asked and the words seemed to snag in the back of her throat.

'Not tonight,' Lick said.

Thereafter, the Canal Street household quickly dropped into

some kind of routine that kept Corissa from her nightmares and Lick from his dreams. Though Corissa was seventeen and Lick just turned thirteen, they lived almost like man and wife and, as if in response, Lick grew physically. Almost overnight. His chest broadened, his chin bristled and he shot up three or four inches. Lick left for work every morning and prostitutes returning to their beds would smile at him and nudge one another and call out crude suggestions because he was a fine-looking young man. But Lick paid them no mind.

While Lick worked, Corissa cleaned the house, washed the clothes and cooked the evening meal. After they had eaten – usually with Momma Lucy too – Lick sometimes went out to listen to music in the tonks. But mostly he stayed home and played his horn on the top step and the Canal Street residents would stop what they were doing and for an hour or so the clock stopped ticking. Those were Corissa's favourite times. She didn't talk while Lick was playing but she watched her brother proudly and considered that maybe life was not so damn scary after all.

Lick loved to blow his horn so! But after he'd finished, he couldn't help but feel a creeping sadness that tangled itself around his heart. He couldn't identify the emotion exactly but he knew its name. 'Sylvie.' Lick spent many a sleepless night picturing his beautiful, pale-skinned sister, decked out in imported dresses and jewellery and giving elegant company in the finest establishments in New Orleans.

I'll go and find her one day soon, he thought.

Naps was released from the Double M on his fourteenth birthday and, when Lick got home from work, he raced right round to Big Annie's. Lick hadn't seen his friend for two years. He hadn't been able to visit him in the Double M on account of his not being family. But he'd heard reports from Naps's momma and his heart was jumping in his gullet as he knocked on the door.

Naps himself came to answer. Naps had grown a good stretch too and he'd lost a few teeth and his cheek bore a jagged scar. It was a beat or two before either boy spoke any. Then Naps's face cracked into a gappy smile and he said, 'If it ain't my own personal fuckin' nigger!'

'You the main man!' Lick said. 'The man with the masterplan!'

And the two boys slapped skin and then hugged. And then the hug turned into an impromptu wrestle that took them stumbling across the sidewalk until they were both sprawling in the dust and giggling. Soon Naps sat astride Lick's chest and pinned him to the street by his wrists.

'You one ugly scarface fuckin' nigger!' Lick said.

'Better mind what you say, Lick boy, ' Naps retorted. 'Or I cut you my own self.'

Lick thrashed about in Naps's grip and eventually managed to throw him off. The two scuffled some more until they ran out of energy. Then they sat panting on Big Annie's step and looked at one another and laughed and shook their heads.

'What you gonna do, Naps?' Lick asked. 'You gonna get a job?'

'Workin's for niggers an' Jews an' fools,' Naps said. 'But I got a few plans.'

That night Lick and Naps went down to Bessie's tonk with a little money that Lick had saved for special. It was the first time either of them had been inside since that night six years before when Good Evans had lain in the gutter with the doohickey sticking from his back. But, for all their experience, the two boys were still young enough to ignore the weight of personal history and Naps laughed when he heard about the joint's name change and he said, 'Guess you better call me Toothless Naps now!'

They took a table close to the bar and they sat shooting the breeze, drinking dime hooch and listening to the house band play some corny old tunes. Once or twice a prostitute came over looking for a trick and once or twice a white good-time boy flashed a dangerous look in their direction. But Naps warned off men and women alike with no more than a glance. Lick noticed that he had an air of authority about him that he'd never had before. He'd always had a way with words but now he had a way with his eyes too that was surely just as eloquent, a 'Don't fuck with me' look that could stop a man at ten paces.

Now the band at Bessie's was no better than average – most folk didn't go there for the music. It was led by Soup Thomas on piano, with a man named Ash Hansen on trombone, Stutter Jackson on clarinet, his brother, Kid Jackson, on drums and Jig on the cornet. Jig didn't have no other name but 'Jig' and he got that name on account of his being everybody's friend. He wasn't much of a horn player but he was a tubby, likeable man who never had a bad word for nobody. Unfortunately, such a pleasant demeanour didn't necessarily help you any in Cooltown.

That night, when Lick and Naps were down at Bessie's celebrating the 'main man's' release from the Double M, some trouble broke out close to the small stage. It wasn't big trouble, just that everyday kind of negro trouble that happens when you mix hard men and hard women with a dash of hard liquor. But it was trouble enough for poor Jig.

Jig was halfway through a cornet solo when an argument erupted between a young prostitute and a squat-looking steam man with devil eyes and forearms like thick oak. It started as just the usual slapping and shoving and it didn't bother nobody. But then the steam man pulled a switchblade from his pocket and there was an almighty commotion as the people at the surrounding tables got themselves out of the way. The look in that steam man's eyes, you could bet he was going to cut the whore real good.

Now Jig was a peaceful man with no mind for violence. But his soul was as honourable as it was simple and he didn't like to see no man beating on his woman whether she be a prostitute or a princess. So Jig stopped his playing, jumped down from the stage and set himself between the fighting couple. He confronted the steam man with quivering lips and what the Louisiana black folk called 'cow eyes' back then – all fear and humility. Soup Thomas's band stopped playing as Jig squared his shoulders and screwed his courage.

'Now, brother,' Jig began, 'ain't no need for no knife play.'

'Who you callin' brother?'

The steam man clearly wasn't in a talking mood. But Jig persisted.

'The way I sees it, you don't wanna hurt nobody, least of all a lady. Jus' a little too much of that there hooch swillin' your system. So why . . .'

Jig stopped speaking and his eyes widened in surprise. At the back of the tonk, Lick and Naps couldn't see what was going on too well. But they knew what had happened. The steam man pulled his blade from Jig's gut and Jig sank to the floor with a soft whimper. For a beat or two Bessie's tonk was silent. Stabbings were a common occurrence in Cooltown but there sure wasn't nobody hardened to the horror. Lick turned to look at Naps but his friend was no longer at his side; instead he was pushing through the crowd to the stage. If there was trouble, then Naps liked to be in the thick of it.

Lick didn't see what happened next but he did hear the shouts and cussing. And he did see the prostitute flee through the door behind the bar and he did see the steam man carried out unconscious and he did see the crowd clear and Naps kneeling over poor Jig, pressing one hand to the knife wound and shaking out the knuckles of the other. Naps had a way with words, a way with his eyes and a way with his fists too. And Lick, slugging dime hooch to calm his racing heart, knew that Naps was a good friend to keep.

Bessie's customers quickly returned to their seats and the chatter buzzed as each told their version at every table. Jig was carried upstairs and someone sent a shooter to find Ma Cooper, the old woman with frantic hair and a gift for the herbs and potions. The crowd were soon baying for more music and, right on cue, Soup Thomas set off upon an easy rag with Stutter Jackson taking the lead on clarinet. But it sure sounded peculiar – thin and unexpressive – to hear the band play without a cornet.

Lick saw Naps talking to Miss Bessie herself right at the front of the stage. And, the next thing he knew, his friend was beckoning him over. At first Lick didn't move. If this was more trouble, then he had no mind to get involved. But Naps was gesticulating wildly and Lick finally sighed and got to his feet and joined his friend. He realized that the liquor was coursing through his system and he tried to keep his mind the right side up. He was greeted by Miss Bessie, smiling broadly. She sure must have been a beautiful woman in her time – her skin was clear and smooth and her dark eyes sparked like two flints – but Lick didn't notice anything but her new false teeth that seemed to jump out of her mouth when she smiled, like they were trying to escape.

'So you Lick Holden!' Miss Bessie said, as if his name was famous. She extended a bony hand to him that showed her age. 'Why they call you Lick?'

Before Lick could reply, Naps said, 'It's due to the way he plays the cornet, Miss Bessie. He blows that horn a real lick!'

Lick didn't know what to say. So he said, 'That's right.'

Miss Bessie nodded and gestured to the band. 'You want to help a lady out?' she said.

'Sure,' Lick replied. Because the hooch was doing the talking.

When the band broke their playing, Miss Bessie took the stage and had a word in Soup Thomas's ear. Soup looked none too pleased and stared at Lick and shook his head. But Miss Bessie was insistent and called Lick over. Lick looked to Naps, who smiled and shrugged, and before Lick knew what he was doing, he was up on stage with Jig's horn in his hands.

'What you say your name is?' Soup Thomas asked. He was chewing a matchstick in the corner of his mouth and his eyebrows were high, like he was permanently surprised.

'Lick, sir. Lick Holden.'

'We gonna play a real hot number. Get folk up and dancin'. You jus' keep up if you can.'

A hot number? Lick suddenly realized where he was and what he was doing and he sidled to the edge of the stage and his nervous fingers jumped up and down on those valves like the pistons on a Mississippi steamer. He looked out at the faces in the tonk – pimps and prostitutes, white good-time boys and gamblers, steam men and drunks – and he said a prayer for the first time since God knew when.

Soup led off on piano, three chords that told the band all they needed to know. Kid Jackson dropped into an easy rhythm – too lazy for Lick's mind – and Stutter set about an unadventurous melody. But Lick liked the sound of Ash Hansen's trombone; he played with a real bluesy feel that put the others to shame. It was a simple, dime-a-dozen, twelve bar blues and, as he lifted the horn to his chops and flicked his tongue across the mouthpiece, Lick thought, I can do this. No. I can do better!

Before he hit that first note, the black folk were just beginning to take to the floor. By the time he'd held that note, clear as a bell, for some eight bars – flattened it, softened it and brought it back stronger than ever – the whole joint was on its feet. Within eight bars, it was no longer Lick following the band but the band struggling to keep up with Lick. He ignored Soup's laboured attempts to rein him in and he raised Jig's horn high to the ceiling and blew until his chops numbed. He played against Stutter's melody, counterpointing, echoing and teasing a performance from the clarinettist like he'd never given before. He indulged in a marvellous glissando with Ash on trombone, sliding between notes with a melancholy relish to make your heart ache. He nursed a new rhythm from Kid's drums until the prostitutes were doing the funkybutt so sexy that even the pee-eyes were flashing their money. And by the time Lick hit that final top C, the tonk was just one body with the ceiling sweating and the walls heaving with quickened breath.

Bessie's hadn't heard music like this in six years; not since Buddy Bolden blew his mind and Lick imagined escape on the climbing scale. But now, as he played, Lick knew that music was not about escape at all. It was about roots, it was about who he was, and, as long as he held a horn in his hand, Lick knew he'd always be at home.

After that first stand-in session, Lick played Bessie's with Soup

Thomas's band every night for two years. Although it was soon accepted that it wasn't Soup's band any more but young Lick Holden's. And when Jig recovered, he was happy to play second cornet to Lick's soaring horn. While Lick blew, Naps worked the tables with quick fingers, sharp eyes and a subtle tongue that sure earned him some good money. He worked quite a stable of girls too, a successful pimp who was fair of mind and fists. But, most of all, he looked out for Lick (though Lick barely knew it), diverting trouble with quiet words and, on occasion, the razor that he kept handy in his back pocket. As Lick's reputation on the horn grew, so did Naps's reputation on the street. Men followed him with their eyes as he walked past and they turned to one another and said things like, 'That's one real smooth smokestack!'

Though Lick played Bessie's tonk by night, he kept his job with Old Man Stekel (the fifty cents or so he received from Miss Bessie was never going to be enough to support Momma Lucy and Corissa too). He played until 4 a.m. most days and was up again at seven to walk to the store in Jones. As a consequence he barely saw Corissa at all. But Corissa didn't object so much. She was happy to see Lick making his way and the extra money sure helped a little and, besides, she now had a suitor, name of Bubble, who thought she was the real fair weather. Bubble was perfect for Corissa, a slow dock worker (his jigs said he lived 'in a bubble') who transformed her opinion of men. Bubble treated Corissa like a lady and, over time, that was what she became.

For two years, Lick's life followed some kind of straight path. He worked, he blew and he treated sleep like a shooter with penny candy, making a little go a real long way. Then, one night in 1915, he took a sharp turn, as welcome as it was unexpected. A tall, red-headed, light-skinned black man watched him play that night and, though Lick didn't know his face, his name was legend the length of the Mississippi.

Fate Marable led a crackerjack orchestra that entertained day-long excursions on the Streckfus Line riverboats. Now, most times, the Streckfus steamers had no cause to stop in the backwater of Mount Marter. But on that particular day, a particular steamer (the *Dixie Belle*) had pulled into the Cooltown docks with engine trouble. And Marable, who was most particular about his music, ended up in Bessie's tonk where, he was told, he would hear the best blues in town.

When Lick stepped off stage at around half three, sweat waterfalling from his brow and his chops humming from exertion, Naps caught him by the arm and his face was alight with excitement.

'Lick boy!' Naps said. 'There's a cat here you gotta meet.'

Naps led Lick over to Marable's table where the long-limbed band leader lounged in a chair in a suit as fine as any white man's. His face was freckled like a child's and in his hand he held a long cigarette with a sickly sweet smell of cloves.

'This . . .' Naps's voice was quivering. 'This, Lick boy . . . This is Fate Marable.'

Lick's heart dropped into his boots and bounced right back up again.

'Pleased to meet you, Mr Marable, sir,' Lick said.

Marable sucked deep on his cigarette and frenched the smoke. His voice was hoarse – like he'd spent too many years shouting over a steam engine – but he spoke with an authority that had a person's ears straining.

'Lick?' Marable said. 'You wastin' your time in this Cooltown ratshop. You ever play New Orleans?'

'No, sir.'

'You read?' Marable asked. Because, as everyone knew, Marable's was a reading orchestra.

'No, sir.'

Marable nodded and smiled and stubbed his cigarette and drummed his fingers on the tabletop like he was playing the calliope.

'You go down to New Orleans, Lick. Brothers down there playin' jazz music so hot their brass be steamin' like the *Dixie Belle*. So you find a band leader name of Kid Ory and tell him Fate Marable sent you. Maybe he'll let you sit in. An' if you ever learn to read, Lick, come find me.'

'Yes, Mr Marable.'

And Lick didn't need no more push than that. The very next morning he was up early planning his move to Storyville, New Orleans, and within a week he was gone. He saw some of the Cooltown folk again (Naps, Corissa and Bubble for starters) but, by the time he eventually returned, others were long gone. Sister disappeared for good; six feet deep in shit, no doubt. Momma Lucy passed away and word arrived too late for Lick to make the funeral. Old Man Stekel too and Miss Bessie and Soup Thomas in a shooting down the Cooltown docks. But Lick knew death too intimately to allow the weight of past and future to affect his decisions any. He always remembered something Momma Lucy used to say, 'Today is a day like any other. But it's surely the only day you got.' Lick Holden had no sense of his place in history, which perhaps explains his inhabiting the sketchy half-world of myth.

The way he saw it, his life was like sheet music: its cast, the notes on the page. And he couldn't read and he never learned and he never joined Fate Marable's orchestra. But he heard the hot jazz resounding in his head and there was one theme that kept repeating and repeating, coming back when least expected in new and subtle guises, played out on different instruments in different keys. So Lick headed down to the Tenderloin (as Storyville was known back then) to look for Sylvie (who wasn't no blood relation). And, as the name of his sister formed on his lips, he smiled sheepishly to himself and spoke aloud: 'When a man called Fate tells you to do somethin', there ain't no point in arguin'.'

I: *Lick and Louis and a brief but significant relationship*

(New Orleans, Louisiana, USA. 1915)
Back in 1915 Storyville, New Orleans, had few things to recommend it and a list as long as your arm to keep a wise man away. Of course there was the music and the atmosphere and the raw alcohol that stripped the mucus from your gullet. But there was violence too, and the kind of crime that could chill your stomach better than sasparilla ice. A fool could lose his wallet, his jacket – damn! – even his life before he'd walked a block. Storyville was the most notorious legalized red-light district in the whole of the United States. And its reputation was well-deserved.

It took its name from Alderman Joseph Story, who clarified the legislation applied to the district in 1897. Now old Joe Story never much liked his name being associated with such an area, but nobody argued any that the title was kind of fitting. 'Storyville': stories unfolded in that district on a nightly basis – tales of sex and gambling, drugs and murder – and concluded before sun-up, often in the most macabre circumstances. Storyville could make Cooltown look like an upstanding community by comparison.

But when young Lick Holden arrived in Storyville in the spring of 1915, with no more than a bundle of clothes, a spare pair of boots and his precious cornet in its battered case, he was in no mind to see the seamier side. So he delighted in the Basin Street bustle and he thought the sun so pretty as it bounced off the windows of insalubrious establishments and picked out the diamond sparkles in the coal on the coal carts.

Most of all, however, Lick couldn't take his eyes from the graceful ladies who promenaded up and down the streets. My! They looked so fine! And they walked in clusters of colour, as if attracted by the shade of their own skin: there were the six-out-seven negroes, there the mulattoes and there the quadroons. Lick was sixteen years old and he'd never been with a woman before, his mind all taken up with music and poverty. But there weren't no women in Cooltown like these, that's what Lick thought. There ain't no women in Cooltown like these! That look like fair weather and smell like spices and walk like they're leading you to the bedroom!

And the women surely scoped Lick Holden too – though he was too green to notice – with his proud forehead and humble eyes and his gait like a real bush negro and his manly height and deep chest. But most of all they saw the way he ran a forefinger over his lower lip like a nervous habit, like he was checking it was still there, slow and sensual and sexual in a way he knew nothing about.

For some two hours, Lick didn't know what he was doing; he just strolled through the streets of New Orleans like a shooter following the scent of his supper. He wandered past the famous Economy Hall, where the great musicians cut their teeth, the Creole tonks of the Seventh Ward and the legendary Congo Square, where freed slaves had danced to African rhythms and Buddy Bolden had blown the hottest music of mythology. There was music on every street corner – it seemed like every man held a brass instrument in his hands! – and the colours were so vivid and the atmosphere buzzed like a trapped hornet and Lick felt as intoxicated as any goddam drunk.

But when the light began to fade, he realized he had to find somewhere to lay his head real quick and he turned down Gravier and began to enquire about a lodging. Only then did he discover how out of place he was, a bush negro who looked and sounded and held himself like a real Country Joe. Folk laughed when he opened his mouth and shook their heads and slapped one another on the back like he was the source of utmost hilarity.

Eventually Lick turned into Franklin and, next to a tonk called Kid Brown's, he asked about a room in a ramshackle boarding house run by a large mulatto lady by the name of Betsy Slim. Betsy was a motherly kind of woman who took one look at Lick and knew he wouldn't survive a night on the Storyville streets, and she took him in and installed him in a second-floor room. She charged him five dollars a week for the privilege – way more than Lick could afford – and the room smelled of fish and its ceiling was stained black from some overzealous cooking. But Lick was just relieved to find some place to lay down his humble possessions and he said, 'Thank you, ma'am! Thank you, ma'am, indeed!'

That night, Lick ate the grit biscuits that Corissa had made him special and pulled on his best boots and cleaned himself up a little and headed down into Franklin Street. Betsy Slim was sitting on the front step, swilling from a growler with two other big-boned, big-breasted women. As Lick walked by, the three of them laughed and nudged one another with heavy elbows.

'You look after yourself, Lick Holden, you hear?' said Betsy Slim.

'Yes'm!' Lick replied. 'Thank you, Miss Betsy.'

One of the women said, 'He sho' got some pretty manners!'

'He fine as sweet wine!' said the other.

Uncertain of his bearings, Lick resolved not to venture too far and he headed straight into Kid Brown's joint, swaggering his shoulders and trying for all the world to change from a smalltown boy into a real city cat. All things considered, Lick's caution was well advised.

Now Kid Brown's tonk had an atmosphere that Lick couldn't finger. It was like the same kind of deal as the joints back in Cooltown only more so. Somehow the music seemed louder, the liquor stronger and the women danced with the kind of sexuality you can taste. And the men? Damn! The men just seemed a whole lot bigger and a whole lot more scary! Each and every one of them exuded a physical presence that kept them from bumping one another like two norths on two compasses.

Lick took himself a table in the corner of the tonk and tried to look inconspicuous and ordered himself a shot of something strong.

He gulped that spirit in one and his throat fired. His eyes swept the room, gobbling up every detail like a baby nursing at the teat. It was a simple kind of joint with barely a nod to good living: a few tables and chairs, a timber bar down one side and a dusty floor that hadn't seen a broom in a while. But it was surely heaving like an old slaver!

Most of the men were sailors, crews from the dozens of ships that docked in New Orleans from all over the world (more than ever since the outbreak of war in Europe). The Storyville natives you could spot with ease. They had that nervous flicker in their eyes that betrayed the confidence of their firm jibs. Most of the prostitutes in this particular establishment were pale-skinned blacks with high cheekbones, unruly hair and noses just-so. On occasion, a young woman would approach Lick's table with sleepy eyes and swinging hips. Lick made polite conversation but he didn't want to dance and he was still a virgin and he wasn't one for a trick. Besides, he found deep-black-skinned women (with a tone to match his own) a good deal more beautiful. Excepting his sister Sylvie (who wasn't no blood relation), of course.

The band in Kid Brown's tonk were top-notch, playing a purity of blues that tickled your gut like a feather. In later years Lick couldn't recall whose band it was that first night in Storyville – because New Orleans spat out high-quality musicians like a shooter spitting pips. But history suggests that maybe Alphonse Picou or Manuel Manetta or even the great Bunk Johnson (who finally found fame in the 1940s) might have been playing.

By the door, a table of Storyville's toughest hustlers were playing cotch for high stakes. There was Morris Moore (without his brother, Godfrey, for once) and the legendary, skew-faced gambler known simply as 'Crook'. Joe Jones was at the table as well, a young drummer with an unhealthy taste for cards. This was when Joe was still a happy-go-lucky fellow with zest for life, liquor and ladies. But it was only a few years later, when his second wife left him, that poor Joe Jones slashed his own throat.

Standing at the bar, there were all manner of peculiar characters. Two young fellows, couldn't have been more than fourteen, were watching the music with rapt attention. One of them, a real chubby kid, had the widest chops Lick had ever seen and they were split in a permanent grin that looked part foolish and part wise. Next to them stood an enormous, broad-faced smokestack in a shirt that strained at the seams. Every now and then, he glanced at the two boys, his leather face folded in concern, like he was their own personal muscle or something.

To the left of this little group stood a terrifying-looking prostitute, famous in Storyville though Lick didn't know it. Her name was Mary Jack the Bear and she was deep in conversation with her pee-eye, a clean-featured brother name of Joe Bright Eyes. But one look at them told you that the power play in this pimp–prostitute relationship was cock-eyed even by Storyville's standards. Mary leaned back on the bar like she owned the joint, one leg bent up behind her and her skirt riding indecently up her thighs. Her face seemed set in a sneer of contempt and every now and then she picked between her teeth with a claw-like nail. Joe Bright Eyes, meanwhile, hunched over the bar and cupped his drink in his two hands like he feared she might take it from him.

It was Mary Jack the Bear who made the trouble in Kid Brown's tonk that night. But it wasn't her that started it and she surely didn't come out of it so good.

Lick had been sat in the corner of the joint for about twenty minutes when he saw the young girl walk in. Her name was Alberta and she was riding high on a cocktail of moonshine and cocaine. She was one of Joe Bright Eyes's walkers and she loved that pimp so much she had no conception of the trouble he got her in. Alberta was a beautiful young thing with milk-chocolate skin, a slim waist and the kind of high ass that brothers described as 'heavenly'. And that night she was rolling her ass to full effect, determined in her stoned haze to get some leverage on her pimp, maybe even drag him away from Mary Jack the Bear. And Lick watched a Storyville story unfold with wide eyes and itching palms.

Alberta leaned up against the bar right between Joe and Mary. She turned her head to Joe, dipped it a little and looked up at him from beneath those long feline lashes. She spoke to him – of course Lick couldn't hear what she said – and when Joe turned his bright eyes to her, she lowered her own with a coquettish kink of her neck. Joe shook his head. But you could tell he was interested, all right. And when Alberta ran a long finger across the soft skin of her lower lip, Joe was transfixed.

Now Mary wasn't going to stand for such a flirtatious display from no little girl who barely knew what it was to bleed and she spat out some cuss words loud enough for most of the tonk to hear. Generally speaking, no prostitute was dumb enough to cross Mary Jack the Bear any, let alone play for her man. But Alberta was as high as Old Hannah at midday and she wasn't bothered none by the older woman. Instead, as if making peace, Alberta sidled away from the bar and over to a bunch of steam men who sat at a nearby table. But then she bent forward, rested her elbows and raised that celestial ass of hers so high and so round that Joe's bright eyes were out on stalks, taking in the apple of her buttocks and the outline of her parting thighs.

That sure did it! There was no way Mary was going to take such cheek from no shooter girl and she marched over to the steam men's table and she pulled Alberta away by the hair and threw her to the ground. Mary was strong as a bear, the way she handled that girl so. And her eyes were bitter-shining and her nostrils flared like two funnels.

'I's goin' outside,' Mary Jack the Bear spat at Alberta. 'You gonna join me?'

Mary stomped out of Kid Brown's tonk like a whole army on the march and every face in the joint was now watching the action unpick. Joe Bright Eyes lifted Alberta off the floor. But, when the young girl turned her face up to his, he looked away. Joe slugged his drink quick time and shook his head slowly from side to side. Years of experience told him there was no gain in fooling with Mary Jack the Bear.

For the next ten minutes or so, Alberta stood at the bar throwing back spirits like she knew no tomorrow. Her confidence had now vanished. She knew she had to face Mary out in Franklin and she knew that prostitute was the toughest in the whole of Storyville. Watching from the back of the tonk, Lick felt like he should say something or do something. But he was rooted to his chair. Besides, he could see the smokestack and the two boys at the bar and even they couldn't bring themselves to look at Alberta, and the kid with the widest chops Lick had ever seen had stopped smiling.

What the hell can *I* do? Lick thought. What the hell's gonna happen?

Eventually Alberta downed her last drink and she walked slowly towards the door of the tonk with only the gentle sway in her step to tell you she was nervous. And, sure enough, the whole joint followed her, the whores and gamblers and sailors and pimps and young Lick too.

Outside, Mary Jack the Bear was leaning against a wooden pillar as cool as you like. But at the sight of Alberta, she straightened herself up and her face twisted with contempt.

'I know you, bitch!' Mary sneered, 'that sleep only with po' white trash.'

Alberta looked terrified but she wasn't going to back down.

'Ain't nothin' tougher than old hide and nothin' better than tender beefsteak,' she retorted.

'You low-down trash!'

By now there was quite a crowd gathered around the two women in a claustrophobic kind of ring and Lick pushed his way to the front. Opposite him, he could see the wide-mouthed kid, similarly transfixed. With every traded insult, the crowd oohed and aahed and laughed and said 'Goddam!' But then, most likely without thinking, Alberta issued a cuss that silenced the crowd and guaranteed the two women would come to blows. She pointed at Joe Bright Eyes, who was hovering in the background.

'You know he tell me he was through with your dirty hide,' Alberta said. 'Guess it mus' be your hustlin' money he gives me.'

That did it! Because there's no worse insult for a whore than her pee-eye spending her hard-earned money on another woman!

Mary Jack the Bear leaped at pretty Alberta and pulled a blade as long as her forearm from her skirts. In an instant, Alberta had a similar knife drawn and the two women were slashing at each other like reeds that whip your legs as you run through the marsh, only a whole lot more vicious. Nobody in the assembled crowd tried to intervene as the fight got way out of hand. Folk just watched, their feet glued to the spot, and they exclaimed 'My God!' when a blade found its target. The two whores knew what they were aiming for – the face, always the face – and they ribboned each other's looks with little care for their own.

The fight can't have lasted more than two minutes – though it felt more like twenty – until both women were lying on the sidewalk, horrifically disfigured and bleeding and moaning and uttering sweet prayers from their cussing mouths. The law officers turned up then and the crowd quickly dispersed, down Franklin or Gravier or back into Kid Brown's. The crazy whores were picked up and taken to the Charity Hospital. The young girl, Alberta, survived, one eye blind and her face like a carved joint. But Mary Jack the Bear – the toughest prostitute that Storyville ever saw – died of her wounds. Just another sorry end to another Storyville tale.

At the sight of the law officers, Lick rushed back into the tonk and took up a position by the bar. His whole body seemed to be pulsing with the horror he'd just witnessed and his breathing came shallow. Lick buried his head in his hands and his face was dripping with sweat like a fever. He'd seen trouble before and plenty of it. But this wasn't like Cooltown trouble, it was more. More violence. More blood. More misery.

I jus' a bush negro, Lick thought. I don't fit in here any and I's not sure I wants to.

He sighed deep and he looked around the tonk. On his left he saw the gigantic smokestack who had resumed his position at the bar and was laughing and joking with one of the two boys. The wide-mouthed kid, however, was staring straight at Lick and his expression was happy and sad all at once, like real good blues music. When their eyes crossed, Lick looked away uncomfortably and tried to order himself another drink. But the wide-mouthed kid came over and slapped him on the shoulder like he was long-lost family or some such.

'Yo, daddy!' the kid said. 'You new in town, friend?'

'What's it to you?' Lick replied and his hands made fists and he chewed on his gums. He looked at the kid and he weighed up his chances if it came to fisticuffs. What he won in height, the younger boy made up for in an extra pound or two around the gut. But the kid didn't seem to be in no fighting mood and he split that wide mouth of his into that enormous grin.

'Tain't nothin' to me, friend,' he said. 'Jus' enquirin'. Real polite, like. My name's Louis. Like St Louis. But everybody calls me Dipper. Not jus' my friends but everybody; so that includes you too. They call me Dipper on account of the size of my mouth.'

Lick nodded, slightly bemused, until Dipper said, 'Watch this!' and opened his mouth as wide as it would go and jammed his whole fist inside, right up to the wrist. Dipper's eyes seemed to swell and pop and Lick began to laugh.

'You see?' Dipper said, extricating his hand from his chops. He was laughing too. 'That's why they call me Dipper. Or Gatemouth. Or Satchelmouth.'

'Right,' said Lick.

'Right,' agreed Dipper, nodding. He leaned in towards Lick conspiratorially. 'There sho' some bad women in this joint. No doubt it's dangerous! No doubt!'

'For sho',' Lick replied.

'But ain't they so fine as sugar from a packet!' Dipper roared and he threw his head back and laughed heartily. And Lick joined in. There was something magnetic about this kid, a kind of sweet-natured innocence that was all the more appealing for its rough context.

'So what's your name, daddio?' Dipper asked. 'If I ain't bein' impolite.'

'Lick. Lick Holden.'

'An' why they call you that?'

Lick thought for a moment.

'It's down to the way I plays cornet,' he said. 'I blow that horn a real lick.'

'You play the horn?' Dipper exclaimed, his chops and bug eyes wide. 'Me too. I's the finest blues man in the whole of the Tenderloin,' he boasted. But Lick's uncertainty must have played on his face because Dipper quickly revised his opinion. 'Anyways, I will be one day. Ain't no point in lyin' any. So. What you doin' in Storyville?'

'I got a recommendation for a position with an orchestra from Fate Marable hisself.'

'You know Fate Marable?'

'Sure. He a personal friend of mine,' Lick lied.

'Damn! An' where's your recommendation?'

'With Kid Ory. You hear of him?'

'Double damn! Hear of him? He only the most famous band leader in the whole of good ol' New Orleans!'

Lick smiled and his chest swelled. He was enjoying showing off in front of his new acquaintance.

'Triple damn, Lick daddy!' Dipper continued. 'I sits in with Kid Ory myself once in a while. But I don't believe he got no room for 'nother cornet.'

'But I gots a recommendation from Fate Marable!' Lick protested, his pride pricked like a balloon.

'Well,' Dipper shrugged, 'we jus' have to go ask him.'

The next day, Lick met Dipper and his same two companions

around noon on the corner of Gravier and Franklin. In the beaming light, Dipper looked a whole lot younger and a whole lot more scruffy than he had the night before. He was wearing a frayed shirt and suspenders and a pair of pants that had been made for a man twice his size and age, rolled up so thick at the ankle that they looked almost like a diaper. The whole effect was so ramshackle it even made Lick look like one smooth brother. But he made no remark.

Dipper introduced Lick to the other boy, Ike, a real handsome child with sharp cheekbones and not much to say, and then to the enormous smokestack. 'Lick Holden,' Dipper said, 'this is Black Benny.' Lick held out his hand and Black Benny wrapped it in his own with fingers as thick and strong as creeping vines. Benny smiled as they shook and his face was pleasing in that broad, African kind of way. But Lick could think of nothing but the sound of his knuckles cracking in the giant's vice-like grip.

'Where we headin'?' he asked.

'Uptown,' Dipper said.

They surely made a funny-looking collection stepping out through the New Orleans streets! Black Benny strode out in front with a dollar grin on his face and his shoulders swinging and his big thighs like tree trunks on the move. Then came Dipper and Lick: Dipper like a shooter playing dress-up and Lick, the Country Joe, with his cornet case bumping against his hip as he walked. Last of all came silent Ike, who trotted in their wake with his eyes buried in the dirt at his feet. Some folk pointed and laughed as the four marched on. But Lick didn't notice on account of Dipper's chattering nineteen to the dozen – about his momma, his music and the Storyville characters they passed on their way – and his making the most peculiar noises. It seemed like every ten paces that Dipper would break wind or belch with extraordinary relish. Then he'd say something like, 'There goes a beauty!' Or, 'If in doubt, let it out!' And he'd laugh so hard and hearty that Lick had to join in.

Eventually they came to an elegant-looking building in the heart of uptown New Orleans, a dancehall by the name of Miss Cole's Cabaret. There were a lot of white folk in this area – men in three-piece suits with watch-chains and jaunty hats and women with bone-china complexions and ruby-red lips – and, as they paused momentarily outside, Lick felt suddenly uncomfortable. But Dipper had no such embarrassment and he marched into the dancehall like it was his own house. Black Benny followed, and silent Ike. And Lick followed behind them.

Inside Miss Cole's it took Lick a beat or two to adjust his eyes to the sombre lighting. But when he did he was dumbstruck by the finery on display. The dancehall had a high ceiling that gave it an airiness that was as different from the claustrophobic Cooltown tonks as chalk from cheese. The walls were hung with scarlet cloth with a sheen like the flank of a well-groomed horse and every single one of the tables was lit by a bright-burning candle sitting in an ornate porcelain holder. The stage was real pretty too, big enough for a brass band and all their friends and family, and raised two feet above the polished wooden dance floor that was as smooth as the ice on a winter bucket. Lick could barely believe what he was seeing. This dancehall had the atmosphere of a church and he couldn't imagine any man daring to speak within these four walls, let alone take to the floor with a girl in his arms.

Sitting at the table closest to the stage were four men of various ages and various shades of blackness, but all dressed as dapper as royalty. Dipper led Lick over to the table and performed the introductions and the men greeted young Dipper like he was one of their own, saying, 'Yo, Gate! Where you been, lil' bro?' and, 'Wassup, Dippermouth?'

The two younger men were Mutt Carey, a skinny negro who was playing first cornet with the Kid at the time, and Johnny Dodds, a crackerjack clarinettist who played with Papa Celestin's Tuxedo Brass Band. But Lick's attention was drawn to the two senior musicians at the table, a big six-out-seven negro as fat as good health who was none other than King Oliver himself and a light-skinned cat with straight hair and pinpoint eyes. That was the man Kid Ory.

'Yo, fellas!' Dipper said. 'This a personal friend of mine, Lick Holden, from Mount Marter. He plays the horn a real lick. Ain't that right?'

Dipper turned to his 'personal friend' but poor Lick was tongue-tied. These men were idols around the mouth of the Mississippi and Lick felt as small as a bug on a shooter's scalp and he was itching to get the hell out of there.

'He sho' the silent type,' observed King Oliver. His voice was like gravel and his expression as stern as an angry mother's.

'He a friend of Fate Marable's,' Dipper said. And Lick wished he hadn't.

'That right?' said Kid, speaking for the first time. He raised his eyebrows and the shadows of a smile played around the corner of his mouth. 'An' how's Mr Marable.'

'Jus' fine, sir,' Lick whispered. His throat was dusty dry.

'An' what can we do for you, Mr Lick Holden?'

'Mr Marable, sir . . .' Lick began.

'Fate . . .' interrupted Ory.

'Fate, sir, he gave me a recommendation. Said I should come to New Orleans and find Mr Kid Ory. You, sir. Said that maybe you'd let me sit in.'

'Fate said that?'

'Yessir.'

Ory looked at Dipper and shrugged. 'You ever hear him play, daddy?' Dipper smiled and looked a little shy for the first time. He shook his head. 'That a horn you got in that case?' Ory said. 'Then you best blow for us, Lick Holden.'

Lick stared at Kid Ory. He looked at Dipper, at King Oliver, Mutt Carey and Johnny Dodds and he couldn't tell if his chest was more likely to collapse or burst. But he gingerly opened his case and lifted out his cornet. How old and tarnished the brass looked in such smart surroundings!

He lifted the cornet to his lips but Kid said, 'Not here, Mr Holden. Take to the stage.' So Lick had to climb on to the stage and blow his horn for the main players of New Orleans music: the legendary Kid Ory, the incomparable King Oliver, the ubiquitous Johnny Dodds, the blues king Mutt Carey. And, though he didn't realize it at the time, Lick was blowing to Louis 'Dipper' Armstrong too, the greatest horn man that ever lived.

Lick never did get to play with Kid Ory's orchestra. Those jazzmen were sure impressed the way he blew so – with a tone as clean as spring morning and fingering tight like elastic – but Kid had no room for another cornet in his band. Instead Kid Ory said, 'Come see me in a few months time, Lick Holden. An' we'll see what we can see.' But Lick never went back.

Now Dipper Armstrong, who, as most folk know, was blessed with a heart as big as a whale, felt sorry for poor Lick, a bush negro on his own in the big city with few prospects. So he cut his new friend in on his regular gig at a low-rent tonk owned by the Italian Henry Ponce. Of course Ponce, a real hard-nosed S. O. B. , didn't pay any more dough for double the music. But Dipper gave Lick half his meagre earnings and it was just enough to scrape by for a week or two.

In fact, Dipper and Lick didn't play together for more than a month before Henry Ponce's tonk was shut down after an altercation with another Italian gangster by the name of Henry Matranga. But Lick learned more about how to blow a horn in that month – in terms of technique anyways – than in all of the six years before. And, truth be told, Louis Armstrong learned a good deal too. Around that time, though he didn't know it himself, Dipper was strictly a blues man who played his horn with the expressive tone and pitch-bending techniques of the most soulful blues singers. But Dipper's style was the product of the Storyville marching bands and he still played to the regulated rhythms of the stomp stomp stomp. Lick, on the other hand, had a head for syncopated beats and he loved to counterpoint Dipper's playing polyrhythmically as well as melodically, blowing in a hot style that Dipper had never heard played so good before.

Sometimes Dipper would rest his cornet and watch Lick blow with an expression of bemused curiosity on his humble face.

'Damn, Lick daddy!' he'd say. 'You blow that horn as restless as a pond skater on the river!'

'You wanna blow the horn real good?' Lick replied. 'You blow with four parts of your body. I play with jus' three: head and heart and chops.'

'So what's the fourth?'

'I dunno, Dipper. I dunno. But I's aimin' to find out.'

For one single month, Dipper and Lick played the sweetest jazz music of Louisiana dreams. But history most likely never heard it and certainly never recorded it or wrote it down. The small crowd who frequented Henry Ponce's tonk were a low-life bunch – drunkards and druggies mostly – who had no ear for fine music and so those precious sounds are lost to time like the fading breath of a final note.

The fact is that, when Henry Ponce's tonk shut down . . . well! . . . after that Lick, with a desperation born of hunger, soon found another gig in another rundown tonk by the name of the 122 (at 122 Basin Street) under the management of a large, cigar-smoking Yankee by the name of Buster Buster. But Louis Armstrong had no such luck and he returned to his momma on Perdido and his job on a coal cart. Now, as far as anyone can say for sure, Lick and Dipper never met again. Lord knows if they fell out (over Lick's gig at the 122, perhaps) or just drifted apart; but there's certainly no record of ill-will and reason suggests that they must have crossed each other in the street every now and again and stopped to pass the time of day. Besides, Louis Armstrong makes mention of Lick Holden somewhere in his later memoirs that have yet to receive publication (since they were mostly scribbled on napkins and the like). He writes, 'That boy Lick. Damn! Daddy taught me the meanin' of the word "hot", all right. He blew that horn so hard you could see the brass sweatin'.'

So – who knows? – maybe one day Lick Holden will receive something of the attention his music deserves; as an influence on Dipper to stand alongside Bunk Johnson, Papa Celestin and King Oliver. But you can't trust to history to grant you your rightful place.

Fate too is a capricious companion who can lift you up or kick you when you're down and just keep on kicking. But a lot of folk confuse fate with the choices they make and that's surely as much of a mistake as moping about the place while your family goes hungry. Now Lick Holden, who was more clean-hearted than any Cooltown negro had a right to be, never made such a mistake and he never suffered the bitterness that goes along with it. But it was his fate and his choices that kept him from his rightful place in history, and who knows where the one began and the other ended?

In the spring of 1916, Lick was in a position that could be rated just about average in the scale of New Orleans jazzmen; better than many and worse than some. Sure, his regular gig was in a low-rent tonk. But he was also on promises from Fate Marable and Kid Ory, which could have been the making of him. Poor Dipper Armstrong, on the other hand, was dragging his coal cart through the streets of Storyville, working a real back-breaker for less than a buck a day.

History tells us that it was Kid Ory who made the first recordings by a black jazzman (in Los Angeles in 1922) and it was King Oliver who found glory in Chicago with his band (which included Johnny Dodds). And maybe those facts don't surprise you any. But Louis 'Dipper' Armstrong went from the coal cart to Fate Marable's orchestra aboard the *Dixie Belle* to King Oliver's Chicago band in the space of five years! Then on to recognition as the greatest damn horn player that ever lived! And Lick Holden? For all his talent and all the promises, he tiptoed around fame's shadow for one brief month alongside Dipper in Ponce's forgotten tonk in the Tenderloin.

And that fact is the product of a meeting of fate and choice of the kind that always has one name. And the name was inevitably 'Sylvie', a name that formed on Lick's chops every time he lifted his cornet, a name that represented fulfilment and damnation in just about equal measures.

Now Lick Holden played the 122 on Basin Street for almost two years and in that time he also got himself married. But the documents of history (in the city marriage register and the *Blue Book* that detailed everyone of Storyville's tonks) are as misleading as a map with no compass. It would be easy to say that Lick soon forgot his search for his light-skinned sister, caught up in the excitement of the Tenderloin (and it sure was exciting!). But that isn't even neighbourly to the truth. Look at it this way. Kid Ory came down to hear Lick play once or twice after a long night at Miss Cole's and it's reasonable to suppose that he made him an offer to join his orchestra. But Lick was happy to play the 122, happy because he figured he'd find Sylvie any day and then he'd take her straight back to Mount Marter.

Certainly Lick was enquiring after his sister from day one, approaching all of the Storyville regulars with his descriptions and questioning. Some of them even misheard his name, assuming he was called 'Look' on account of his search for this mysterious woman. Others shook their heads and said, 'Any woman who needs that much findin' can't be nothin' but trouble.'

As for Lick's marriage? Well! That's a whole book in itself that could tell folk all they need to know about the nature of relationships in the Tenderloin back then. After six months at the 122, Lick – just like most other jazz musicians at the time – decided to try his hand at a little pimping. Of course Lick's bush-negro heart wasn't much suited for the rigours of running whores, but he did take on a local girl by the name of Beatrice (Bea for short) and when he looked out for his girl from the stage at the 122, Lick felt every inch the city cat. Little did he know that Bea had had her eyes upon him from day one and she was fixed on catching him the way she wanted.

Lick may have called himself a pee-eye but there was no questioning who took control.

Bea was just about typical of a young Storyville prostitute. She was around nineteen years old (with a couple of years on Lick) with deep blue-black skin, a pretty figure and pouting lips that were undeniably sexy. She was certainly fine but as tough as worn shoes and she had that view of men – part contemptuous, part needy – that might as well be described as 'realistic'.

The first time she peeped Lick was in a seedy shine-joint on Poydras when the night was counting upwards from one and the place was filled by nobody but Storyville's own. On that particular occasion, the main entertainment was what was known as a Battle Royal in which a dozen brave negroes were blindfolded and enclosed in a makeshift boxing ring for a last-man-stands, winner-takes-all type of affair. As usual, Black Benny was fighting that night and as usual Black Benny won with something to spare, handing out fearful beatings with flailing fists and elbows and knees and feet. Not that Lick saw any of this, covering his eyes with his hands while trying to appear like he was watching with the rest. Of course, none of the other men noticed Lick's cowardice. But Bea saw it, all right! And she resolved there and then to make Lick Holden her man because, all things considered and with few reservations, a man who feared violence was a better prospect than most in Storyville.

So, after that, Bea began to weave her life with Lick's, real subtle-like, so the Country Joe wouldn't notice. When Lick came off stage at the 122, Bea interrupted his path with a coy smile and a delicate turn of the head. When she danced, she got her angle just right so that Lick got a grandstand view of her firm buttocks or rounded breasts or whatever part of her body she chose to show him. And when, after a week or two, Lick began to smile at the sight of her, Bea would turn away and lower her eyes as if wholly embarrassed by such attention. Within a month, Lick was hooked like a fish to the bait and, even as she reeled him in, he was so bush that he still figured like it was him who'd done the catching.

Truth be told, it's doubtful whether Bea ever turned even one trick on Lick's behalf. Certainly the other pee-eyes laughed at his attempts to pass as one of their own, especially when they saw Lick spend a good part of his hard-earned wages on food and fine cloth and jewelley for the demanding Bea. And, when Lick and Bea walked into the 122, they leaned into each other and whispered, 'Here comes the pimp and her whore!'

Of course, what the mocking pee-eyes didn't figure was Lick's attachment to Bea, which arose from her taking his virginity. Following about a month of flirtation, Lick took her to his room at Betsy Slim's and she fucked him so good that his mouth gaped and his eyes squeezed tight shut and his groin ached to do it again and again. After that, Lick would follow the girl like a dog following the butcher's cart and he'd do just about anything she'd say. Even to the point of marriage.

In fact, it was on the very day of their wedding (March 1917) that Lick first saw another side of Bea's character, the violent side. The two of them had moved out of Betsy Slim's to a two-room apartment on Basin Street and, when they returned there from the simple marriage ceremony, Lick said to her, 'Mrs Beatrice Holden! It sure got a nice ring to it!'

'Bea Holden!' Bea replied and then she burst out laughing. 'I ain't beholden to no man.'

Lick was determined to assert his rights as a husband, however. So he looked at her with serious eighteen-year-old eyes and he said, 'You my wife now, Bea! An' you do what I damn well say!'

'Don't you raise your voice to me, Lick! Don't nobody raise their voice to me!'

'This my house!' Lick said. 'An' in my house I do what I goddam please!'

'So you think you a real powerful negro now? You think you the cat that got the cream?'

Lick was breathing heavily. He wasn't angry but he was sure determined to show his new wife who was the boss.

'No, Bea . . .' he said. But he didn't get any more out before the girl picked up a cooking pot and brought it ringing around the side of his head and he slumped to the ground like a sack of beans. Wasn't that a fine way to start a marriage?

Officially Lick and Bea were married unto death. They certainly never divorced. But in practice the marriage lasted for eight months of violent fights (that twice landed poor Lick in the Charity Hospital) and passionate making-up. It would be easy to label Lick a fool for staying in such a relationship so long. It would be easy to label him a typical 'shine nigger' for walking out on his wife. But the truth, as usual, is a whole lot more complicated than the facts. With his uncertain background, Lick had little notion of what marriage might be and no idea of love outside the emotions he'd felt for his mother and grandmother and sisters. So it's not so surprising that he couldn't figure the connection between love and lust any. And it's not so surprising that he still considered Sylvie – his sister, for landsakes! – in terms of the former when his unconscious was filled with images of the latter that left him shaking his head. And all the while Lick kept blowing his horn at the 122 and enquiring about Sylvie from anyone who'd listen and making up with his wife as if there was no tomorrow. In the end, it was a combination of these three that caused Lick to leave New Orleans.

Although Lick never knew it, Storyville's best days were long gone even before his arrival, the number of tonks shrinking year on year. Eventually, with the advent of the Great War and the institution of army and naval bases in New Orleans, pressure built from the federal government to shut the Tenderloin down (since so many soldiers and sailors were becoming dangerously entangled in the night life). It took until October 17, 1917, before the mayor of New Orleans finally caved in and agreed that prostitution should be declared illegal. It was also on this very day that Bea Holden discovered she was pregnant and it was only one day later that Lick finally heard word of Sylvie. Fate surely weaves its patterns and no mistakes. And just because you don't like them any, it doesn't mean they are not there for you to see.

When Bea realized she was pregnant, she flew into some kind of rage. Hadn't she done everything possible to guard against it? She squeezed her muscles tight during intercourse as her momma had taught her and she always jumped bolt upright when Lick was spent and douched herself clean just as soon as she could. Sitting alone in their Basin Street apartment, Bea rubbed her hand across her stomach and worked herself to a fury. It must have been Lick's fault, the way he liked to hold her so after sex. It must have been Lick's fault with his bush-negro semen that could impregnate a woman just with the smell of it. It must have been Lick's fault with his big old doody that pressed deep into her very womb. It must have been Lick's fault.

'An' I damned if I get myself cut by no backstreet quack!' Bea exclaimed.

True, knowing Lick's personality, a child might tie him in better than she'd manage on her own. But, the way Bea saw it in such a black mood, she wasn't sure she wanted him no more anyways. Besides, Lick might be scared off at the prospect of providing for an extra mouth and he'd run away with another whore or go searching for that sister of his that he was forever talking about. This thought just blackened Bea's mood further, so that by the time Lick returned from the errands he'd been running, she was waiting on the bed with a serious blade clenched in her right fist.

Lick burst into the flat with a brown paper package full of groceries and a smile the size of Texas spreading across his chops.

'Wassup, sweet pea?' he cooed. But that smile was soon wiped from his face.

Bea leaped from the bed and hurled herself at her husband, blade to the fore. She didn't say nothing but a primeval, guttural sound emerged from her throat, a growling mixture of anger and fear.

'Damn!' Lick shouted as he evaded the first swing of the knife by the breadth of a hair. 'What the fuck got into you?'

But Bea didn't reply. She slashed the knife again and this time she caught Lick across the biceps and he yelped in pain. Desperately he tried to grab his woman by the wrists, but her fury made Bea as strong as an ox and he couldn't get a grip the way she wielded that knife.

'What you doing, Bea?' Lick shouted, pressing his palm to the wound to try and stem the bleeding. But there was no talking to Bea as she came at him again.

'You no-good nigger fuck!' Bea screamed. And this time she went straight for Lick's face, thrusting the sharp tip towards his chops. Lick raised his left hand just in time to block the assault so that the blade impaled his palm. As Bea tried to extricate the blade from his flesh, Lick brought his right arm swinging round and caught her square on the cheek. Bea fell sideways and hit her head hard on the wall, leaving her dizzy. Lick was breathing heavily and his hand smarted something bad and his eyes were pin-pricked with tears.

'My chops!' Lick exclaimed. 'Why you have to go for my chops?'
Lick ran a bloody finger over his precious lips.

'Bitch!' Lick said and he marched out of the apartment and right out of Bea Holden's life.

That night Lick slept on the floor of the 122, courtesy of Buster Buster. The manager didn't ask Lick how he came to be bloodied so – such wounds were both too commonplace for comment and rare enough to be embarrassing – and he even let Lick off from playing, what with his cut hand and his horn being trapped in the Basin Street apartment with his crazy wife. But the next night he fully expected Lick to take the stage, though Lick had been slooping all day and was drunk as a sailor.

'You don't play, I don't pay,' Buster Buster said.

'They shuttin' down Storyville anyways,' Lick said (because the closure was the talk of the tonk). 'An', besides, I don't have my horn.'

'You gonna let your woman keep your horn? Next thing I'll fit you out a corset an' a pretty wig an' I'll put you to work myself!'

'Better she keep my horn than she bust my chops,' Lick said. And he fell off his bar stool and Buster Buster shook his head and left him well alone.

Lick scrabbled on the floor amid the butts and wood shavings and chicken bones. He tried to get to his knees but his eyes were misty and his limbs were unresponsive to his wishes. Yet his mind was as clear as a bell and it peeled with Sylvie's name so loud that he feared it might split his head.

This what happen when I's drunk, Lick thought. This what always happen when I's too drunk or too tired or the mornin' sunshine look so pretty on the river or the music so deep that I feels it in my chest! I always thinks about Sylvie when I too fucked up or too happy or too sad to do nothin' 'bout it. Where she? I 'spect to find her in the shit on the floor in the lowest goddam tonk? The shit that people step on without thinkin' any? Ain't nobody step on Sylvie! No shakes I can't find her, I such a goddam lowlife! Sylvie with the elegant folk, airin' and gracin' in fine dresses and good company. No shakes! No fuckin' shakes! Where she? Where she?

'Where she?' Lick spoke the words aloud as he hauled himself to his feet, clinging to the bar like it was a boat in rough weather. He bit on his lolling tongue and he sucked on his lips in concentration. 'Where she? Where she?' he said, so loud that all the early evening folk were staring.

Lick stumbled along the length of the bar to where Buster Buster was standing, talking to the only other white man in the joint, a real slick-looking, outta-town type of fellow in a tailored suit with polished shoes and a silver watch-chain protruding from his pocket. Lick pushed between them. 'Where she?' he said to Buster Buster. And the manager winced at his breath. 'Where she?' he said to Outta-town.

'Get away from me, nigger!' the man said. And he turned to Buster Buster. 'This the kind of tame negro you let into your establishment? I'll kick his booboos ass way up north. Uncivilized fuckin' savage!'

'Where she?' Lick said again. All insistent.

'Lick!' Buster Buster exclaimed. 'Get outta Chicago's face! You wanna be killed jus' for being a dumb nigger?' And then, to the outta-town called Chicago, 'Calm down, Chicago! Lick Holden's my main horn man an' he a good kid. Jus' drunk, that's all. Lookin' for some sister of his. That's all he does. Just lookin' for his sister.'

'You seen her?' Lick said. 'You seen her, Missa Chicago, sir? Name of Sylvie. Beautiful, light-skinned, real Italian-looking. Beautiful and with all the airs and graces of a fine lady. Not my blood sister. Oh no! Not my blood sister. But my sister no doubt!'

Chicago laughed. 'You sho' one desperate fuckin' nigger an' no mistake!'

'You seen her, sir?'

'Beautiful, you say? Light-skinned and beautiful and goes by the name of Sylvie?'

'That's her!'

'Where you from, boy?'

'Mount Marter, sir. Yessir. Jus' up the Mississippi. Mount Marter, sir. I down in New Orleans to find my sister.'

'Well! You lookin' in the wrong place!'

'You seen her, sir? You really seen her?'

'Sho' I seen her.'

'Where she?'

'Mount Marter,' Chicago's face cracked with hilarity. 'I seen her in Mount Marter jus' yesterday. I stayed there the night, travellin' down from Chicago. Beautiful? Light-skinned? By the name of Sylvie? I *seen* her, all right, boy. If you catch my drift . . .'

But Lick was of no mind to catch nothing but the lovesickness he'd caught from birth. Although, of course, he didn't know its name right there and then. Lovesick for his sister? Was that the devil's own work or destiny's light-fingered plan? And sometimes those two can surely look like family.

And Lick was of no mind to be caught neither. Because Lick Holden was falling from birth. Sure he sometimes moved from side to side and sometimes he even had the sensation of moving upwards. But he was always falling. Or perhaps sinking would be a better description. Like a man caught beneath the bottom of a riverboat who cannot tell which way is up as his lungs are gasping for breath.

So Lick Holden – the jazzman who taught Louis Armstrong the embryonic hot style – fell back to Mount Marter the very next day. Kid Ory made for LA, King Oliver for Chicago and Louis Armstrong joined Fate aboard a Mississippi steamer. But Lick fell back to Mount Marter on account of his sister Sylvie (who wasn't no blood relation). It was another two years before he finally tracked her down and she was surely keeping the fine company he expected. Only it didn't look so fine any more.

Lick never did see his wife Bea again neither. He never knew that she was pregnant (for she was both too proud and too crazy to go looking for the no-good negro) and he never saw her slide into cocaine abuse and that ugly kind of prostitution that guts a woman on a nightly basis. He was long gone by the time she died a syphilitic death at the age of twenty-nine and he never saw his son. Fortis Holden Junior was born in April 1918 and lives to this day. Fortis has nothing of his father's but the six-out-seven negro skin, the colour of black coffee, and a swatch of his musical talent that still strums a tame guitar blues in a Crescent City bar. He also owns a battered old cornet that he buffs and polishes as if it were the most precious possession in the world, a token reminder of another melancholy Storyville tale.

V: *The coffee-coloured woman*

(Heathrow, London, England. 1998)

The coffee-coloured woman looked a million dollars. And as she strode through the terminal, people stared at her, men and women alike. She just had that look. Maybe she was a film star or something.

Husbands voiced this thought aloud to their wives – 'Isn't she on TV?' – and wives tugged at their husbands' sleeves when their gaze lingered a little too long. It wasn't so much the way she was dressed (though she looked immaculate in a fitted cashmere rollneck and flared black trousers that billowed rhythmically as she walked). It wasn't her beauty either (though men unconsciously licked their lips as they looked her up and down and enjoyed the gentle 'S' of her body). She just had that look, that poise of someone who's used to strangers' eyes.

Anyone who allowed themselves more than a passing glance, therefore, was surprised to see the coffee-coloured woman join the queue to Economy Check-In that wound more than fifty suitcases around two pillars. The woman certainly looked First Class. And people wondered: what's her story? Nobody saw how nervous she was because she'd spent a lifetime not showing. Nobody considered she might be broke, dressed in expensive gear like that. Nobody realized she felt that loneliness that is bestowed on a woman by a thousand different men. And nobody got close enough to sense the shroud of desperation that enveloped her, thinner and more invisible than her perfectly applied make-up.

When she finally reached the front of the queue, the official at the desk was flustered by the crowds. But when he looked up at the woman he found his breathing faltered for a moment and he automatically reached to his forehead and began to paste his hair over the bare skin of his receding temples.

'JFK?'

The woman nodded silently.

'Passport and ticket,' the official said.

The official studied the woman's photograph and he took the chance to study the real thing too. She was, he read, forty-five years old. Ten years older than him. But if anything, her age made her sexier still, as if her beauty were enhanced by its slow passing.

She had strong features. Her eyes were hidden behind wrap-around shades. But her nose was long and straight, her lips full and her cheekbones high enough to cast attractive shadows. And her skin? Her complexion was the colour of milky coffee with an eggshell sheen. It was the kind of skin you wanted to smell and touch, to see if it had the delicate scent and silken texture that you conjured in your imagination.

She wasn't 'black black'. That was the way the official put it in his head. Not 'black black', nor half-caste. Probably an American. Because they have all kinds of different mixtures over there.

As he stared at her and saw the distorted reflection of his face in her sunglasses and she stared mutely back at him, the official felt himself bristle with irritation. As if she were somehow looking down her nose at him. Of course she wasn't. But this is something that men feel with beautiful women. Especially white men with beautiful black women. It's as old as race.

Look at her in her shades! he thought. Just who does she think she is?

So he put her right at the back of the jumbo in the middle seat, where the air is at its stalest and she'd have to clamber over two sleepers on either side if she wanted to stretch her legs. Just because he could.

Despite her apparent sophistication, the coffee-coloured woman wasn't an experienced flyer. And what she knew of flying, she didn't much like. So when she settled into seat 42G, she immediately took off her shoes and closed her eyes and hoped to fall asleep. She stretched and curled her toes across the rough carpet, a childhood habit, and she tried to think lightweight thoughts that might help the plane stay in the sky.

'Bob Peck!'

She was disturbed by the man saying 'Bob Peck!' and she opened her eyes to find a florid, jowly American squashed into the seat next to her. He reminded her of the Birmingham truckie. She did that a lot, made comparisons with her more memorable clients.

'Bob Peck!' the man said again.

He said his name like he was saying 'Happy Christmas!' or 'Congratulations!' and he extended a pudgy hand towards her. She lightly squeezed two of his fingers. His hands were like her father's, the fleshy, pink digits, the blunt nails and the arrogant grip. She refused to meet his eyes. Not even through her shades. Instead she looked at the neat trim of his moustache, the flesh that bulged above the collar of his pinstripe shirt and the Disney tie; a birthday present from his daughter, she guessed.

'This your first time in England?' Bob Peck asked. 'It sure is a swell country.'

'No,' the woman said. 'I'm English. I live here.'

Bob Peck laughed, a big throaty laugh (like the psoriatic undertaker) that shook the spare flesh on his neck.

'I could have sworn I'd met a fellow American. Blimey! Isn't that what you say? Blimey?'

The coffee-coloured woman smiled without teeth and her lips seemed to retract into her mouth. She didn't reply. She turned her head to the other side and allowed it to rest on her shoulder. She didn't have much time for Americans with their witless enthusiasm and their dubious moral certainties.

She thought back to an American client she'd had some ten years earlier. He was a black preacher who was touring Britain's Pentecostal churches and had a waistline as big as his bank balance. She remembered the way he yelped, 'Maybe baby. Maybe baby.

Maybe baby. Baby. Baby. Baby.' And then, 'Surely!' The memory made her smile, a full toothy grin that peeled her glossed lips until she covered her mouth with her hand. But if she hated Americans so much, then what was she doing on a plane for New York?

A young man sat down next to her on the other side. He was wearing baggy jeans, a grubby T-shirt and a wispy beard that covered his chin like a stain and he carried a plastic bag full of duty-free cigarettes and bourbon. His hair had the colour and texture of wet straw and he pushed it nervously from his forehead. His eyes were a curious mixture of innocent and knowing, like a naive character who's just happened to see too much. He apologized pointlessly as he sat down – so he had to be English – and he smiled sweetly. The coffee-coloured woman resolved that, in the event of a crash, she would definitely cling to his arm rather than the American's. And she closed her eyes.

The woman had twice been to see the black preacher speak during his time in London. Those two visits to church were her first for more than twenty years and she found herself intrigued by the smells and sounds and colours of worship. This black church bore little resemblance to the Catholicism of her childhood. Her memories of mass were of bowed heads and Latin and men whispering to one another with the expressive faces that Italian men do best. It was as if faces had to be covered and voices lowered for fear of seeing or maybe disturbing the mysteries of worship. But this Pentecostal church? It was loud and proud and on its feet, a vibrant collage of colours and singing and movement.

Put simply, she saw the Pentecostal church as expressive of a blackness she'd never been allowed to engage. Put simply, she knew how her father would have reacted to such an overt display of faith. He would have shuffled uncomfortably from foot to foot with unintelligible sentences on his breath that all included the word 'respect'. But he wouldn't have been surprised to find his daughter in such a place. Because, as far as he was concerned, her very life was disrespectful. At first she had thought this was because she was black. In time she realized it was because black was what she was. And that, in the eyes of both her father and herself, was different.

'MASTURBATION! FORNICATION! ... Jesus said ... ADULTERY! JEALOUSY! ... Love the Lord your God ... THE DEVIL! SATAN! BEELZEBUB! ... with all your heart and all your mind and all your strength ... STRENGTH! HE SAID. PRAISE JESUS! AMEN!'

The coffee-coloured woman could remember every word of the preacher's sermon and, in retrospect, she wondered if he was really any different from her father: all style over content with hypocrisy dancing invisibly around him like a victorious boxer. For all the show, she'd identified little useful blackness in the Pentecostal church. She knew that the congregation expressed their race in spite of their church rather than through it. And she thought of all the other misunderstood mechanisms of Negritude that she had tasted and rejected as if they were bad habits or addictions: the men, the movement, the politics of alienation and the alienation of politics. Born into an opposed status, she could see little redemption in choosing new oppositions to replace the old. The coffee-coloured woman knew that she was, in one sense of the word, exotic. Not because she was 'foreign' – she was as English as her passport – but because she was strange and bizarre and unusual and this was the only kind of blackness she understood.

'Exotic.' It was a word she had used on her business cards for more than fifteen years. She wondered if her clients had ever found her 'exotic'. Probably not. And she wondered if it was possible for a person to find *themselves* 'exotic'. Could a woman think of herself as strange and bizarre and unusual? And if she was not exotic then what was she?

She sat bolt upright in her seat and she saw that they had been airborne for an hour and she hadn't even noticed. Her sunglasses had slipped on to her lap and her eyes were wide in the artificial half-light that passes for night on an aeroplane. Next to her Bob

Peck was sleeping and his breathing came heavy. But the skinny English lad on her other side was watching the movie, though, seeing his neighbour jolt from her daydreams, he removed his earphones and looked at her curiously.

'You all right?' he asked.

'These things test a girl,' she said and she smiled for a moment before realizing that she'd engaged her professional smile, a wet, lascivious expression. She zipped her mouth and the young man looked confused. She was old enough to be his mother. What on earth did she think she was doing?

'Have you got the time?' she asked.

The young man didn't own a watch. But he eagerly called a stewardess who showed him her wrist. He wrinkled his forehead and grinned at the coffee-coloured woman. 'English or American?'

'American.'

'Half past three.'

'Morning or afternoon?'

'They're six hours behind us,' he said. 'Afternoon.'

'Thanks,' she said. And she caught herself doing it again, that professional smile that would make him think his luck's in. She cursed inwardly. Old habits died hard. She pushed her sunglasses back on her nose and sighed deeply to signal the end of the conversation. But the young man wouldn't let it go that easily.

'This your first time?' he asked.

'Yes,' she said. 'First time.'

In spite of herself, she answered easily. Maybe conversation seemed superior to the puzzles in her head. Or maybe she couldn't help but be flattered by the attentions of a twenty-something. It didn't happen so much any more.

'Business or pleasure?'

'Family,' she said.

And the young man laughed, a frank, open laugh that was charming and unselfconscious.

'A bit of both and a lot of neither, then,' he said. 'Where are you heading?'

'Harlem.'

'Harlem?'

'Yes, Harlem. I've got a great-uncle on West 126.'

'West 126?'

'Yes, West 126. Why are you repeating what I say? Do you know it?'

'I'm sorry. Do I know it? West 126? Yeah. I know it. Rough area.'

'I heard that.'

'You'll be all right, though. You'll be fine.'

'What do you mean?'

'I mean you'll be all right. It's different for me, isn't it? But you'll be all right. You're black.'

'I am, aren't I?' the coffee-coloured woman said. And she smiled again. But this was an amateur smile, only a flicker from a laugh, and the young man smiled too.

I like this boy, she thought.

'I'm Jim,' he said and he offered her his hand. They shook and Jim's smile widened. She noticed that his hand was smaller than her own but his grip was strong and confident. She said nothing.

'And you are?' Jim prompted and she hesitated for a moment. 'It's only your name,' he said and his furrowed eyebrows kissed above his nose. 'Not a commitment or anything.'

'Sylvia,' she said. 'My name's Sylvia. After my grandmother.'

'And what do you do, Sylvia?' Jim asked. But he saw the defensive shutters close in her eyes and he quickly added a footnote. 'Not that it's any of my business.'

'No. It's fine. I'm a prostitute. Retired. And a singer. Unemployed.'

The woman was surprised at herself. She was never so brazen. But the combination of the aeroplane's confined space and the potential liberation of her pilgrimage had given her a fuck-it streak that made her feel giddy. Jim was staring at her and his expression was non-committal.

'Really?'

'Yes. Really.'

'A singer?' he said and his face unfolded into a smile so cheeky that she couldn't help but return it. After a moment he went on, 'And a prostitute?'

'Yes.'

'Retired?'

'Yes.'

Sylvia pulled back a little. She wanted to see if he was mocking her. Maybe he was and maybe he wasn't but his face was kind.

'Have you met any prostitutes?' she pushed.

'One,' Jim said. 'She gave me crabs.'

'That's terrible.'

'Not so bad.'

'It could have been worse.'

'Exactly,' Jim nodded.

Again Sylvia thought for a moment. There was a silence between two strangers and she felt she had to fill it.

'I've never had crabs,' she said seriously and Jim nodded to that too. Then the corners of his mouth began to twitch until he couldn't hold it in and he giggled manically and he looked, Sylvia thought, like he was about thirteen years old. And she joined in, a full and unashamed laugh that sounded like it had been a long time coming. And Bob Peck, the fat American in the neighbouring seat, woke up, opened his bleary eyes and shook his head at the two strange English people. And the coffee-coloured woman and the young man laughed until a stewardess asked them to keep the noise down because they were disturbing the sleeping passengers.

V: *Sylvia tells her story and gets lonely. Jim listens and gets drunk*

(Manhattan, New York, USA. 1998)

Sylvia knew she'd fallen on her feet and she didn't want to screw it up. But while Jim was in the shower she had to look around. She couldn't help herself; it was force of habit. Years spent paying suburban house calls to frustrated husbands (or occasionally wives) had left her incurably nosy and she loved nothing better than to rummage through an underwear drawer or a jewellery box while the man slept off his sex in the soiled marital bed. She never stole anything – she was a hooker not a thief – but she did like to try on the pastel slips she'd never choose and the earrings she'd never afford. Of course there was no underwear nor jewellery in this palatial Manhattan apartment. But there were plenty of other knick-knacks to prick her curiosity. And while she heard the rush of the shower, she knew she was safe enough.

Sylvia picked up an abstract African sculpture, smooth stone and entwining curves. It was heavier than she'd expected and she almost dropped it. Gingerly she replaced it on the heavy mahogany side table.

What the hell is this place? she thought.

When they'd disembarked at JFK, Sylvia and Jim had shaken hands with a formal stiffness. Jim wished her luck with her great-uncle in Harlem. And Sylvia wished Jim luck too. It was only then that she realized that she'd dominated their hours of chatter on the plane and she knew next to nothing about him. She was embarrassed. Because her initial introversion had given way to a cascade of personal information in the artificial intimacy of their neighbouring seats and she now wished she'd shown some restraint. And God knows what she was wishing him luck *for*. But everyone needs luck, don't they?

They consciously went their separate ways. After all, they were still strangers. But the predictable patterns of fate (or embarrassment, which often works the same way) ensured they found themselves standing next to one another again in the queue for immigration and neither of them knew quite what to say. Whereas their conversation had come easily in the sky – tongues loosened by that piquant mix of boredom and alcohol – it was now lumpy and awkward.

At passport control they chose different windows. Sylvia was intimidated by the thick-set officer who looked her up and down like a vet inspecting a stray dog. He looked, she thought, like the Danish software engineer with the reluctant wife – all bushy moustache and luncheon-meat complexion – and she felt her hands getting clammy.

'What's your purpose in visiting the United States?' the officer asked.

'Holiday. Just holiday. A few weeks.'

'What's your employment?'

'My employment?'

'Your job.'

'I'm a singer,' Sylvia said. 'Jazz.'

'Are you intending to work?'

'No.'

'You sure about that?'

'Sure.'

'You have a return ticket?'

Sylvia showed the officer her return ticket and she was tempted to use it there and then. Arsehole, she thought. Maybe it's because I'm black. Fucking Americans. Asshole. Fuckin' A1 asshole!

She met Jim again at baggage reclaim and they exchanged goofy small talk. Like, 'You're following me, aren't you?' and, 'We must stop meeting like this.' Jim helped her to haul her newly bought luggage from the conveyor belt and he slung his one drawstring sack over his shoulder. He loaded her cases on to a trolley while she went to check her face. Then they walked together through the exit and into America.

'Goodbye again, Sylvia,' Jim said.

'Goodbye again, Jim.'

The two of them shook hands once more and then Jim rocked back on his heels and shifted from foot to foot.

'How are you getting to Harlem? Someone meeting you?'

'No. I'll get a cab.'

'It's late.'

'What's the time?'

'Must be getting on for eleven. Do you want to share?'

'What?'

'Do you want to share a cab? I'm heading to Midtown. You're on my way. Or I'm on yours. Kind of.'

They walked out on to the terminal concourse and the chill spring night bit their cheeks. Jim hailed a taxi with the ease of a New York pro and, as she clambered into the back of the cab, Sylvia asked, 'You've been here a lot?'

'A few times,' Jim said.

The driver was a chunky white guy with a beanie hat pulled low on his head and his shoulders hunched over the wheel like he'd been physically designed to drive a taxi (in fact he reminded Sylvia of a cabbie who'd been one of her Tuesday regulars – but somehow more American). As he pulled out of the rank, he cut up a fellow cab and he snarled 'Come on!' with the intonation of a game-show host before pulling away with a judder.

'Fuckin' mook!' he exclaimed and then turned what there was of his neck to look at Jim from the corner of his eye. 'No offence.'

'None taken.'

'So where you folks heading?'

'Make for St Patrick's,' Jim said. 'I'll direct you from there.'

'You English?'

'That's right.'

'I love the English! Benny Hill! You got some crazy mothers over there!'

'We sure have. Some crazy mothers.'

Jim slipped easily into Americanese. He turned to look at Sylvia and his eyes were laughing and she smiled at him. But it was a nervous smile.

For the next ten minutes they rode in silence and they watched the big American cars jousting on the busy highway. Every now and then, the driver would lean back and shout out a landmark – 'On your right, that's the borough of Queens! You know Queens? Named for Queen Catherine! You know that?' Sylvia felt her heart thumping against her chest. New York seemed like a daunting place: a city on fast-forward where every sentence ends in an exclamation mark. Not so much a melting pot as a sack of shingle in which the multi-million stones blunt and sharpen each another in equal measure. It should have been the perfect city for Sylvia; a city of lost souls.

But I'm just too tired, she thought.

Maybe it was the jet lag.

Sylvia sank lower in her seat and buried her chin beneath her rollneck and hid her eyes behind her shades once again. She noticed Jim had his face pressed to the window like an excited kid.

And he's even seen it all before, she thought.

'We'll take the bridge,' the driver shouted. 'Give you folks quite a view!'

As they crossed the Queensboro Bridge and Manhattan blew up in front of them like a peaking graph, Jim turned to look at Sylvia and his eyes were dancing.

'Look at it!' he said. 'No matter how many times I see it, it always gets me.'

Sylvia nodded and licked her lips but she couldn't bring herself to look out of the window. Jim turned momentarily to the view but then span back to Sylvia as if he realized he'd missed something.

'You all right?'

'I'm fine.'

Jim nodded and scratched his fuzzy beard thoughtfully.

'Look,' he said, 'don't take this the wrong way, but it's late to be heading to Harlem. Especially if you don't even know whether your uncle's going to be there.'

'I'll be all right.'

'I've borrowed an apartment in Manhattan. From a friend. He's not there. Three bedrooms. Why don't you come and spend the night? You can go up to Harlem in the morning.'

Sylvia looked at Jim and pushed her shades back to rest on her hairline. At the sight of her eyes, Jim smiled and said, 'Waddya say sweetheart?' in a Jimmy Cagney accent.

'I'm not going to sleep with you,' she said quickly and she immediately regretted it. Because clearly such a thought hadn't entered Jim's head. His face threw a curious mixture of expressions, from blank to confused to panicked to blank again.

He doesn't want to sleep with me, she thought. He thinks I'm too old. I *am* too old. Shit!

Sylvia felt her cheeks prickle and her ears burn and her lips purse and dry. Jim stared at her in silence for a moment or two as if he hoped that some words might make their own way out of his mouth. He blinked and he bit his tongue and he cracked his knuckles.

Eventually he smiled and said, 'I'm not offended. But you can stay anyway.'

Sylvia was doubly grateful.

She relived this exchange as she looked at her face in the vast mirror that lined one wall of the apartment's living room. She felt her face heat again and the blush gave her coffee-coloured complexion a pinkish glow that made her look younger than she was. She traced each crease of her face with her eyes, as if she was trying to remember a complex journey on a map. She remembered her intention to start face exercises; cheaper than a lift and much more reliable. She opened her mouth and stretched her jaw and lips. Her teeth, she thought, looked old and worn, protruding from her gums with a yellowish-brown tint like a sepia photograph. She poked out her tongue and even that seemed to mark her age.

Young people's tongues, she thought, are pink, gorged, sexual. Mine is pale and flaccid.

As she stared at her reflection, Sylvia found that her face slowly faded and vanished like a cheap movie effect. This didn't worry her. It seemed like the natural progression of the ageing process that was taking place before her eyes. She looked through herself at the room behind: the split-level, polished wooden flooring, the elegant glass coffee table; the tasteful throws and drapes; the many African artefacts; the enormous window that opened up on the famous Manhattan skyline like a cinema screen. And she felt profoundly sad.

I don't belong here, she thought. I don't belong anywhere.

Sylvia picked up an African mask from the side table. It was an ugly-looking thing with wild eyes and a screaming mouth. She held it to her face and then, on lowering it, she found that her face disappeared once more.

She wondered at her assumption of Jim's intentions. It wasn't so surprising. She could divide prostitutes neatly into two camps: those who were waiting for a Prince Charming to sweep them off their backs and those who knew that all men were the same. Generally most of the girls she'd known had started out as the former and ended up as the latter. And she was no different. What's more, the experienced girl felt an illusion of control over their lives and their sexuality. But that too passed in time. Sylvia knew that she had been defined by men: by her father, by her punters and now by a kid who saw she was too old.

She thought bumper-sticker thoughts.

My other woman's the wife. Prostitutes do it standing up. Lying down. In parked cars. Hotel rooms. Alleys. Prostitutes don't die, they just . . . They just what? Survive?

At that moment, Sylvia squeezed the mask in her hand a little too tight and her fingers splintered the wood. Just then, Jim appeared at the doorway with a towel around his waist. He'd shaved off his patchy starter beard and he looked younger than ever. His chest was scrawny and hairless and pale.

'I'm sorry,' Sylvia said. 'I broke the mask.'

'Never mind,' Jim shrugged.

'Is it valuable?'

'No. Just tat. Do you want to go get a drink?'

Sylvia stared at him and he ran his hand through his damp hair. He shivered unconsciously. Water was dripping on to the floorboards from the corner of his towel. Sylvia felt her sense of dislocation growing. She'd spent years wondering who she was. Now she wasn't sure where she was or what she was doing either.

'A drink, then,' Jim said and, before she could reply, he disappeared into the master bedroom and emerged moments later fully dressed, counting the notes in his wallet and tucking his keys into his jacket pocket.

'Ready?' he asked.

At the door of the apartment block, Jim nodded to the uniformed security guard who said, 'Good night, Jim'.

'See you later, Benny,' Jim replied.

They took a right up Fifth Avenue and right again down East 52nd. The one o'clock streets were near deserted and the cold air had a texture all of its own. Despite her heavy woollen overcoat and cashmere sweater, Sylvia found herself shivering and she clasped Jim's arm as they walked and he didn't object. Sylvia was excited. The streets had a smell she couldn't put her finger on – an almost fateful quality – and the buildings were so tall you couldn't see their tops however much you craned your neck.

'Everywhere's shut, Jim,' she complained. 'It's too late.'

'I know a little place,' Jim said and he pointed to a small, tacky neon sign further up the street. An illuminated shamrock enclosed the words 'Irish Tony's'.

When they opened the door, a soft bell sounded and all the bar's customers looked at the new arrivals. In other lifetimes Sylvia might have felt intimidated. But she'd seen her fair share of seedy dives. Besides, there were only four or five other punters – old white men with sallow skins, empty glasses and full ashtrays – and the barman (who looked like one of her Monday-night quickies) greeted Jim like a long-lost friend.

'Jim!' the man exclaimed. 'It's been a while.'

Jim smiled and lit a cigarette.

'How are you, Tony?'

'Where's complainin' gonna get me? You here a stretch?'

'Not sure. Maybe a couple of days. Maybe a few weeks.'

'Yeah? What you up to?'

For a moment Jim looked a little pained before his expression relaxed and be shrugged nonchalantly. 'You know how it goes.'

'For sure,' Tony said. 'I hear you. You on your own?'

Jim touched Sylvia lightly on the arm. 'With my friend. Tony, this is Sylvia. Sylvia, this is Irish Tony.'

'Sure is a pleasure to meet you, Sylvia.' He shook her hand. 'And what can I get you folks?'

For a moment, Jim glanced at Sylvia with enquiring eyes. Then he seemed to think better of it and turned back to the barman.

'Two Nigerian Guinness,' Jim said.

'Two what?'

'Nigerian Guinness. Nigel G.'

'What the hell's that?'

'Come on, Tony! You've made it for me before. You pull the Guinness and then you just add a splash of blackcurrant on top. Nigerian Guinness.'

'You serious? You drink that shit?'

'It puts hairs on your chest,' Jim said and Sylvia smiled at the thought.

The pair of them turned from the bar and selected an empty booth by the door. Jim lit another cigarette straight from the last. He looked exhausted, like an exhausted little boy. And Sylvia thought what an odd couple they must make, a pasty-faced kid and a knackered old whore. It was a thought that made her smile grimly.

'I don't drink Guinness,' she said.

'No? You should start. It . . .'

' . . . puts hairs on your chest,' Sylvia finished the sentence.

'It will make you grow up big and strong.'

'I'm already grown up.'

'It keeps you young,' Jim said finally. And Sylvia realized that Jim was in his element and there was no point arguing.

Irish Tony brought over their drinks and set them down without a word. But his expression was warm and friendly.

'To Nigel G,' Jim said and raised his glass.

'Nigel G.'

Sylvia took a sip. It was good. Fruity and smooth and with a gentle kick. Like an alcoholic milkshake.

'I don't drink much,' Sylvia said.

'I do,' Jim replied and he took an enormous gulp of the black liquid as if to prove the point.

'You were going to tell me about yourself.'

'I was?'

'Yes. You were.'

'You first.'

'I've told you everything.'

'No, you haven't. You've told me you're a hooker (retired) and a jazz singer (unemployed). That's not a lot to go on. For starters, you haven't told me what you're doing in New York.'

'I'm looking up my great-uncle.'

'I know that. But why?'

'Why not?'

'Come on. You've got a story and it's a good one, I bet. Tell me.'

Sylvia looked at Jim over the rim of her glass and he smiled back at her. There was something about him that she couldn't figure. Like he was a knowing fool, as innocent as a rosebud and as tired as flowers a week after the funeral. And it was this 'something' that made Sylvia want to tell him. Or maybe it was her desperation.

Because nobody had wanted to hear her story before and she'd felt it slowly suffocating in her chest for longer than she could remember (because stories need to be aired to survive). So she tried to tell him who she was, she tried to tell him what she was doing and she tried to tell him her story. And, as it came out, she almost began to understand it herself. And, as she spoke, Jim drank Nigel G right under the table.

An hour and a half later, at the tail end of the tale, Jim suddenly stood up.

'I'm drunk,' he announced.

'Were you listening?' Sylvia asked.

'I was listening. But now I'm drunk.'

Irish Tony called over from the bar, 'You all right, Jimbo?'

'Drunk,' Jim replied.

Tony laughed and said to Sylvia, 'You'd better put him to bed, sweetheart.'

This time, as they walked the two blocks back to the apartment, it was Jim who held Sylvia's arm. And she laughed every addled step of the way as Jim tripped and stumbled down the quiet street.

'Good night, Jim,' the doorman said as they entered the lift.

'I'm drunk, Benny,' Jim replied as the doors slid together.

In the apartment, Jim pointed a vague finger across the living room before stripping with uncoordinated awkwardness to his shorts and collapsing in the master bedroom. Sylvia found another bed in a beautiful room of deep blues and aquamarines and she undressed and slipped beneath the soft sheets. But she didn't want to sleep because she never liked to go to bed alone. What's more, her story was still unpacking itself before her mind's eye and she remembered a time when she watched a drunkard called Flynn (a boyfriend not a punter) attempt the impossible when he tried to cram twenty cigarettes back into an empty box. And she knew such an effort required a machine's precision. So, after half an hour or so of irritable fidgeting, she got up and padded across the living room. And she didn't even think to slip into a T-shirt.

She knocked at Jim's door.

'Jim,' she whispered.

She opened the door a crack and heard the sounds of contented sleep snorkelling. Slowly she eased her way into the room – she didn't want Jim to wake up – and slid into bed next to him. She curled her naked body around his back and he didn't stir. He smelled rancid – of alcohol and cigarettes – but Sylvia didn't care. He smelled just like Flynn.

At around six o'clock, Sylvia suddenly shot awake. Jim was talking in his sleep, loud exclamations and full sentences in an indecipherable language. After a while, his dreams subsided but Sylvia now felt uncomfortable. She wondered if Jim would remember her story in the morning. Did she want him to? She got out of bed again and returned to her own room. She lay on her back with her hands behind her head and her breasts flattening into her armpits. She thought through the previous evening and the tale that had unfolded in Irish Tony's dive bar. She was wide awake. Sylvia didn't like to go to bed alone but she wasn't used to waking up any other way.

'Did I tell you my surname? Di Napoli. Sylvia Di Napoli. Can you believe that?'

Jim looked blank and lit a cigarette. Although she rarely smoked, Sylvia instinctively reached for the pack and sparked one of her own.

'Di Napoli. You see what I mean? It's Italian. It means "from Naples". I've never even been to Italy, let alone Naples. And I hardly look Italian, do I? My family's Italian, you see. Well, American-Italian anyway. White American-Italian.'

'White?' Jim puffed smoke and peered at Sylvia through the haze of his own making. Then he supped at his Nigel G without taking his eyes off her.

'You see?' Sylvia said. 'You see what I'm saying? I was something of a surprise, I can tell you. My mum and dad were not expecting a little black baby.'

'You were adopted?'

'No! That's the point. Are you listening? If you're not . . .'

Sylvia tutted to herself in frustration and gulped a heavy sigh. She sat back in the booth and looked away for a moment. It was hard enough for her to explain and if Jim wasn't going to listen, there was no point in trying.

On the wall above the bar where Irish Tony was idly polishing glasses, there was a black-and-white photograph of a boxer, posed punching from the picture. She vaguely recognized him. What was his name? Barry something-or-other. The grainy image made him look somehow Hispanic. But she knew he was Irish.

'I'm sorry,' Jim said. 'Carry on.'

Sylvia sipped her drink. The Nigerian Guinness was beginning to taste sickly. She gazed at Jim steadily and licked the creamy foam from her top lip. Jim blinked.

'My dad left when I was born. My mum had been in London, like, seven months and my dad just upped and left. Typical fucking Italian man with his brains in his bollocks. I mean, he came back in the end and I suppose he acted like my dad as best he could. But he never let her forget it. Me neither. Those are my earliest memories. We had a flat above the restaurant on Dean Street in Soho and, when they fought (like, every fucking day!), he'd stalk around the apartment, hitching his trousers and smoking his cigars. "Jesus Christ, Bernadette! How the fuck I end up with a black kid? You think I look black ah you? You think I look fuckin' black ah you? So what I do that was so wrong, Bernadette? Why you have ah go and screw a coon?"'

As Sylvia impersonated her dad, she started to raise her voice and the faces of Irish Tony's few other customers turned to stare at the beautiful coffee-coloured woman and the young white man. Then she said the word 'coon' with bitter enunciation and the faces buried themselves in their drinks and backgammon. Jim laughed.

'That's a good impression.'

'That's how he spoke,' Sylvia said. And she began to laugh too. 'I swear that's how he spoke; his sentences punctuated with grunts. "Hey!

Bernadette! What you ah want me ah do?'' Like that. Like a gangster movie or something.'

'So who's your real father?' Jim asked.

'I don't know.'

'She never told you.'

'She always said she was faithful. Right up till she died. I hadn't seen her for about twenty years and she was still saying the same thing on her deathbed. "Sylvia. You gotta believe me. I never sleep with no man but Pops. Take the Virgin herself as my witness." That's what she said.'

'When did she die?'

'About six weeks ago.'

'I'm sorry.'

'It's OK. She wasn't my mother any more anyway. Being a mother's a lot more than just giving birth, you know. A whole lot fucking more. I swear, if I ever have kids . . .'

Sylvia stopped for a moment. The sentence seemed to have tripped her like a cracked paving stone.

'If I'd had kids I'd have been a real mother to them; a real tea-on-the-table, bedtime-stories, brush-your-teeth kind of mother. You can't just . . .'

Again she stuttered and her voice cracked a little. Her thoughts were freewheeling and her brain was struggling to keep up.

'You know what? I reckon my mum hated me. I mean, my dad came closer to saying it. But I could tell from her eyes. I hadn't seen her for twenty years and I could tell from her eyes.'

Sylvia reached her hand across the table as if she were stretching for a life line. Either Jim didn't notice or he chose to ignore it. Instead he lifted a lazy arm and signalled to Tony at the bar. He raised his eyebrows at Sylvia.

'You want another drink?' he asked.

Sylvia shook her head. Her hand settled on a cardboard beer mat that she now flipped between her fingertips.

'Another Nigel G!' Jim called out to Tony before turning his attention back to his companion. 'So. What were you saying?'

'It doesn't matter.'

Sylvia bowed her head a little and began to tear the beer mat into thin strips, like toast soldiers for a boiled egg. Her face was a picture of concentration – as if this were the most testing task in the world – but her mind was elsewhere. Jim watched her and he knew that she'd retreated into her own story, shutting him out.

'So,' Jim said again. 'So. Why are you looking for your great-uncle?'

Sylvia stopped her origami. She wasn't sure she had the will to tear more cardboard. Let alone keep talking.

'It's a long story.'

'Carry on.'

'Do you want to hear?'

'Yes.'

'I mean. Do you really want to hear? It's a long story.'

'Yes. I want to hear. Tell me. Please.'

'Well. Like I say, it's a long story. I mean, I only found out most of it when I went back to see my mother. Of course I knew bits and pieces but Mum and Dad didn't like to talk about their past. You know what I mean? It was like they looked at me and I was all they needed to know. And it was like I wasn't really a subject of polite conversation. What's that saying? "Children should be seen and not heard." Fuck that! I wasn't to be seen or heard or fucking mentioned if they could help it! I . . .'

'Just start at the beginning.' Jim interrupted.

'What?'

'Just start at the beginning and tell me the whole story.'

'The beginning. Right.' Sylvia sucked her gums for a moment and polished her teeth with her tongue. 'You mind if I smoke another cigarette? I don't usually smoke but I don't talk about this stuff much.'

'Help yourself.'

Sylvia lit another cigarette and dragged deep. She placed her palms flat on the table, wedging herself in and she began to talk in a steady monotone, as if that would lend objectivity to what she said.

'My mum and dad were both Italian New Yorkers. You know, like, typical fucking Italian New Yorkers, from big Catholic families that ate pasta dinners around huge tables with red-check tablecloths. It's not like I

162

know that for sure but that's how I picture it in my mind. You know what I mean?

'My mum came from Harlem and my dad from Queens. I don't know much about my mum's background but she told me she was an only child (so that throws my pasta-dinner fantasy straight out of the window). I don't know much about her parents either. Her father died when she was a kid. I know that. She lived with her mother. But I get the feeling they didn't get on and that's why she moved to England with my dad. I remember one time when Mum and Dad were fighting in the kitchen. My dad said to her, "You want me ah send you back ah Harlem, Bernadette?" Something like that. Some kind of threat. Other than that, I just know that my mum was born in 1925. And that's about it.

'My dad. I remember he used to reminisce sometimes when I was a kid. Usually when he got drunk. He'd sit in this great big chair in the living room by the gas fire and he'd just talk. Not to anyone in particular. Definitely not to me.

'His family came from Brooklyn. They ran a pizza restaurant. A successful one too. And, by the time my dad was born, they owned three restaurants – two in Brooklyn and one in Harlem (or maybe the other way round) – and they'd moved out to Queens. When my dad grew up, he managed the Harlem restaurant. That's where he met my mum. I think she must have been a waitress. "She was a fuckin' A1 Italian beauty." That's what my dad used to say. Like he was talking about a prized possession, like a car or something. "A fuckin' A1 Italiano with legs up ah here and thick black hair and olive skin." Sometimes he'd look at me and he'd be, like, "So what the fuck happen ah you? Jesus Christ!"'

Sylvia paused and pursed her lips and blew smoke rings. Jim felt like he should say something. 'Nice bloke,' he commented. Sylvia raised her eyebrows and Jim noticed that they weren't really her eyebrows at all, just thin lines of paint that wrinkled with her forehead.

'So that's where they met anyway,' she continued. 'At the restaurant. And they fell in love over the pizza dough and melted mozzarella. Very fucking romantic.'

Again Sylvia paused, as if she'd run out of words. This story was proving to be quite an effort and Jim realized she needed encouragement.

'So when did they move to England?' he asked and Sylvia sighed heavily.

'The year I was born. 1953. They didn't just move to England, though. They, like, eloped or something. I don't know why. Someone didn't approve of the marriage. I think it was my grandmother. I think mum took care of her or something like that. Because Mum certainly wasn't a kid when she married Pops. She was, like, twenty-seven. Twenty-eight maybe.

'Anyway. They ran off to England in 1953. So I was conceived aboard the Queen Mary. Can you believe that? Maybe my father was some black sailor or something. A child of the fucking ocean. That's me. A fucking nowhere baby.

'Dad had this plan. He was going to open a chain of pizza restaurants in London. 'Di Napoli's Pizzerias.' He started this pizza place down in Dean Street in Soho. You know Soho? Just off the square. And that was as far as he got. Thirty years later and they were still churning out bad pizzas in their one restaurant and making fuck-all money. It was a good idea but about twenty years too early. Either that or it was my fault. Because the marriage was never the same again after I was born.'

'I'm sure that's not true,' Jim said. Just because he thought he should make the right noises.

But Sylvia bristled. 'What do you know?'

Jim drained his second Nigerian Guinness and looked at her through the bottom of the glass. Her face was distorted, her features stretched and painful.

'I don't know anything,' he admitted and he smiled thinly. Sylvia felt her expression soften, not so much against her will as in spite of it. Cinema phrases like 'If I was twenty years younger' span through her mind until she put a stop to them. When I was twenty years younger, Sylvia thought, this skinny, good-hearted white boy was not the kind of man I was looking for. That was half the problem.

Irish Tony called over from the bar, 'You need another drink, Jimbo?'

'What do you think?' Jim replied. But his eyes never left Sylvia's.

164

'What you say?' Tony asked.

'I said, "What do you think?"'

'I think you do.'

'That's good. I think I do too.'

Jim curled his index finger around the rim of his glass, scooping up the leftovers of creamy foam like a window cleaner. He sucked it up and a little dollop slipped from his finger and landed on his chin. His tongue flicked out to catch it, pink and pointy, like a lizard's.

'You like to drink,' Sylvia observed.

'Yeah,' Jim nodded. 'I like to drink.'

Irish Tony delivered Jim's next Nigerian Guinness and Jim lifted and gulped, as if to illustrate the point. Then he sat back in his chair and belched discreetly into his fist.

'What about your great-uncle?' he asked.

'Who?'

'Your great-uncle. Where does he fit in to all this?'

Sylvia sighed and lit yet another cigarette. If her companion was going to get so determinedly drunk, then she wasn't going to worry about the odd smoke.

'Mum and Dad,' she began, 'they didn't stay in contact with the rest of the family. Not as far as I know. Not a Christmas card or a birthday card. Nothing like that. It was the way Pops wanted it. "It's better this way, Bernadette," he used to say. "Why anybody need ah know our business? You think they gonna understand? Why you want them ah know our shame?" He used to say stuff like that. And when he said the word "shame" he'd look at me like I'd stabbed him in the heart.

'Anyway. Pops died five years ago. I heard about it. But I didn't go to the funeral. I mean, he didn't like me and I didn't like him. Why should I go to the funeral just because he was my dad? Fuck! He probably wasn't even my dad. Know what I mean?

'But when my mum got sick a couple of months ago, she asked me to go and see her. I don't even know how she found me but she said she was dying and I thought, shit! Why the fuck not? So I went to see her, still living in that flat on Dean Street (though they sold the restaurant a decade ago. Now it's a wine bar, isn't it? All suits and bottled beer). I swear, Jim, she looked at me with hate in her eyes.'

Sylvia paused and looked up at him. He liked it when she said his name and he felt his feet twitch inside his trainers. She seemed to invest that one syllable with some kind of seductive quality.

'What did your mum want?' he asked.

'She wanted me to get in touch with this uncle of hers in Harlem. Apparently she'd been writing to him every now and then for forty years. She just wanted him to be told when she died.'

'So what did you do?'

'What did I do? I wrote to him, didn't I? When she died, I wrote him a letter. Just to let him know.'

'What's his name?'

Sylvia retrieved her purse from her pocket and flipped the popper. She pulled out a crumpled scrap of paper and carefully unfolded it.

'Fabrizio Berlone,' she read. 'Apartment 8, 426 West 126th Street, Harlem.'

'So?'

'So what?'

'So he wrote back to you and told you to come and visit.'

'No,' Sylvia said. 'He never replied.'

'He never replied?' Jim repeated. And he swilled the last of his drink around his teeth. 'So what are you doing here?'

Sylvia looked at her feet. She suddenly felt very stupid. Jim looked at her. He suddenly felt very drunk.

'I thought . . .' she began. 'I thought he might be able to tell me.'

'Tell you what?'

'Who I am,' Sylvia said quietly.

For a moment there was a silence between them that Jim felt heavy on his shoulders. He knew that he had to say something but the words that formed in his head were inappropriate. But then they teetered on the edge of his mind and fell out of his mouth like clumsy kids slipping off a wall.

'He's probably dead,' he said and immediately cursed himself.

Sylvia stared at him. 'Probably,' she said. 'Thanks.'

'But even if he's alive,' he said, trying to make amends, 'even if he's alive, your great-uncle can't tell you who you are. Nobody can tell you who you are. You've got to work that out for yourself.'

'Yeah?' Sylvia said. 'Where did you read that?'

'Dunno. Some problem page.'

Jim suddenly stood up.

'I'm drunk,' he announced.

'Were you listening?' Sylvia asked.

'I was listening. But now I'm drunk.'

Irish Tony called over from the bar. 'You all right, Jimbo?'

'Drunk,' Jim replied.

Tony laughed and said to Sylvia, 'You'd better put him to bed, sweetheart.'

I: *Black's my name*

(Mount Marter, Louisiana, USA. 1920)
Sylvie shared her last name with her mother, Marlin, her aunt, Kayenne, and her grandmother, Momma Lucy. Sylvie Black, that's what she was called. Sylvie Black. And with her pale complexion and delicate features, the name surely struck her as ironic before she even knew there was a word for such a thing. While all the rest of the kids in Kayenne's household took the last names of their fathers (however fly-by-night or no-good these men might have been), Sylvie was stuck with the name of her great-great-grandmother. Now Momma Lucy, who was herself born a slave to the Fredericks of Jackson Hill (and wasn't there a further irony in that?), could tell Sylvie little about this woman. But she knew that Elizabeth Black was a real African lady whose husband (Momma Lucy's grandpappy) died soon after arrival in the United States of America.

'Black'. Sylvie sometimes wondered where the name came from. Maybe white folk just got lazy when they were naming a new batch of slaves from market. And here she was, even paler than some of the white ladies who would do their damnest to stay out of the high sun!

Sylvie took the name 'Black' because there just weren't no other name for her to take. Her father was a white good-time boy who'd headed into Cooltown to lose his virginity on his eighteenth birthday. And nobody knew no more about him than that. Sometimes Sylvie plotted out this white boy's life history as it might have developed. Maybe he went straight off to college in Chicago or even Boston or New York. Maybe he trained as a doctor and he saved a hundred lives, or as an attorney in a sober suit and a starched white collar. Maybe he was a good son to his father who took over the running of their plantation at the age of twenty-one and always treated negroes with a fair hand. Maybe he was now married to a beautiful lady who wore the finest dresses, her hair in golden ringlets. Maybe he now had more children – three children, Sylvie imagined. Two boys and one girl. Her half-siblings! – and he taught the boys how to ride and he bounced the little girl, his favourite, on his knee.

Sylvie wondered if her father would somehow recognize her if they passed in the street. Perhaps she would catch his eye as he walked and he would stop and his brow would furrow and then he would turn and call after her, 'Sylvie! My Sylvie!' As if he would know her name!

One might have expected young Sylvie to bear some resentment towards her father, who got his kicks from her momma's body and then paid her fifty cents and left her to die in childbirth. But folk don't always think how you expect, least of all black folk who've had the sense fucked out of them before they are born. So Sylvie resented her mother instead. She resented poor dead Marlin who couldn't even tell her her father's name.

I could have had a real name, Sylvie thought. Not a slave name that binds me tight with its short history! A real name with an endless leash of generations behind it that could let me run straight out of Cooltown, away from Mount Marter, maybe even right out of Louisiana State! I could be somebody else!

The way Sylvie saw it, she wasn't just part slave but part slave-owner too. And try as she might, she couldn't find no balance on this seesaw. Just a whole lot of confusion.

That was how Sylvie thought. As a shooter anyways. Later Sylvie grew into what she was and she tried to make the best of it. Just like the rest of us.

Now, at the age of twenty-two, Sylvie lay back on the soft bed with the clean white covers that smelled of rose petals and she tried to figure out what had brought her to this situation. Was it her fault? Was it her destiny? Or was it simply who she was? These three questions all sounded kind of the same to Sylvie, though she couldn't be sure, because the atmosphere in that building wasn't much conducive to thinking. She could hear Annalise's tuneless singing on the stairs and Septissa in the apartment below, screaming at her two kids like they were somehow to blame. Septissa! What kind of a dumb name was that? A name that belonged in the medicine chest!

Irritably Sylvie ran a finger around the base of the tight bodice that pinched her ribcage uncomfortably. She wanted to take it off. But it was such awkwardness to remove and, besides, she knew that she was supposed to be getting ready. Too tired to be naked, too lazy to be dressed. That's whore mentality all over, Sylvie thought.

There was a knock at the door of her apartment. Slowly Sylvie swung her legs over the side of the bed and tottered across the room. She felt like she was drunk. She wished she was. She caught sight of herself in the pretty looking-glass that stood next to the window and she paused for a moment and her eyes prickled like a nettle sting. Time was when she could stare at her reflection for hours and delight in her milky complexion, the soft curls of her hair and the sensual curves of her breasts and hips. But not any more.

Sylvie opened the door to find Sweet Elly bent over on the landing, hitching her stockings beneath her elaborate skirts. Sweet Elly straightened up, took one look at her and laughed infectiously.

'Girl!' Sweet Elly exclaimed. 'You still not dressed? Goddam! Forgive me, sweet Jesus, but you is lookin' for trouble!'

Sylvie smiled and stood aside and Sweet Elly walked into the apartment with that curious cocksure strut of hers that only seemed to accentuate her innocence. With her bright blue eyes and blonde wig, Elly could have passed. No doubt. But, despite Sylvie's pressing, the thought had barely entered her mind.

Sylvie thought back to one such conversation.

'Elly,' Sylvie had said, 'what you doin' this for, girl? 'Cos you sho' know you could pass and I ain't lyin'.'

'Pass? How could I pass round here when folk knows me so well?'

'Not round here, Elly. Not in Mount Marter. But you could go some place else.'

Sylvie remembered the look on Elly's face all too well. That wide-eyed, vacant look of non-comprehension that made her so popular with the white good-time boys.

'But where would I go?' Sweet Elly had said.

Where would she go? Elsewhere! Anywhere! Everywhere!

This memory came back to Sylvie as she watched Sweet Elly preen in front of the mirror with vanity born of innocence and she heard the irritation surface in her own voice.

'What you want, Sweet Elly?' she asked.

Sweet Elly span around and her face looked so forlorn that Sylvie had half a mind to hit her.

'You mad at me, Sylvie?'

'No, I ain't mad at you.' Sylvie's tone softened. 'I jus' busy, that's all. You knows I gots to get ready. So what is it you wantin'?'

'Can you borrow me a garter?' Elly asked. 'Mine's all snapped and frayed and ugly.'

'I told you you shouldn't let no man undress you,' Sylvie said, smiling. 'You know that's one expensive mistake to make.'

'It's his money, honey.'

'An' that's the truth, Ruth.'

The two women smiled at each other. 'It's his money, honey.' 'And that's the truth, Ruth.' It was a kind of call and response between all the *plaçage* women. Sometimes it reminded Sylvie of the call-and-response hymns that church folk sang, kind of like a prostitutes' spiritual. But only Sylvie thought of herself as a prostitute. The others said they were 'mistresses' or even 'girlfriends'. Even when they saw one of their number thrown into the street with their kids in tow because of a forthcoming marriage or, sometimes, just out of plain boredom. Some of these girls were as naive as could be!

Sylvie took a selection of pretty garters from her small chest of drawers and Sweet Elly insisted on trying each one. She cooed over the soft silk and ribbons and delicate lace.

'You sho' got the prettiest clothes, Sylvie,' she said.

'They ain't clothes. They's a uniform.'

'You bad, Sylvie!' Elly laughed. 'Why you got to be so cock-tempered all the time? You sore as a drunk's head at sun-up. 'Cos you know it's true. Johnny don't buy you nothin' but the finest. You always got the prettiest clothes, you got the prettiest room and the prettiest damn bed too, with all them soft covers and lace pillows. You the princess of this buildin', Sylvie Black. An' you act jus' as spoiled too!'

'T'ain't no bed,' Sylvie said flatly. 'A bed's a place where you can relax. That jus' my office so why can't I make it as comfortable as I likes it?'

Elly sighed and tutted and shook her head from side to side. Sylvie stared at her and she felt the irritation rise in her chest once again. It's not her fault, she told herself. Elly jus' a fool. But if that ain't her fault, then who the hell's to blame?

Sylvie opened the door of the apartment.

'I gots to get ready, Elly,' she said. 'You know how mad Johnny gonna be if I keeps him waitin'.'

When Elly crossed to her own apartment opposite, Sylvie stood for a moment in her doorway. She could hear a soft breathing sound from the murky shadows on the landing. Maybe rats again. As Sylvie's eyes got used to the gloom, she made out Cecil, Septissa's youngest, weeping quietly in the corner. Cecil was a beautiful child with caramel skin and blonde-tinged curls that climbed out of his head like snakes. He reminded Sylvie of her dead brother, Falling Down. All her instincts told Sylvie to sweep little Cecil up in her arms, to hold him to her breast and to tell him that everything was going to be all right.

But it's not gonna be all right, she thought. Better let the shooter get used to the world as it is.

And she shut the door and lay right back down on that bed.

When Sylvie Black was growing up in Cooltown, she always knew she was different. Sure she did. 'Different' was who she was. She could tell as much from the way folk looked at her, not just black folk but white folk too. Some blacks looked at her with a kind of jealousy that most times showed itself in sneering disdain. Others smiled as she passed by, like they were pleased that one of their own could be so fine-featured and ladylike. As for the white folk, their expressions were harder to read. Leastways at first. Later Sylvie realized that their emotions were exactly the same: jealousy or pleasure. And it didn't much matter since both these emotions derived from the same mean spirits. The truth was that people saw her whiteness or her blackness. And they liked or hated the one. Or they liked or hated the other. Simple as that. And the only certainty was that she – Sylvie Black – was different. Even as a child, Sylvie Black was a beautiful, pale-skinned negress whose very being made men look inside themselves and confront the sex they found there.

When she was younger, she dreamed of washing the blackness right out of her system. She dreamed of elegant white gentlemen with whiskers and white manners and the money to buy her anything she wanted. She dreamed of social occasions and wealthy households and black servant girls who would drop their heads when they spoke to her for fear of meeting her eye. She dreamed of passing.

Sylvie couldn't figure quite when her attitude had changed. But changed it had. Sometimes she traced it back to the night of Kayenne's funeral some nine years before when she'd sung her heart out on the Cooltown jetty.

She'd been at the service. Of course she had. Kayenne was like a mother to her. But she hid herself at the back of the congregation because she was already working the whites-only Cooltown tonks and she knew that church was no place for a whore (whether that was the preacher's decision or God's own). Then she followed the parade down Canal Street to the docks where her brother Lick blew the sweetest blues hymn that a woman ever heard. She couldn't help herself.

Back then, at the age of thirteen, she was already dressing like a fine white lady. But the sound of Lick's horn? Damn! It was so tragic she wanted to laugh. It was so beautiful she wanted to cry. It was just so fucking *black* she had no choice but to sing. And she stared into Lick's coal eyes and envied the African soul she saw there, a shooter who was born to express himself with all the power that a white child devotes to *keeping himself inside.* She wanted to talk to Lick that night, didn't she? No. She wanted to throw her arms around his neck and never let him go, to smell his kid's sweat and to taste his salty kid's tears and to feel the strong beat of his heart against her chest. But was that the correct behaviour for an as-good-as-white sister and her black brother? Even if there wasn't no blood connection?

Other times Sylvie figured her attitude had changed during her spell in New Orleans some four years before. She remembered a night when she was working Emma Johnson's French house at 335 Basin Street. Now that establishment was surely the dirtiest high-class tonk in the whole of the Tenderloin, with more than fifty girls (of all different colours) performing all kinds of heinous acts for the exclusively white clientele. There was Olivia, the oyster dancer, who placed a raw oyster on her forehead and shimmied it down the length of her body (across her breasts and belly and crotch and thighs) before flicking it from her foot to her forehead and starting again. And she never dropped that oyster once. There was Madame Johnson herself, who'd built quite a reputation with her 'sixty-second plan' which excused any man from payment who could last a full minute with her. According to Madame Johnson, no man could resist her 'special technique' when she chose to really turn it on (even though, in 1915, she was almost sixty years old). And there were the sex circuses that groups of girls performed on stage on a nightly basis, involving lesbianism, sado-masochism and even children on occasion (because Emma Johnson was a woman with no shame when it came to making money).

Now Sylvie took to the stage just once when a number of the stage girls (who were all the worst abusers of narcotics and alcohol) were too sick to perform. She refused to participate in the shows but she danced and stripped and heard the men cheer. The longer Sylvie was on stage, the harder she found it to look down on those men with their tongues hanging out and their hands in their groins. So she closed her eyes and threw back her head and lost herself in the music and she remembered the way she'd danced as a child in those funeral parades back in Cooltown.

When she came off stage, the tyrannical Madame Johnson met her with a face like fire.

'What the shits you think you're doin', girl?' she snapped.

Sylvie stared back at her, uncomprehending.

'You think . . .' the madame was so angry she could barely get the words out. 'You think that white men come to my establishment to see some crazy African nigger dancin'? You fuckin' wrong, girl, you hear me? You way wrong. Even the men what want to sleep with some blue-black nigger don't want to be reminded of what they doin'. You may got pale skin but you the blackest nigger I ever seen!'

And Madame Johnson had Sylvie thrown out into Basin Street there and then and told never to come back.

Truth was, Sylvie was none too sorry to leave Emma Johnson's. Because Emma Johnson's was a French house, she'd been employed mostly for fellatio and her seventeen-year-old mouth was sick of the taste of it. But the madame's words – 'You the blackest nigger I ever seen' – wrapped themselves around her heart and they wouldn't let it go. In fact – just as she had believed as a child, just as she said to Sweet Elly often enough – Sylvie could have passed with no trouble at all. But she came to believe that her blackness would always show itself in the end, like a jack rabbit poking its nose from the warren. And Sylvie learned to love that black part of her, or respect it anyway.

She used to say to herself, 'Black blood must be real strong if it can find its way past all the whiteness in me.'

Sylvie thought about all these things as she lay on her bed in the *plaçage* apartment in Jones and the thoughts weighed her down so she couldn't get up to ready herself for the evening. She thought and she thought but she always came to the same conclusion. The way she had it figured, it was always music that set her blackness free, like it was some kind of alarm call to the slumbering giant of history that was inside her. And she couldn't explain it no better than that.

When she heard music . . . Well! She found herself transported to another place entirely, a place where the barefoot dancing bore about as much relation to white folk's orderly dance-floor rituals as water to neat gin; where the melodies told stories as simple as nursery rhymes and as complex as great literature; where the syncopated rhythms hypnotized you like evening sun on the river; where the singing told who you were better than the particularities of your face.

In her mind's eye, Sylvie fantasized about how music might take human form. The music of her imagination played on an unknown landscape of rocky outcrops, dusty earth and exotic trees beneath a bad-tempered sky that raged and burned. The music of her imagination smashed into tiny shards of glass that were caught in a swirling eddy of wind. Rays of sunshine illuminated this little whirlwind and imbued the glass fragments with a rainbow of colours. Then torrential rain filled the music with water, giving consistency and nascent shape. Slowly, so slowly, the eddy stopped spinning and a coherent form began to emerge like a butterfly from a chrysalis, stretching its limbs with the agony and ecstasy of new life. As the being solidified, so it darkened and stretched until there, at the pinnacle of Sylvie's imagination, stood the most handsome black youth that evolution ever saw, tall and dark and as naked as nature. Suddenly, for one moment, she followed the young man's eyes to the far side of a lake where a beautiful black princess sat. She was naked but for an elaborate seashell head-dress and she was transfixed. Then she was gone. Now the young man stared straight at Sylvie with eyes that crossed oceans and cut her back to her roots. And when he opened his mouth and his white teeth shone and his pink tongue flicked across his lips, Sylvie's breathing stuttered and her fingertips clenched around the white covers of her bed. Sylvie was lost in a dream that seemed more real than any life. She felt her breasts swell and her belly flutter and her skin shimmer. She felt teeth biting down on her lower lip and a caress as soft as breath between her legs. She happily drowned in her imagination; she gulped the fantasy into her lungs and wrapped her arm around her head and buried her nose in the musk of her own shoulder. Her pelvis tilted a little and she gasped and she sank back into the soft mattress as the young man sank back into the past.

As her dream faded, Sylvie heard the knocking at the door, although it took a second or two to connect the sound with any action. She opened her eyes wide and her forehead was damp with perspiration and her chest was heaving. She ran a hand between her legs and shuddered at the touch of her own fingertips. Her underwear was wet and she slipped her panties off and discarded them under the bed.

The knocking was insistent. It had to be Sweet Elly. But what the hell could she want now?

Sylvie opened the door with cuss words already forming on her lips. But she was silenced by the sight of Johnny Frederick standing in the doorway, nineteen years old and dressed to the nines in a tuxedo and white scarf. His lips were smiling but his eyes were as pig-mean as ever and, at the sight of the half-naked Sylvie, even his mouth flattened out. Half a century after abolition and the Fredericks still had their stake in the Black family, all right.

Sylvie had to think on her feet.

'Hey, honey child!' she cooed. 'I jus' knew it was you. But I thought I was meetin' you at the ball.'

Before Johnny could get a word out, she had pressed her lips against his and pushed her tongue into his mouth. The sour taste of tobacco was almost enough to make her retch.

Johnny half-heartedly tried to push her away.

'You not ready?' he said.

'Like I said, Johnny, I knew it was you.'

'But you not ready.'

'I always ready for you, sugar,' Sylvie said and she ran her hand mechanically across his groin. She shuddered at the feel of his penis, a reaction that he misinterpreted for excitement. But Sylvie knew that this game was only ever getting a whole lot harder to play.

Johnny jabbed two clumsy fingers between her legs and felt her wetness as the two of them stumbled back to the bed. He was excited now and he dropped his jacket to the floor and his hands were eager at his dress shirt and fly. Sylvie was cold-sweating, running her mind through all the ways she knew to cope. But it was hard to detach her spirit from her body with no time for preparation.

Johnny pushed her to the bed and squashed the air right out of her. She felt his erection against her belly and she tried to guide him home with her hand, anything to speed the ordeal. But Johnny hissed 'Don't!' and pinned her to the mattress by her wrists. His penis nudged around her crotch like a drunkard's key and Sylvie squeezed her eyes and bit on her tongue to stop herself from crying out. He's better than most, she told herself. He's quicker than most. She was overwhelmed by the stench of the tobacco on his breath and the wax in his hair. She turned her head to one side and grunted to encourage him. She felt his wet tongue on her cheek and then he was inside her – finally! – like an eel thrashing about in a cooking pot. One. Two. Three. Sylvie counted the thrusts. He'd never made ten. He was quicker than most.

When he was done, Johnny Frederick dressed quickly – as he always did – and he didn't say much or look at her any. So Sylvie watched him instead. Coldly. She watched him pull his pants on and she wanted to laugh at his pink bottom like a pig's and his chubby legs that rubbed together at the thigh and chafed bare, hairless patches. She watched the way his heavy round shoulders spoiled the line of his suit and his growing paunch sat on the waistband of his pants and his neck bulged from the collar of his shirt. He glanced at her over one shoulder and his wide upturned nose looked like a snout. His sparse moustache was surely intended to make him look older. But it had the opposite effect. Johnny Frederick had the body of a man twice his age and only the downy hair on his upper lip marked him out as nineteen years old. What would a slaver pay for a physical specimen like this?

'I be waitin' downstairs,' Johnny said. And he quickly turned away from her. Sylvie liked that. Sex with Johnny was quick and ashamed and impersonal. Which felt just about right. As far as she was concerned, if you were going to fuck with contempt then the further it stayed from the ideal the better. *Love*. What in God's name was that?

When Johnny left, Sylvie lay stock still on the bed for a further minute or two. Whatever energy she'd been building to get ready had now been fucked right out of her. She was numb all over and melancholic as grey skies. She knew that some of the *plaçage* women actually enjoyed sex with their men (a mark of emotional commitment that would lead to nothing but trouble, as sure as night follows day). Others despised every second of it. And these women were so fearful of discovery that they developed reputations as 'the greatest fucks'. But Sylvie? With every one of Johnny's visits, she just got colder and colder and on good days she felt like she was listening to two other fuckers in a room down the corridor. For Sylvie, sex confirmed who she was just as surely as it destroyed who she might be. She was being nailed into a cheap coffin and she didn't even have the spirits to cry out.

Sylvie could feel Johnny Frederick's semen seeping from inside her and she reached a detached hand between her legs. She raised her hand to her face and she watched the way the glutinous white substance webbed across her splayed fingers. For years she had thought that, because white men's semen was white, a black man's semen must be black. How the whores at Emma Johnson's had laughed when she'd said as much! But Sylvie had never fucked no negro so she still wasn't sure of the truth.

She sighed deep like there was nothing but poison in her lungs. At least she didn't have to wash herself out since she'd been fucked since the age of thirteen and her bleeding stayed regular as clockwork. Sometimes she thought that her body simply couldn't figure what colour baby it was trying to make. Sometimes she thought she must be a hybrid; she was different, all right, a different kind of animal altogether, as sterile as a mule and bred to carry a white man's baggage.

I ain't white, Sylvie thought. And I sho' ain't black. Maybe Sweet Elly's right; maybe I could pass as good as her. But I ain't never going to pass as no black woman.

Sylvie's throat constricted and her lungs seemed fit to bust. Her face contorted and she wrapped herself up in her arms, her fingernails drawing blood from her shoulders. 'Lord Jesus!' she wept and she closed her eyes tight and she tried to see the beautiful black young man she called Music. But he was buried so deep inside her that she couldn't find him nowhere.

I: *Brother and sister*

(Mount Marter, Louisiana, USA. 1917)
When Lick Holden returned to Cooltown towards the end of 1917, he found that the old place had changed again. This discovery didn't bother him any. By now, Lick had experienced so much change in his young life that he was sure he'd be shocked if anything stayed the same. In some ways, Lick figured he was returning home. But in others he felt like he'd left his home with his wife back in the Tenderloin. Not the apartment! No sir! But the battered old cornet that he'd been given by Professor Hoop when he left the Double M. Because a jazzman without a horn is like a preacher with no congregation, all pent up inside with no audience to hear him.

First off, Lick stayed a while with Corissa and her husband Bubble in the Canal Street apartment. Lick was surely surprised by the first sight of his sister. Her skin-and-bone figure had filled out into a matronly kind of shape with hips like two saddlebags and her pinched face was now set in an expression of permanent joviality, like she was always on the point of laughter. There was no doubting that Bubble, who was as slow as a turning steamship, showed Corissa love that smarter men could never provide. He was a hard-working man who put money on the table every day and had no time for boozing and no desire for other women.

When Bubble returned home of an evening, he would hang his hat on the hook by the door and sit down in Kayenne's old corner rocker. Corissa brought him a pot of fine-smelling coffee and then Bubble would pull off his boots with a grunt and an honest sigh of pleasure. In his first few weeks back in Cooltown, Lick would generally be sitting in the shadows of one corner or other; maybe supping coffee of his own or sometimes from a growler of beer (if

Corissa'd had any money to spare). When he spotted his brother-in-law, Bubble would raise his eyebrows and say, 'Howdy, Lick.'

'Yo, Bubble,' Lick replied. 'Tough day?'

'Yip.'

'That coffee . . .' Lick tried. 'That coffee sho' smells good.'

'Yip.'

The two men would then sit in silence for up to ten minutes, Lick watching Bubble as he tried to figure out something to say – it's like starin' at the workin's of a broken watch, he thought. Eventually Bubble would begin to flex his toes and then he'd examine his old boots.

'Lick,' Bubble would say seriously, 'when I's a rich man, the first thing I's gonna buy is a new pair of boots. Give a man a good pair of boots and he can walk all the way to Philadelphia.'

'Sho' 'nuff.' Lick nodded.

It was the same exchange every night and Lick never did figure out why Bubble should think of walking to Philadelphia (except because it was a place he knew he'd never visit that might as well be on the other side of the world, for landsakes!). But suffice it to say that Bubble was not what you might call a conversationalist.

As soon as he could move without seeming impolite, Lick decided to go stay with Naps. Even then, Corissa protested. 'You belong here with your family,' she said.

But Lick took hold of both her hands and spoke to her like the big brother he'd always been (though she had four years on him). 'Corissa,' he said, 'now you knows I love you. But you's a married woman now and a married woman has a responsibility to look after her husband. And Bubble surely needs your lookin' after.'

'You think so?' Corissa said.

'Damn straight. Ain't nobody could look after Bubble like you do.'

And he kissed his sister on both cheeks and hugged her so tight that she was gasping for breath. Then he left the apartment and the echo of his feet on the outside staircase had Corissa biting her lip.

Now Naps had scored himself a fine little game in the two years since Lick went to New Orleans. After Miss Bessie, the popular Cooltown madam, died in 1916, Naps took over the running of her tonk and called it Toothless Naps's (partly from respect for the passing of the old lady and partly because of his own lack of teeth). Naps had surely turned the ramshackle outfit into the most popular honkytonk in Cooltown. Of course all the tonks in Cooltown were booming back then (with travelling business on the increase after the closure of Storyville). But Naps certainly had a way of attracting the finest girls. First off, he must have been the only pimp in the whole of history who never bothered his own girls to squeeze the lemon any. He'd just say, 'I don't mix business with business,' and pull that gap-toothed smiled. What's more, he was so mean and so kind to them all at once that they were too busy apologizing and thanking him to ever contemplate taking their talents elsewhere. And, if nothing else, Naps looked after those girls. Any cleek who stepped out of line had Naps himself to deal with and rumour had it that he had a whole closet full of guns, from shotguns with a kick like a mule to miniature one-shot rings that he could wear on his trigger finger.

Naps set aside a suite of rooms for Lick at the back of the tonk. There wasn't much in the way of furniture but it was comfortable enough with a bed in one room and a big tub in the other for soaking away your troubles. When Lick arrived at the tonk one afternoon in February of 1918, Naps took one look at him and began to laugh.

'You sho' made your fortune in New Orleans, Lick boy!' he said. 'You one po' fuckin' negro!'

Lick looked down at his threadbare suit and one suitcase that was bound together with string and he began to laugh too.

'I left all my fine clothes outside,' he said. 'Didn't want to embarrass nobody in your chicken-shit joint.'

'What you say?' Naps rasped, feigning anger.

'You heard me.'

Naps approached Lick and puffed out his chest and raised his hand like he was going to punch him or something. 'Say it again.'

'Chicken shit!' Lick said.

Naps put his hand on Lick's shoulder and his angry face cracked and he pulled Lick towards him and embraced him like family.

'My personal fuckin' nigger!' he said.

That night Lick took a table in the tonk and kicked back and listened to the music (some sorry-ass blues, he thought) and watched Naps at work. His old friend buzzed between the tables like a hornet, pouring drinks for drunkards that didn't need them, introducing new faces to the card tables and ushering girls towards beetroot-faced white men with sweat stains on their shirts. Every now and then, Naps would bring Lick a drink and raise his eyebrows. Every now and then, Naps pushed a girl in his direction and he would shake his head and Naps would laugh and shrug his shoulders.

Late on, one of the girls – a young blue-black whore, couldn't have been more than fifteen, with puppy-fat thighs and a nose like a dough ball – was falling down stoned and she spilled a drink over some steam man. Naps was on the spot at once. He placated the customer with free liquor and a fine cigar and he took the girl to the corner of the room, where he slapped her real good until a slug of blood was crawling from her nostril. The girl ran out back and Naps whirled back into the room with a wide smile on his chops. Lick winced and drank jick spirit until he had to wipe his watering eyes on his sleeve.

It must have been pushing 5 a.m. before Naps pulled up a chair at Lick's table. Lick looked out the door and the sky was that pale grey that washes out any colour and leaves you feeling melancholy.

'You workin' hard,' Lick said. But he didn't look at his friend.

'Workin'!' Naps exclaimed. 'I ain't workin', Lick boy! Workin's for niggers an' Jews an' fools. I jus' makin' money an' havin' myself some fun.'

'Like when you beat on that girl?'

Naps stared at Lick and chewed on his gums and lit a cigar with a flourish. 'For sho',' he said.

'Coulda been Sister or Ruby Lee.'

'Coulda been.' Naps nodded. 'Coulda been but it wasn't. Because they both dead, Lick boy.'

Lick turned to look at his friend. Naps's face was half-hidden in an opaque sheet of smoke. Naps leaned forward and touched him lightly on the arm.

'It's a hard world, Lick boy. It's a hard, shitty world full of hard folk that you wouldn't piss on in a fire. People change, you hear me? People change because they gotta change to survive in a hard world. But that's why you my personal nigger, Lick. 'Cos you never change. You still as innocent as the day your momma slapped you to make you breathe. You like a shooter who never learns to hear the crack of his pappy's strap; you jus' keeps on comin' back for more. An' that's why you play the horn so good. The music stops you from turnin' into a hard motherfucker like the rest of us. You my personal fuckin' nigger because you innocent enough for the two of us. An' that's why I's one hard negro an' I always gonna look out for you.'

Naps squeezed Lick's arm and sat back in his chair. He sucked long on his fat cigar and he supped straight from the bottle and he looked kind of embarrassed. Lick didn't say nothing. Because it had always been Naps that had the way with words.

'So, Lick boy,' Naps said. 'Why you come back to Cooltown?'

Lick shrugged. 'Because they were closin' down Storyville and there weren't no work no more. Besides, I had some trouble with a crazy whore.'

'You can't lie to me, nigger,' Naps said.

He was watching Lick seriously and Lick drew a deep breath.

'I's lookin' for Sylvie. I heard she was back in Mount Marter.'

'I ain't seen her, Lick. An' you knows I been keepin' an eye out. Ain't nobody seen her.'

'Sho'. But I knows she's here.'

Naps nodded and threw his head back and stared upwards. He watched the cigar smoke rise and dissipate in the bright lights of the ceiling lamps. He knew what he had to ask and he already knew the answer. But the question still had to be said aloud.

'Why's you lookin' for her?'

'Because she's my sister. Because Sister an' Ruby Lee an' Cheese too, they's all gone. Because I only got three sisters left an' Corissa's happy with Bubble an', last I heard, Sina was up in Chicago an' I surely ain't gonna see her again in a hurry. Because I gotta look out for Sylvie jus' like you looks out for me.'

'But she ain't your blood sister, Lick.'

'As good as,' Lick said quietly.

Lick didn't want to talk about this no more and he didn't like the way that Naps was staring at him with eyes so intent that they burned his heart like sun on tinder.

'Like I said, Lick boy,' Naps said, speaking slowly, 'you can't lie to me. An' the way you look when you talks about Sylvie . . .'

Naps whistled through his teeth.

'I jus' gotta find her,' Lick whispered. He was staring at his feet. 'That's all.'

'Dangerous,' Naps said.

The next day, Naps was up with the cock – there's surely never been no negro who slept so little (perhaps a mental scar of the Double M) – and he woke Lick with some coffee and a pail of cold water. Lick burned his tongue on the coffee and splashed his face and said, 'What the fuck you wantin' this time of the mornin'?'

'The devil sleeps late,' Naps replied. 'An' I's aimin' to stay one step ahead. 'Sides, you surely don't think I lets you board with me for nothin', Lick boy. I's a businessman.'

Naps led Lick out of the tonk around 10 a.m., just as the day was beginning to cook. Naps wouldn't let on where they were heading and he didn't talk any. He just strolled up Canal Street and touched his hat with the same polite smile for hard-working whores and idle churchwomen alike. Lick trotted behind him and took deep breaths to try and clear his fuzzy head of the previous night's jick. But the air was as hot and as wet and as sticky as his mind.

They walked into Jones. They walked past Old Man Stekel's store, which looked kind of dilapidated since Dov had taken over the family business. Lick contemplated stopping to pay his respects but Naps was striding ahead, a man with a purpose.

They finally halted in uptown Mount Marter, rare black faces among the well-to-do white folk, outside a store by the name of Murphy's that sold everything from Coca-Cola machines to gramophones. Murphy was an Irishman who was, Naps said, 'jus' as sharp an' jus' as poisonous as a rusty nail'. Naps led Lick into the small, claustrophobic shop and Lick pestered him with 'What the hell we doin'?' questions until he pointed to a cornet that was laid beneath a glass panel on a counter like an altar. It was the most beautiful cornet Lick had ever seen, polished so bright that he could make out the pimple bumps on his cheeks. And when Murphy took it out of the case, the valves were so smooth that Lick whispered 'Damn!' and he wanted to play it then and there.

Naps just shrugged. 'How you gonna lead my band without a horn?' he said.

Lick wanted to say thank you but the words caught in the back of his throat as he fingered the instrument that fitted his handspan like it had been made special. And Naps smiled because Lick didn't have to say nothing.

'You gonna work for a living,' he commented. As if that was his only motivation.

Lick must have led the band at the Toothless Naps honkytonk for well over two years before he found Sylvie. But, truth be told, his playing (leastways with the band) never touched the heights of his collaborations with Louis Armstrong down at Henry Ponce's Storyville joint. This was partly because of the inadequacies of the other musicians (though Lick employed his old friends Jig – every man's buddy – on second cornet and the funky style of Ash Hansen on trombone) but mostly because Lick's mind and therefore his music were all taken up with Sylvie. Where previously Lick had blown his horn so that he could take the time to search, he now looked for her – desperately, so desperately – in the music itself.

In those half-times when late becomes early and Old Hannah has just begun to peep her head up to smile over the shimmering Mississippi, Lick sat on the edge of the tonk's stage and played a brand of blues to the emptying bar that left his chops humming. Lick blew as though Sylvie could hear him – wherever she was, whatever she was doing – and he surely believed it because he knew his sister had music in her heart.

Sometimes, these late nights, husbands would be making their way out of the bar with hangovers that pumped like pistons and their shirts unbuttoned to the breast after an evening's jiggery with a whore. Sometimes these men were stopped in their tracks by the lilting melodies that moaned to them like their wives on their wedding night. And their mouths dried and they left with their chins on their chests. Sometimes Naps listened too and he wondered how loss could be made to sound so beautiful and he swallowed tears that he didn't understand because he couldn't admit the resonance in his soul. Sometimes Naps interrupted Lick's playing with applause just because he couldn't stand to hear the blues played so. And he rinsed good whisky through his gap teeth and said, 'That's the African shit, Lick boy.' Because that's what Naps called it – Lick's style of blues – the 'African shit'.

Of course, there's no chronicle of Lick's playing back then. While New Orleans was full of writers and wannabes and musicians who went on to recordings and greatness, Mount Marter was nothing but a backwater that was swallowed whole in the urban sprawl of the 1950s. So you might say that Lick Holden's music was prehistorical (or mythological, if you prefer) and lived only in memories that died with their witnesses. Some folk, however, still remember a story that a young white jazzman used to tell in New York in the 1920s when he was (too frequently) drunk. This kid (who pioneered a free jazz that wasn't touched again for more than twenty years) recollected a trip he took with his mother and father down South from their home in Davenport, Ohio, around the fall of 1918. He recalled sneaking out one night – he was only fifteen – and drinking in 'some smalltown joint where a negro played a style I'd never heard before. And that's when I was bitten by the jazz bug.'

Now this was some three years before Bix Beiderbecke first heard Louis Armstrong blow in Fate Marable's riverboat orchestra and it's only a small leap of logic that says he was talking about Lick Holden; just as surely as Bix died an alcoholic's death of pneumonia at the age of twenty-eight.

It was the summer of 1920 before Lick's search concluded and, truth is, he'd just about given up. Lick had been playing Toothless Naps's tonk night after night with no sign of his sister and Mount Marter was a small town where most negroes were on first-name terms. So he was forced to conclude that the man called Chicago, down at Basin Street's 122, must have been spinning him a lie. The way he saw it, he was never going to see Sylvie again and he resigned himself to hearing his sister's voice only in the music that he played from his head and his heart and his chops. He figured that he would surely sense his sister if he ever got close; that he would feel the hand of destiny on his shoulder. But that certainty of fate sure don't make it no easier to predict.

Then, one steamy night when Lick was blowing with a passion born of his frustration, he saw Naps talking to a man at the bar, a tall coffee-faced boogerlee with immaculately straightened hair and a smart suit. Although Lick had never seen the man before, he knew who he was at once: Harry 'Gage' Absolom, who led a reading orchestra for the white parties uptown. Most of the negro musicians in Cooltown despised Gage as a 'sell-out' and a 'no good boog', partly because he played safe music that even white folk could dance to and partly because he was rumoured to earn more than a hundred dollars a week. There were also rumours about what went on at these parties. Although nobody knew for sure because no negroes were admitted besides the musicians and they were too well paid to be telling no tales.

As for Lick, he wasn't one to be making such judgements. Because Lick was a clean-blooded brother who'd seen enough badness to know that condemnation was always hot on the heels of guilt. And Naps? Naps would talk to any man for the opportunity of a buck or two.

So, when Lick finished his easy jazz number, he headed down from the stage to join Naps and Gage at the bar.

'Lick boy!' Naps greeted him and clapped him on the shoulder. 'This here is Gage Absolom. I sho' you knows the name.'

'Sho' I do,' Lick said and he took the opportunity to check out Gage up close. The half-caste had, Lick considered, inherited the worst looks of both races: a squashed nose, thin lips and mean eyes the faded grey of high clouds. His expression was as empty as the white folk's church on a weekday and just as disconcerting.

'Gage be lookin' for a third cornet,' Naps said. 'Thought that maybe you'd like to help out.'

'Sho' I would, Mr Absalom, sir. But you knows I don't read.'

'No problem,' Gage said. 'Way you play, you keeps up with us no doubt.' His voice was thick and harsh, like the sound of a river tide sucking back over a pebble beach.

Lick and Gage shook hands. Lick smiled his open smile with his jibs pulled back from his teeth. Gage licked his thin lips.

Lick rehearsed with the Harry Absolom band for two days. Though he read no music, he picked up their set like a shooter picking candy. There was no improvisation and the melodies and arrangements – though founded in the blues – were so plodding and simple that they seemed childish to his ear. But the money was sure good.

At the end of the second rehearsal – it was a Thursday afternoon – Gage called Lick to one side and pressed ten dollars into his hand. 'You buy yourself a tux 'cos you gotta look spic and span,' he said.

'An' you makes sho' you arrive on time tomorrow. Seven o'clock sharp.'

'Arrive where?' Lick asked.

'The Montmorency Hotel.'

Lick did as he was told and, the next day, the man in the tailor's in Jones said that he looked 'every inch the Major Dee'. Lick didn't know what that meant but he took it as a compliment. He polished his cornet real good and walked out of Cooltown at half past six. He arrived at the Montmorency with ten minutes to spare and hung around the tradesmen's entrance, as jittery as a dog hunting a jack rabbit. If Lick had known what he would see that night, he'd have sure been a whole lot more nervous. In fact, if Lick had known what to expect, he might not have taken the gig at all. And maybe he never would have seen Sylvie again neither; the sister that turned out to be fulfilment and damnation in just about equal measures.

Now, as most folk know, in the years leading up to abolition, the racial soup in southern Louisiana was spicy on the palate, with all varieties of whites and blacks and every crossbreed in between. Of course, in the half-century since 1864, a whole lot had changed (in New Orleans most of all). But Mount Marter was a small town with a small town's conservatism and it clung to its archaic rituals with the determination of rigor mortis.

One such ritual was the *bals de Cordon Blue*. These had died out in New Orleans right along with the nineteenth century but in Mount Marter they were still going strong. They were also known as the 'quadroon balls', where wealthy white good-time boys would seek out fine-looking, pale-skinned black mistresses (mythologized for their sexual prowess). Often these men would lodge their women in what were known as *plaçage* apartments and they would pay for their every need. You could call these women girlfriends or you could call them whores; but it didn't make no difference when the men tired of their favours and kicked them penniless into the street.

It was just such a quadroon ball at the Montmorency Hotel that night, although Lick didn't realize it at first because the women looked so refined and so damn white. And besides, he'd never heard of such a thing.

The Harry Absolom band began to play at 7.30 on the dot and the easy-paced music gave Lick plenty of time to look around. His heart was pounding. He'd never been in a place so fine! Not even Miss Cole's Cabaret in New Orleans! He began to blow too loud and Gage Absolom flashed him a warning glance from the piano. Clearly this was some restrained kind of occasion. Lick took in the elegant curves of every table and chair and the shining polish of the dance floor and the lush fabrics of the curtains and carpets. And he was surely tickled by the pompous white men in tuxedos like his own. Because who'd ever heard of white folk waiting tables?

At around 8 p.m. the guests began to arrive and Lick's eyes were out on stalks. Women arrived in groups of two or three and stood by the bar smoking their cigarettes French style and crossing their willowy legs like doors on the latch. The good-time boys pitched up – mostly drunk as skunks – and they smoked fat cigars and they adjusted their pants and patted their foreheads with silk handkerchiefs. Couples entered arm in arm and the women had the strut of trained walkers and their partners looked kind of nervous but still scoped the fine ladies at the bar.

At first Lick had no opinion on the whole scene except for the sensation that he'd never realized a white party could have an atmosphere so hot. But then he checked one girl – the first to take the dance floor with her boyfriend – and he thought, the way she moved so, that she must have at least an ounce of black in her. And gradually Lick began to figure it out. He examined each girl in turn and he realized that, whatever the make-up and blonde wigs and fine manners, they were negroes one and all. And Lick understood the nature of this 'white party' and his lungs pinched and the tone of his cornet faltered.

Now Lick Holden, with innocence enough for two, was never the kind to judge nobody by the colour of their skin. But this whole situation? Damn! It was enough to make a black man feel like the worst kind of cuckold. Because Lick knew the stories of slave rape. Of course he did. In the first instance, he knew that white and black never bred with no choice on the black side. And he surely felt sick to his stomach and his legs were unsteady and his prayer bones near buckled. Lick felt like a sell-out to his deep black skin that shone like polished mahogany in the sun. He was a real Uncle Tom nigger!

He looked around the other faces in the band – mixed-race and six-out-seven negroes about half and half – and their expressions were empty, unseeing and unseen, as invisible as any sensible black man allows himself to be. Lick tried to figure how he could get himself out of such a situation. But he knew there was no chance of that without causing the kind of fuss that led to white-folk trouble; and that was the worst kind of trouble of all. Especially when he was stuck uptown, a good ten minutes' running from the relative safety of black Cooltown. Instead, therefore, Lick reined in his playing even more; he pulled back on his cornet until he was doing nothing but playing the right notes. Of course the white folk, with no ear for music, never noticed the reticence of the third horn. But, the way Lick saw it, he was damned if he was going to give them the black music that told who he was clearer than any photograph, for landsakes! And Jesus Christ hisself, who knew all about persecution, would surely excuse the blasphemy!

As the night progressed, Lick blew in some kind of haze. The room was hot and his eyes blurred with a mixture of sweat and tears. He saw folk gradually take to the dance floor until the boards bent under the weight. He saw the white men watch appreciatively as the quadroon mistresses shimmied in front of them with just enough black suggestiveness mingled with white propriety. And then he saw Sylvie.

At first he couldn't believe it was her (after all, he hadn't seen her for more than six years). But he blinked his eyes clear and he knew there was no mistake. She was dancing with a pig-faced white boy whose eyes never lifted above her chest and whose chops slobbered like an overheated dog's. Her dark curls bounced seductively on her neck and, every now and then, her split dress flashed a milky thigh. And her face was just as empty as a steam man's coffee cup.

Sylvie turned to look at him then, as though she felt his eyes like a ray of sun through a window at dawn. And her dark eyes widened and her lips formed an 'O' and she looked just as scared and just as plain embarrassed as a shooter caught robbing in a white man's store.

Lick felt the blood rushing around his head until he couldn't think straight. Every part of him burst with emotions as conflicting as they were numerous: joy and sadness and anger and sympathy and love and hate and lust and revulsion. All at once. If Lick had been an orator, he'd have dropped his cornet there and then and shouted his feelings for all to hear. If Lick had been a fighting man, he'd have stridden across that dance floor and punched that white boy to the ground and taken his sister into his arms. But Lick was a clean-blooded musician.

So he blew the hottest jazz that any white man ever heard, a sound that soared over the Harry Absolom band like an eagle over Africa, a sound so loud that, back in Cooltown, Naps walked to the door of his honkytonk and turned his ear to the sky. And one by one the other members of the band stopped their playing and stared at Lick with their mouths agape. Because Lick blew with more conviction than any orator and stronger than any fighting man. Lick blew until he could *see* the music; until he could see the music as a proud black man who looked down on the white folk from the heights of a hilltop. Lick blew with four parts of his body for the first time: his head that thought of joy and sadness; his chops that spoke of anger and sympathy; his heart that pumped with love and hate; and his groin that ached with lust and revulsion. Lick blew until the four winds ran right out of breath.

He was bent double, gasping for air, and the quadroon ball was stopped dead in its tracks. Gage got up from his piano and looked nervously at the shocked white faces that would turn to anger in an instant. He walked over to Lick and bent down beside him. With his breathing so deep, Lick sucked in Gage's fear and came quickly to his senses.

'You better fuckin' pass out, Lick Holden!' Gage hissed.

'What?'

'You better fuckin' faint, go down, collapse. You best die if you don't want these folk to kill you!'

Lick didn't need no second asking and he sank to his knees and closed his eyes and threw himself prostrate across the stage.

'He's fittin'!' Gage shouted. 'Lord Jesus! He's fittin'!'

Lick felt strong hands lift him by the thighs and shoulders and he was careful to rest his cornet on his chest. He heard a woman's voice say, 'He all right?' – could it have been Sylvie? – and Gage barking, 'Clear the way. Clear the way there.' White voices said 'he don't look so sick to me,' and 'Fuckin' nigger,' and 'I kill him my own self.' But his pallbearers carried him on until he felt the sticky breeze of the outside air on his face. He was laid on the ground and a slap stinged his face. But Lick didn't even wince, let alone open his eyes. Someone was bending over him and Lick could smell the alcohol on his breath. 'I never wanna see this nigger again. You can call a doctor or leave him in the gutter but I never wanna see this nigger again. That clear?' Lick heard Gage say, 'Yessir! Never see that nigger again, sir!' in that dumb negro voice that white folk so liked to hear. A door slammed and there was silence. Lick opened his eyes and found Gage looking down at him. His jibs were tight but not unkind and his mean peepers didn't look so mean no more. His lips were thin and his eyes were small but not so thin or so small as a white man's.

'What the fuck you doin,' Lick Holden?' Lick didn't say nothing.

'You never come back here again, negro, you hear me?' Gage said. 'You never come back here.'

Gage turned back into the hotel and Lick whispered, 'Thanks, Gage.' But the band leader didn't hear him.

Lick found himself in the alley behind the hotel. There was nobody about and he lifted himself gingerly to his feet. He was relieved to find that he still clasped his cornet in his hand. 'You sho' one lucky nigger!' Lick said aloud. 'You sho' one lucky, fool-ass nigger!'

Lick walked out down the alley and his every breath was as loud as rushing wind and his every footstep resounded like a gunshot. He knew that if any white man saw him now, he'd surely take a beating. Or worse. Lick came to the end of the alley and heard footsteps approaching from around the corner. His stomach lurched and he stood stock still. But it wasn't no white man. It was Sylvie.

'You all right?' she said.

'Fine.'

'I heard you was in New Orleans.'

'I was. I was lookin' for you.'

Sylvie nodded. Her eyes were puffed with tears and she blinked and her fingers trembled on the handkerchief she held. Lick felt so much love for her but he couldn't control the anger he felt too.

'So you a white man's whore,' he said. 'In fact you's lower than a whore.'

Sylvie licked her lips and she smiled a bleak smile.

'What's lower than a whore?' she asked quietly.

'A slave.'

Sylvie nodded and sighed deeply.

'What colour am I, Fortis?' she asked.

'You's black.'

'An' say I have children by a white man. What colour they be?'

'They black, of course.'

'One day . . .' Sylvie said. ' . . . The way I sees it, one day the whole world gonna be black and the white folk won't be able to do nothin' about it because they be black too.'

Sylvie walked up to Lick, real close so that he could feel her breath on his neck and smell her scent like a meadow after rain.

'You play music real good, Fortis,' Sylvie whispered.

'You ain't heard me play for many years.'

'I always hear you, Fortis. I always hear you.'

The way Sylvie looked at him . . . Well! Lick felt all twisted up inside like his guts were a length of rope caught round a steamer's wheel. He couldn't think of nothing to say. He thought of music but his cornet hung silent against his thigh.

'I play with my whole body now,' he said quickly. 'I play with my whole body because of you. My head and my chops and my heart and my . . .'

Lick's words tailed off. Sylvie pressed a hand to his head like she was feeling for a fever. She kissed him gently on the lips like a mother saying good night. She pulled him towards her until she could feel his strong African heart against her own chest.

'And what, Fortis?' she breathed.

Lick felt the tug in his groin as Sylvie pulled away. But still the right words wouldn't come. Sylvie shut her eyes for a moment and then she opened them again like she was taking control of herself.

'Johnny'll be lookin' for me,' she said flatly. 'I gots to go.'

And Sylvie Black turned away from her brother who wasn't no blood relation and she didn't look back.

BOOK TWO

Dissonance: a combination of notes that sounds discordant; in classical music, dissonances generally require resolution to consonances; in jazz, many milder dissonances are elements of the harmonic vocabulary.

I: *A crude and subtle story*

(Soho, London, England. 1968)
Sylvia Di Napoli was a late developer, both physically and sexually. But when she started, everything changed, like a shift in key or a twist in narrative, with that mixture of the crude and the subtle that needs the perspective of distance to spot.

While her schoolfriends discussed bra sizes and tucked their blouses tight into their skirts to accentuate their busts, Sylvia wore long cardigans that hid her stubbornly flat chest. Occasionally she stood naked and wet from the bath in front of the mirror and she wondered if she would ever be a woman. Or maybe her gender was as uncertain as the colour of her skin. When her schoolfriends talked of boys and exaggerated what they'd done and underestimated what they'd be prepared to do, Sylvia sat quietly and pretended she understood what all the fuss was about.

She didn't have her first period until she was fifteen years old. She was waiting tables after school in the Di Napoli Pizzeria, with its atmosphere of male sweat and rich coffee, when she felt the wetness between her legs. Sylvia dropped the plates she was carrying and the customers shook their heads and she ran into the kitchen with tears in her eyes.

'Mama!' she cried.

Her mother was busy chopping vegetables and she didn't pause or look up. But she told Sylvia to take a bath and wait for her to come. An hour later and Sylvia was still sitting in lukewarm, pinking water and, when her mother finally opened the door and the draught blew in, Sylvia sneezed repeatedly.

That night, she heard her parents arguing.

Her mother said, 'Poppa! She just have her first period.'

'An' she have ah drop the plates?' her father replied. 'You think the customers come ah see some bleedin' spook in my restaurant? She bring me nothin' but shame, Bernadette. Nothin' but shame!'

Sylvia bled heavily for more than a week and her stomach cramped so tight that she was sure her guts were eating themselves. At its worst, she whimpered in pain until she heard her father's footfall at her door. Then she bit on her sheets and buried her face in her pillow.

On the eighth day, Bernadette Di Napoli sent her daughter to the doctor, who prescribed her the contraceptive pill, and the bleeding stopped. When Pops discovered this, he beat her to tears and then he beat her to silence. And he took her to confession. She knelt in the cubicle and at first she couldn't speak for sobbing.

'Bless me, father, for I have sinned,' she whispered.

But she couldn't say any more because she thought her whole life – indeed, her very self – was a sin.

In spite of her troubled home, Sylvia Di Napoli was a good student. At the age of sixteen, she passed her O levels and she stayed on at school with dreams of A levels and college. But destiny didn't give a fig for her dreams and neither did her parents. And, to a child, destiny and parents (especially parents without love) are often much the same thing.

Sylvia was the only black pupil in her school until she returned for the beginning of the sixth form in the autumn of 1970. And she wasn't even 'black black'. That's what her friends said. 'Not like Sidney Poitier or Sammy Davis.' Then a new boy started; a tall, dark-skinned Jamaican by the name of Dalton Heath who had the strapping body and serious demeanour of a full-grown man.

During their first lesson together, the English literature teacher, a late-middle-aged spinster called Miss Hart who wore her hair in a bun and perched her spectacles on the very tip of her nose, asked Dalton if he 'would like to tell the class about the immigrant experience in London'.

Dalton stood up and smiled thinly. 'I was born here,' he said and sat down again. And Sylvia admired him for that.

His voice was like honey dripping from a comb.

From the beginning, Dalton gravitated towards Sylvia. At first, she assumed it was a connection of colour and nothing more. Because Sylvia didn't see the beautiful black woman that now stared back at her from the mirror. Besides, none of the white boys had ever been interested. Or never admitted as much anyway.

In October of 1970, Dalton asked Sylvia to a Friday-night dance in Camden Town. Sylvia told her mother that she was going to the flicks with her friends and her mother begrudgingly let her off work. Sylvia met him at Tottenham Court Road station and he kissed her on the cheek and told her she looked like a princess. Nobody had ever said anything like that to her before, not even close. The Northern Line was Friday-night busy and they had to stand and Sylvia clung to Dalton's jacket for balance. Then she wound her arms around his waist. The other (white) boys that Sylvia knew were chopstick thin and wore their hair long and could recite the lyrics to 'Space Oddity'. But Dalton felt wholesome, immovable, like an oak that gives you shelter in a storm.

The dance was held in a church hall off the high street. It was decorated with multicoloured bunting and helium balloons that rested on the ceiling. There was no live band but the disc jockey played music that Sylvia barely knew, everything from big band jazz to Weather Report, from Diana to Marvin to James to Bob Marley's nascent sound. But it was the people that fascinated Sylvia most, hundreds of black kids all gathered in one place, with impeccable manners and their hair slicked just so. The boys wore sharp suits that showed off every ridge of their thighs and buttocks. Some of them even wore shades. The girls fell out of tight dresses designed for white women who wouldn't know a square meal if it was set before them on a plate.

Dalton introduced her to a good number of people who were as friendly as family. But Sylvia only had eyes for him, with his stone features and neat haircut with a texture that called to her adolescent fingertips. She noticed that when he smiled a flame flickered in his eyes like the pilot light of a sleeping furnace. They danced and they talked and they danced some more and Dalton held Sylvia by the hips, his fingers kneading her flesh, both strong and gentle all at once. Sylvia drank some rum punch that was sweetened with condensed milk and tasted as good as a soft drink. She felt a little dizzy. Dalton drank nothing but water.

Just before 11 o'clock the DJ played the last record, a slow number by Louis Armstrong that had recently topped the hit parade on the back of a James Bond film. Dalton held Sylvia close and she rested her head on his chest and she could hear the strong beat of his African heart against his broad ribcage. Sylvia draped her arms around his neck and their movements slowly synchronized. She stared into his flickering eyes and he could taste her sweet breath on his lips. Dalton felt a swelling in his groin and he tried to pull away a little, looking for just one moment like the sixteen year old he was. But Sylvia felt his hardness too and she pulled him closer, enjoying the heat of his erection against her belly, and she kissed him and his mouth tasted like nature.

'And we got all the time in the world for love,' Louis Armstrong sang with aged authority. 'Just for love. Nothing more, nothing less, only love.'

And Sylvia believed him. For maybe the first time, she could see a future that was made of more than dreams because it wasn't drowned out by the mysteries of her past. For maybe the only time, Sylvia saw those mysteries as an adventure to be explored in another's arms. Because, within a year, such optimism had been torn out of her for good and Louis Armstrong had died in his sleep. And all the time in the world – time past, time present and time future – had been compressed within the seemingly cruel fate of her coffee-coloured skin.

After that first night, Sylvia and Dalton went out together at least twice a week or as often as Sylvia could sneak away from her parents. Sometimes they drank coffee in one of the Greek Street dives, sometimes they sat in Soho Square and laughed at the androgynous fashions, and sometimes they went back to Dalton's home in Chalk Farm for mugs of tea and thick slices of bun and cheese. Dalton was the eldest of five and his younger brothers and sisters bounced around the small flat like fleas in a matchbox. Dalton's father was a small, silent man who'd passed his serious expression on to his son and he sat in the corner of the living room poring over the *Racing Post* with a ballpoint pen, his shirt undone to the navel.

As for Dalton's mother, it seemed like she never left the kitchen. She was a robust woman with a smile like sunshine and she always had the radio on full blast and sang along to all kinds of music in a rich church voice that came from deep in her chest. Sometimes Sylvia joined in, nervous at first and then with growing confidence. Dalton would shake his head and smile with his flickering eyes and Mrs Heath said things like, 'Gyal can sing! Sing it loud and proud!' Sometimes Sylvia almost felt like one of the family.

Sylvia and Dalton made love for the first and only time on Valentine's Day 1971. Sylvia had wanted to for months but there was little opportunity to be alone and, besides, Dalton was a boy with morals as tight as his face.

They bunked afternoon school and took the bus to a friend of Dalton's council flat in Notting Hill. His name was Tupper Ricketts, a blue-black Jamaican who greeted his friends with a Black Panther salute. He wasn't in that day but he'd given Dalton a set of keys and winked at him in a knowing and infuriating way.

Sylvia found it hard to relax at first, in a stranger's bedroom that smelled of incense with posters of Charlie Parker and Marcus Garvey on the walls. But she drank sweet white wine from a plastic tumbler and Dalton drank some too and they looked into each other's eyes and somehow kissing seemed a lot easier than conversation.

They made love long into the afternoon, until the rush-hour traffic hummed on the West Way and the street lights threw shadows across the bed. They made love with a piquant mixture of tenderness and enthusiasm, of nervousness and certainty. Sylvia gasped with every one of his movements, hearing her breath as if from a distance. She ran her fingers over the taut muscles of his chest and she clung to his buttocks to hold him inside. She closed her eyes and watched his shadow dance amid the purples and oranges and yellows. She opened them again and she loved the intensity in his face and the veins that pulsed in his forehead and she hollowed her lips and bit on her tongue and spread her legs so wide she thought she might snap in two. And when he fell into drugged sleep, she pressed herself into his body and stroked his back with her fingertips.

This is a moment outside time, she thought. A moment of significance.

Walking back down Dean Street in the early evening chill, the first-time lovers ignored their usual care to avoid being spotted. Perhaps they were still caught up in the heady emotions of the afternoon or perhaps the abandon of their sex had left them reckless or perhaps they felt a new bond that needed the affirmation of discovery. If this last is true then they got their wish, because Sylvia's father came running from the pizzeria with a face like an angry bull's. His wife was behind him and she pressed her hands to her mouth and she said, 'Oh God! Oh God!' again and again, like a prayer or a magic spell. Sylvia clung to Dalton's arm and he stopped still where he was. His face remained impassive but he raised his chin a little and licked his lips.

'Who the fuck . . .' Di Napoli snarled. But he didn't even allow himself to finish the question (let alone Dalton to answer) before he slammed his heavy fist into the boy's stomach. Dalton buckled at the waist and dropped to his knees with a gasp like a dying horn. Di Napoli brought his knee up into the boy's face and Dalton crumpled on to the pavement.

'Nigger fuck!' Di Napoli shouted.

Sylvia caught her father by the arm. 'Poppa! No!' she cried. But he pushed her aside.

A crowd gathered, fashionable young people with faces like blank paper. One of them said, 'Shame!' and another said, 'Somebody call the police.' But nobody moved and Di Napoli whirled round and growled in his Italian-American accent, 'What the fuck you staring at?'

Sylvia, with her lips trembling and her knees shaking, positioned herself between her father and Dalton's still body. Di Napoli turned towards her and his nostrils snorted and he raised his hand high above his head like a baseball pitcher.

'No, Poppa!' Bernadette Di Napoli shouted. 'Luca! She your daughter, for chrissakes!'

For a moment Di Napoli looked confused and he was suspended in mid-movement like a wax dummy at Madame Tussaud's. Then he lowered his fist and caught Sylvia by the wrist and dragged her into the restaurant.

'She no fuckin' daughter of mine!' he snarled. And Sylvia knew that was why she'd escaped a beating; a lack of love rather than its surfeit.

Luca Di Napoli took Sylvia out of school the very next day. He didn't tell her that's what he was doing. But when she picked up her school bag in the morning, he spoke to her without lowering his newspaper. 'Sylvia!' he said. 'You stay home today and wait tables.' And she knew what that meant and she knew she would never go back and she was right.

Sylvia saw Dalton Heath just once more. It was a couple of days later, around 7 p.m., when Dalton walked sheepishly into the pizzeria behind the small figure of his father. Dalton's right eye was swollen like a dark bubble and his lip was stitched and he winced with every step. Mr Heath's face was sterner than ever and he was smartly dressed in a pressed suit and clean shirt and polished brogue shoes. Di Napoli appeared from the kitchen and he was smoking a cigarette and he blew smoke into Heath's face.

'What you want?' he asked. 'I don't want none of your type in my restaurant.'

'You and I,' Heath said quietly, 'We need to talk.'

'Outside,' Di Napoli said and he looked back at Sylvia, who was standing in the kitchen doorway with emotions fluttering across her face like moths against a window. He jabbed a finger in her direction. 'You stay here. And you better clear those tables or there's gonna be trouble.'

Standing in Dean Street, Di Napoli towered over the small Jamaican and threw his shoulders back like a peacock fanning his feathers. But Heath wasn't flinching.

'You got somethin' ah say?' Di Napoli said. His chest was heaving like a barrel at sea.

'Nobody lays a finger on my son but me.'

'Say what? You fuckin' spooks is all the same. You want Sylvia? Take the little bitch! I never wanted nothin' ah do with her anyway.'

'Your daughter . . .'

'My *daughter*? She ain't my daughter. Just another fuckin' illegitimate negro.'

Di Napoli's face was so red it looked like it might burst. But Heath was as calm as dry heat and it would have taken an expert to notice the way his lower lip jutted and quivered a little. There was a moment of silence.

'She's your daughter,' he said eventually. 'You're not a father, that's true. But that's different.'

'You got somethin' ah say so say it.'

'I said it. Nobody lays a finger on my son but me.' Heath raised himself on to his tiptoes and confronted Di Napoli's stubborn jaw. 'Nobody.'

Inside the restaurant Sylvia stared through the window at Dalton's figure and Dalton looked back at her. His proud shoulders were slumped and his battered face looked grotesque; or was it just a trick of the lights that bounced off the glass? The more Sylvia stared, the further away Dalton seemed until he was no more than another of the ghostly reflections that played in semi-transparency on the pane. And then he disappeared altogether and Sylvia could see nobody but herself and she lifted her hand to her face and she followed the movement of her fingers in the reflection. And as she felt her fingertips gently stroke her cold cheek, she couldn't be sure which image of herself she was touching. She tried to see through the window into the street again but she couldn't manage it. And, besides, Dalton was gone.

Di Napoli burst back into the restaurant with a forced smile on his face and he spat the words 'fuckin' niggers' like they might lend him some credibility. Some of his regular customers looked up and laughed and met his eye. Others took man-sized mouthfuls and sniffed and shut their ears. Sylvia stared at the monstrous reflection of her father in the window – like a bad caricature by a Leicester Square artist – and she turned, as numb as bereavement, and she walked through the door and up the stairs into the family flat.

Luca Di Napoli was about to go after her but his wife caught him by the arm and said, 'Leave her, Pops. Just leave her alone.'

Sylvia was gone before dawn the next morning with nothing but a small suitcase and emotional baggage too heavy to bear. It took just a week for her to turn from a virgin schoolgirl to a prostitute turning her first trick. But time works like that sometimes, a piece of string with kinks and loops and knots that unravel into freefall. Besides, the way Sylvia came to see it, she was born to be a prostitute, a confusion of love and lust, raised with no faith in the former and no reason to restrain the latter, destined to live in an alienated body. Perfect prostitute material.

The first man Sylvia slept with for money was a friend of Di Napoli's called Emilio Casati, a middle-aged tailor with a shop on Brewer Street and more kids than he knew what to do with. Sylvia was wandering the streets of Soho. She'd spent two nights at a schoolfriend's and she couldn't go back there again. She'd half-expected her parents to come looking for her but they hadn't. She had no money and nowhere to go and she meandered down Tottenham Court Road in a daze of uncertainty and unlove.

Casati called to her from across the street. 'Sylvia! Sylvia Di Napoli!' He bustled across the traffic and he smiled a yellow-toothed smile. His fading hair had a yellowish tinge to it too and his fingernails were dirty. 'Why ah you not atta school?' he asked. Half a lifetime in London hadn't eroded this accent.

Sylvia looked at him and she began to cry. At first she cried because she'd found somebody to cry on. But she kept on crying because of who that person was, a friend of her father's whom she barely knew and had never liked. Casati put his bulbous arms around her and hugged her to his chest and smelled the fresh cherry blossom of her hair. Sylvia pressed her face into his shirt. It was as damp and clammy as a towel for washing.

'I've left home,' Sylvia said. 'I'm sorry, Mr Casati.'

'There, there,' Casati soothed. 'There, there. Hey, Sylvia, you a big girl now. You ah call me Emilio. Uncle Emilio. You ah think I ah not gonna look out for you?'

He took her to a dingy hotel nearby and he smiled to the man at the desk and spoke to him in whispers. The man had pointed rodent features that twitched like a rat's around trash. He nodded and he raised his eyebrows and every now and then he threw his head back in a disreputable-looking tick, as if to say, 'You're kidding me.'

Casati led Sylvia upstairs to a second-floor room with a bed and a sink and brown-patterned wallpaper in circular swirls. 'I ah jus' gonna make sure you all right,' he said.

Sylvia sat on the bed and she buried her face in her hands and she spluttered a thank you.

'What ah you thank me for?' Casati cooed and he knelt behind her and slipped off her cardigan and held her shoulders like a concerned father, as if Sylvia had ever known such a thing.

'A beautiful girl like you? You ah be OK. Trust me.'

Casati slipped his arms around Sylvia's waist and cupped her breasts in his hands. Sylvia stopped crying and sat stock still. Casati curled his fingers beneath the hem of her T-shirt and lifted it over her head in one swift movement. Sylvia didn't object and she didn't help him either. Now he knelt above her and unfastened the buttons of her jeans. She winced a little as she heard the elastic of her underwear complain and she lifted her buttocks to ease them off because she'd only packed five clean pairs.

Sylvia heard Casati unbuckle his belt. She thought the sound of metal on metal was like handcuffs fastening. She stared at the brown circles in the wallpaper and she watched the way they undulated as the bed began to move. She tasted the cold sweat that was beading on her upper lip and she smelled the man who had the same fetid scent as her father. She felt the synthetic softness of the bedcover as she rucked it beneath her fingernails that bit into the flesh of her own palms. But between her legs she felt nothing. No. Less than nothing. An absence.

When Casati was done, he sniffed and cleared the phlegm from the back of his throat like a bad taste. He spat it into a handkerchief and zipped his trousers and looked down at Sylvia's body. She was still and she wouldn't meet his eyes. He liked that. He laid two pound notes on the small bedside table and he shut the door quietly behind him.

Sylvia didn't move until there was a knock at the door. Then she sat up quickly and pulled on her T-shirt and hoisted her jeans. The stench between her legs turned her stomach and she vomited in the sink and she kept on vomiting like she wanted to throw up the soul that had gone bad inside her. She heard the door open and the ratty man from the front desk said, 'You're sick on the bed, love, and you have to pay for cleaning.'

Sylvia looked at the man through her retching tears and she shook her head. The man's face was impassive. Slightly amused, perhaps, with a wry look in his eyes and his lips flickering up at the corners. His head jerked back in that same curious tick. You're kidding me.

'What do you want?' Sylvia asked.

'Time to go, darlin',' the man said. Even her father could never have invested the word 'darlin'' with such loathing.

'But he paid for me to stay.'

'Who paid?'

'Mr Casati.'

Now the man did smile. In fact he laughed (if you could call such a noise a laugh, a miserable sound like an engine dying).

'He paid for an hour, love. And an hour's what you've had. That's your lot.'

'But . . .' Again Sylvia retched and the man shook his head and laughed some more. Because he'd seen it all before.

'Look, sweetheart,' he said. He used terms of affection like a quack prescribes placebos. 'Look, darlin'. You can stay if you like. But you'll have to work it off. Know what I mean?'

The man picked the two pound notes from the bedside table.

'This'll do for starters. And I'll expect the same tomorrow, love. OK?'

So Sylvia Di Napoli became a prostitute and she worked out of the Majestic Hotel on Goodge Street for almost a year before she saved enough money to rent her own place, a tiny bedsit just north of Soho. In the early 1970s, she went through five or six pimps who beat her up and took her money (a little more of the one or a little more of the other). But she was tougher than any man and outlasted them all. Sometimes she drank vodka and dropped acid with other girls in a drinking den on Dean Street and, when she walked past the pizzeria at three or four in the morning, she would look in the darkened windows and consider ringing the bell. But she never did. Sometimes, when she was high, she liked to say, 'I've had more men than I've had hot dinners.' And she laughed at the truth of it until her lungs hurt.

Most girls don't survive such a lifestyle for long. They sink into madness or addiction or they give it up for a Prince Charming who turns into a frog or they end up bleeding their life away in a dark alley on a winter night. But Sylvia wasn't most girls. And when her fellow prostitutes told the sad stories that had led them to such a life, she said, 'I was fucked in the womb, sweetheart. I was born to whore.' And she smiled a smile so vicious that the younger girls knew she meant what she said and they thought, I hope I never turn out like that.

In the mid-seventies, when she was in her early twenties and she'd grown into a woman who turned heads and brown sugar was in fashion, Sylvia managed to move upmarket. She worked the celebrity circuit and accessorized the party crowd and draped herself across king-size beds in expensive hotel rooms and took cocaine and counted her money. Other such women called themselves 'escorts'. But Sylvia knew what she was and she knew she was good at it.

In 1982 she finally shacked up with an alcoholic jazz pianist called Flynn and she moved south to his garden flat in Tulse Hill. She liked Flynn because he told her, 'You're not a prostitute, you're a singer.' And, though she knew he was wrong, she liked the senti-ment. She didn't want a man who appreciated her for what she was; she wanted a man who couldn't see it. She kept working out of Soho – of course she did, Flynn made no money – but on Friday nights the couple had a regular gig at a small bar in Streatham where Sylvia sang jazz standards and Flynn accompanied her in blind admiration (and blind drunk). It would be good to say that Sylvia had the voice of an angel, an undiscovered talent who sang her pain as expressively as a crying infant with a musicality learned in the womb. Good but not true. Because if Sylvia had such a voice it was buried deep inside her – packed down by a thousand errant fucks – and she sang prettily enough, but with all the polish and depth of cheap linoleum.

From the day she met Flynn, he was trying to drink himself to death. And, when he finally succeeded in 1993, Sylvia was more relieved than sorry. It was around the same time that she'd heard that her father had died and even that provoked greater emotion, albeit of the bilious sort. She found Flynn's body on a bright summer's afternoon when even London smells of fresh-cut grass. He was slumped over the kitchen table, face down in a puddle of bile and God knows what, and two wasps were courting on the collar of his shirt.

He was fucked before I met him, she thought and she necked a capful of neat vodka before pouring the rest down the sink. That's why we got on.

The way Sylvia saw it, Flynn was the kind of man who would die this kind of death. The way Sylvia saw it, she was the kind of woman who would find him. And, over time, such a certain fate (real or perceived) loses its tragedy and resonates as emptily as a bad joke in good company.

After Flynn she kept the Tulse Hill flat and she kept working as much as she could. She still had the regular Friday-night gig in Streatham but her career as a prostitute was beginning to wain. For a while – maybe even a year or more – Sylvia didn't notice. At first it seemed like the regulars who'd grown old with her were just drifting away to golf courses and retirement bungalows on the south coast. But she had fewer and fewer new clients and she found herself stooping to advertisements in the local press for 'exotic massage in intimate surroundings'. Later she even changed the wording to 'intimate massage with exotic, mature lady' and she found the word 'mature' enormously depressing.

Sylvia finally lost her singing job in 1997 when the bar was bought up by a chain of themed pubs that pumped Irish rock over brand-new sound systems. That same week a white twentysomething with compassionate eyes and a smug mouth responded to her ad in the local rag. He said that he didn't want to sleep with her, just to talk, because he was writing a book featuring a middle-aged hooker. Sylvia made him a cup of tea and charged him £40 and she told him nothing because her story wasn't for sale. And she gave up prostitution on the spot. Although she didn't really see it like that. Sylvia felt like prostitution had given up on her, with her fortysomething face and her fortysomething breasts and hips.

For six months Sylvia did nothing. She had a little money saved and she drank it and she tried to avoid the 44-year-old question of who she was. Prostitution had defined her for her entire adult life and now even that sorry identity was no longer her own. If only she had faced the fate that was her past, perhaps her tragedy would seem a little less mundane. But only the lucky ones among us see fate lit in neon like the multicoloured advertisements in Piccadilly Circus. Sylvia suppressed her past, her fate, her very *self*. And nobody could blame her for that. 'What am I doing here?' It's a difficult question at the best of times. Often it's a whole lot easier to simply not ask it than to reply 'I don't know.'

So why had Sylvia come to New York in search of her great-uncle? Directly, it was because she knew she was no longer a prostitute (because Emilio Casati was long dead). Directly, it was because a young Jamaican called Dalton Heath gave her a glimpse of pride in her colour. Directly, it was because her father taught her to hate; to hate him and to hate herself, and it took her forty-five years to see the contradiction. But the truth? The truth is that fate is both as crude and as subtle as a key change in music or the twists in a narrative. And the truth is where you want to see it, so long as you've got enough moral energy or enough moral despair to get up and go looking.

I: *Two hookers, one white boy and a dirty old man*

(Harlem, New York, USA. 1998)

What the hell am I doing here?

Jim's belly was churning and he squeezed his eyes tight shut as the cab bounced up Lexington Avenue at an unhealthy speed. He was horribly hungover and it took all his concentration to keep from vomiting. He had thrown up in a New York cab once before and the Korean driver had threatened him with a baseball bat, emptied his wallet and left him stranded on the Lower West Side. He didn't want to repeat the experience.

Jim hugged his stomach and opened his eyes a crack. The spring sun was blinding bright, bouncing off the skyscrapers' windows with an intensity that hurt his head. Sitting next to him, Sylvia was a picture of cool, her shades steady on her nose, her gaze fixed out of the window, her mind in forty-five years' worth of different places. But Jim saw the way her fingertips picked at the quick of her nails and he knew that her insides were in turmoil too, though for an altogether less prosaic reason.

He looked at her closely. The sunshine was unforgiving to her middle-aged skin, picking beneath her foundation and identifying each line and wrinkle with a callous, intrusive persistence. She looks haggard, he thought with some surprise. Forty-five years old and she looks it.

'Nnnngh!'

In spite of himself Jim let loose a pained groan and Sylvia turned her head. Even through her sunglasses she could see that he was pasty almost to the point of translucency, and she found herself smiling unsympathetically. She'd seen enough drunkards in her life.

'Are you all right?' she asked.

'Fine,' Jim muttered. 'Fine. Just groaning.'

He closed his eyes once again and tried to distract his mind with the big question. What the hell am I doing here? he thought.

This was just about typical of him because he was one of life's pinballs, bouncing between jobs, continents, emotions, stories and identity crises like that ballbearing around the flashing table. He was a slacker long after Generation X had signed up for proper jobs. He was a traveller who always forgot his toothbrush and found foreigners incomprehensible. He was a happy-go-lucky kid who needed a drink to preserve his mood. He had lived enough stories to fill a book (or two) but he wasn't much of a one for talking about himself and when he did it stank of bullshit. And his identity crisis was that he knew who he was too well. Where most people – Sylvia for one – spent their lives trying to find themselves, Jim was trying to forget.

He blinked his eyes open and stared out of the window as the steepling skyscrapers gave way to brownstones north of Central Park. He clutched his chewing stomach as his mind ruminated on that one question.

What the hell am I doing here? he thought. And he had no great desire to find out the answer.

The taxi pulled up at traffic lights and the driver, a black guy, turned in his seat. He addressed Jim.

'Where you going exactly?' he asked.

'That,' Jim muttered, 'is a good question.'

Sylvia fumbled in her purse for her great-uncle's address.

'West 126th Street,' she said. 'Number 426. Are we nearly there?'

The lights turned to green and the driver indicated, pulled in on the right and pointed to a large, crumbling brownstone on the other side of the street. The ground floor of the building was taken up with a record shop, Mo's Music, that blared loud hip hop from its open door. A couple of B-boys in baseball hats and hoodies were lounging out front.

'That building right there,' the driver said.

Jim paid him and the unlikely pair got out.

As they approached Mo's Music, the two men on the pavement began to giggle. One whispered to the other and then they exchanged high fives and laughed out loud. Jim and Sylvia stopped at the door next to the music shop and stared at the numerous buttons. Some were marked with names, others were not. But there was no 'Fabrizio Berlone' and none of the buttons was accompanied by a number.

'Apartment eight,' Sylvia said. 'Do I count from the bottom or the top?'

'From the top,' Jim guessed.

Sylvia pressed the buzzer and flattened her ear to the intercom and they waited. Jim sucked his teeth and turned away from the door to find that the two B-boys had circled behind them and they were looking Sylvia up and down.

'What's your problem?' Jim said. He was in a fragile mood and the question came out more aggressively than he'd intended. But the two men were unfazed.

One of them pulled his baseball hat low over his eyes. 'Woooweee!' he whistled and he shook his head appreciatively. His friend joined in. 'Woooweee!'

'Pam Greer is . . .' said the first.

'Jackie Brown!' said the second.

'Pamela Greer is . . .'

'Jackie Brown.'

Jim couldn't help but smile. There certainly *was* something of the film star about Sylvia and he was suddenly proud to be seen with her.

'She's old enough to be your mother,' he said.

The door buzzed and Sylvia pushed it open. 'Less of the old,' she said and she went inside.

The hallway was old and tatty. Blue wallpaper, faded with age, bubbled from damp plaster and the tiled floor was covered with

218

threadbare rugs and litter. A staircase with a rickety banister circled upwards, maybe five floors, and Jim and Sylvia looked up its middle uncertainly.

'What did they say?' Jim asked.

'Who?'

'I don't know. Whoever buzzed us in.'

'Nothing. They just buzzed us in.'

'Creepy,' Jim whispered. 'This place could use a lick of paint.'

He looked at Sylvia. She was biting her bottom lip like a nervous child and curling her hair around her fingertips.

'What are you going to say?' he asked.

'What do you mean?'

'To your great-uncle. Assuming he's here. What are you going to say?'

'No idea,' For some reason, that seemed to stiffen her resolve and she marched up the stairs to the first bend. 'Come on, then.'

Apartment eight turned out to be on the fourth floor, just high enough for Jim to feel the full force of his hangover and regret his smoking. The door was open and the two of them looked at one another nervously.

'You take me to all the best places,' Jim said.

Ignoring him, Sylvia quietly pushed the door and made her way inside with the soft feet of a burglar. 'Mr Berlone?' he hissed. 'Mr Fabrizio Berlone?'

A gloomy corridor led into the middle of the apartment. At its end was a tiny kitchen. There was an uncovered loaf of bread on the table and a half-eaten tin of nondescript pink meat with a cockroach teetering on the rim. Sylvia winced and Jim moved ahead of her. On either side of the kitchen there was a door. The door to the right was shut tight, the door to the left slightly ajar. Jim turned to look at Sylvia and silently pointed to each door, shrugging his shoulders and asking for her decision. She chose the door to the left.

'Mr Berlone?' Jim called. 'You in there?' And he pushed into the room and momentarily disappeared from Sylvia's view.

'That,' she heard him say, 'that is not a pretty sight.'

Sylvia hurried after him into the left-hand room. The light was so murky that, at first, she could not see what Jim was talking about. Besides, the stench of urine was strong enough to negate any other sense. But then, as Sylvia pinched her nose and her eyes grew accustomed to the half-light, she saw what Jim was staring at. And he was right. It wasn't pretty.

In a rocking chair at the far corner of the room sat an old man, eighty, ninety, maybe even a hundred years old. His eyes were closed and his head lolled back against the wicker. His complexion was not so much pale as colourless and his skin looked bizarre against the dyed ink black of his hair. A line of phlegm strung from the corner of his mouth to the dip of his chin. He was wearing a frayed denim shirt, a woollen cardigan, ancient brogue shoes, socks and no trousers. His underpants were around his ankles and one hand cupped his testicles while his penis lay sleepily against his thigh.

'Fuck!' Sylvia breathed.

Jim approached her holding a magazine that he'd picked off the floor. He held it up to her face. It was hardcore pornography and the open page held a picture of a naked woman, sitting with her feet behind her head.

'How the hell did she get into that position?' he hissed.

'Practice,' Sylvia whispered flatly. 'What happened to him?'

'Probably wanked himself to death.'

'In the time it took us to climb the stairs?'

'I suppose so.'

'You're sure he's dead?'

'No,' Jim said. 'I don't know. How do you tell?'

'Prod him.'

'*You* prod him.'

'If he's dead, why are we whispering?'

'Respect,' said Jim loudly. His voice seemed to echo around the room and he began to giggle manicallly. Sylvia giggled too and she looked around the walls for a light switch, finally locating one by the door.

Sylvia flipped the switch and the light came on and Jim exclaimed, 'Jesus Christ!' Sylvia span around to find the old man sitting up in his chair. His eyes were wide open and he was carefully wiping the phlegm from the corner of his mouth.

'Who the fuck are you?' he said and his voice sounded like wind in a chimney.

'Sylvia,' said Sylvia.

'And who's he?'

'Jim,' said Jim.

'Wadda fuck you starin' at?' the old man said to Sylvia (whose eyes and mouth were gaping). 'You a prostitute and you ah never seen a dick before?'

Sylvia couldn't reply. Her mind was confused and she looked from the old man to Jim. But Jim's eyes were blazing with the same questions.

'Where's Rosetta?' the old man continued. 'She ah sick or somethin'? Je-sus Christ! An' they send me a fuckin' negro. That's jus' great. If I wanted a fuckin' nigger I'd have asked for one. How old are you honey, anyway?' The old man squinted. Sylvia was dumbstruck. 'Fuck! You nearly as old as me. Fuckin' A! I could ah pick up an old timer like you down the parish lotto on a Tuesday. An' who's this fuckin' boy? I may be getting old but I sure as hell don't ah bat for both teams, you hear me?'

Sylvia swallowed drily. She suddenly realized what was going on because she'd paid a few house calls like this in her time.

'Are you Mr Berlone?' she asked. 'Are you Mr Fabrizio Berlone?'

'Course I'm Mr Berlone. Who the fuck you think I am? The Pope? An' what's that accent of yours? English? Not just a nigger but an English nigger. That's just ah fuckin' great!'

'Mr Berlone,' Sylvia said calmly, 'I am not your hooker, I'm your niece . . . well . . . great-niece. My name's Sylvia. Sylvia Di Napoli.'

Berlone stared at her but for a moment or two he said nothing. Now it was his turn to be struck dumb. Eventually he opened his mouth but it took a while for the words to follow.

'An' who's he?' he asked, pointing a bony finger at Jim. 'He ah your boyfriend?'

Jim and Sylvia looked at one another.

'Just a friend,' Jim said.

Berlone nodded and he was silent again as he appeared to process the information. Then, slowly, his mouth split into a smile so fragile that it looked dangerously like it might tear his face.

'Now this,' Berlone said, 'this is what ah might be termed an embarrassment!'

He began to laugh, an appealing, catchy laugh that rattled deep in his chest.

'I guess I got ah caught with my pants down,' he said and he laughed so hard that he began to cough and cry. Sylvia looked at Jim. He was laughing too. But whereas Sylvia had previously been calm, she was now too disturbed to join in.

'You get my pants?' Berlone said to Jim. 'Next door. Over the chair.'

And Sylvia said, 'I'll get them,' before Jim could move. She had to get out of the room.

For a moment, she stood in the gloomy passage and sucked a deep breath. But the air was so rancid that it didn't help at all. Her mind was busy and empty all at once. She'd seen this before – the lonely old fucker in Belsize Park, the war veteran who liked to commemorate Poppy Day, the ancient queen who discovered he'd been living a lie at the age of seventy-five and was determined to make up for lost time.

She pushed the opposite door and found a musty bedroom lit only by the bare bulb of a light in a small adjoining bathroom. There was no furniture in the room apart from a single upright chair and the unmade bed. Its sheets were covered in all kinds of unidentifiable stains that she had no urge to identify. Water dripped from a damp patch on the ceiling into a half-full saucepan on the floor with a musical sploshing noise. The one window was covered by a colour-less blanket that hung loosely from two nails. The walls were lined with dozens of dusty old ledgers, stacked four or five high. Sylvia considered nosing around but thought better of it. She picked up the trousers from the back of the chair – baggy, forties-style suit trousers – and hurried from the bedroom.

Berlone was talking to Jim, his face so animated that Sylvia couldn't believe she'd thought him dead just minutes before.

'You get ah my age,' Berlone was saying, 'an' you still got the car but you ain't got no licence. You hear me?'

Jim nodded but his eyes betrayed his non-comprehension.

'You wanna dance the four-legged shuffle but you can't find no partner. An' you still got the pen but you fresh outta ink.'

'Oh,' Jim said. 'I see. So you fuck prostitutes?'

The old man laughed again. It was a full-bodied laugh that looked like it might finish him off if he wasn't careful.

'Fuck 'em? I ain't fucked nobody in thirty years. That's what I'm sayin'. 'Sides, my skin so dry I'd probably catch alight with some woman rubbin' up against me too hard. He he he! No. I jus' like ah watch. Keep ah me from gettin' old.' Berlone looked at Sylvia. 'No offence, honey.'

'That's fine,' she said flatly. 'Whatever makes you happy.'

'He he he! Exactly! Whatever ah makes me happy.'

Slowly Berlone got to his feet – stiffly, like he hadn't stood up in years – and took his trousers from Sylvia with a bony hand. He bent down awkwardly and slipped each leg over his shoes. His movements were so painful that Jim started towards him to help but the old man's eyes warned him off. The whole operation of putting his trousers on took a good couple of minutes and, when he finally zipped and buttoned, his expression was briefly triumphant.

'Good pants these,' he said. 'Schwarz tailor in Brooklyn.'

Gingerly the old man lowered himself into his rocker once again and breathed heavily with the effort. He lifted his face and stared intently at Sylvia.

'So you ah Bernadette's little girl,' he said. 'I should ah known. You look jus' like her. Same eyes. Same proud face.'

'Except I'm black,' Sylvia commented. And Berlone waved a dismissive hand.

'Ah! Black or white, it's not such a difference. So your mama passed on?'

Sylvia nodded.

'That's a real shame. But she died happy, right?'

'Yes,' Sylvia lied.

The old man shook his head and leered creepily.

'You a fuckin' awful liar. You were nothin' but fuckin' trouble for your mama from the day you were born. You know that? She wrote me. You were nothin' but fuckin' trouble.'

Sylvia's expression was unchanged.

'So what you doin' here?' Berlone asked.

'I want to know who my father was.'

'An' you come here ah ask me? What your mama say?'

'She said it was Pops.'

'So maybe it was Pops. That's what Bernadette told me too. In her letters. An' she ain't gonna lie ah me. It's not like she was comin' back ah Harlem or nothin'. You hear me? So maybe it was Pops. You certainly got a streak ah him inside you. He was one stubborn son of a bitch. A real big-balled cocksucker.'

'I always thought so,' Sylvia said and Berlone began to smile again and the two of them stared intently at one another – the foul-mouthed old man and the ageing hooker. Jim looked between them silently. There wasn't much in the way of a family resemblance.

'Look,' Sylvia said slowly, 'I just want you to tell me what you know.'

For a moment the old man closed his eyes and shook his head gently from side to side like he was exercising his neck. When he opened his eyes, he was looking directly at Jim.

'What you say your name was?'

'Jim,' Jim said. 'Jim Tulloh.'

'An' what you thinkin' Jim Tulloh?'

Jim shrugged. 'It's none of my business.'

'So make it your business.'

'I think,' Jim began and then he stopped again and sighed softly. 'I think . . . let's face it, Mr Berlone, you're an old man who's seen a lot of life and you're not going to see a whole lot more. I think you should stop fucking about and tell your niece whatever she wants.'

Berlone nodded and smiled. 'I like this kid. A real straight-talker. So. Tell me, Miss Sylvia Di Napoli, what you wanna know?'

'I told you,' Sylvia muttered. 'I want to know who my father was.'

'An' I told you. Way I know it, your father was Luca Di Napoli an' I don't know no different. Perhaps you lookin' in the wrong place. You hear me? Fuckin' A!'

'What are you saying? I don't understand.'

Berlone sighed and looked to Jim again. 'She always this slow?' he asked rhetorically. 'Pass me a cigar. That box on the table.'

Jim opened the box and selected a fat Cuban that he handed to the old man. Berlone reached for a silver cigar cutter from the pocket of his cardigan, snipped the cigar with rheumatic fingers and held it between his teeth. He flourished a silver lighter and puffed blue smoke into the already fuggy atmosphere.

'These things'll kill me,' he said. 'He he he!'

Sylvia and Jim said nothing.

'Let me tell you a story,' Berlone began. 'You ever hear about your grandpops? Name was Tony Berlone. My brother. *Tony Berlone.* It got a good ring to it, don't it? He was the fuckin' man. A real big-hearted motherfucker. An' we were tight like that. You hear me? Tight like that.

'Back in – when was it? Musta been the fall of 1923. Tony an' me, we ah opened a nightspot in the Jungle; that's what we called the area round 133 back then. Right between the Cotton Club an'

Connie's Inn. The Rose. That's ah what we called it. The Rose. An' it was a happenin' joint, you got that right! The Cotton Club? That was where the rich Manhattan motherfuckers went for the show. Paris had nothin' on that place; swanky table clothes, high-yellow chorus girls, feathers and thighs, the whole ah fuckin' kit and caboodle. Now Connie's Inn, that place was damblack. Full of whites, for sure. But they were that intellectual type who just wanted to listen to the new jazz music. At the Rose, we had a different attitude. The music was important – sure it was. We had everyone from Armand J. Piron's orchestra to W. C. Handy playin' blues. Back in the twenties, we even had Fats workin' as a delivery boy. But we ah concentrated on the relaxed atmosphere. The Rose was a place to come an' pick up a girl, drink a little liquor and smoke yourself some mooca. Whatever you was wantin'. A real old-fashioned speakeasy. You hear me?

'I tell you. Back then, I was like ah twenty fuckin' years old an' we was makin' some serious fuckin' moolah. Clearin' a couple of Gs a night. Easy.'

'So?' Sylvia said coldly. 'What's your point?'

'All right, already! Je-sus! You wound tight, honey!'

'So, the point is, winter 1924, we thinkin' of expandin' the business. We heard of real good opportunities out West an' I travelled cross country to LA. Took fuckin' days. Anyway, as it turned out, those LA joints were done up as secure as a caboose. Legitimate businessmen or hoodlums, made no odds, there was no way those West Coast boys were gonna let a New York I-talian cut a piece of the action, no matter how big his balls were. You hear me?

'So. Anyway. I made it ah back to Harlem around December '24 and Tony'd been ringin' the changes at the Rose without no consultin'. He'd got some new girl singin' full time – a real moolie but with all them high-society airs – an' he got the hots for her somethin' bad. She'd jus' come up from the deep south, like two months before. An' I'm talkin' way deep. Said her name was Sylvia.'

'My grandmother,' Sylvia interrupted. She was hanging on to his every wheezing breath. 'She was a jazz singer?'

'Tha's right. You was named for her.'

'I was named for her,' Sylvia repeated. 'Go on.'

Berlone had begun to cough. His chest was rattling and his eyes were pale. For all his hard attitude, this story was wearing him out.

'Go on,' Sylvia insisted.

'Now . . .' Berlone began again. But his words were immediately swallowed, awash with racking phlegm. Jim looked nervously at Sylvia. He was worried they were pushing the old man too hard. But Sylvia could barely contain her impatience.

'Now Tony . . .' Cough. 'Now . . .' Cough, cough. 'Now I knew Tony was a big-hearted son of a bitch but I'd never seen him like that before. Cupid had hit him. Pow!

'Like, me an' Sylvia, we was never close. I'll admit that dame sang like an angel but she had too many secrets for my likin' and there was ah something about her . . . Some real bush manner that I couldn't put my finger on. She said she was from some I-talian family down South. But, the way I remember it, she never told their name. An' she ah never liked me much either. That's why after Tony got took in '27 – God rest his soul . . .' – Berlone paused and crossed himself – 'That's why I didn't see none of your mother. Even as a baby. Even when Sylvia was gettin' kinda famous, the year she spent singin' with Smack Henderson's band . . .'

'She sang with Smack Henderson?' Sylvia interrupted. 'What? Fletcher "Smack" Henderson?'

'Sure she did. For a little while anyway. Before she got so deep into charlie that she ah fuck'd up her voice. Then she had nothin' and nobody ah look after her but your mother. 'Cos she weren't gonna come ah me for help.'

Sylvia's face was flickering with emotion long suppressed. But she was too used to hiding her feelings for them to be seen through the thick atmosphere. Not by Jim. Certainly not by the old man, who was lost in his memories.

''Sides,' Berlone continued, 'when are we ah talkin' about? Must be '34. We shut down the Rose when Tony got sick. After that, I was workin' protection for Jonny Numbers. Around '34 I musta still been in the clink.'

'What for?' Jim asked.

'They said I off'd some negro grifter, just up from Louisiana, behind St John the Divine, a smokestack who was cuttin' in on Jonny's bag. But they couldn't prove nothin' an' I weren't ah too concerned. So weren't I the dumb mook? Like I said to Jonny's lawyers, "This is ah one big city an' it take a real small world to put me and a corpse in the same place at the same time an' no one give enough of a fuck about no dead nigger."'

A lump caught in Jim's throat and he fixed his gaze on the old man. Berlone looked momentarily embarrassed and averted his eyes.

'Anyways. I'm digressin'. That's age for you. People think you lose the plot but that ain't it. You still got ah the story. But it gets a whole lot more complicated and nobody wanna hear it no more. He he he!

'Anyway. I was sayin'. A month after I got back from LA, January '25, Tony decides he gonna marry Sylvia. Mother of God, you shoulda seen the fuss! None of my family at the weddin' but me! An' four months after that, Sylvia gives birth to your mother, Bernadette. So you see what I'm sayin'?'

Berlone paused and stared at Sylvia. Sylvia stared back and licked her lips but her face was blank as her mind tried to process this lost history. She blinked a couple of times. She didn't get it. But Jim? He got it straight away and his breathing came quickly.

'You see what I'm sayin'?' the old man said again.

Sylvia said nothing but Jim answered for her.

'Seven months,' Jim said, unable to hold it in. 'Sylvia had only been singing at the Rose for seven months. Tony Berlone couldn't have been Bernadette's father.'

'Butter bingo!' the old man exclaimed. 'About fuckin' time. Tony

228

was raisin' some other cocksucker's kid but he was so took up with this Sylvia dame that he didn't give two hoots.'

Jim turned to Sylvia. He could barely make her out through the thick smoke from Berlone's cigar. But he could see that she was swaying gently on the spot, her eyes closed.

'Who was my grandfather?' Sylvia asked.

'How the fuck do I know?' Berlone said with unkind relish. 'But, judgin' by your complexion, I'd say he was some jigaboo from down South. If Tony ever knew, he wasn't tellin'. Though I 'spect he was glad his new wife didn't give birth to no nigger. I guess fortune lent a hand. You know what they say, Sylvia Di Napoli? Bad blood skips a generation. So ain't you little Miss Unfortunate that you the one what turned out a negro.'

Berlone's body began to shake again with that infectious laugh. But now it had a cruel edge that pricked Jim's spirit.

'Who'd've fuckin' believed it,' Berlone spluttered. 'Me. Related to a fuckin' spook!'

Jim's eyes darted to Sylvia. One hand pressed to her forehead, she stepped backwards and leaned herself against the wall. Her shoulders were heaving.

'I've got to get out of here,' she said, her voice as pained and numb as fingers in snow. 'Get some air.'

Sylvia stumbled out of the door and her footfall was heavy in the passageway and the door of the apartment banged against the wall and she didn't bother to shut it fast behind her.

'He he he!' The old man was laughing again and Jim felt anger rising in his gut and chest. 'Let me tell you, Jim. That's the trouble with the truth. It don't please nobody but itself. You hear me? Just like the old numbers game.'

Jim crouched beside the old man. 'Who was her grandfather?'

'I don't fuckin' know,' Berlone said. But he heard the gravity of Jim's tone and he added, 'I swear it. I don't know.'

'How can we find out?'

'I don't know. God's honest truth.'

'Not good enough,' Jim said. His voice seemed to have dropped an octave and his hands were making fists.

'Je-sus! Maybe you could try Chicago. Far as I remember, Sylvia had some sister there who married a minister. Apostolic Church of All Saints. Something like that. An' Sylvia used to go visitin' on her sometimes.'

'Whereabouts in Chicago?'

'I don't know. What am I? A fuckin' road atlas?'

At that moment, there was a knock at the door and a nervous-looking dolly blonde walked in. She was wearing knee-length black boots and a clinging red dress cut low at the chest and high at the thigh. She was at least thirty but trying to look sixteen. Her mouth was fixed in a smile that looked friendly at first and then ghoulish.

'Rosetta,' Berlone exclaimed, 'where the fuck you been?'

'Hey, sweetie pie! Baby got caught on the subway. I didn't know you had company. You want me to dance for the pair of you?'

'He's jus' leavin',' said Berlone turning to Jim. 'Unless you get your rocks off seeing an old man gettin' his.'

'No,' Jim said numbly. 'I'm leaving.'

But he didn't move.

Berlone began to fumble with the button of his trousers. Rosetta approached him, her lips pursed in a kiss. 'Let me help you with that, sweetie pie.' Now Jim made for the door.

'Jim!' Berlone called him back. 'Tell me somethin'. Why you helpin' Sylvia out?'

'She's my friend,' Jim replied instinctively. Although he remembered that he'd only met Sylvia the day before.

'Bullshit!' Berlone exclaimed. 'Let me tell you what I learned in the clink. Nobody do nothin' for nothin'. As simple as that. It's a fact of life.'

'Your life,' Jim commented drily.

'Yeah? Well, a word of warnin'. A nigger bitch will fuck you like a pro and then she'll fuck you up like a pro. You hear me?'

'You're talking about your niece.'

230

'But she ain't my fuckin' blood,' Berlone said. But Jim was already out of the door.

Out on 126, Jim found Sylvia sitting on the pavement with her feet in the gutter. She looked incongruous with her elegant posture and elegant clothes set off against the blowing litter and the dusty curb. The two B-boys were still hanging outside Mo's Music but they weren't bothering her. Two kids rode close by on bicycles but Sylvia didn't flinch. And she didn't look up when Jim sat next to her. Her face was blank. She didn't look upset. Maybe just a little tired.

'What did he say?' Sylvia asked. Her voice was even.

'Not much.'

'Did he say anything about me?'

Jim weighed the options in his mind and made the wrong choice. 'He said you'd fuck like a pro.'

A guttural noise emerged from Sylvia's throat – 'Hngh!' – like an attempted laugh. Jim lit a cigarette but he didn't like the taste. After two drags he flicked it into the street.

'Did you see the hooker?' Jim asked. 'Rosetta?'

'Yeah.'

'I think she just dances for him. Imagine! Stripping for an old fucker like that.'

Sylvia said nothing. Jim thought for a moment. Again he made the wrong choice.

'Sylvia,' Jim said slowly. 'Have you ever done that?'

Jim had hardly got the words out before Sylvia span towards him, the flat of her palm stinging his cheek. Her eyes were alight and her face twisted in anger.

'Who the fuck do you think you are?' she spat.

'I'm sorry. I just . . .'

Sylvia made to get up. But it was as if she was too weak. 'Fuck!' she said. Jim pawed at his tender cheek and lit another cigarette. It tasted as foul as the last but this time he was determined to persevere.

'You want one?' he asked. But Sylvia didn't reply.

For a full minute they sat in silence. The two B-boys watched them from the other side of the road and whispered to one another. They'd wondered how this scrawny white kid and Pamela Greer fitted together. Now they knew. Jim and Sylvia looked unhappy enough to be a couple. However unlikely.

Eventually Sylvia spoke and her voice was full of uncried tears. 'What am I going to do?' she asked.

Jim didn't reply for a second. Just to give his brain time to engage before his mouth.

'Berlone told me you had a great-aunt in Chicago,' he said at last. 'We . . .' He paused. '*We* are going to Chicago.'

Sylvia turned her face to him then. But his mind was elsewhere and he didn't see what was clear in her eyes.

What the hell am I doing here? Jim thought. I'm going to Chicago. That's what I'm doing. OK.

I: *Magic city*

(Uptown, Chicago, USA. 1998)
Sylvia was tired. She put it down to jet lag but it wasn't that at all. Her past was catching up with her.

My past is catching up with me.

Sylvia thought about that expression.

And if it's catching up with me, then I must be tiring because my past's not going to accelerate now, is it?

She was sitting with Jim in a bar and grill on Chicago's North Pier, which noses into the expanse of Lake Michigan. It was one of those themed joints (Irish, of course) and the menu was divided into sections called things like 'Donnegrill' (for meat) and 'Ennisgallon' (for beers). And the individual dishes had unpunnable, unironic names like 'De Valera Burger' and 'Michael Collins Club'.

Jim was talking in that aimless way of his; remarking how strange it was to eat a lump of mince that was so specifically anthropomorphized. He swilled beer, chomped red meat and smoked a cigarette all at once.

He had tracked down the Apostolic Church of All Saints in a two-dollar guidebook and he was making plans for a trip down there the next day. Sylvia watched him blabber and swill and chomp and puff (like the obese vicar from the Forest of Dean) and she felt her top lip curl in distaste. She was beginning to find his enthusiasm for this wild goose chase disconcerting, irritating even. It was almost like he wanted to find out who she was more than she did herself. And that made her feel a little guilty and a lot more tired. She'd never liked a man who appreciated her for what she was; she liked men who couldn't see it. And what the fuck was she anyway? Prostitute (retired). Singer (unemployed). The way Sylvia saw it,

233

labels that needed brackets for accuracy weren't exactly worthwhile tools of identity.

She picked up a tepid chip and grease ran down her forefinger. 'Do you have to smoke while I'm eating?' she said.

Jim exhaled happily. '*You* smoke.'

'Hardly.'

Jim shrugged and stubbed his cigarette and swallowed a mouthful of beer. Sylvia began to suspect that his interest in her past was more about him than her, as though he was jumping on the first pilgrim's bandwagon out of the Town of Empty Stories. And that thought got her back up. What was she doing with this white boy anyway (who was young enough to be her son)? What could he offer her?

Unfortunately, the answers came to her before she'd even finished with the questions and they seemed to hang over her like a personal rain cloud in a cartoon. Without Jim she was alone and she didn't want to be alone any more. Without Jim she wouldn't even have made it this far (since he'd paid for the tickets to Chicago and found the church). Without Jim, what would she be doing? Nothing. And this was better than nothing. Even if, as far as she was concerned, it would take some kind of miracle to find an answer to her personal mystery. And she couldn't see much room for magic in a place like Chicago, a concrete city, dressed in Lycra, fed to bursting on reconstituted offal that was named after Irish republican heroes.

She sipped on her vodka and slimline tonic and watched Jim devour the remains of his burger. He licked his fingers and caught her eye and raised his eyebrows to ask if she minded. She shook her head and he began to help himself to her leftovers. Sylvia didn't know whether to laugh or wince.

That was one thing about her new companion, a feature that she identified but found hard to explain. It was that 'knowing fool' thing again. Beneath that tatty old I-drink-for-England topcoat, there was a boyish enthusiasm that he sometimes couldn't suppress.

Sylvia recalled their flight to Chicago. When their plane descended

234

into O'Hare, Jim had been overexcited and pressed his face to the perspex like a nerveless kid. When he saw the city's skyscrapers reaching for the heavens like a hundred great Babels, he hadn't been able to contain himself. 'Look!' he'd exclaimed. 'God! Look at that!'

Sylvia smiled at the memory and shook her head. Jim was a confusing character. She corrected herself. Confused.

'Why are you doing this?' she asked.

Jim called the dozy waitress. On her lapel she wore a pin that read 'I' followed by a red heart and a green shamrock. He ordered another beer. 'Doing what?'

'Helping me. Why are you doing this?'

'I thought you wanted to find out where you come from.'

For some reason, Sylvia felt herself bristle. This was about trust and honesty and those were two impostors she generally avoided. 'But why?' she spat. 'I mean, what's it got to do with you? Was it my idea to come to Chicago? No, it wasn't. It was yours. So what the fuck do you want? Why are you doing this?'

Jim stared at her and lit a cigarette. His movements were infuriatingly slow and deliberate.

'Sounds to me like you're asking why *you're* doing this. Like you've started telling this joke and now you're scared it won't be funny. I tell you something: it definitely won't be funny if you don't tell the punchline.'

'No!' Sylvia snapped. 'You! I want to know why.'

'Just because.'

'Just because what? Nobody does something "just because".'

Jim shrugged. He looked momentarily bewildered. 'I do,' he said.

Sylvia had her eyes on him and he couldn't meet them. They seemed to ask an embarrassing question and he felt his forehead heat and his palms were damp. She got up then and Jim thought that she might be about to walk out. But she leaned across the table and took his face in her hands and kissed him lightly on the forehead. Her touch was cold and dry.

'My white knight,' she said. She'd intended to sweeten this with suitable spoonfuls of irony and detachment. But that's not how it came out, not to Jim anyway. And he coughed into his hand.

He called over the waitress for the second time in a minute and ordered more drinks: another beer, a bourbon to chase it and a second for moral support.

'Let's get drunk,' he said. 'This is our drunken tour of America.'

'Are you always drunk?'

Jim considered this for a moment. 'Not always.'

Sylvia sipped on her vodka and bit her top lip. 'I had a friend once,' she said. 'Watched him drink himself to death.'

Jim met her eyes and shook his head slowly. 'There are some things you should do on your own,' he said seriously.

But the conversation eased a little as they drank. Sylvia knocked back more vodka than she was used to and she began to tell Jim stories of her days whoring in London. She told him about the comical punters she'd had – the wigs and the corsets, the foot fetishists and the adult babies; about the psoriatic vicar and the black preacher who yelped like a pig; about the virgins who messed their jeans and turned their heads to stop her seeing their tears. She told him about the time she had sex with a junior minister in a black cab outside the Houses of Parliament. She told him how Brian G— wrote a song to her that topped the charts in '78 and Jim laughed and shook his head in disbelief.

Then she told him about her first love – a handsome Jamaican when she was just seventeen years old – and Jim felt briefly uncomfortable. As she spoke, her eyes blurred for a moment before she blinked them clear and hard. She described the only time they'd made love and, in spite of herself, her voice took on a momentary softness and Jim examined his shoes. She remembered the way Dalton told her that she was a princess and briefly she looked like a teenager again.

Now Jim stared at her. He was so drunk that her features misted a little like a flattering photograph. He was so drunk that he thought this was quite the saddest story he'd ever heard and he didn't notice Sylvia's tearful eyes since he was too busy mopping his own.

'He was your first love?'

Sylvia nodded.

'I don't think I've ever been in love,' Jim said morosely. 'If I was, I'm not sure I'd even know.' And he wondered vaguely at the way the words seemed to rattle in his chest and Sylvia noticed the noisome scent of something unsaid hanging above their table and she waved it away with her hand.

'So,' she said briskly. 'What about you, Jim?'

'What about me?'

'Ever since I met you . . .' Sylvia began and she giggled (because how long had it been? Less than a week). 'Ever since I met you, you've said you'll tell me about you. Come on, Jim the drunkard. Spill the beans.'

Jim looked at her seriously. He put a cigarette in his mouth and lit it. It was the wrong way round and he got a choking mouthful of filter smoke. He stubbed the butt end irritably.

'It's a long story,' he said, swigging on his bourbon.

'So tell it,' Sylvia said and she sat back in her chair.

Jim cracked his knuckles like he was about to deal a deck of cards. He cleared his throat. 'Well . . .' he began.

Fifteen minutes later, Sylvia leaned forward on her elbows. She was shaking her head in a bemused kind of way and Jim looked pleased with himself, relieved even.

'I don't tell many people,' he said.

Sylvia shook her head and said, 'I can imagine.' And her sarcasm was lost in the toped haze.

She had heard some alcoholized tales in her time but this one really supped the dregs. After all, she'd been lied to by professionals – pimps and politicians and all the low-life scum in between – and she knew the structure of a good fabrication all too well. A real tear-jerking, dry-mouth, gum-chewing kind of fib? It needed a grounding in truth, a thread of mundanity, an implausible twist or two and, most of all, a why-would-I-lie? defensiveness. But Jim? He'd gone all out with that excessive verve that smacked of amateurism more surely than the faking of a novice tart.

She tried to piece together his preposterous yarn in her head. He said he'd taught in Africa. Kind of believable, although she couldn't imagine what Jim knew enough about to teach. But it didn't much matter since his tale immediately began to weave new lace for the borders of fancy. Something about a coup, something about a witchdoctor, something about a mythical chief. And he'd been the hero, hadn't he? Of course he had. It was his story.

Initially Sylvia was angry. Because hadn't she told him the God-honest truth (however bizarre it sounded)? But she soon had to admit a grudging respect for such audacious absurdity. There she was opening her heart about her one lost love and Jim had replied with a story too implausible for an airport novel. There was some dark comedy about it that appealed to her. And it was made all the more appealing by the fact it was so clearly unintentional.

Besides, did the truth really matter so much? She knew that the best stories were those that both worked for their teller and revealed something about him. And this insane yarn clearly worked for the smiling Jim and illuminated his confusion like a light bulb in a whore's knicker drawer. And perhaps she could learn a thing or two from such fabrications. Perhaps she could invent a story of her own – of a happy childhood, a fulfilling past and an optimistic present – and she could go home. But home? That was the problem. Because she knew she'd be going back to nothing.

Sylvia watched the way Jim drained his glass and lit a satisfied cigarette and she concluded she was almost flattered that a kid should still want to impress her ageing self with his lies. She found her mouth was twitching in a smile. But she didn't want to say anything. Because he'd wake up sober in the morning and his embarrassment would easily be punishment enough.

Outside, the air was biting as they stumbled back to their hotel (a dull, corporate affair) and Sylvia clung to Jim's arm. This was partly for warmth and partly to ensure he stayed vertical because he was nearly as drunk as the ophthalmologist from Aachen (who'd been drunk in a curiously indefatigable and German kind of way). Jim put his arm around her shoulders and hugged her into his chest. Her hair smelled like ripe fruit and people stared like Americans at this odd couple who stumbled along like contestants in a three-legged race. As for Sylvia, she half-closed her eyes until she was peeking through her false lashes and she tried to conjure the streets of Soho on a chill autumn evening with that poised young man striding next to her with a face like stone. But Jim walked too slowly and he lurched from foot to foot and the image was hard to sustain.

On the corner of Michigan and East Ohio, a black man wearing a red bow tie and a crescent in his ear approached them, brandishing a bundle of newspapers. Despite his smart dress, his right eye was bloodshot, bruised and swollen.

'*Last Call*, sister?' he said to Sylvia.

Sylvia said, 'No thanks'. But Jim said, 'Heads! No! Tails!' And he laughed at his own joke and the man glared at him. And Jim drunkenly thought that a sense of humour should be a prerequisite for a street hawker and maybe it was no wonder that this guy had been punched.

In the hotel room they were sharing, Sylvia immediately began to undress and Jim turned his back on her and closed his eyes.

'What are you doing?' she asked. Her voice bubbled with giggles.

'Nothing,' Jim said and he squeezed his eyes a little tighter and began to whistle, soft and pissed and nonchalant.

Sylvia slipped between the ice linen and her skin goose-bumped and she began to shiver. 'I'm cold,' she complained. 'Can't you come here?'

Jim turned around and looked at her where she curled beneath the blankets. Her lips quivered a little and her eyes were bright. He approached her awkwardly and sat on the edge of the bed.

'You know that story you told me . . .' she began.

'Sure.'

'Was it all true?'

Jim stared at her. 'Sure.'

Sylvia smiled at him, amused and happy. 'We're on a mission, aren't we?'

'A mission,' he said. 'Yeah. A pilgrimage.'

She raised herself on one elbow and kissed him on the cheek. 'Bless you, my white knight,' she said.

She turned herself over, closed her eyes and she was asleep at once and she dreamed of a much younger man whose name was Dalton Heath. The caked make-up on her cheeks that she'd been too drunk to remove left brown marks on the white pillows, as if her skin itself left stains on all it touched.

For a moment, Jim sat on the edge of Sylvia's bed and he fingered the trace of her lips on his cheek. Then he stood up and stripped down to his shorts and he climbed gently into his own bed as if he was scared of waking his neighbour. He looked at the coffee-coloured flesh of Sylvia's shoulders and he sucked on his gums before reaching to turn out the bedside light. He lay in the darkness and he stared at where the ceiling had to be – how else could it be spinning? – and he didn't sleep a wink because, though he didn't realize it, he was bewitched in Chicago. And this the city that Sylvia thought had no room for magic.

Across town, just some five blocks west, a comparable scene was unfolding in a similar hotel room (with identical Formica panelling, brass fittings and ashtrays by Ceramix of Detroit). There was another mixed-race couple (another young man and another prostitute). But in their case, there was no confusion on either side about the nature of the relationship.

The man was sitting on the edge of the bed. He was looking down his naked body and counting his toes. Because he'd once treated a man who'd lost two toes after a particularly enthusiastic week of promiscuity, a phenomenon he couldn't explain to this day. But *his* toes were all there.

He shook his head and his dreadlocks whipped about his face.

Why was his mind as cloudy as fermenting *kachasu*? It had been like that ever since he'd arrived. And how long ago was that? Four days perhaps. He had lost track of time like a tribesman loses his way on a rainy season night.

He looked over his shoulder at Sophia – was that her name? – as the young prostitute smoked a cigarette and practised her pelvic tilts. Her heavy breasts pancaked beneath her armpits and she repeatedly blew wisps of dark hair from her forehead. He suddenly felt revolted with himself and he spoke to the girl for the first time since their congress.

'Excuse me, my dear. Would you mind desisting from these extraordinary contortions? I am finding them most disturbing.'

Sophia shrugged. 'Your money, sugar,' she said. And she lay back on the bed and pulled on her cigarette and started her buttock clenches instead.

How many hookers had he fornicated with in the last few days? Maybe twenty. And the relief that sex gave him from his dreams was temporary. But it was less frustrating than his attempts at celibacy and at least he had learned a great deal about these exotic harlots. To his dismay, they seemed to take no pride in their work.

Prostitution is the oldest profession in the world, he thought. Surely there should be nobility in such a fact.

He had begun by sleeping predominantly with black prostitutes. But he discovered that, in this strange city, they fucked as badly as their *musungu* counterparts. He resolved, therefore, only to sleep with white prostitutes on the grounds that a change was as good as a rest (even if the urban myths of unathletic *gulu gulu* were surprisingly accurate).

The truth was that, ever since the magic sleep and his departure from Zimindo, his dreams had been getting worse. Or better. Clearer anyway. And mercantile sex was only ever going to treat the symptoms, not the cause, like the painkilling properties of a *guruve* root to treat a family-curse headache.

He picked up his cigarette papers and the small bag of marijuana from the floor. He couldn't believe that Americans paid good money for this dope that was only related to *gar* as closely as one of those third cousins that your *makadzi* insists you meet. No wonder they referred to it as 'shit'.

He constructed a joint with nimble fingers and he savoured his first taste of the pungent smoke and his brain began to gurgle. He stared out of the hotel window across the cityscape of enormous skyscrapers that would have dwarfed their Queenstown counterparts like great eagles soaring above the *boka* birds. They looked like the fossilized fingers of the *shamva* spirits reaching up to Father Sun himself and begging forgiveness.

No wonder my dreams are so strong, he thought. This strange city is a magical place indeed.

When he had suffered the *zakulu* illness at the age of thirteen, he had immediately realized that his perception of the world would never be the same again. Reality and dreams, history and myth, physical and metaphysical, past and future – all these things were as singular as conception. For most people, the world was a place of earth and water. Sometimes rivers cut across the land and promontories jutted into the great lakes and oceans; but earth and water were still well defined. And where they were not defined, the people found their feet stuck in the mud and they turned to him for help. But for him? Well. The world was as viscous as at its beginning – before Father Sun turned up his heat – too thick for swimming but wet enough to drown you. He remembered the first lesson he had learned in his earliest dreams with Cousin Moon: Father Sun melts and Father Sun bakes and this is the first mystery.

He had never known a time, however, when his uncertainties had been so certain. His dreams had begun to overtake his waking hours so successfully that he found the only time he could think through the issues with any clarity was when asleep. During the day he had begun to experience all kinds of strange hallucinations.

While walking by the great lake that bordered this peculiar city, he had seen a young girl floating face down on the surface some twenty feet away. Stripping to his waist, he splashed into the icy water and dragged her to the shore as an excitable crowd gathered. She was a beautiful young thing with dark skin and perfect features and her cropped head was covered in an ornate seashell head-dress. But she was as thin as famine and as cold as good beer. Desperately he tried to resuscitate her, filling her lungs with his air and whispering the *zakulu* spells that he'd learned as a boy. He heard the people laughing behind him and he span around on his haunches. 'Are you people savages?' he cried. But they laughed all the harder and when he turned back to the girl, he found that he had been trying to resuscitate a piece of driftwood and the head-dress was actually a swollen sanitary towel, snagged on a nail.

On another occasion, he came across a vagrant who played the trumpet and had an unseemly bulge in his trousers. He stopped to listen because he was reminded of the music that Kudzai loved to listen to with her monkey ears (that were the most hilarious thing he'd ever seen) and he felt suddenly homesick. He closed his eyes and revelled in the melody, an old spiritual called 'The Far Bank of the Jordan' (though he didn't know it). However, when he opened his eyes again, he found the tramp was metamorphosing. First the clothes faded away. Then the tramp's beard receded into his face and his complexion dissolved to the colour of turning cream. Right in front of him, the tramp grew pert breasts and full hips and his lips and nose thinned and his cheekbones lifted and his raggedy hair untangled itself and cascaded in soft curls down his shoulders. Soon the tramp's only remaining mark of masculinity was the dark penis that hung between his legs, swaying a little in time to the music. Then the trumpet itself began to sing; literally, in a lush woman's voice with just the faintest hint of brass.

'There is only one love story,' the trumpet sang. 'All love is the same. There is only one love story. Love bears no shame.'

For a moment, he stared at the grotesque apparition, rooted to the spot. Because, for all his metaphysical experience (including many nights in the company of Cousin Moon's eccentric taste for the metaphor), he had never heard a trumpet speak or seen a woman who was quite so well endowed. So he turned and he ran until his lungs ached and he found himself outside a quiet deli. And he went inside and ordered himself a banana ice-cream soda to calm his nerves.

His worst experience, however, came in the sparse landscape that this strange city described as 'a park'. He was walking across the thirsty lawns between the trees that looked like they had been dead for centuries when he came across a number of amateur artists with their easels set up before the lakeside. He had been smoking 'shit' and, if not high, he was certainly climbing and he looked over the painters' shoulders and engaged them in conversations they didn't want to have. Because who was this peculiar, well-spoken black man with the raggedy clothes and wild hair and wild eyes?

He walked among the artists, nodding his head and looking out to the skyline, until he came across . . . a *musungu*. Not just any *musungu* (since, in his experience they often looked alike) but the same *musungu* he'd seen during his five-day dreaming, the same *musungu* he'd known during the Zambawian coup six years before, his old friend, his comrade, his *gar*-buddy. But the *zakulu*'s brain was understandably so scrambled that he couldn't put a name to the face.

He called out but the *musungu* didn't reply.

This artist had his canvas set up opposite another artist, an elegant, middle-aged, coffee-coloured woman who reminded the *zakulu* of Zambawian billboards for skin-lightening cream. Their two faces wore identical expressions of fixed concentration. They stared at one another, they stared at their canvases, they held up their brushes to judge proportions.

He sidled behind the *musungu* to take a look at his work. It wasn't a picture of the woman at all but a rather bad self-portrait. He gulped. By now he was fully aware that he was hallucinating yet again and he resolved to ride the experience. He walked to where the woman stood and he looked at her picture too. He wasn't surprised to find it was another bad self-portrait.

He knew what he had to do.

He lifted the woman's canvas from its easel. She looked at him strangely but he didn't say a word. He carried it to the *musungu* and swapped the pictures. The *musungu* didn't even blink as he lifted his canvas and, in turn, set it on the woman's easel.

'There!' he said. And the pair continued painting.

He stared at the woman's picture again. For goodness' sake! As far as he could tell, it was the same self-portrait she'd been working on before. He sighed and didn't bother to check the other painting because he knew that dreams – even real ones – have a suggestive logic that is a good deal more infuriating than helpful. Besides, he remembered Cousin Moon's fundamental tenet: few people understand the full meaning of dreams. And those that do are mad.

Instead he tutted and he said, 'For goodness' sake!' And the apparitions disappeared and he found himself standing in a storm drain, waist deep in all kinds of shit, with the group of artists watching him curiously.

That had been yesterday.

Now he sucked deep on his joint and lay back on the bed as stoned constellations twinkled before his eyes. The young prostitute knelt over him and massaged his temples as he absentmindedly watched her large breasts sway gently above him like ripe mangoes in a mango tree. He vaguely wondered whether he wanted to fuck again. No. He needed to work out these peculiar occurrences in his tired mind. There was one thing of which he was sure; the real trouble of this confusion between dreams and reality came in reverse. If it was problematic to mistake dreams for reality then the other way round was a whole lot worse.

He remembered walking back from his encounter with the artists – both real and imagined – his trousers dripping with sludge and slime. He'd been approached by a smart black man who wore a bow tie with a crescent-moon insignia (surely a symbol of Cousin Moon).

'*Last Call*, brother?' the man said.

'Last call for what?' he replied irritably.

'The last call for the one true way.'

He stared at the man. Perhaps this was the sign he had been searching for. But he was exhausted and nervous and untrusting.

'Why do you call me brother?' he asked.

'We are all brothers,' the man said and he smiled sternly.

It was at this point that he snapped. He was more fed up with the grotesque imagery and oblique references that these metaphysical signs seemed to assume than at any time since the five-day sleep. If his ancestral spirits, Cousin Moon or even that barn-sized eagle, had something to say to him, then they could damn well say it in plain English, Zamba or any other mutually convenient language. And if his history had to make a confession then it was about time to spit it out.

Without thinking, he lunged for the man and grasped him by the throat and shook him with African strength. The man struggled to get free and his newspapers scattered all over the pavement.

'You're a wriggly one,' the *zakulu* shouted. 'The truth always wriggles when you try to pin it down.'

And the wild-eyed dreadlock punched the immaculate representative of the Nation of Islam smartly in the face so that he fell to the ground.

'*Kuripe zvi Tuloko vaseme di zvozva!* But you? Your bottom speaks in riddles!'

And so some do-gooder called the police and Musa the *zakulu* had to do his firefly vanishing trick to avoid arrest. And so Musa was overwhelmed by the magic city of Chicago and he resolved to wait for a sign that he might understand. And so he had sex with *musungu* prostitutes until he feared for his toes.

I: *That shit's even true of the simplest twelve bar blues*

(South Side, Chicago, USA. 1998)
The old man was certainly fond of digression, like a jazz trumpeter that gets wrapped up in the improvisational potential of a specific phrase; something that never happened to the original blues men, like Buddy Bolden, Louis Armstrong (before '38 anyways) and Lick Holden, of course.

'Y'all don't know me. Y'all don't know nothin' 'bout me 'cept I'm the one gonna finish this story and you 'spect it to sound as clear as the music from this ol' horn. But let me tell you somethin', sugar pie. In fact, let me tell you three things about stories because there ain't nothin' so damn complicated as a story (except the jazz and I's not stupid enough to think you understand that any).

'So. Whatever else I's gonna say – no. Don't interrupt me none. If it still don't make no sense later, then you can ask me questions – whatever else I's gonna say, remember this. There ain't no story so important as the one you tells about yourself. Because everybody got their own story don't they? Some kinda fairy tale or scary tale that gets them outta bed at sun-up or leaves them buryin' their face in the pillow. And these stories are practised until they's word perfect. They told upside down and back to front and inside out. They told to friends and enemies and shrinks and barmen. And, believe me, I knows 'cos I's so old even the sun call me "sir".

'Anyways, the point is that no story set in stone. You hear me? He he! Look at the young white boy nodding like he understand what I mean. Dreadlock there, he know the truth. What about you, sugar pie, cousin of mine (I like the sound of that!); you understand me?

'No story set in stone. You think about that, sugar pie, and I know you knows my reasonin'. An' that's why I ain't never written no book because

247

them pages ain't nothin' but a prison an' that's somethin' only black folk understand. An' that's why true jazz don't live in no music book or on no compact disc. It live in your head an' your chops an' your heart an' your sex – don't ask me where I heard that! – an' a story jus' the same. If a story don't change any, then it probably ain't worth hearin'. OK?

'An' another thing. If them pages restrict a story, then there ain't nothin' restrict it so bad as your own mind. You 'spect it to mean one thing, then you can be sure it really mean somethin' else. I jus' leave you with that an' you let it sit in your stomach like grits on a hangover. 'Cos all stories are love stories when you thinks about it. But that don't make them no simpler; jus' like jazz.

'Last thing I tell you is that stories don't have no beginning, middle an' end. That jus' a dumb-ass fantasy told by teachers to schoolkids 'cos they plain too lazy or too damn stupid to tell it like it is (the teachers, I mean). Fact is that stories have a vibe jus' like love. Jus' like St Paul hisself tells it; as real as this table and as see-through as the air on top of one of them skyscrapers. And I can see you know what I sayin', sugar pie. I can see it in your eyes even though you don't know it your own self.

'Let me tell it like it is to all you young folk (an', cousin of mine, you still young even though you don't think so). Let me tell it like it is. The mouldy figs come to this ol' town and analyse the jazz music like that's gonna make them understand it any. Truth be told, jazz has its patterns and its predictabilities. But, trust me, any time you think you got it figured, it gonna play a trick on you. Because in jazz music the future, the past and the present are all happenin' right now. You think jazz facin' one way an' it turn right round on you like a nigger bein' chased 'cross the bayou. An' that's true of the simplest story and the simplest jazz. Damn! That shit's even true of the simplest twelve bar blues. An' don't you forget it.'

Jim and Sylvia took a cab across the Loop. They weren't talking much because Jim was preoccupied and Sylvia was vaguely waiting for him to confess the previous night's lies. But they agreed there was something ominous about the day. Sylvia thought it was because of the vivid dreams she'd had (though she didn't want to talk about them) and the oppressive weather that sat heavy clouds on the city like bales of cotton on a pack horse. And Jim? He'd woken with a crick in his neck that made it painful to turn his head. Sylvia didn't understand the significance of this until Jim explained with a smile, 'It makes it too hard to turn around'.

Sylvia laughed and dug steely fingertips into the flesh at his nape. 'You need a massage,' she said and Jim winced.

The cab turned away from Lake Michigan heading south-west of Prairie Avenue and pulled in opposite an imposing red-brick building, the Apostolic Church of All Saints. Jim and Sylvia looked at one another and smiled nervously and raised their eyebrows.

'We're here, then,' Jim said.

'We are, aren't we?'

The driver turned round in his seat and coughed and licked his lips. 'You guys sure you wanna get out here?'

'What do you mean?' Jim asked.

'I gotta tell ya, this is one rough area. Pimps and prostitutes and guns and gangs and all sorts. I jus' sayin', you wouldn't catch me down in this neighbourhood. Jus' sayin'. You sure you wanna get out here?'

'Oh,' Jim said.

But Sylvia was already out of the door and handing the cab driver a ten-dollar bill. 'We're sure,' she said. Then she turned to Jim and her eyes were laughing. 'Come on, my white knight.'

They stood on the pavement as the cab pulled away. Sylvia tilted her head and looked up the façade of the church. Above the red brick, there was Roman-style lettering in chipping gold paint: 'And The Word Was Made Flesh And Lived Among Us'. At one corner of the church's front there was a large wooden signpost covered in a fluorescent green poster: 'Get High On Jesus'. The wall by the main entrance of heavy oak was tagged with graffiti: 'South Side Devils'.

Jim slowly looked around the surrounding streets and he had to turn his whole body because of his sore neck. How he wished he hadn't cricked it! Chicago's South Side looked, he thought, like a war zone. Sometimes, when he was in New York, he'd visit some rough neighbourhoods just for the buzz of it; parts of Brooklyn and the Bronx and even the projects on Staten Island that the locals called 'Shaolin'. But this? It seemed like every second apartment had been gutted by fire and the crack addicts were sparking rock on every street corner and kids clocked each other's colour with raised eyebrows and gang signs. And there wasn't much question that he and Sylvia stood out like pussycats at a dog fight and Jim felt the glare of a dozen pairs of eyes and his throat parched and he lit a cigarette.

'I think,' he said quietly, 'that we should go into the church.'

Sylvia was still scanning the heavy oak door. She didn't look round.

'Padlocked,' she said.

'Shit.'

There was a gang of six young men approaching them. The oldest couldn't have been more than seventeen. They all wore orange rags around their foreheads and baggy jeans with the crotch brushing their knees and they walked with a roll in their shoulders, like walking was an exercise in cool.

'Shit,' Jim muttered again and this time Sylvia looked round.

The tallest boy walked forward and turned his head to the side a little as if, Jim thought, he was sizing up his jugular for a clean cut. The boy had close-cropped corn rows and one sleepy eye that rolled white into his head.

'Yo, Rockerfeller!' the boy said. His voice was unnaturally high. Comical in another situation. 'You lost? You wanna spare a nigger da Benjamins get you back uptown?'

'I'm sorry?' Jim said and the boy kissed his teeth and shook his head and the other boys laughed and said, 'You tell him, Tweet,' and, 'Tell him the shits, Tweety Pie.'

'You German muthafucka?' the boy said.

'English.'

'English? So how's about I tax yo' vanilla ass. You on the South Side now, bro, and you don't pay, you don't play. You hear me? You better front mo' cheddar 'fore I put a cap in you like a damn fool muthafucka. You hear me?'

The boy patted his jacket and raised his eyebrows and stared at Jim with his one good eye.

'I hear you,' Jim nodded. But he had no idea what the boy was talking about.

Jim realized that Sylvia was now standing at his shoulder and he manoeuvred himself in front of her. There was no need for her to get involved.

'What you lookin' at, bitch?' the boy said and the other boys cheered and joined in.

'Raggedy ol' Pam Greer-lookin' ho!' they shouted. 'Take your teeth out and suck it bitch!'

Jim looked at Sylvia. Her eyes were blazing but her expression was calm. He knew he was way out of his depth.

'Your mama teach you to speak like that?' Sylvia said. She was staring directly at the boy they called Tweet and he looked momentarily disconcerted.

'You English too? Damn! An English nigger. That don't give you no right to talk about my momma, bitch,' he said.

'If I'm a bitch then your mama's a bitch.'

'I warnin' you!' the boy said. And his squeaky voice seemed to jump another octave. He patted his jacket again and Jim suddenly understood what the gesture meant. But Sylvia wasn't finished.

'What the fuck happened to your voice? Your mama must be a bitch to give birth to a pencil-dicked dog like you!'

The boy blinked his sleepy eye. Then, in a flash, he had his gun drawn from his jacket. A heavy Desert Eagle with a chrome handle and dark barrel. He trained it on Sylvia, side on, like he'd seen them do in the movies.

Jim said, 'Fuck!' But Sylvia said nothing.

'How about I fuck you up real good, gran'ma?' the boy spat.

'At least you didn't say you were going to fuck me.'

'Maybe I put a bullet in yo' head and fuck the hole.'

'You could do,' Sylvia sneered. 'Just about the right size for your pencil dick.'

Jim saw this exchange with a mixture of terror and detachment. He felt like he was watching a film in which the top billing (himself, of course) was about to be blown away with the story half-told in some kind of clever-clever directorial sleight of hand. He suddenly regretted his ominous feelings. And, what's more, he found himself looking at Sylvia in a different light. Of course she'd told him her stories of whoring on the London streets. And they'd made him laugh and wince and shake his head. But they'd sat incongruously with the elegant, soft-spoken woman who was lost inside her own self. Now she was making her stories true with fearless and unthinking relish. Now it was like she'd been stripped to the essence and Jim had the ignoble thought that maybe she was *just a prostitute* after all.

'Look . . .' he said. And he pulled out his wallet and began to leaf through the small denomination dollar bills.

But Tweet was in no mood for reasoning.

'I don't want yo' chump change, punk! How 'bout I put a bullet in yo' bitch an' see how you like that?'

Jim watched Tweet's fingertip play around the trigger. The boy wasn't shaking at all. He was calm; he'd actually done this before. Jim looked to Sylvia like she might have an answer. But she was just staring straight ahead. And the only clue to her predicament was in the pulsing muscles of her jaw and the strung tendons of her neck. Jim closed his eyes.

At that moment, there was the sound of brakes and tyres squealing and Jim flashed his eyes open again. A polished black Lexus mounted the pavement where they stood and screamed to a halt. It had tinted windows, shining alloy wheels and an engine that roared like a jet plane at take off. An enormous man in a black suit leaped from the driver's side. His head was shaved and his skin shone like polished mahogany and the flesh of his neck wrinkled up like a dog's. Around his neck hung a heavy gold crucifix, maybe six inches high, on a thick gold rope and at his throat he wore a white dog collar like gang colours. He had a voice like a booming bass line.

'What you think y'all doin', Tweet?' he said.

But Tweet didn't look round. 'This ain't none of yo' business, pastor.'

'You pull a gun on the doorstep of my church and you think t'ain't none of my business? You a fool, son. An' you know I put a bullet in you my own self 'fore I let you shoot nobody else. May God forgive me.'

Jim looked from Tweet to the pastor to Sylvia to the other boys. The boys' bravado had vanished and they were now silent and cowering. Jim began to feel slightly unreal. He'd seen some strange stuff in his twenty-five years – in Africa especially – but this was right up there with the strangest.

For the first time Tweet turned to the pastor. But he kept the Desert Eagle trained between Sylvia's eyes.

'She disrespected my momma, pastor,' Tweet said. The boy suddenly looked small and young and lost, like a kid caught shop-lifting.

The pastor laughed and it was a noise like rolling thunder.

'Boy, I diss your mother my own self. She's a no-good crack fiend and you know it. What you think this is? An eye for an eye? Weren't these folk who took your eye, Tweet. You hear me? You wanna put a cap in some gang banger then that's your own business and ain't nothin' I can do about it. But you ain't gonna pop nobody on the doorstep of my church. You hear?'

The pastor paused and wove his fingers and cracked his knuckles. He smiled and ran his thumb around his collar.

'My! It sure is hot today,' he said. His voice sounded almost bored. 'I feel like I might jus' have to take off my jacket. And you know what happens when I take off my jacket, Tweet. You don't want me to take off my jacket, do you, boy?'

Tweet blinked. With his bad eye, it was a strange, retarded-looking expression. Slowly he lowered his gun and pouted his lips. The pastor's smile broadened and he walked right up to him and the other boys began to back off. They wished they were somewhere else. The pastor gently lifted the Desert Eagle from Tweet's hand and felt its weight in his own enormous palm.

'Sure a nice piece,' he said.

'You can't take my gun, pastor!' Tweet protested.

'Can't?' the pastor's smile just grew and grew until his cheeks seemed likely to tear. He looked at Jim and raised his eyebrows. 'Can't?' he said again before turning back to Tweet. 'I tell you what, son. You collect your piece off me at service on Sunday.'

'Pastor! I . . .'

'Ten-thirty sharp. Don't be late.'

'But . . .'

The pastor yawned. 'It sure is warm and sticky. I suggest you get your black ass outta here 'fore I take off my jacket. You hear me? Now.'

Tweet dropped his head in assent and the pastor offered him a huge hand: 'You put it there, little bro.'

Reluctantly, Tweet took his hand and they shared a convoluted handshake.

'Much love,' the pastor said.

'Peace out,' Tweet replied. And he began to walk away, his cronies in tow.

'Peace,' the pastor said. 'You hear me, Tweet? Peace.'

The pastor turned to Jim, his smile still fixed in place. Jim realized that his own mouth was wide open.

'You folk lost or somethin'?' the pastor asked.

'Something like that,' Jim said. But the pastor wasn't listening. He was watching the gang amble down the street. They were arguing and Tweet's sparrow voice said, 'What's I s'posed to do?'

'Look at them in their baggy pants!' the pastor said. 'I understand why they packin' guns and on crack and gang bangin'. But their clothes? In my day a cat would never be caught in no suit that didn't fit him just so.'

The pastor's voice was laced with affection and he shook his head and absent-mindedly clicked the Desert Eagle's safety and stuffed it in the pocket of his suit. Jim looked at Sylvia. Sylvia looked at Jim and her face suddenly twisted and her chest heaved and she bent double and vomited on to the pavement. She rested her hands on her knees and spat bile.

'I guess she's not from round here,' the pastor commented drily and he reached a responsible-sized set of keys from his trousers.

Inside the church, they sat on cold wooden pews and it was Jim and the pastor who did most of the talking while Sylvia took deep breaths and mopped her forehead with a tissue. Jim rested his hand on Sylvia's shoulders and he regretted his earlier unkind thoughts. Because Sylvia was on a mission and he of all people should have understood the vagaries of her identity. She was a prostitute, sure. But *just* a prostitute? When is anybody *just* anything?

The pastor handed Sylvia a glass of water and shook his head and said, 'Take your time, sister.'

'Reverend Joseph T. Jackson the third,' he announced and wrapped Jim's hand in his mighty paw that was as cool and dry as snakeskin.

'Jim,' said Jim. He felt like he was shaking the hand of a comic-book superhero.

'My friends calls me Boomer on account of my voice. Ha ha! You see? No need for no microphones when I'm preachin' an' it all saves us money for the Lord's own work. As for everyone else? They call me Pastor. An' you can choose whatever sits most comfortable on your tongue.'

'OK, Boomer,' Jim said. And he cleared his throat. 'You've got some strange methods.'

'How so?'

'I don't know. I just meant . . . with those kids . . . and your car. You just looked like . . .'

'A gangster?' Boomer laughed and that same throaty rumble vibrated in the back of his throat and echoed around the rafters of the empty church. 'Let me tell you somethin', Jim. The Lord works in mysterious ways an' what's good enough for him don't get no argument from ol' Boomer. You hear me? 'Sides, these kids don't know no other game. They don't even know they own selves an', sorry to say, that's the most common affliction for black folk today. Am I right, sister?'

Sylvia sipped on her water. She said nothing.

Jim spoke up: 'I know what you mean.'

Boomer looked at him seriously. 'Then you an exception,' he said slowly. But Jim was sure he was thinking something else.

'So,' Boomer said. And he clapped his hands together and the deep crack ricocheted off the walls. 'What're you folks doin' down in my parish? You ain't come to see me 'bout no weddin', that's for sure.'

Jim looked at Sylvia but her head was buried in her hands and she was kneading her temples with her fingertips. He ran his tongue across his lips. He wanted a cigarette but he couldn't light up in church.

'We're looking for someone,' he said and Sylvia's fingers stopped their work.

'Who's that?' Boomer asked.

'Well. There's the thing,' Jim said. 'We don't know.'

It took Jim about half an hour to tell Boomer the whole story, including five minutes of the pastor's patient prompting while he checked every word he said with Sylvia's motionless head and closed eyes. He told the pastor everything he knew; about Bernadette Berlone who met Luca Di Napoli at a pizzeria in Harlem. He told him about the couple's emigration to England and the Di Napoli restaurant in Soho. He told him about the shock of Sylvia's birth – 'She was black and her parents were white,' he said. 'I figured,' Boomer replied. And he skated over the nightmare of her childhood with phrases like, 'Her father didn't deal with it very well'.

He told Boomer how Sylvia ran away from home and saw nothing of her parents for the best part of thirty years. He didn't mention the prostitution because . . . well . . . what was the point? He told him about Sylvia's great-uncle, Fabrizio Berlone, and the ramshackle Harlem apartment and the hooker called Rosetta and Boomer laughed like an earthquake. He told him about Sylvia's grandmother who moved north to New York and married Tony Berlone and gave birth to Bernadette four months later. He told him how Grandma Sylvia used to visit Chicago once in a while to see a sister who'd married a preacher at the Apostolic Church of All Saints.

As Jim spoke, Sylvia raised her head a little. She couldn't believe how much he remembered of what she'd told him. Had anybody – *anybody* – ever listened to another as generously as that? Now that her stomach had settled, she sneaked a glance at him from the corner of her eye; she bathed in the gentle tone of his voice, the humble way he struggled to meet the pastor's eye, the sincere anger that simmered beneath his telling of the saddest moments of her history. It was strange to hear someone else recount her life story. It was as if the various twists and turns suddenly slotted into place like the jigsaw chapters of a book. And, for the first time, she felt a sense of inexorable progress towards a conclusion, a denouement that was already written, committed to the page, waiting for her to choose to read it. For a brief moment, Sylvia felt comfortable with who she was. Or comfortable with the question anyway, because she was sure it had a definite answer, however difficult. But then Jim finished her story and the pastor spoke up and the moment was lost.

The church was as silent as religion. A car backfired in the street outside and Sylvia looked up. Boomer was staring at her with eyes that mixed sympathy with a hard quality she didn't understand. She met his gaze and it was like he saw right through her and she blinked.

'Where is the wise man?' Boomer said. 'Where is the scholar?

Where is the philosopher of this age? Has not God made foolish the wisdom of the world?'

'Excuse me?'

'Corinthians,' Boomer said absentmindedly and he pinched the bridge of his nose between thumb and forefinger. He looked tired, jaded. 'So. Sister. You tryin' to find out how come you're black?'

'I suppose.'

'Then let me make it easy on you. You're black the same reason as me; 'cos you got African blood in you. Simple as that.'

'But I need to know where it comes from.'

'Africa,' Boomer said shortly and lapsed into silence. Sylvia sucked her gums and said nothing.

Jim tutted. He couldn't stop himself. 'Aren't you going to help us?' he said.

For a full minute Boomer still said nothing and the quiet echoed just as loudly as his voice. But he just sat there, motionless, like he was concentrating on the hardest mathematical problem.

Eventually Boomer answered Jim's question. But he was talking only to Sylvia. 'Sure I'll help you,' he said. 'But let me give you a piece of advice first. OK?'

'OK,' Sylvia said.

'Seems to me like you're on a journey . . .'

'On a mission.'

'Exactly. On a mission. You got a lot of questions for answerin' an' maybe they get answered an' maybe they don't. An' if they're answered, then maybe you like those answers an' maybe they nothin' but more questions. You hear me? Point is, only thing you can be sure of is that you'll still be as black as today. Understand? An' that somethin' you gotta figure out for yourself.'

Boomer sighed. It was as if this arcane explanation was just too exhausting.

'Like Jesus Christ himself, Sylvia,' he said. 'You know Jesus?'

'Not personally.'

'Jesus Christ walked into the wilderness for forty days an' nights an' Satan tempted him with possessions an' power an' glory. But Jesus wasn't gonna listen to no devil an' he returned to Galilee. Now Jesus was on a mission, he was on a journey. But he finished up right where he started from an' the only things he learned were 'bout his own self.'

'Because of the devil,' Sylvia said flippantly.

'Exactly!' Boomer enthused. 'You got the devil on your back?'

Sylvia smiled thinly. 'I've just got Jim,' she said.

'Exactly!'

Jim had been listening intently. He had no idea what Boomer was getting at. But he realized that he was getting at him and he didn't understand why. He shifted uncomfortably where he sat.

'Are you saying I'm the devil?' he asked, disconcerted.

'We're all the devil to each other, Jim. An' we're all God too. You hear what I'm sayin'?'

'I hear it,' Jim said bitterly. 'I just don't fucking understand it.'

Boomer frowned and he put his finger to his lips.

'This is a house of God, Jim,' he said. 'You remember that. You're in a house of God where even Satan don't dare cuss.

'Now,' he continued – he was suddenly smiling cheerfully, as if it as now all said and as clear as an open window – 'let me tell you what I know. I've been pastor of this parish the best part of fifteen years. 'Fore that, I was trainin' up in Detroit. But you don't wanna know 'bout that. Till I came along, I know this church'd been in the same family since its foundation in 1917 by a preacher by the name of the Reverend Isaiah Pink an' his wife, Mrs Thomasina Pink. I figure Mrs Thomasina must've been the sister your grandmother was visitin'. Guess that makes her your great-aunt. Anyway, Isaiah an' Thomasina died a long time before I got here. The only pastor I ever knew at this parish was the Reverend Isaiah Pink Junior. An' he died in – when was it? – must've been the fall of '84.'

Boomer paused for dramatic effect. But Sylvia was impatient. 'And his widow?' she prompted.

'Whose widow?'

'Isaiah Junior. He never married?'

'No!' Boomer scratched his head. 'He married, all right, an', way I heard it, that was one sad story. They say Isaiah Junior was a difficult man. An', believe me, if a congregation's prepared to say the pastor was "difficult", then you can guarantee that he was an awkward S. O. B. (may God forgive me). Anyway, Isaiah Junior didn't marry till late in life an' then he married a girl some twenty-five years younger. I think she was a small-town schoolteacher from Rock Island or some place like that. An' she died just one year after they were married. Way they tell it, Isaiah was never quite the same again. In fact, truth is, nobody remember whether Isaiah was difficult before his wife died or only after. I guess it don't much matter no more.'

Jim interrupted. 'So we've hit another dead end,' he said and he glocked his tongue against his palate.

'Son,' Boomer said. 'You a typical white boy 'cos you both impatient and you give up too easy. You may's well let me finish what I know before you start talkin' 'bout no dead ends.

'See, Isaiah Junior's wife – don't think I ever knew her name – was taken in childbirth an' if there's one thing more tragic than that, then I'd like to know it. 'Nuff to turn me into a doubting Thomas sometimes. But the daughter survived, a little girl by the name of Coretta.'

'Did you ever meet her?'

'Coretta? Sure I met her. I conducted Isaiah Junior's funeral, didn't I? She was thirteen years old, bright as a button an' feisty as good chilli. She's a typical preacher's daughter (an' with a father like hers that ain't no surprise): no interest in no religion or Jesus Christ an' all caught up in black politics an' that "back to Africa" talk that makes the young people think they know where they're comin' from. Even when she was thirteen years old!

'I seen her a few times since too. She comes back to visit once in a while an' I swear she's grown up into a fine-lookin' young lady, the kind to make a pastor say double prayers. Ha! Even Boomer, an' I never been much of one for prayin'!

'But I ain't seen her a few years now. Last I heard she was teachin' at Northwestern an' I am pretty sure she still there 'cos she always lets me know when she moves on. Teachin' African history or somethin' like that at the Gold Coast campus. Professor Coretta Pink. Now ain't that some title!'

Jim and Sylvia looked at one another. The Gold Coast campus of Northwestern University was only three blocks from their hotel. Sylvia felt her heart beat a little faster. Maybe the conclusion to her story was just around the corner after all, just over the next page.

'Pastor . . .' she began.

'We're friends, ain't we, sister? You call me Boomer.'

'I'm sorry. Boomer, can you tell me . . . This may sound like a stupid question . . . but, can you tell me, the Pinks . . . were they black?'

Boomer stared at her intently for a moment until his face cracked into that same broad smile.

'You ever hear of white folk callin' their daughter Coretta?'

Boomer said that he'd drive Jim and Sylvia back uptown. 'Last thing I need is your blood on my conscience,' he said. And when Jim smiled, Boomer wrinkled his forehead and said, 'Serious.'

They jumped into the pastor's Lexus (Jim in the back, Sylvia up front) and the stereo blasted Billie Holliday's plaintive tones way louder than she ever sang herself.

'Do you know what it means to miss New Orleans
And miss it each night and day.
I know I'm not wrong. The feelings getting stronger . . .
The longer I stay away.'

Sylvia closed her eyes and she sang along. She must have sung this melody a thousand times down in that wine bar in Streatham. She knew every note upside down and back to front and inside out. She remembered how Flynn could never get the texture just right and, when she complained, he'd say, 'But it's a sad song!' And she'd think how 'sad' was a black-and-white word. Not a blues word at all.

Boomer couldn't help but stare at her as she sang and twice he almost crashed the car. When the song faded he cleared his throat.

'You ever thought about singin' in a choir?' he said.

'Not really.'

'What about New Orleans? You ever been there?'

'Me?' Sylvia said. She was surprised that he could even think she might have visited such a place. 'Of course not.'

'So where you think about when you sing that sad song?'

Sylvia considered for a moment. 'Notting Hill,' she said. 'In London.'

'There you go,' Boomer said, as if this proved a point he'd never made. 'That's your problem. Y'all need to be thinkin' 'bout the Big Easy.'

Boomer pulled over in front of the small turn-of-the-century building on East Oak that was dwarfed by the skyscrapers on every side, a Peter Pan type of building that never grew up.

'Northwestern,' he said and Sylvia took his hand and kissed him on the cheek.

'Thank you for your help, Boomer,' she said. 'Wish me luck.'

'You don't need no luck, sister. God's on your side.'

'Are you sure?'

'Sure I'm sure. God's always on your side,' Boomer said and he slipped a pair of mirror sunglasses on the end of his nose, despite the darkening skies.

Jim jumped out of the back of the car. He tried to say goodbye to Boomer but the pastor seemed to ignore him. Then, as he walked towards the double doors of Northwestern's Gold Coast campus, he heard the buzz of the electric window behind him and Boomer called him back. Jim turned around and raised his eyebrows. 'What?' he said. But Boomer beckoned him closer and wouldn't say another word until Jim had bent forward and rested his arms on the car's window.

'What?' Jim said again. He was grateful for Boomer's help for Sylvia. But he was sure that the pastor didn't much like him. And the feeling was mutual.

'Remember,' Boomer said quietly.

'What?'

'"It ain't where you're from, it's where you're at." You got that?'

'Got it,' Jim sighed. He was fed up with this doublespeak. 'What's that? Corinthians again?'

'Rakim Allah.'

'A Muslim?'

'A rapper.'

Jim nodded and Boomer smiled broadly. Boomer smiled a lot but this was, Jim thought, a different kind of expression. A benefit-of-the-doubt type of smile.

'Peace, brother,' Boomer said and he revved the Lexus's engine. Jim backed away from the window and the car pulled away with a macho roar.

'Peace,' Jim said quietly. He noticed Sylvia looking at him quizzically from the steps of the building and he shrugged.

They were met at the door by an officious security guard; the kind of middle-aged black man who likes nothing better than to look down his nose at other black people (the Tooting bank manager, Sylvia thought).

Jim said, 'We've come to see Professor Pink.'

The security guard scanned down his clipboard and said, 'Third floor.' His voice was almost coy, like he was giving out privileged information and they didn't know how lucky they were. 'Elevator on the left.'

He allowed Jim and Sylvia to walk in just so far before he called them back.

'You folks better sign in,' he said and he tapped his ballpoint deliberately on the thick visitors' book.

Sylvia tutted irritably and scrawled her signature. Jim did the same and then he caught Sylvia by the arm and pointed to the entry above their own. The name was illegible but, in the column headed 'Company/Purpose', the visitor had written, 'I am on a mission from the past.'

'On a mission,' Sylvia repeated the words like a magic spell.

'Ominous,' Jim said.

Sylvia bit her lip. *Ominous*, she realized, wasn't the right word. In fact, what she felt was way too visceral to be limited by a dictionary.

Out of the lift, they turned right through the double doors marked Department of Ethnology and Archeology. They both sniffed the air slightly dubiously. The atmosphere had that institutional smell that reminded Jim of school assembly and Sylvia of hospital check-ups with scornful young doctors. Behind a desk a bespectacled woman with a red-wine complexion didn't look up from her needlepoint.

Sylvia took the lead. 'We're looking for Professor Pink.'

'Who's that?'

'Professor Pink. Professor Coretta Pink.'

'Not here,' the woman said and narrowed her eyes to concentrate on a particularly tricky cross-stitch. Jim imagined this woman kept a flask and a tooth glass in the drawer of her desk. Sylvia's irritation grew.

'When will she be back?'

'Don't know.'

'Is she in a meeting?' Sylvia pressed. 'Teaching? On holiday?'

The woman sighed and lowered her work. She looked at Sylvia for the first time and her face registered mild surprise. 'You a relative?'

'Her cousin,' Sylvia said. 'From London.'

'But she's in Africa,' the woman said. Now that she had some bad news to deliver she was a whole lot more enthusiastic. 'On a dig. She's gone for the whole semester. At least another two months.'

Jim raised his eyebrows. Somehow he wasn't surprised. The

weight of the weather, his stiff neck, the brush with Tweet, the extraordinary pastor, the entry in the visitors' book . . . He thought of straight-to-video detective thrillers where the hero turns to his partner and says, 'I don't buy it. It's all too easy. Too clean.' He looked at Sylvia. Her chin had dropped to her chest. He touched her on the shoulder and she span round and her eyes were wet and shining. She looked at him bitterly like he was somehow to blame.

'You said it was a joke.' Her voice was thick and rasping. 'You said it was a joke. Well, that's one great fucking punchline.'

Jim turned to the receptionist. She'd given up on her needlepoint and stared at the two of them and licked her lips. This was more interesting than her tapestry cushion cover. This was better than the daytime soaps.

'Can we see Professor Pink's office?' he asked. 'Perhaps we could leave her a note.'

'Sure,' the woman said. She was now being over-the-top helpful, a bit player in a story more interesting than her own, like a walk-on extra overacting her one scene. 'Fourth door.'

Jim nodded and headed off down the corridor. He caught Sylvia by the wrist and roughly pulled her after him. Whatever Sylvia thought, Jim's feelings of prescience (instinct, foreboding – whatever word you wanted to use) left him certain that this little chapter wasn't yet played out. He stopped in front of the fourth door. The plaque said 'Professor Durowoju' and he was momentarily confused. He looked back towards the receptionist, who had, of course, turned in her seat and she was staring after them like a rubber-necking driver. She widened her eyes to say that they had found the right office and Jim shrugged and pushed open the door.

'After you,' he said. And he shoved Sylvia in ahead of him.

The office was late-afternoon gloomy and Sylvia's eyes took a moment to adjust and her nose twitched at a scent that was both familiar and exotic while she heard Jim fumble his hands against the wall. 'Can you see a light switch?' he asked. But Sylvia didn't reply. She was peering at the man who sat in the chair beneath the window with his feet on the desk. In the half-light, she could only make out his silhouette, the thick snakes of his hair and the whites of his eyes and teeth. Then Jim said, 'Got it!' and he flicked on an overhead light and she found herself staring at a handsome man with haunted eyes and unruly dreadlocks and the charred black skin typical of most Africans. And he was staring back at her.

'Are you real?' the man said. Then he shook his head like he was trying to rattle some sense into it. 'No. It doesn't matter. Are you Sylvie? Or Sylvia?'

'My name's Sylvia.'

She was transfixed by this man's appearance. She was both sure she'd never met him and certain of his familiarity. 'Do I know you?' she asked and the man smiled, an eerie expression, ironic and full of melancholy.

'I was a friend of your great-great-great-great-grandfather,' he said obtusely. 'And I am here to pay a debt. And that's a lot of greats. But he was a great man.'

Slowly Sylvia turned to look at Jim, although her eyes stayed with the black man throughout the gentle parabola of her head. Then she focused on Jim and saw that his expression was captured in a polaroid of comic disbelief, his face, eyes and mouth stretched wide.

'Musa,' Jim said, his voice barely above a whisper.

'Jim,' the *zakulu* said. He was now beaming a bright-toothed smile. 'I knew I'd remember your name the moment I saw you! Thank Tuloko that you have finally arrived! I fear that one more hallucination and I would have lost my mind; one more prostitute and I would have lost my toes!'

'What the hell are you doing here?'

'I have come to tell you, Jim,' Musa said ominously. 'We must head south.'

IV: *Tongo the hero*

(Zimindo, Zambawi, Africa. 1998)
Chief Tongo Kalulu was walking south from Zimindo village with nothing for company but a small twist of *gar* and a one-person helping of *kachasu* that swilled viscously around the bottom of a recycled Coca-Cola bottle. His legs knew where he was going but the bureaucracy of his brain still had the information in an admissions file marked 'Pending'. He was on that kind of journey.

Tongo had never felt quite so lonely; nor had he realized that loneliness could be as pernicious and painful as the *putsi* fly larva that hatches beneath your skin, gorges itself on your innards and cripples you within a week. It was eight days since Musa had left for God knows where and the chief missed him like a brother. Chipampe, the village simpleton, had gone to the *zakulu*'s kraal and reported back that he was nowhere to be seen. Of course, as he was a simpleton, nobody believed him. But Tefadzwa 'Ngozi confirmed Musa's absence and bemoaned the fact that there would be no witchdoctor to bless his daughter Stella's marriage. Tefadzwa had harangued the chief with metaphors as though Musa's absence were somehow his fault saying things like, 'A wedding with no *zakulu*? *Maiwe*, Tongo! It is like a totem ceremony that's snubbed by the ancestors. It is like a *makadzi*'s *pau pau*, good fun but utterly without function.' But Tongo hadn't been listening because, as they spoke, Kudzai was packing for her return to the city.

Six days ago Kudzai had left. She'd caught the early-morning bus (the cryptically christened 'Number 17 (*In Memoriam*)') and Tongo had seen her off with a breezy expression on his face for the benefit of the curiously watching villagers.

'Because Musa is not here,' he explained. 'After the scare with the baby, we thought it was best that Kudzai be near a hospital. My child's a feisty one. He can't wait to get out. She'll be back soon.'

And the villagers said things like 'Good idea' and 'Right you are, chief', even though they knew he was lying as surely as chickens laid eggs, because hadn't the *zakulu* said that Kudzai needed at least two weeks of bedrest?

It had all gone wrong on the day of the scare, the day that Tongo met the seductive Bunmi Durowoju (aka Coretta Pink), Professor of Ethnoarcheology at Chicago's Northwestern University. Tongo felt gut-knottingly guilty for the events of that day, even though his pietism had solidified to such an extent that he'd managed to convince himself that he'd said and done nothing wrong. If Kudzai (who was herself quite possibly an adultress) couldn't trust him, then what was a good husband to do? And though that sentiment seemed resoundingly hollow (even to Tongo), its echoes were loud and long enough to drown out any more reasonable assessment.

Tongo had relived that day through all the most selfish filters of memory. He recalled how he had entered the sleeping hut to find Kudzai writhing in pain with her womb weeping blood into the bed blanket like unborn tears. He recalled his panic, his screams for the *zakulu* and the agonizing hour spent pacing up and down, convinced that his wife was on the doorstep of death. He recalled Musa's hands on his shoulder, the reassuring platitudes, the way he'd ignored the *zakulu*'s warning to rush, ever devoted, to his stricken wife's side.

In the hut, he found Kudzai sitting up – and wasn't his heart full of love for his wife and forgiveness for the worry she'd caused? He asked the two *makadzi* attending her to leave and he felt his face crease in an expression of tenderness worthy of the most concerned husband. But Kudzai looked through him as though he were as transparent as the ancestral ghost who's yet to admit his own death.

'What do you want, Tongo?' she said. And her voice was barren like the maize store during a drought.

Tongo's throat constricted. He had planned his every word: declarations, apologies and justifications. He'd planned his every expression: dignified, tragic and forgiving. But now he found his face was as a grey sky and it seemed like there was nothing to be said.

I love you, he thought. I love you as the Great Chief Tuloko loved Mudiwa in the springtime of their union (only more so because I am not a god and have none of the ease of divine adequacy). Mine is a love that gorges roots and pushes buds through the soil into the light of Father Sun; a love that carefully unfolds delicate leaves and swells a strong stem and colours petals with magical intuition; a love that blooms proudly and turns its face to the sky and sways in the summer breeze. A love that wilts in autumn, that browns and rots and regenerates the earth. A love that hibernates in winter, that humbly sustains itself beneath the rain of your tears and the wind of your anger and the frost of your heart. I love your twisting hair, your almond eyes, your fruity nose, your soft mouth. Even your monkey ears (though I don't see the resemblance myself). I love your swelling breasts, your woman's hips and your belly that grows with a child that surely can't be fed on anything but my love. I love you.

But Tongo just said, 'I don't know. What do *you* want?'

'I want to go back to the city. I want to see my family.'

The chief stared at his wife and the door of the hut banged in the breeze and a shadow passed across his face (synchronized with the shadow across his heart) until Kudzai couldn't see his expression.

'Right,' he said. And he left the room.

His wife may as well have died. That's what Tongo thought. Because he had that ache of a bereaved spouse which men, with their low thresholds for such pain, never intend to experience (for they don't just marry younger women for the passing perkiness of their breasts). What's more, her death would surely have been preferable to the ignominy of a divorce that now seemed so inevitable.

Chiefs were not supposed to get divorced. Traditionally, a hapless wife would have been banished to a sunless corner of the kraal and replaced by a superior version. Although, in fact, since the fidelity of Tuloko (the first and greatest chief) to his wife Mudiwa was legend, most of his descendants had avoided polygamy and the sense of inadequacy that went with it. And those that had married more than once were remembered with derogatory monikers like Tapezwa the Unsatisfied and Roving-Eyed Rupayi. Generally speaking, the chief's marriage was regarded as a model for his people and, while a little whore-crawling was understandable, divorce was unheard of. Until now.

So Tongo strode through the Zimindo bush under a dark cloud, both literal and metaphorical. For he wasn't surprised to find that Father Sun had no desire to confront him eye to eye and had sent his fluffy black sky-soldiers to taunt him with their heavy wit before pissing on his head from a great height. Sure enough, it began to rain and Tongo was surprised to discover that his bucket of self-pity had room for another drop or two yet.

He sheltered under a *musasa* tree whose trunk bore an uncanny resemblance to an old man's face and he swigged the sour *kachasu* dregs from the Coca-Cola bottle. He leaned back against the trunk and he watched the rain begin to puddle on the ground and he tried to enjoy the promising smell of wet soil. He found himself thinking about his chiefly lineage. He wasn't sure why thoughts of his forefathers should have wandered unchecked into the forefront of his mind (unless they'd sneaked in alongside the nicknames of the shameful polygamists) but now that they were there, they proved remarkably difficult to shift.

He remembered the stories his father had told him about his ancestor, Mhlanga, who had led a local rebellion against a particularly tyrannical and vicious *musungu* District Officer at the turn of the century. Mhlanga had had his lips cut off as a curb to his insidious speeches. But he had returned to the village unembarrassed by his grotesque physiognomy. 'The *musungu* may spoil my looks but they won't stop me smiling,' he'd announced.

And what about Tongo's great-grandfather, Francis, who had

converted to Christianity after betting with a monk about his capacity for celibacy (an ill-conceived wager if ever there was one)? During the 'Protected Village' resettlement of 1967, he had been shot dead along with twenty others for supposed recalcitrance. The local missionary who had baptized him pleaded for Francis's life only to be told by the British sergeant-major, 'Don't worry, padre. We'll leave St Peter to sort out his own.'

Even Tongo's own grandfather, Shingayi (who had understandably changed his Christian name from Bartholomew), had been a son of the revolution during the independence war. Sometimes Tongo, who remembered the *mboko*'s face as if from a dream, liked to picture Shingayi fighting alongside Zambawi's first President Adini throughout the southern campaigns.

Tongo thought about all the noble chiefs in his personal history – a line that stretched (theoretically anyway, for he didn't believe it) as far back as the Great Chief Tuloko himself – and he couldn't help but wonder whether heroes were actually made rather than born. Because what chance did *he* have of heroism? There were no wars to be undertaken, no revolutions to instigate and no good fights to fight. He would have lost his lips for justice, died for his race, killed for his nation, wouldn't he? But for goodness' sake! These days, even a healthy day's hunting was out of the question since most of the interesting animals were under 24-hour protection for the viewing pleasure of honeymooning *musungu* tourists. His title was no more than an archaic sinecure, grudgingly respected for the sake of nebulous tradition but practically as meaningless as a bride's virginity.

So what chance did he have of heroism? None. And, more to the point, his marriage would surely not have fucked up if he'd been out in the bush fighting for the Zamba's honour or tracking a rogue *shumba*. Because he would have returned to a triumphant welcome and Kudzai would have opened her legs and been grateful for the privilege. And, if she was tired, she'd have pointed him in the direction of the village whores and said, 'Go on! You deserve it!' And those strumpets would have paid *him* for a consignment of top-class genes on the off chance that they might drop the chief's bastard issue. But instead?

Instead the rain had stopped and the *kachasu* was finished and his head was splitting like an overripe *mazvoe* berry. Instead he could look forward to posterity sniggering behind its fingers over the memory of Tongo the Divorcee. Instead the various committees of his mind flicked through the 'Pending' file and argued about the enclosed proposal to visit the Professor of Ethnoarcheology. But their debate was purely academic, since the matter had already been decided by his executive legs at the whim of the self-obsessed little despot who was currently dozing against his left thigh.

Tongo tutted to himself as though somebody was there to hear him and he examined the empty Coca-Cola bottle ruefully. He should really get going if he was going to make it in daylight. But he was suddenly overcome with lethargy and, in spite of himself, he sat down, leaned his head back against the dimpled chin of old man *musasa* and began to construct himself a skinny five-puff joint.

He recalled his conversation with Bunmi the previous week. Initially, this was merely to conjure her clean features and undulating shape for his own lubricious amusement. But, much to his annoyance, he soon found himself contemplating what she'd said: about the head-dress the archaeologists had found, how the artefact explained who the Zamba were. Tongo remembered his impassioned response and he felt his face heat uncomfortably. Was it embarrassment or just a *gar* flush? Because didn't he stand by his words? The Zamba knew who they *were*, all right; they had to because they'd spent so long defining themselves in opposition to what they were not. But now?

I know where I come from, Tongo thought. It's where I *am* that causes the problems. How I envy the *zakulu* who jumps through time like a soaring *nzwa* frog that leaps into a lake with nothing to fear but the mouth of a yawning crocodile. For me, the past is a lush battlefield populated by heroic chiefs who are noble warriors all. And the present? It crumbles beneath my feet like erosion and the future is as unreclaimable as scorched earth.

Tongo sucked on the quickly shrinking *gar* butt and began to wish he'd constructed something more substantial for himself.

By the time he reached the ruins of Maponda dam, Father Sun was poking his head from behind his menacing minders to say good night and the tired shadows stretched out behind their painters as if to suggest it was time for bed. It was the chief's first visit to the dam in a couple of years (though its collapse threatened the fertility of all the surrounding land) and he found something melancholy in what he saw, like the dissipated aftermath of a failed rebellion. Downstream, Maponda river had burst across its former floodplains with evangelical fervour, surrounding trees and gentle hillocks like crowds teeming around hated symbols of the status quo. New channels had cut through the surrounding terrain in various directions like typically diverging ideals. But their support soon seeped away into the porous dust until there was no trace of their existence but the inconsequential pools of dirty water that were gradually evaporating. Even the river itself had now almost shrunk to its previous size and only the ruined dam wall bore testimony to past cataclysm.

Upstream, Maponda river had narrowed considerably, exposing several dry lakes that studded its new floodplains. It was in one of these that the archaeologists had set up camp, though it was an unimpressive looking affair; a few Land Rovers and a shambolic arrangement of tents.

Pacing quickly towards the dig, Tongo almost tripped over an archaeologist who was lying in an undulation and tugging ferociously on an unhealthily large joint that would have finished off even Musa (who was a superman of all things smoking). Despite the archaeologist's expansive beard, the chief saw from his eyes that this kid couldn't have been more than about twenty-three and the young man greeted him in such an extraordinary accent that Tongo accepted it as English only for a lack of plausible options.

'Hey dude! Wassup?'

'I'm Chief Tongo Kalulu,' Tongo said formally. 'I've come to see Professor Durowoju.'

The young archaeologist rubbed his eyes and tried to sit up. But without success. 'Chief, eh? That shit rocks, man! You getta boss people around and cool stuff like that? That's crazy shit, man! Some crazy shit!'

'Indeed,' Tongo said blankly.

He liked to think he had an ear for American slang (with all the movies he'd seen when at Gokwe) and he remembered Bunmi's use of the same expression. But he still couldn't fathom how 'shit' could be 'crazy'. So he looked at the young man with what he hoped was a suitably contemptuous aspect and he said, 'My friend, you want to watch out for the weed. If you're not careful, you'll forget who you are.'

The stoned young man began to laugh. 'Fuckin' A, man!' he said. 'Fuckin' A!' And Tongo was surprised to realize that a loss of identity was precisely this *gar*-head's aim. The chief knew he'd never comprehend a *musungu* and he wondered why he bothered to try.

Tongo stopped at the lip of the dry lake and he looked down into the basin. A group of four beards were talking animatedly on the opposite bank but his eyes quickly homed in on Bunmi's figure. She was kneeling as if in prayer some ten yards away and Tongo's breath shortened and he tried a jaunty 'Hello!' but it snagged in the back of his throat like a *boka* bird's squawk. The professor didn't look up, so Tongo took the opportunity to look her up and down as an *'ndipe* monkey assesses a particularly perilous jump. She was very differently dressed to their last encounter. He could see the soles of her safari boots and the outline of her buttocks beneath beige shorts. The muscular triangle of her back was barely hidden by a tight and grubby vest with a sweat smudge that traced the curve of her spine. And she wore a back-to-front baseball cap with the word 'Cubs' embossed in gold.

Tongo swallowed and licked his dry lips. 'Bunmi,' he called again and this time his voice was reassuringly steady.

The professor looked round and if she was surprised to see him it didn't show. She got to her feet and walked towards him and he noticed that her eyebrows were raised a little in the middle in an unspoken 'So *there* you are'. But all she said was 'Hey', a non-committal greeting by an American's enthusiastic standards.

'You said I should come and see the dig,' Tongo began.

'Right.'

'So I did.'

'Right. How's your wife?'

Tongo sniffed. 'She's gone to the city. She hasn't been well. Two weeks' bedrest. Witchdoctor's orders.'

Bunmi nodded. She reached her arms above her head and arched her back and closed her eyes in a seemingly ecstatic stretch. Then she looked westwards towards where Father Sun was sliding beneath the horizon's bedspread and the black clouds were lined with soft purple light. Bunmi's face adopted an expression of fixed curiosity, like she'd never seen a sunset before.

'She called me a prostitute, didn't she?' the professor remarked absent-mindedly. '*Hoore*. I've been reading up on my Zamba vocabulary.'

Tongo was taken aback. Bunmi's tone was conversational but that only made her comment all the more disconcerting.

'She's a bit . . .' Tongo began and he shrugged. Because he didn't know how to finish the sentiment. A bit what? He had to stop himself making that universal insanity gesture with his index finger at his temple. But, unfortunately, that effort didn't halt the words 'crazy shit' slipping meaninglessly from his mouth.

Bunmi nodded as though that made perfect sense. 'Where I come from,' she said, 'sister call you a ho and you gotta get clinical on her ass.'

'Clinical,' Tongo agreed. He liked the way the professor's

language could slip so easily into coarse colloquialisms. Even though he hardly understood them. He was nodding too.

Bunmi smiled and Tongo smiled too.

He noticed that the professor was holding a small toothbrush in one hand. 'What are you doing?' he asked.

'Cleaning.'

'Your teeth?'

She unfurled the fingers of her other hand to reveal what looked like a small grey pebble. She carefully brushed away a little more dirt from its surface. '*Cozaka*,' she said. 'They're all over the place. This little guy's travelled all the way from the Mozolan coast. Now a mollusc doesn't make a journey like that for no reason!' The professor's eyes were fixed on the chief. They made him feel uncomfortable. 'You've got to use your imagination,' she said. 'Come on. I got something to show you.'

Tongo followed Bunmi from the bed of the lake towards the largest of six tents. The day was fading fast and he shivered unconsciously, partly because of the closing light and accompanying chill and partly because he didn't fancy walking back to Zimindo at night. Mostly, however, because he remembered that Maponda river was a notorious blackspot for witches and *shamva* and ghosts. It was the dark time of the month when Cousin Moon barely winked and Tongo knew those spirits would like nothing more than to catch a lonely chief out on his own while Father Sun slept.

They ducked under the canvas flap and Bunmi lit an oil lamp. Tongo found he could just about stand upright if he bent his head forward a little. Inside there was an inflatable bed, a single chair and a small desk. The professor self-consciously started gathering strewn underwear and she said, 'Sorry about the mess,' while Tongo picked up a framed photograph from beside the bed and a proud, big-featured black man stared back at him, his jaw set stubbornly towards the camera.

'My dad,' Bunmi said.

'He's not smiling.'

'No. He was a preacher. He's dead now.'

Tongo nodded. He wasn't sure what to say. Bunmi's tone was strangely cold. She sounded almost as though she was associating 'not smiling', 'preaching' and 'death'. He felt confused.

'Are you a Christian?'

Bunmi made a noise that sounded like a curious mixture of laugh and curse. 'No,' she said. 'You?'

Tongo shook his head. 'My great-grandfather was. He was shot.'

'For being a Christian?

'I don't think so. But I'd rather not risk it.'

The chief stared at the professor. He couldn't take his eyes off her but she didn't seem to mind. It was warm in the tent and he licked his salty upper lip. The atmosphere, he thought, smelled strongly of a woman; ripe and sweet, almost sickly, like fruit that's about to turn. It reminded him of Kudzai's room at Gokwe Teachers' College, where she used to invite him for a late-night cup of chicory and she'd talk about jazz and he'd cross his legs and bide his time. It seemed like such a long time ago that he almost felt like he was recalling someone else's memories (just like Musa, Tongo thought, who told good stories about his totem life as a baboon).

'Look at this,' Bunmi said and he looked. Although he wasn't sure what it was he was looking at. He followed her pointing finger to a tatty object that hung over the back of the chair. It seemed to be made of string and cloth and seashells, a twisted mess like flotsam on the shore of the Great Lake to the West.

'What is it?'

'The head-dress.'

'Oh,' Tongo said. 'Of course.' Because he didn't know what else to say.

In spite of himself, he was disappointed. He'd imagined some ornate crown of shimmering mother-of-pearl, intricately worked and awe-inspiring. But this? It was nothing more than a chewed rag, the kind of thing that was left on a wife's washing line when an 'ndipe troop had been playing dress-up with her clothes. And this was supposed to be a definitive expression of Zamba culture? It looked about as expressive as a used hankie.

Catching Tongo's bemused countenance, Bunmi said, 'You have to engage your imagination,' and she carefully slipped her forefingers through the threading and lifted the head-dress into the light. Her expression suddenly lit up and her voice was vibrant.

'Look at these,' she said. 'The *cozaka*. Of course they're grey now but you're got to picture them bleached white in the sun and there'd be a whole lot more of them besides, like maybe 5,000. Of course, *cozaka* don't mean anything any more. But once upon a time these were more precious than diamonds for the Zamba, rare shells from a coastline they'd never seen. Now all that's left of the frame is string. But you see the tiny threads there? That's silk. Mostly rotted but once upon a time it would've been woven throughout. And you see those smaller shells? *Jobe*. They must have come from Mozola too. And what about that scrap of cloth? You see that? We haven't ID'd the pigment yet but I figure it might even be indigo. Imagine that! Indigo. Where the hell did that come from? Could be as far as Addis. Ethiopia, Tongo. You ever been to Ethiopia?' Tongo shook his head. 'So you see what I'm saying.'

Bunmi paused. She was no longer looking at the chief but holding up the ragged artefact and painting pictures on her mind's canvas. Tongo's imagination was similarly inspired but not by the head-dress. He felt like Bunmi's excitement was almost tangible and if he could only catch it he'd reel her in like deep-water *kapenta*. He loved the way she was so inspired by an old rag. But that couldn't be the only source of her inspiration!

'A queen. Or a princess maybe,' Bunmi was saying. 'A real *African* princess.'

Reverentially she laid the head-dress back on the chair and when she turned back to Tongo her eyes were glistening like black onyx. She was standing so close to him, her face at the level of his chest and those gems turned up towards him. He could smell her gentle musk, feel her breath like Kupile, the west wind, who's known to comfort the mourning with her soft breeze. Tongo blinked, very slowly, and there was no Kudzai on his eyelids. His wife was gone.

The professor looked like she was about to speak but couldn't find the words. The unspeakable question, Tongo thought. All women are the same about this moment, a moment that must be grabbed like a chicken hypnotized by a python. And that's what men are for.

He reached for her and slipped his arms around her neck until he cupped her head in his palms. He licked his lips and pulled her too him and closed his eyes. He guzzled her scent and sensed the heat of her body. And he bit down on his tongue and collapsed in pain when Bunmi raised her knee sharply into his groin.

'What the hell you think you're doing?' she said. 'Damn!'

But Tongo couldn't say a word. He was face down in the soft rubber of the inflatable mattress and his eyes were streaming. He could hear Bunmi ranting with that detached clarity that only pain can bring and he felt a small lump rise in his throat that he feared might be a testicle running scared. He squeezed his hands tight between his thighs and he wondered how he'd come to this; he, a chief, playing hunt-the-*choko* in the intimacy of his own scrotum. And, for the first time, he began to admit liability for the departure of Kudzai (or at least to lay the blame squarely upon the shoulders of his bruised *chongwe*). He remembered one of Musa's favourite sayings: 'If you defecate in the bedroom, don't be surprised when the whole house smells like shit.' Exactly. 'Tongo the One-Balled Divorcee', that's how they'd remember him.

The professor's tirade continued for about ten minutes, during which time she cursed her way down from the generality of men to the specifics of Tongo and all the way back up again. Occasionally the chief attempted to unstick his mouth from the rubber to try to explain himself. But the smallest movement sent a spiteful needle of pain roaming about the most surprising parts of his body (a node behind his ears, a spot beneath his armpits) and he didn't manage to utter a word.

Eventually Bunmi's fury started to fade and she began to wonder whether she'd inflicted rather more damage than intended. For the most part, Tongo was now lying completely still and then, every so often, his body would spasm alarmingly. Bunmi felt somewhat uncomfortable. After all, he'd only tried to kiss her and a clumsy castration was undoubtedly harsh retribution for such feeble advances. What's more, it was hardly likely to go down well in the Zimindo village where the chief was both notably popular and . . . well . . . the chief.

'Are you all right?' she asked nervously and the chief made a whining noise. He might have been trying to say, 'Fine.' Or possibly, 'Dying.' He tried to sit up then and when she saw his expression she had to bite down on her lip to stop herself laughing: his face was bizarrely cartooonish with one eye wide and the other squeezed and his nostrils turned out and his lips inverted.

'Sorry,' she said. 'You caught me by surprise. It was a reflex action.'

The chief didn't reply. His lineaments appeared to be locked. So Bunmi said, 'Take your time. I'll be outside. When you're . . . y'know . . . ready.'

She was sitting around the fire with her fellow archaeologists when the chief finally appeared, walking gingerly, one bandy foot swinging after the other. The night was so dark that he was barely illuminated by the flickering flames. But she thought there was something rather charming in his manner, a kind of shame-faced dignity, a pride that begged her to keep their little secret to save him from further humiliation.

'Sit down,' she said. 'You want some food?'

Tongo perched, awkwardly, on an upturned beer crate.

The other archaeologists welcomed Tongo warmly (with the exception of the *gar*-head, who was nowhere to be seen. Presumably asleep in a ditch, dreaming the dreams that first sent the hyena mad). This was partly because, despite their months in Zambawi, these young men hadn't met many Africans and they were eager to mix with the natives. But it was mostly because Tongo seemed, despite his eminent status, so winningly humble with that pained, apologetic look on his face. And you can bet that when they returned to America and reflected on their time 'in the field', Tongo's humility was an attribute with which they benignly pigeonholed all Africans.

For his part, the chief soon forgot these young men's names because they all seemed to be called things like 'Chip' and 'Bud' and 'JD', named, so Tongo assumed, after all-American consumables.

They were cooking mealie porridge and Tongo asked if he might show them how it was done to make proper Zambawian *chadze*. They watched in admiration as the chief dexterously mixed a small quantity of meal with one part cold water and one part milk into a consistent paste before adding the boiling water slowly, a cupful at a time. And Bunmi looked on with wry amusement, enjoying the way the chief squatted uncomfortably on his haunches and patiently taught the beards to copy his every action and ensure lump-free *chadze*. Occasionally, as the men cooked, Tongo glanced up at Bunmi and smiled nervously and Bunmi smiled back.

While they ate Tongo listened respectfully as the archaeologists discussed the perils of C-14 dating and he even tried to show interest in their humour.

'How many archaeologists does it take to change a light bulb?' Chip (or was it Bud?) asked eagerly.

'I don't know,' Tongo said.

'We don't change light bulbs,' Chip guffawed. 'We leave that sucker right where it is and try to imagine what the light must've looked like!'

The archaeologists observed Tongo expectantly and remarked, 'Good one, huh?' and 'You get it?' And he smiled, broad and bemused, and he tried an enthusiastic nod.

'Quite so! Quite so!' he exclaimed before adding, 'In Zimindo we have no electricity, of course. So we are not big light-bulb changers ourselves.'

At first the assembled beards weren't sure whether the chief was joking. But he raised his eyebrows a little and gave them licence to laugh.

After dinner Tongo entertained them with stories with the ease of a natural raconteur. He told them about the time his drunken friend Kamwile got so stewed at a Gokwe party that he thought he was Idi Amin and began to attack all the student teachers. He told them about the woman from Zimindo who was caught with more than fifty pairs of stolen shoes in her kraal and the way the villagers had spread the rumour that she must a witch who'd given birth to a *chongololo* (this story was somewhat spoiled by the fact that Tongo couldn't remember the English for *chongololo*). He recounted the tale of the long-celibate *zakulu* who controlled the weather with his moods and was struck by lightning while spying on unsuspecting newlyweds.

Tongo rolled a small joint and passed it around the fire, warning the beards to be alert for its notoriously flatulent qualities. As they smoked and the conversation descended to a bawdier level (that made Bunmi tut indulgently), the chief told them about Musa the *zakulu* who sang the praises of the sex life of baboons (from the vicarious experience of his totem life). He was enjoying himself, despite the dull ache in his groin, and he began to show off.

'How I would love to be the chief in a troop of *gudo*,' he enthused. 'You have no problems with your wife and kids. You may choose a favourite partner but that only means she gets to pick your fur more regularly than the rest of the girls. The chief is like a god: as many women as he likes in one day and they don't complain or ask for a pretty frock or the price of a pair of shoes. You think you have to pay *lobola*? Of course you don't! The only time you'll see the girl's mother is if you fancy a romp with an older woman!

'As for the *gudo's chongwe*? My God! It is shaped like an umbrella. When he is pumped up, spokes like *zvoko* thorns leap out from the sides of his pride and joy and the girl won't move for fear of rupture. Any time the chief wants to plough a new field? You can bet the she-baboons will let him have his way. Those ladies don't answer back, I can tell you!'

The young men around the fire roared with delight. It wasn't just the outrageousness of Tongo's stories; it was the way he told them with his eyes wide and his hands reliving every piece of the action. As for Bunmi? She couldn't help but enjoy his nonsense, his boasting boyishness, his vitality.

'And they don't kick you in the *cojones* either,' she remarked.

'What's that?' Tongo asked. He was still laughing.

'The she-baboons. They wouldn't kick you in the groin.'

'Not just the baboons,' Tongo said, adopting a serious tone. 'Who would possibly dare to kick the chief in the *choko*? *Maiwe!* She would have to be quite some woman to attempt such a thing!'

The young men were now uniformly so high that singing seemed like a good idea and JD – it was definitely JD because he was the one with the least impressive beard – produced a guitar and began some clumsy three-chord strumming. All the beards joined in tuneless versions of songs by Paul Simon, Bob Dylan and the like.

Bunmi looked at Tongo across the fire and his smile was fixed in place like a coat hook. She caught his attention and spoke to him with her eyes and he replied loquaciously and they got up with one mind and moved out of earshot. At first they stood face to face but neither felt comfortable and they began to circle around one another like courting *boka* birds.

'Sorry about the singing,' Bunmi began.

'That was *singing*? I assumed it was a *musungu gar* ritual. And I'm never surprised by *musungu* antics.'

'How are your . . .'

'*Machoko*? Don't worry, professor; they are as tough as *mapole* conkers. I fear it is more my pride that may require surgery.'

'What? You never been turned down before?' Bunmi started to giggle but her laughter was cut short when she saw the indignation in Tongo's face. 'I am the chief,' he said simply.

Tongo began to walk away. 'Come on.'

'Where are you going?'

'Now it is my turn to show you something.'

'OK.'

The chief led the professor away from the camp and back to the dry lake. It was now so dark that she stumbled as they walked down the bank and she caught his arm. He held her hand for support.

'I tell you something,' Bunmi said. 'You're quite a storyteller.'

She could barely make out Tongo's shape but she knew he was shrugging.

'I am a Zamba,' he said plainly. 'The Zamba are storytellers. Americans are fat, Nigerians are smug and the English are ugly. We have no fast food and nothing to be smug about except our good looks. So we tell stories and make love like champions.'

They sat down on the far side of the lake and the chief let go of the professor's hand. He lay back on the bank and put his arms behind his head. The professor sat with her elbows on her knees and felt peculiarly awkward. The beards had stopped singing and their camp fire glowed no stronger than a distant candle and it was quiet enough and dark enough to hear the whispers of the unspoken (even if you couldn't quite make out what they were saying).

'What about you?' Tongo asked quietly. 'What's your story?'

'What do you mean?'

'You're American. I've never been to America and I will never go there.'

For a moment they lapsed into silence again, a silence that was ear-splitting in its emptiness. Because Bunmi was shy. She didn't know where to begin, what to say or what he wanted to hear. But she did want to tell him *something*. She started talking generally about Chicago, about Lake Michigan, the remarkable skyline and the basketball team. And Tongo listened but he wasn't interested. 'What about you?' he asked. 'Where did you grow up?'

She told him about downtown Chicago. A tough neighbourhood, she said. She told him about the gangs and the drugs and a childhood friend called Lakisha who was caught in the cross fire while jumping rope outside school. But Tongo shook his head and said, 'I don't understand.'

So she talked about her father, the Reverend Isaiah Pink Junior. Stiltedly at first. She told how he used to impose a sun-down curfew right until she was thirteen years old. She recalled his moral polemics from the pulpit and the way he used to farm her out to the good women of the parish. She remembered how he disapproved of all her friends and the time she took a wupping when he saw her talking to a boy. 'Only two things get you outta this place,' her dad used to say. 'The good Lord an' study. An' you take care of the one an' the other'll be jus' fine.' But the reverend had been wrong. Because the more she studied, the less the church seemed to matter. And Tongo said things like, 'is that so?' as if her stories confirmed everything he thought. And every time she dried up in embarrassment, he prompted her with another question. What about her mother? She had died in childbirth and the reverend had never talked about her and Bunmi didn't even have a photograph. Her father's family? From down South, she thought. She guessed they were plantation slaves.

'You were right,' Tongo said.

'About what?'

'When you said we are all Africans originally.'

'Of course. My ancestors were African slaves.'

Tongo shook his head. 'I meant your story. It sounds like an African story. You take the head-dress, professor. Do whatever tests you want. I'll sign the papers. For I can trust a fellow African with our culture, I am sure.'

Bunmi looked at him then. She wanted to see his face, to figure out what he was thinking. But he was still staring straight up at the sky and his expression was passive. What was she doing talking to him like that? She felt comfortable and uncomfortable all at once; trusting enough to talk to him, uneasy now she had. She cleared her throat.

'You said you wanted to show me something.'

Tongo glanced at her. As he looked up, her features seemed perfect to him, silhouetted against the sky like love's shadow upon the wall of the sleeping hut.

'You see Zamba,' he said – his voice was reflective, thoughtful, detached – 'the moon from whom we take our name? We call him Cousin Moon because of his relationship to the Great Chief Tuloko, who first made a deal with Father Sun to defeat the caitiff *shamva* who stole our offerings of food, precious stones and ritual objects that nobody understands any more. Can you see him? It is the time of the cycle when he is barely winking. Some people say that Zamba is lazy to fade from our skies every month. But they are as foolish as the chickens that play chicken with Number 17 (*In Memoriam*). For Cousin Moon is not a god like Father Sun. He was born a man who fell upwards into the sky precisely to save us from a god's wrath. So is it surprising that he finds his new status exhausting? It is not. And once a month, he tries to shut his eyes and he weeps because he will never know the earth as he once did.

'Look! The stars are his tears and that is why they shine so brightly when Cousin Moon winks. You see, professor, we are the Zamba; we live in the Land of the Moon. Our struggles are as numerous as the stories that make us and they are populated by heroes whose names are immortal. We are simple Africans who don't know much. But you can be sure we know where we come from.'

Bunmi couldn't look at Tongo then. But she knew that she needed to touch him and she bent towards him and lay her head against his chest until he unconsciously slipped his arm around her shoulders. She closed her eyes and wondered if this was who she was, an African woman under African skies. For his part, Tongo continued to stare at the moon, at the winking hero who gave the Zamba his name, more celebrated than even the Great Chief Tuloko. And he kept his eyes open because he knew who had returned to look back at him from his eyelids, her face a reflection that reminded him of what he was not.

Instead, he began to sing and, in spite of himself, he chose songs that, he felt, belonged to Kudzai, working back through Al Jarreau to Nina Simone to Louis Armstrong.

'We have all the time in the world. Just for love. Nothing more, nothing less, only love.' Tongo sang to the stars. And Bunmi nestled her face into his chest and rested her hand on his stomach.

'You can sing,' Bunmi said quietly.

Tongo laughed. 'Better than your archaeologist friends, anyway.'

'Sing an African song. Sing something Zambawian.'

The chief thought for a moment before softly beginning the folk song his mother had taught him as a child. Maybe it was the silence of the night or the acoustics of the dry lake's hollow or the ache that still hovered around his bruised groin, but even Tongo had to admit that his voice sounded good, resonant and meaningful.

'*Sikoko kuvizva sopi vadela, zvumisa vabe pi kupe zvade. Sikadzi kuzvizvi, kadzi dacheke, putela makadi nade. Tela makadi nade. Chi kupe vechela chi vipe kupe vasi, jamije opi ne opi. Mboko vezvo belabe chikadzi kakasi ku vasi Tuloko zvopje. Zvopje. Vasi ku fonge luzvopi.*'

If Tongo had sung in English, then how would Bunmi have reacted? But he didn't. He sang in Zamba and she didn't know enough to translate. So she bathed in those enigmatic phonemes and created new stories from the mysteries of those same building blocks. And she held him tighter and she didn't notice his muscles contract when he saw the shadowy figures coalesce on the far bank of the lake, illuminated by no more than the wink of heroic Cousin Moon. And she didn't hear his own tears that were as silent as the stars.

IV: *Six months later*

(Zimindo, Zambawi, Africa. 1998)
'Have I ever told you the story of Fate and Choice? I thought not. It is a good story but a privilege of the zakulu.

'Let me see. There was once a chief by the name of Vamaloko. As you can tell from his name, he lived some four generations after the Great Chief. Vamaloko was a good man, perhaps a quarter as good as Tuloko himself (which is unsurprising) and he ruled over a time of fabulous prosperity for Zimindo, in which the kingdom spread out in all four directions and even upwards so that the boka birds knew their ruler. Unfortunately, however, Vamaloko had the same attitude to procreation as the zaffre orchid (quality over quantity, if you see what I mean). Consequently he only had two sons, identical twins. Their names have long been lost to the past but the dreams of Cousin Zamba have told me that they are to be known as Fate and Choice for the purposes of this story.

'Now you know that identical twins are as rare as Kupile's anger. But this pair were a whole lot rarer than that. Generally, there will be a distinguishing feature or two to identify difference, but Fate and Choice were as two egg yolks from a maize-fed chicken. They were exactly the same height, they ate the same food and they both had identical scars on their knees from the time they simultaneously tripped over either end of the same log. Even their own father could not tell them apart. When one of his sons allowed the chief's herd to wander unchecked into the quicksands of Kalanga, Vamaloko shook his head and told the villagers, 'My Choice let me down.' But it wasn't. It was Fate.

'Of course, when the brothers were young, their identical appearance bothered no one, especially since their characters seemed equally the same. Apparently the brothers liked to play pranks on the villagers but they were soon forgiven because they were apparently so helpful in times of trouble.

288

In fact, Fate was the only trickster but he attributed half his escapades to his brother and the villagers knew no better. Conversely, Choice was the only considerate brother but he felt no need to claim his do-goodings for himself.

'Only when Vamaloko was killed, out of the blue, in a one-off Felati raid did the brothers' identities become a problem. For the chief had not named his successor and even the zakulu could not bring themselves to make a decision. If they had known the facts, they would certainly have agreed upon Choice. But they were as gullible to Fate's deceptions and Choice's humility as anyone else. In the end, the head zakulu, an ancestor of mine who is remembered in archaic Zamba as Kolonpoje (that is, 'The Hedger'), decided that the two brothers should rule jointly.

'At first this shared chieftainship posed no difficulties. Choice proved himself to be a tough ruler who expected hard work from his people but ensured their rewards were great. Fate adopted a more apathetic style, taking credit for successes and shrugging off failures with a 'Don't blame me'. However, the people, of course, did not know which chief was which and so they soon found themselves changing allegiances, both real and deceived, on an almost daily basis. Fate had his heroes. They were often good men whose only crime was to share Fate's blessing. Choice had his heroes too; generally humble scrappers with the weight of moral certainty on their side. But the two amorphous armies were hugely outnumbered by the undecideds in the middle who didn't know which mob to join and consequently maintained the peace by their sheer weight of numbers.

'Eventually, such a confusion of authority would have led to the Zamba's first civil war. But Fate and Choice, although distinct personalities, shared one congenital defect, a weak heart. And they both died in their sleep on the same night and some said it was the work of Father Sun, who could not bear to see his people torn apart.

'Now comes the interesting bit. The two brothers had only one wife between them, a young Mozolan girl by the name of Tupiwa. And nobody, least of all Tupiwa herself, was quite sure whom she had married. At the ceremony, her husband had presented himself as Choice. However, by now, everybody knew that Fate was a compulsive fibster, and who would dare make a guess on the truth of the matter? Sometimes villagers would ask Tupiwa how she could have married under such circumstances and her answer depended on her mood. Sometimes she said, 'It was my Fate.' At others, 'It was my Choice.' And both answers were accompanied with a philosophical shake of the head.

'When the brothers died, it transpired that Tupiwa was already pregnant and she gave birth to a son. Arguments raged as to what to call this little boy since the identity of his father was uncertain. But in the end everybody ran out of energy and the matter was still unresolved and so the new chief was known simply as Name. He grew up to be an unremarkable ruler who, unusually, is remembered only by his name with no adjunct to his moniker. He is not Name the Maize Eater or Name the Crooked Chongwe. Just Name.

'And that is the end of the story. The only interesting thing to point out is that zakulu rarely tell this story. Because they worry that the people will be confused to discover that their chief could be a descendant of either Fate or Choice. After all, the zakulu themselves are often confused. Generally – though not always – when a chief is weak-willed, the zakulu will say things like, 'What do you expect of the issue of Fate?' But when he is a hero they say, 'Thank Tuloko that Tupiwa took her Choice!' As for me, I understand that a wise man recognizes the contradiction in ascribing heroism to Choice and therefore Fate (if you follow me). For does not heroism come in many different guises?

'So it seems to me, my friend, that every chief faces a decision concerning his ancestry. And, in taking it, his lineage is determined.'

Even for October, the very height of summer, the sun was unbearably hot. Gudo hid in the trees, shumba slept like only shumba can and the cattle swished their tails and dreamed of a shearing. Even the kapenta lurked at the bottom of Maponda river and complained about the heat of the water closer to the surface. Because what was the point of avoiding the fisherman's cunning only to be boiled in your own home? As for the villagers of Zimindo, the women worked slowly in the fields with no time for gossip and the men couldn't decide whether to drink the cold bottled beer or to empty it over their heads. Sibongile, an albino, looked like an incognito film star in her floppy hat and enormous sunglasses and everybody felt sorry for the blistering skin on the backs of her hands. Some of the men who'd read newspapers brought from the capital blamed the heat on 'global warming' (although they couldn't imagine England or Russia or Germany suffering like this). But Musa the *zakulu* had a different explanation: 'Father Sun fears he has been forgotten in this modern world,' he said. 'He has decided to remind everybody who's boss.'

Musa and Tongo were sitting in the concrete house that was the centrepiece of the chief's kraal. It was hardly the ideal venue on a day like this because the amateur design of the house was such that it maximized both winter cold and summer heat. However, Tongo had just purchased a second-hand sofa from Queenstown (Zimindo's first piece of soft furniture) and he was determined that it should receive maximum usage. Besides, these days the concrete house was no longer just a tribute to Tongo's vanity but a functioning home with (apart from the sofa) a paraffin stove in the corner, a woollen rug on the floor and a bookcase against one wall which carried half a dozen battered archaeology textbooks that Tongo intended to read.

They were listening to one of the cassettes that Musa had brought back from his journey. It was a collection of Dixieland featuring Papa Celestin, Bunk Johnson and the like. Tongo was vaguely irritated that the *zakulu* should have developed a love of jazz on his travels, because hadn't that music originally been his shared connection with Kudzai? As far as Tongo was concerned, there was something intrusive, even tactless, in Musa's new-found interest and his mood tended to bristle when he caught the *zakulu* tapping his fingers to the rhythms or nodding his head in a meaningful and pretentious way.

Although Musa had been back in Zimindo for the best part of four months, the two friends had barely spoken since his return.

There were various reasons for this. In the depth of his heart, Tongo still felt a poignant sense of shame about the events that had roughly coincided with the time of Musa's departure. Of course he wanted to tell the *zakulu* (as both his friend and adviser) everything that had transpired. But Musa had the annoying habit of knowing (or at least *appearing* to know) all the facts before they passed Tongo's lips. On the very day that Musa returned, Tongo had cornered him in his kraal, desperate to outpace the wildfire village gossip.

'An archaeologist,' Tongo had begun and his heart was beating so fast that he feared the clumsy words might block his aorta. 'Bunmi.'

'Ah yes,' Musa replied, nodding with pronounced condescension. 'Professor Durowoju. Or should I say Coretta Pink?'

'You know her?' Tongo stuttered. Even for a *zakulu*, this seemed astonishingly accurate divination.

'I wouldn't say I know her. But Chicago's Northwestern is a most pleasing campus.'

On hearing this Tongo immediately decided to leave it at that. Because he had no desire to tell his version if the *zakulu* already knew the truth of the story.

For his part, Musa had been quite the recluse since coming home. These days he was walking with a pronounced limp but he deflected any questioning with a stern glance or an enigmatic shrug and the villagers invented stories that told how Cousin Moon had trodden on Musa's foot or how the *zakulu* had donated a toe or two for the sake of a particularly powerful spell (which was, in fact, but an acorn's throw from what had happened). He'd told nobody about the destination or purpose of his journey and when Tongo had pushed him, he'd replied, 'It is personal, my friend. A negotiation between myself and my past.'

Sometimes Tongo would not take such an answer and he said things like, 'Come on, *zakulu*! I am your chief; I have a right to know.'

But Musa just smiled and replied, 'I think you will know soon enough. I believe that we may soon have some visitors and you shall see for yourself.'

And though Tongo was desperately curious to know what the *zakulu* meant, he had no desire to pander to Musa's inscrutability, which came across as patronizing in the extreme.

In fact, the specific reason why the *zakulu* and the chief now sat next to one another, smoking *gar* on Tongo's new sofa, was not social at all. Officially they were meeting to discuss Stella 'Ngozi's proposed divorce after only five months of marriage. It seemed that her husband Tatenda, a placid character with a smile to match the size of his heart, had caught her with her thighs gripping the waist of George, a travelling soap salesman and noted libertine. While infidelity was hardly unusual (even in such a small village) it was certainly rare for a wife to cop off with a morally flexible huckster in the primary months of her union and the situation was threatening to get out of hand. Tatenda's uncles had already returned the *lobola* plate to the 'Ngozi kraal in expectation of a full repayment and, for the first time in Tongo's experience, Stella's father, Tefadzwa, was stuck for a metaphor.

Tongo sucked deeply on the joint and handed it to Musa as he exhaled. He was sweating profusely and the heat and the *gar* had successfully joined forces to dull his thinking.

'We are agreed,' the chief asked deliberately, 'that a divorce is not desirable?'

Musa eyed the chief cautiously. He didn't say anything but lugged voraciously on the marijuana and followed this initial toke with a few sharp breaths to ensure maximum impact upon his brain.

'What example does divorce set?' Tongo continued. 'If every unhappy couple decided to split up at the sniff of adultery, we'd be a village of divorcees. We cannot allow that to happen.'

Musa began to blow smoke rings. 'Are you speaking as a chief,' he asked quietly, 'or from personal experience?'

'What are you suggesting?' Tongo snapped.

Musa smiled. 'I am suggesting that we regard the situation

sympathetically. I agree that divorce is not appropriate. But we have to look at things from Tatenda's point of view. After all, everybody knows that the hoist of Stella's underwear is as temperamental as the Congolese flag.'

'Meaning?'

'Meaning her knickers come down at the first sign of trouble. And do you really think Tatenda was not cognizant of this fact? Of course he was. But he knew that an amateur who fucks like a pro, fucks like a pro. And that's what he wanted to marry. Tatenda does not care about the infidelity. Or at least he does not care about that nearly so much as the fact that Stella was doing the vertical *gulu gulu* with a man like George who's been known to bore his *boerwors* into any animal or vegetable with an appropriate depository. Minerals too, I shouldn't wonder.'

Tongo was about to say something. But Musa held up his hand and sucked on the joint. He wasn't finished, although he paused for a moment while he ruefully contemplated the *gar* butt.

'It seems to me,' the *zakulu* continued at last, 'that we must divorce the divorce from the adultery, as it were. The adultery itself is insignificant; it is the perception that matters and I will convince Tatenda of that fact.

'"During the time of drought," I shall say, "when you are away with your cattle for days at a time, do you care if your wife burns her *chadze*? You do not. But if she is cooking for you, your father and your friends and the mealie meal is black as coal and just as bitter? Then you are embarrassed and angry. Even *that* is grounds to send your wife back to her people wearing the charred saucepan upon her head."

'There is undoubtedly an amicable solution to this issue. But I must have the chance to talk to Tatenda and Stella alone. So you must ensure their families don't get in the way like the thirsty *jubu* roots that strangle even the smallest violet; especially that ridiculous bombast Tefadzwa. OK?'

'OK,' Tongo said. 'But what are you going to say to them?'

'It is simple. Stella must agree to be more selective in her adultery. She can't just give up her *pau pau* to every fruit picker with a sculptor's hands. If she is going to be unfaithful, then Tatenda must not know about it or at least he must be able to pretend he does not. So she will agree only to perform *gulu gulu* with men who have as much to lose as herself rather than troublesome yobs who love to show off by carrying their conquests' brassieres in their knapsacks.'

'And Tatenda? Do you really think he will accept such a proposal?'

'Aah!' Musa exclaimed emphatically. He was enjoying his scheming because there was nothing a *zakulu* liked more than to meddle in the fate of others. 'This is the brilliant part! I will persuade Tatenda to visit a different *hoore* every month with money from the housekeeping. That way he will no longer be jealous and the moral high ground will slip from beneath his feet like a sand dune.'

Musa stubbed out the joint and looked at the chief expectantly. For a moment or two, Tongo was speechless. Perhaps the *zakulu*'s travels had addled his brain because this was the most preposterous proposal he'd ever heard.

'So that is your solution, *zakulu*? The bride continues her infidelity while the groom pokes hookers? That's quite some counsel!'

'Calm down, old friend,' Musa said smugly. 'I know it is not perfect but what good is a perfect solution in an imperfect world? Ideals are for the fairies, pragmatism's for people. Do you really think Stella will stand for her husband going with a *hoore*? – "Excuse me, dear, I'm just popping off for my monthly fix of the other." Of course she will not! And as for Stella's wandering *pau pau*? She undertakes that she will not sleep with a man who boasts about the feat. Tell me, Tongo, have you ever met a man who can resist dissecting his congress in the smallest possible detail in front of the widest possible audience? No? Neither have I!'

Now Tongo stared at his friend. There was no doubt about it; he grudgingly had to admire the *zakulu*'s expertise in all matters marital. For a magical dreamer who commuted between past, present and future like an African swallow between continents, he had a remarkable grasp on humanity's prosaic staples; especially since Musa himself avoided wedlock like a chicken avoids the cleaver (indeed, if a girlfriend ever decapitated the *zakulu* in a moment of unmarried pique, Tongo suspected his friend's legs would keep on running).

The chief unpacked a small amount of *gar* into a strip of newspaper and he rolled it thoughtfully in his palm. He could feel the sweat beading on his temples and upper lip. On a day like today, what else was there to do but get stoned?

'What that couple need,' Tongo said slowly, 'is a baby. If all relationships are triangular, then that is surely the point.'

He contemplated the marijuana creation that was beginning to take shape in his hands. He knew that Musa was watching him and he knew it was one of the *zakulu*'s special looks that somehow managed to be condescending and sympathetic all at once. Musa cleared his throat expressively but Tongo wouldn't meet his eye.

'Wise words, chief. You've learned a lot,' he said. Then he paused, as patient as he was expectant. But Tongo said nothing. 'So that's the plan.' Another pause and Musa's patience finally collapsed. 'So. Come on, then. What happened?'

Still Tongo couldn't look up. He concentrated on his joint and wondered at its construction. It was a beautiful cone, absolutely symmetrical with smooth sides and apparently seamless seams. But he knew that the proof of a reefer was always in the smoking. He had seen uniform little numbers like this before that had come to pieces at the first drag or been rendered unsmokable by an invisible hole no larger than a pinprick. He'd also smoked the odd stubby brutus that had sent him to *gar* heaven despite looking like an ugly midget's *chongwe*. Fact was, it was the basics that mattered: good-quality ganja, tightly packed. The rest was all just cosmetics.

Tongo knew what Musa was asking and he certainly wanted to talk. After all, hadn't he waited nearly half a year for such an opportunity? But when he thought back to that definitive night at the dry lake near Maponda dam, his throat constricted and the words lingered reluctantly in his gullet like cowardly warriors in a trench. He opened his mouth but nothing came out except meaningless fillers: numerous 'wells', a sprinkling of 'to be honests' and at least a dozen 'it's a long storys'. At one point, he even managed to say, 'Well, to be honest, it's, well, a long story. To be honest. Well. To be honest, it is.'

Musa prompted him gently. 'Come on, old friend, spit it out. As I am your *zakulu*, you cannot say anything I do not already know and as your friend I promise nothing I know will shock me.'

Tongo looked up then and, for a moment, chief and *zakulu* were eye to eye. Then the words began to fall out of his mouth with all the force, honesty and lack of subtlety of the breach of Maponda dam.

He told Musa how Kudzai left him to return to Queenstown to stay with her family. He described how he felt – the self-righteous anger, the sense of betrayal – and he wasn't trying to justify himself, only to tell it how it was. He outlined the long walk to Maponda and the thoughts he'd had. He recalled his musings on heroism, bemoaning his lack of opportunities like a growing boy complains about no seconds. 'If a chief is not a hero, what is left?' he wondered. 'You're not even a footnote. Your only contribution to history is in your absence.' And Musa shook his head and bided his time. Tongo skipped over the clumsy pass he'd made at the beautiful professor and his battered *choko* (because, honest or not, there was no need to compound his memories of that humiliation) and he talked instead about cooking *chadze* for the archaeologists and recounted the stories he'd told around the camp fire.

Musa was listening attentively. 'But what happened?' he said.

Tongo gazed at his friend, his expression a tribute to melancholy. He sparked the joint. Fortunately it was a good one.

Tongo jumped then to his conversation with Bunmi. They'd been sitting on the shore line, gazing at the tears of Cousin Moon. She described her city and her childhood, cagey at first, then open, trusting. She leaned her head against his shoulder and she smelled like homecoming and he thought the moon seemed to be winking saucily and he felt the weight of destiny's hand on his shoulder (the way a boy feels the hand of his *mboko* at the *temba* initiation). He began to sing. And Bunmi asked him to sing something Zambawian.

Tongo dragged on the joint. His head was buzzing as he sang out loud: 'And the boy with the voice that rings over cool water sings words that nobody hears. And the girl wearing seashells, the noble chief's daughter, has drowned in a pool of her tears. She drowned in a pool of her tears.

'So there were three faces because love had three corners, that never could meet eye to eye. And men made the rituals and women were mourners for the love that was destined to die. To die. Love like a child's first sigh.'

The last note faded and Tongo licked his lips. He passed Musa the joint and rubbed his eyes with his hands. He was beginning to feel fatigued. He noticed the *zakulu* was eyeballing him intently. 'What?'

'Nothing,' Musa said and he began to shake his head like he was trying to rattle something loose. 'Did you know there are only thirty-four stories? And most of them are as inbred as the people of Chivu Province.'

The chief blinked. Perhaps he was more high than tired. 'What?' he said again. Although he wasn't sure he wanted to know the answer.

'Yours is number thirty. The most divisible. So?'

'So what?'

'So you saw something. You must have seen something. Tell me, my friend, what did you see?'

Tongo suddenly appreciated that he wasn't high or tired at all. No. He was forlorn, dazed and saddened by the recollection of a memory he'd kept under lock and key for so long. It wasn't that he was sad about what had happened (although that was true). He was more depressed by the near-miss of what hadn't and it was a feeling that filled his gut like the post-traumatic stress of the soldiers of independence; a guilty, welling sadness that might break out at any moment. To his surprise (since he wasn't the type), Tongo realized he was about to start crying. And this realization came too late to do anything about it and huge man-sized tears (that couldn't have been mistaken for droplets of sweat) began to stream, embarrassing and ostentatious, down his cheeks.

'Strong stuff, this *gar*,' Musa observed tactfully.

'I looked across the lake,' Tongo spluttered. 'I don't know why but my eyes pricked with tears then too, and Bunmi was clinging to me like a *makadzi* clings to her lost childhood. I don't know. My vision was blurred with tears of course, but I swear the landscape coalesced before me. I can't explain it, Musa! One moment I was looking at a scrawny *zvibo* bush and the next it had transformed into a young girl – as thin as famine and as desperate as disease – with her arms thrown out to her sides, locked in agony. Next to her a baobab dissolved into an *mboko*, a *zakulu*, I think, with a guilty hunchback and a stolen staff in his hand that he examined with two knots for unseeing eyes.

'I looked to Cousin Moon, I can tell you. I raised my head to the heavens and I prayed to our greatest hero, for I am not a *zakulu* and I am not supposed to witness such visions. But what did I see? A shooting star transformed into a mighty eagle that swooped into the distance faster than time. And when I blinked and returned my gaze to the far bank, there was a girl standing there who must have been called Beauty, for who else could have given her substance to such an abstract? Her thighs were two ebony sculptures of the finest Makonde workmanship; her hips were leg-crossingly promising; her stomach was muscular, rippled like sand caressed by Kupile's gentle touch; and her breasts were sexy enough to dry out a drunkard. She was dressed like a queen in her nakedness, for she wore nothing but the seashell head-dress that I'd heard so much about. But this wasn't the one I'd seen. It was a radiant masterpiece of perfect whites and deep purples and silk that shimmered beneath the winking Cousin Moon. And below this glorious crown, she had the face of . . .'

Tongo's emotion suddenly got the better of him and the words collapsed into heavy, choking sobs. Musa was bemused. Of the mortals he'd known who'd seen Beauty (if it was indeed her), Tongo was certainly reacting most peculiarly. But he patted the chief on the shoulder and kissed his teeth sympathetically.

'Whose face was it, my friend?' he asked. Although he already suspected the answer.

'Kudzai's,' Tongo wept. 'It was Kudzai's.'

'Oh.' Musa nodded. So it had been Beauty, all right. Because, among *zakulu*, this was one jade whose taste for melodrama was as celebrated as it was shameful.

The two friends sat in silence, punctuated only by Tongo's sniffs. Musa watched the joint burning wastefully between the chief's fingertips. But he didn't say anything. He was somewhat confused, surprised as ever that knowing the story could be of so little use. That was something he'd learned on his travels, especially from the new passion he'd found in music. Because a story is no more a movement from here to there than a journey (where the travelling is always more important than the arrival); to describe a story as an assemblage of words would be as foolish as to describe music as an assemblage of notes. For couldn't Louis Armstrong inject a lilt of happiness into the most tragic song? Didn't he undercut sweetness with an artist's sense of pathos?

Tongo's tears seemed to have subsided. But he showed no sign of finishing the story, so Musa decided there was nothing for it but to bite the strap like a *temba* initiate.

'So that was when you did it,' Musa suggested.

But Tongo didn't reply.

'My friend. Don't punish yourself. Your wife, carrying your child, I might add, left you; you'd just seen Beauty in all her provocative glory and a gorgeous woman was holding you like the deal was done and dusted . . .'

Tongo looked up sharply. 'No!'

Musa hesitated. 'No what?'

'No, I didn't fuck Bunmi!'

The *zakulu* was now totally flummoxed. It didn't help that the chief was staring at him defiantly, nostrils flaring, as though he'd accused him of the most heinous crime. 'Why not?' he asked carefully. 'And if not, what in the name of Tuloko are we talking about?'

Tongo sighed and wiped the streaking tears from his cheeks. He began to shake his head slowly from side to side.

'You were right all along, *zakulu*,' he said seriously. 'I am in love with Kudzai.'

While Tongo was smoking pungent *gar* and crying on his best friend's shoulder, his son was crying too while Kudzai changed his pungent nappy. Even after a few weeks, she still struggled with the folds and knots that other women made look so simple and she cursed in frustration. And Tongo (his father's idea) caught her mood and wailed all the louder until she swooped him up in her arms and force-fed him a nipple (nature's comforter). Motherhood, she reflected, could be a lonely business. But she remembered something the *zakulu* had told her: for a man, the baby completes the marriage. For a woman, the baby completes herself. And whatever else Tongo senior had given her, he'd given her that.

'Look at you,' Kudzai cooed. She was smiling down at the baby's pudgy face. 'Look at my little boy. You need Mummy, don't you? But one day you'll grow up to be a head-strong bastard just like your father. You'll break all the girls' hearts.'

Gently disconnecting her son from her breast, she laid him on the bed mat and wrapped him in a blanket (despite the heat), careful to cover every inch of his sensitive skin against the sun. As she worked, she sang Billie Holliday (the baby's favourite): 'Mama may have, Papa may have. But God bless the child that's got his own, that's got his own.'

Kudzai walked out into the yard with her baby against her

shoulder. An old man was standing outside and, at the sight of her, he bowed respectfully. But with the sun so strong, she barely broke stride to acknowledge him before entering the concrete house opposite.

Even as she entered, she was already saying, 'Could you take Tongo for a moment, I need to . . .' But her sentence was cut short and she smiled nervously. 'Have you been crying?'

Her husband wiped his face self-consciously. 'Just sweat,' he said. 'It's hot out there.'

Kudzai studied Tongo and Musa curiously. As usual, the *zakulu* looked like he might pack up laughing at the sight of her (something she never understood). 'What have you two been yakking about?'

'I was telling Tongo a story about heroes,' Musa said.

'A story about heroes?' Now Kudzai laughed as she deposited the baby on his father's lap. She patted Musa affectionately on the knee and kissed both Tongos on the cheek. Her husband's face was burning up. 'A story is where heroes belong!' she said. 'I'm going to Mapandawanda's store. Junior's grizzling and I want to buy some Calpol. Did you know Tefadzwa's waiting outside? I think he wants an audience.'

Kudzai hurried from the room. Her lips were split in that gummy smile. She loved to see Tongo holding his son; there was a kind of tender incompetence about him that melted her heart. She paused at the door. 'Don't smoke in front of him, will you? We don't want him to grow up as much of a *gar*-head as his father.'

Tongo nodded and Musa said, 'Of course not.' Kudzai stepped outside, barely able to suppress her giggles.

The chief bounced his successor thoughtfully up and down on his knee. The baby had recently learned to smile (unsurprisingly precocious, according to Dad) and he was determined to practise. Musa was playing peek-a-boo and the child gurgled appreciatively.

Eventually Tongo spoke. 'I am a chief,' he reflected. 'I am born of heroic stock.'

Musa shook his head. Some men were never satisfied. 'I think fatherhood suits you just fine,' he said.

Unsupported, the baby's head lolled backwards and he couldn't right it by himself until his dad helped him lift the weighty cranium to the vertical. Tongo contemplated his son seriously as the little boy began to blow bubbles of saliva and dribble down his front.

'Do you think he looks like me?' Tongo asked and Musa made a great show of examining and comparing their every feature.

'Well,' Musa concluded at last. 'At least he's got your ears.'

I: *Six months earlier*

(New Orleans, Louisiana, USA. 1998)
Ear? This is ashtray. Ashtray? Ear.

Jim was holding the ashtray to his right ear. A moment earlier, the phone had rung in the bar and he had instinctively answered the ashtray.

I am obviously drunk, he thought. I say 'obviously' because, in the first place, I am formally introducing my ear to this ashtray and, in the second place, I am always drunk. That's what Sylvia said.

Jim was right. He was dead drunk. How long had he been dead drunk? Well. How long had he been in . . . Where was he? New Orleans. Three days. So he'd been dead drunk for three days. That was it. He wasn't happy drunk (or at least *sparky* drunk) like he'd been with Sylvia throughout the majority of their whistle-stop American tour. He was dead drunk, morose drunk, drunk as a skunk, drunk as a punk skunk about to blow chunks. Or something.

How long had they been gone, her and Musa? They were getting close, those two. When Jim had told her he knew an African witchdoctor, she'd thought he was bullshitting. And now here she was gallivanting around the Big Easy with the very same. How long had they been gone? He looked at his wrist irritably. But he didn't own a watch.

Long enough for me to get dead drunk, he thought. Again. Three days of being dead drunk. Because *three* is a crowd.

Jim drained his glass and waved it at the landlady. 'Molly,' he said. 'Another Nigel G.'

Molly smiled maternally. 'Right up, Jim boy.'

That's one thing about me, he thought. Known in drinking holes from New York to New Orleans. Now that says something.

He was propping up the bar in Malone's, an Irish establishment on Decatur in the French Quarter. He wasn't sure what was so Irish about it. Of course they served Guinness and had pictures of the Pope, Jack Kennedy and, bizarrely, Gerry Adams on the wall. But perhaps the real point was that, in America, pubs were Irish as surely as Koreans owned cornershops and McDonalds employed Mexicans.

That said, Jim didn't know of any other Irish pubs with a predominantly black clientele, the smell of Cajun cooking, the hot, syrupy atmosphere of a steam room and a lazy ceiling fan that did no more than stir the mix. In the corner by the window an ancient, wizened little man strummed an uneven guitar blues with arthritic fingers like root ginger and the pale sun illuminated the eddying dust around him. And there wasn't much Irish about such a sight. Even Molly, the aptly named landlady, was an enormous middle-aged black woman with greying hair tied up in a headscarf and breasts like two melons in a slingshot.

Molly set Jim's drink before him and he thought the blackcurrant cordial looked quite pretty the way it flecked the creamy white head. He thanked her and nodded towards the blues man.

'Who's that? I've not seen him before.'

Jim asked the question like he was a regular.

'That's Fortnightly,' Molly replied.

'Why do you call him that?'

She looked at Jim like he was stupid. 'Because he comes in fortnightly and plays the blues and sings a little,' she said and she eye-smiled with whites that were flecked red and brown.

'OK.' Jim shrugged and he tipped his head back and drank like an Englishman until the glass was half-empty and he spanked it back down on the counter with a satisfied smacking of his lips. At the far end of the bar, a wave of laughter burst from the cluster of local drinkers (that included Jim's new friends Chillidog and Tompy). Jim looked up and the men were all watching him, wearing grins as wide as the Crescent City itself.

'You can sure drink, Jim boy!' Tompy exclaimed.

'Nigerian Guinness,' Jim replied. 'Puts hairs on your chest.'

He smiled a crooked, drunken smile and the men smiled back and raised their own glasses of purple-black liquid.

'Here's to Nigel G,' Chillidog pronounced seriously.

'Nigel G,' Jim concurred and he lifted his own glass and belched magnanimously. The local men guffawed and supped on their drinks and Jim felt like a missionary for the merits of Nigerian Guinness.

'Where your partners at, Jim?' Chillidog asked and Jim waved a dismissive hand. But Chillidog persisted. 'Where the *zakulu*, Jim?' he said and he turned to his companions. '*Zakulu* mean witchdoctor in African,' he explained. 'A real African witchdoctor! Now ain't that somethin'!'

Jim felt his irritation resurface. Musa's burgeoning celebrity only fuelled his growing resentment.

'They've gone to some voodoo museum,' Jim said.

'An' you didn't wanna go with?'

'Me? No way. I think voodoo's a . . .'

Jim caught himself just in time. He looked at the faces at the bar and they were intense; not a smile among them.

'What you think, Jim?' Chillidog asked and if his eyes weren't exactly dangerous they certainly held a warning.

Jim sipped his drink and bought some time.

'Voodoo?' He paused. 'I think it's a black thing.'

The local men looked at one another and their expressions cracked and they laughed uproariously, slapping each other's shoulders and bending double and saying things like 'There it is!' and 'Sure 'nuff! It's a black thing, all right!'

Jim watched their laughter with a bemused expression because no one had ever found his every comment so funny before. But, inwardly, he breathed a sigh of relief that he'd not said the wrong thing. Because his lack of faith in New Orleans voodoo wasn't strong enough to support tempting fate. Besides, whether Sylvia believed him or not, he'd experienced enough crazy juju in Africa, and who was to say that voodoo wasn't just as powerful?

Jim looked at the scene in front of him and felt a drunken moment of clarity. For pretty much the first time since their arrival in New Orleans, he had a sense of authenticity. It felt, he considered, just like the instant when the junior gangster called Tweet had pulled a Desert Eagle on Sylvia in Chicago's South Side a few days before. Only this time he wasn't too shit scared to appreciate its resonance before the second hand ticked on.

Jim thought about it like this. New York? That was different; a place apart, a self-contained city state. Or maybe he just knew it too well. But elsewhere in America? As far as he could see, if you tore off the thick bubble-wrap packaging and stripped the veneer of themed pubs – Irish, *obviously* – and 'Have a nice day' smiles, there were all kinds of colourful cultures just screaming to get out. But it was seamy, unprocessed, potent stuff that threatened the illusion of homogeneity. And New Orleans voodoo was a prime example.

When the three pilgrims had arrived three days before and booked themselves into a ramshackle apartment block on Chartres, Musa and Sylvia were already as thick as thieves, chattering about God knows what and falling silent whenever Jim tried to overhear. So Jim explored the French Quarter on his own, munching on Lucky Dogs and trying to avoid spoiling the photographs of snap-happy Japanese. He sidestepped walking tours of nodding Germans, open-top buses of idle Americans from La La Land or Texas and gaggles of drunken Brits. He got drunk on cold beer in jazz hotels that had super-friendly doormen and an impressive array of 'N'awlins' merchandizing. He got drunk on bourbon in bars that had cultivated seedy atmospheres and lacquered chipboard panelling. He sobered up on coffee as thick as molasses, paying tourist prices for a shot of fat-free creamer. And he concluded that New Orleans was about as authentic as a theme park where commercial spin was given the status of myth, the colourful locals were unpaid street performers, and souvenirs masqueraded as artefacts. It was a place where history was told in ad slogans and bumper stickers; where histories were drowned out by the international chatter; where history had imploded to fit neatly into a gift-wrapped box. Or at least that was the way Jim had it figured.

But then, two days before, Jim had stumbled into Malone's, quite by chance. An Irish pub, for fuck's sake! He had been wandering down Decatur and the heat was suffocating when he came across the drab sign and the Guinness symbol. Inside the black people stared at him and they raised their eyebrows when he ordered a Guinness with blackcurrant.

'With blackcurrant?' the barmaid asked.

'Sure,' Jim said. 'It's called a Nigerian Guinness. A Nigel G.'

'Whatever you say.' The woman shrugged and the men around the bar began to snigger and she kissed her teeth as she pulled the drink and Jim felt a little uncomfortable.

'Why Malone's?' he asked.

'What's that, honey pie?'

'Why Malone's?'

''Cos we an Irish pub. That's why.'

In spite of himself, Jim smiled. The barmaid put his drink in front of him and looked at him with milky eyes and a bored expression and she was just the right height for her heavy breasts to sit on the bar like they were too tired to hold themselves up.

'Who's Malone?' Jim asked.

'That's me, honey. Molly Malone. Jus' like the song.' Her mouth twitched for a second like she might start smiling. 'I'm an Irish-American,' she said. 'Ain't that right, boys?' And the men around the bar muttered, 'That's right, Molly' and 'Sure 'nuff'. She stared at Jim some more and she watched the way bemusement was dancing across his face. 'You got a problem with that?'

'No. Not at all.'

Molly leaned forward on to the bar, conspiratorially, and Jim looked down her magnificent cleavage.

'The way I see it,' Molly said, 'ain't no such thing as "an American" these days. 'Cos you got Italian-Americans, Irish-Americans, native Americans an' African-Americans. But s'all bullshit! You think any of them Italian-Americans ever been to the Coliseum? Course they ain't! The only Coliseum they know's in Vegas! You think any African-American been to Africa? Course not! They wouldn't survive without their southern fried chicken! But they still don't call themselves no Americans an' I jus' figure that's plain stupid. Me? I 'bout as African as Elvis Presley an' as Irish as Bill Cosby. But I got an Irish name that was found on some plantation or other and my poppa called me Molly on account of he liked the song. So why in God's name can't I open an Irish pub? No reason. That's why.'

Jim smiled broadly and extended his hand to the woman. 'Jim.'

'Well. Pleased to meet you, Jim,' she said, taking his hand. 'I'm Molly. But you knows that already.' She winked at him and then, without warning, she threw back her head and laughed so heartily that Jim was quite taken aback and he had to wipe her spittle from his face.

'The way I got it figured, honey pie,' Molly continued, 'every name got a story.'

She turned to the men at the far end of the bar and singled one out. 'Yo! Tompy!' she called. 'Come here.'

A small, stocky man in his early thirties approached with a friend at his shoulder. Tompy had a sweet, innocent face that looked on the verge of tears. His companion was a gangly individual with laughing eyes and a bitty beard on his cheeks.

'Miss Molly?' Tompy said.

'Tell Jim here how you got the name Tompy,' she said and Tompy's expression immediately changed. His eyes widened, his mouth pursed and his cheeks pinched with embarrassment. His friend started to laugh.

'I ain't tellin' nobody that story,' Tompy said. 'Sides, everyone knows it already.'

'Jim don't,' Molly said.

Tompy's friend leaped in. 'I tell it,' he said. 'I *love* to tell that story.'

'Chilli!' Tompy interrupted. But his friend wasn't going to be distracted and he turned to Jim and his eyes were dancing.

'Now it happened like this,' the man Chillidog began. 'See, years back, Tompy – yo! What's your real name, Tomps? I can't even remember! – Tompy had a reputation for bein' kinda unlucky with the ladies. Ain't that right, Tomps? He got played by some no-good hos an' bitches an', on one occasion, he only jus' managed to avoid the altar. You hear me? Anyways. One day, Tompy comes into this here bar an' he wearin' a smile like a cabaret nigger an' we're all, like, "Damn! What happened to you?" An' Tompy look like he fit to bust to tell us but he tryin' to play it cool. "I met a lady," he says. "A real fine white lady from Paris, France." An' we, like, "Shit!" 'Cos Tompy ain't had a woman so long his paws as hairy as a bear's!'

'Now that ain't true,' Tompy interjected. But the storyteller ignored him.

'So we're sayin', "Damn, my brother! You knock the boots or what?" An' Tompy looks all coy an' he says, "Only all night long!" An' I swear he look as happy as a dog in a butcher's shop!

'"Lemme tell y'all," Tompy says. "First off, the young lady – a real beautiful little chicken – was all *'Non! Non! Non!'* But soon she sayin', *'Oui! Oui! Oui!'* An' when we was done, she was moanin' like she was right at the gates of paradise!" So I looks at Tompy here an' I says, "What was she sayin'?" "I dunno," he replies. "Jus' some French stuff. *'Tompy! Tompy! Tompy!'* Yelpin' it over an' over again. Jus' like that." "Tompy?" I says. "What the blazes that supposed to mean?" An' Tompy jus' shrugs 'cos he don't know neither.'

'Tompy?' Jim asked and the man nodded.

'Sure, Jim. "Tompy." Leastways, that's how the brother heard it. Ain't that right, Tomps? He say she moanin' "*Tompy! Tompy! Tompy!*" an' he look as proud as a muthafucka!'

'Now, Chilli,' Molly scolded. 'Ain't no need for language like that.'

'I'm sorry, Miss Molly,' Chilli said and he paused and blinked respectfully before turning back to Jim. 'So. Anyways. We all standin' round this bar tryin' to figure what this "*Tompy-tompy-tompy*" thing might mean when we see this Creole hoverin' around our little group like a bad smell. Now I ain't never seen this light-skinned brother before – what 'bout you, Tomps?'

'Never seen him before,' Tompy confirmed.

'But he jus' come right up to us like he an old friend, you hear me? "Tompy?" he says. "Your woman sayin' that when you got your groove on?"

'"That's right," Tomps says proudly. "It's French."

'"I know what it is, brother," the Creole says an' he look like he 'bout to bust his gut with laughter. "I know what it is," he says – an' this is the killer, Jim! – "*Tant pis?* It mean 'Never mind!'"'

Chillidog stared at Jim and his face looked ready to twist with the humour of it all. But, at first anyway, Jim was nonplussed.

'You see, Jim?' Chilli laughed. 'There ol' Tomps gettin' busy like he the mack daddy an' this white chicken bouncin' on his dick – 'scuse me, Miss Molly – an' all the time she moanin', "Never mind! Never mind! Never mind!"'

Chillidog buckled at the middle and began to howl with laughter. But Jim could only force a smile and he looked at the unfortunate Tompy, who ducked his head and fingered a matchbox that was sitting on top of the bar.

Molly Malone was watching Jim with a placid expression. 'Like I tell you, Jim,' she said, 'every name got a story.'

Jim waited for Chillidog's hilarity to subside – a full minute! – and then he said, 'What about you, Chilli? Where does your name come from?'

The man wiped his streaming eyes on the back of his hand. 'Chillidog?' he said importantly. 'They call me that on account of my liking for chilli dogs.'

This time Jim did laugh and Molly Malone laughed too and even Tompy raised a smile. 'I told you every name got a story,' Molly chuckled. 'But some surely a whole lot better than others!'

Two days later, when he was dead drunk, Jim thought back to this conversation and he considered the truth of Molly's words. Every name's got a story. He thought about Molly Malone, named for a song; about Tompy, whose very name was a pinprick to his ego; even Chillidog had a story behind it and, if you didn't like *that* story, you could easily make up another. And Sylvia? Sylvia Di Napoli? A black woman with a name as Italian as pizza? That name was half a book in itself. And what about Musa? As far as Jim knew, Musa had no surname. He was just Musa the *zakulu* and it was a story right there. But Jim Tulloh? There was nothing to be said about such a name. It was an apathetic kind of moniker; a classless, colourless label that showed no initiative of definition, making do instead with the rudimentaries of nationality and gender.

Jim muttered to himself. 'It's all Musa's fault,' he said and, even in his drunken haze, he realized he wasn't entirely sure what he meant by that. But he suddenly felt very depressed and it took him a minute or two to finger the reason for that too.

The point was that, before Musa showed up, Jim had a new story unfolding by the day. And it wasn't Sylvia Di Napoli's story or his story but *theirs* (with a good enough plot to let him forget himself). It was the story of how they met on an aeroplane; how she told him her life in Irish Tony's bar; how he dealt with her great-uncle in Harlem, that nasty old pervert called Fabrizio Berlone; how they travelled to Chicago and were rescued from a shooting by a minister by the name of Boomer Jackson. It was a convoluted tale of identity that wound them together like lovers' fingers at the end of a tear jerker. It was a crazy shaggy-dog joke populated by absurd characters, dead ends and half-truths that tumbled towards a punch-line that would seem inevitable with hindsight. But then Musa appeared – *Musa!* With his charisma and his mysticism, his driven certainty and his attitude of I'm-a-witchdoctor-and-what-I-say-goes

– and Jim was suddenly struck from the equation like another absurd, dead-end, half-truth character.

As soon as Musa appeared before them (as if by magic) in that Northwestern office belonging to Dr Coretta Pink, Jim noticed the change in Sylvia. He knew from past experience that Musa tended to provoke one of two responses in a woman: either she ran from his haunted eyes like a savvy virgin or she was captivated like a rabbit in headlights. And, however savvy, Sylvia was certainly no virgin.

Although she had a good ten years on Musa (still less than the twenty she held over Jim), Sylvia fawned over the witchdoctor like a young girl from the first. It was the little things Jim noticed: the way she walked a mite too close to him through Chicago's streets; the way she absentmindedly removed a dreadlock from his bowl of rice at dinner that evening; the way she kissed his cheek a shade too long when they said goodnight prior to their early-hours flight to New Orleans the following morning; the way she gave him her window seat without a thought (although she knew how Jim liked to watch the land fall away beneath the aeroplane's wings).

And, of course, they began to exclude Jim from their conversations. When Jim asked what they were doing in New Orleans, Musa replied, 'We are here because this is where we must be,' and Sylvia looked at him witheringly. And when Jim asked why, Sylvia shook her head and tutted and said, 'Because it is,' as if that was the most obvious thing in the world. Jim was used to such unexplained pomposity from Musa (it came with the job of *zakulu*), but from Sylvia it was harder to accept. The way he saw it, Musa had arrived on the scene and whisked them off to New Orleans on an abstract promise and they'd been there for three days and their *search* – for what? Jim had almost forgotten – hadn't progressed one step. But Sylvia lauded Musa as if they'd been lost without him (which was an affront to Jim's pride, because they'd mostly been getting on just fine).

Jim did corner the witchdoctor alone in their apartment one

night when he had been drinking and Sylvia was washing her hair (two activities Musa eschewed in favour of his 'shit' and tangled dreads).

'Musa,' Jim said.

'Jim.'

'Why are you here?'

'You're drunk,' Musa observed.

'Yes.'

'I am here because I dream of a huge eagle who infuriates me with his manner. I am here because I dream of a princess who drowned in the chief's seashell head-dress and I wake to find no more than driftwood and a woman's intimate equipment. I am here because I dream of a light-skinned woman with a *chongwe* like a black cucumber who sings with the voice of a trumpet. I am here because I dream of Sylvia Di Napoli and James Tulloh and I do not yet understand why.'

Jim blinked and licked his lips and found himself swaying slightly, as if the breeze of Musa's madness might knock him off his drunken feet. 'You're stoned,' he said.

'No,' Musa replied patiently. 'I am here because my destiny is in the past.'

'You mean the future,' Jim assumed.

'No, *musungu*,' Musa said. 'The past.' And he shook his head smugly and Jim felt dizzy and irritable.

But the worst for Jim had come the night before, when he had introduced Musa and Sylvia to the crowd in Malone's bar. Molly, Tompy, Chillidog and the rest had welcomed Jim like an old friend and treated his companions just the same. But when they discovered Musa was a witchdoctor – a fact he was never shy to announce – he soon became the centre of attention. Musa sat at a round table in the middle of the pub and Jim was forced to the edge of the group by the circling men and he hovered twitchily. Sylvia sat plum next to her new idol and looked up at him from beneath her false lashes.

'Show us your powers, witchdoctor!' challenged a bulbous man whose name Jim didn't know. He had a face that looked like the reflection in the back of a spoon.

'*Zakulu!*' Musa corrected him gravely. And he shook his head from side to side as if gently ridding himself of the suggestion. 'We learn our trade in the dreams of Cousin Moon that we suffer in the delirium of the *zakulu* illness. And the truths of the Great Chief Tuloko therein are as secret as the fantasies of a pubescent boy about the friend of his mother.'

The assembled New Orleans men stared at Musa as though he were part genius and part madman. And it was the desired *zakulu* effect.

Some of the men made disgruntled noises and said things like, 'Jus' one demonstration, man!' and, 'Brother sho' full of shit!' Others, with Tompy at the forefront, took the opposite view. They said, 'T'ain't nobody mess with the hoodoo,' and, 'Sure 'nuff!' and, 'Ain't that the truth!' And throughout the heated exchange of views Jim felt his annoyance simmer while Musa's expression was as serene as a summer's evening as the argument panned out just like he knew it would.

Eventually, beneath the growing disquiet, Musa spoke with soft-toned authority. 'I'll show you a trick,' he said. And immediately the whole bar was silent, except for Jim who made deliberately loud sighing noises and whistled through his teeth and shuffled his feet on the floor.

Musa picked up a matchbox and removed its innards and held up the rectangular sleeve between thumb and forefinger. He focused his attention on Chillidog.

'Chilli,' Musa said, 'Do you think I can push you through the opening in this box?'

'Say what?' Chillidog replied and his voice was as tense as a high wire.

Musa repeated himself: 'I will push you through the opening in this box.'

And the local men began to murmur, 'No way!', 'Brother gone crazy!' and, 'Now wouldn't that be somethin'?'

Lazily the *zakulu* got to his feet and he signalled to Chillidog to do the same. Musa made a great and solemn show of preparing himself – cracking his neck and going through all manner of elaborate stretches – and an expectant hush descended on the group. He set the matchbox sleeve on Chillidog's chest with one hand and he closed his eyes and furrowed his brow as if in the deepest concentration. Then he drew back his other hand and slowly extended his index finger. He stared into Chillidog's eyes and the man timidly met them with his own, which welled with nervous tears. Musa's lips moved in silent exhortation, a prayer to Tuloko perhaps? Then, with surprising force, he rammed his index finger through the matchbox sleeve and poked Chillidog firmly on the chest. Chillidog yelped in shock and stumbled back over a chair and landed on his backside and rubbed his sternum ruefully. The other men looked on with confused expressions but Musa was smiling broadly. He was extremely pleased with himself.

'You see?' Musa announced. 'I pushed you through a matchbox!'

A great rumbling noise began to roll up through Musa's stomach and to rattle his chest. His whole torso convulsed and then his mouth burst open and he threw his head back and he laughed like thunder with his dreadlocks shaking like catkins in a gale. He bent himself double and he clutched his sides. He wiped his watery eyes and he said, 'Oh dear, oh dear!' and, 'Goodness me!' And the surrounding men stared at him blankly for the briefest moment before catching the bug of hilarity. One by one, they too began to laugh until the whole pub shook to the humour of Musa's weak joke as if it was the funniest thing in the world. Tompy rocked back and forth and slapped his thigh and squeezed his sad eyes tight shut. Chillidog lay back on the floor where he'd fallen and wailed with laughter and bicycled his legs in the air. Sylvia's face contorted and her painted eyebrows took an unnatural shape and she hung on to Musa's arm and buried her face in his shoulder.

Only Jim and the man with a face like the reflection in the back of a spoon didn't laugh. Jim raked his teeth over his bottom lip and his eyes were fixed on Sylvia. He remembered that the most metaphysical thing about Musa was his charisma and that, frequently, the 'magic' itself was no more than diversionary. He saw the way Sylvia's false nails rucked the material of the *zakulu*'s T-shirt and an unnamed sensation knotted his gut.

Later, when Musa had accepted all kinds of plaudits and pats on the back with practised modesty, Jim caught him by the arm and led him to a corner table. He was surprised to hear his voice come strained and angry.

'Musa!' he began.

'Yes, Jim.'

But at that moment they were interrupted by the man with a face like the reflection in the back of a spoon. He was drunk and confrontational and he laid a vaguely threatening hand on Musa's shoulder.

'That sure was some chicken-shit stunt you pulled back there,' the man rasped.

Musa blinked as the haze of alcohol hit his eyes. He removed the man's hand with a firm but gentle gesture.

'Excuse me,' Musa said politely. 'At present I am conversing with my friend. Be so kind as to leave us alone.'

'I talk to who the fuck I want. An' at the moment that's you. So since I talk to who the fuck I want an' at the moment that's you, I'm talkin' to you. You got that?'

The man shoved Musa a little and Musa swayed back and smiled placidly. 'Of course,' he said.

Jim was going to intervene but the *zakulu* raised a hand.

'That sure was some chicken-shit stunt you pulled back there,' the man repeated. 'Some chicken-shit stunt! You wouldn't know real hoodoo if it bit yo' muthafuckin' jungle-nigger ass! An' you wanna watch out in this ol' town 'cos there sure 'nuff real witch-doctors who bounce yo' black ass back to Africa 'fore you got time to say your prayers. You don't talk the talk if you can't walk the walk, you got that?'

This time the man pushed Musa a little harder and Musa's smile widened.

'Be so kind as to leave us alone.'

'Fuck you!'

'Would you like to see some real magic?'

'Fuck you!' the man snarled and his face scrunched and Jim was sure they'd come to blows.

'Be so kind as to leave us alone,' Musa repeated and he closed his eyes for just one second. And the man with a face like the reflection in the back of a spoon disappeared. And Musa opened his eyes again.

Jim stared at Musa and then at the place where the man had just stood and then at the crowd around the bar, who were chattering animatedly and hadn't noticed the altercation, let alone the vanishing. He swallowed.

'Where did he go?' Jim asked.

'I sent him back to his wife. Poor woman. Drunk-ass jungle-nigger muthafucka!' – Musa beamed serenely ' – to use the vernacular. Now. You wanted to talk to me?'

Jim licked his lips and tried to focus his mind and remember all the things he'd wanted to say. But he'd quite forgotten. This was typical of Musa, he thought, to throw a magical spanner in the works.

'I . . .' he began and Musa nodded patiently. But no more words would come. the *zakulu* patted him on the head, at once comforting and patronizing.

'You are troubled,' Musa said. 'You think, what's old Musa doing here, my old friend from Zambawi? What's he doing here with his dreaming and his manner as sexy as a she-baboon on heat? Why does he come and spoil my little *musungu* adventure? Well. Let me tell you, Jim. I am here for Sylvia because I owe her a debt from the past and that is not something you can hope to understand. You are troubled because I have brought you to New Orleans and you don't know why. To be honest, *musungu*, as I previously expostulated, I am not fully cognizant of the reasons myself. But I am the *zakulu* and you must trust me as I trust my dreams. You are also troubled by the relationship I have formed with Sylvia. It is that alone among your troubles which I cannot help. You are troubled because you are jealous and jealousy is as personal and pernicious as an STD.'

'Jealous?' Jim spluttered.

'Of course.'

'I'm *not* jealous!'

Musa stared at him and craned his neck forward and narrowed his eyes to two needle points. Jim felt uncomfortable.

'Of course you are not jealous,' Musa said slowly. 'My mistake.'

But the next day, when Jim was dead drunk on Nigerian Guinness and Musa and Sylvia had been gone for hours on their visit to the voodoo museum and he was thinking how every name but his own told a story, he remembered Musa's comment and, in his drunken haze, its truth began to seep into his mind like a spillage absorbed into a paper napkin. He sipped on his sixth pint of Nigel G and he shook his head from side to side as if that might loosen the idea. But no luck.

Why the hell should I be jealous of Musa and Sylvia? Jim thought. And as soon as he thought that, the answer sneaked up on him like a child on tippy toes and, before he knew what was happening, he found himself saying 'Oh!' at the top of his voice. 'Oh! Oh fuck! Oh shit!'

The men at the far end of the bar – Tompy and Chillidog and the rest – looked at him with curious eyes. But Jim didn't notice. He gulped his Nigel G, sparked a cigarette and stumbled towards the table by the window where the old blues man called Fortnightly was strumming the same old blues. Jim pulled deeply on his cigarette and nodded at the man who acknowledged him with a tilt of his head and seemed to launch into the next twelve bars with a little more vigour. Jim sat down next to him and – as drunk as a skunk –

he began to sing. He bent his head down, squeezed his eyes shut and sang the blues with as much authenticity as a pissed English boy could muster.

'I came here to lose myself . . .' he began. And he revelled in the 'dow dowdow dow dow!' of Fortnightly's chords.

'But I found someone else.
Now she ran off with a witchdoctor and I'm left on the shelf.
Woh yeah! I got those identity-crisis blues!
When you can't forget yourself, it surely turns you to the booze!'

Jim opened his eyes and the locals at the bar were laughing themselves silly. But that only seemed to fuel his desire to sing and he buried his face in his hands and launched into a second verse.

'For the first time in my life
I figure that I'm in love,
But my baby's a dirty whore. Lord Jesus! Heavens above!
Woh yeah. She'll fuck anyone who'll pay!
But when it comes to me? I just don't get no play!'

Surely if he hadn't been so drunk, Jim would have noticed the sudden break in the laughter in the bar. Certainly he'd have noticed when Fortnightly stopped strumming the guitar. But he was so drunk that the new silence just seemed to give him more space to fill with his voice and he began to sing a cappella; louder than ever, freestyling lines with little sense of their metre, melody or meaning.

'Yeah she a low-down hooker!' His voice was rasping. 'Not even much of a looker! Kind of elegant, I guess! But way past her best! False eyebrows, lashes and nails! Probably got false breasts as well! I can't help but love her! But she's old enough to be my mother!'

Jim was shaking his head from side to side, shouting the words as they came to him, lost in his bitterness and jealousy. Only when he opened his eyes a crack did he see the two figures standing in the doorway. Then he opened his eyes wide and the sounds stuck in his throat like coins in a vacuum cleaner. Musa and Sylvia were watching him. He looked at Sylvia and her lips were quivering and her eyes filled. How long had they been standing there? Jim scanned the rest of the faces in the bar and he quickly found his answer. He turned back to Sylvia just in time to see the door of Malone's bar swing behind her. He looked to Tompy, Chillidog and Molly. But they wouldn't meet his eyes. He looked at Musa and double-taked. The *zakulu* appeared to be standing in a pool of blood and (perversely, Jim thought) he was staring fixedly at Fortnightly. Jim looked at Fortnightly and the old man shrugged.

'Ain't nothin' wrong with lovin' a hooker,' Fortnightly said. 'My momma was a hooker an' I sho loved her.'

It was the first time Jim had heard him speak.

And Jim got uneasily to his feet and ran drunkenly from the bar, brushing past Musa, who seemed frozen like a statue. He shouted Sylvia's name into the street but he was blinded by the sun and he couldn't see anything. He was panicking.

Typical woman to run off, he thought. And, as he tried to blink back his streaming tears (part emotional, part sun-pricked), Sylvia's heavy fist smashed into his nose and his tears were now uncontrollable.

'How dare you?' Sylvia wailed. 'Fuck you! You jumped-up little fucker! How fucking dare you?'

And Jim crumpled to the pavement like a sack of shit and his mouth and nose and eyes filled with blood and he thought his heart might burst.

I: *Finding destiny, losing digits*

(New Orleans, Louisiana, USA. 1998)
Taxi drivers, pseuds and greetings-card romantics have been known to claim that Greek has fourteen different words for love. Any Zambawian will tell you that their native tongue has twenty-one words for *hoore* – not a synonym among them – and Musa had had frequent cause to use them all (even before his recent obsession with the idea of paid sex as some kind of psychological panacea). Never much of a one for 'monotamy' (as he liked to call it when speaking English), the *zakulu* had spent most of his adult life with various streetwalkers, brothel workers, *kwensters* (city girls) and *gwaashters* (rural girls) and even the *polopeji* (a kind of Zambawian specialist that defies sexual translation). Consequently he was undismayed to discover that Sylvia – the focus of both his history and his destiny – was a retired hooker (or *machekamadzi* in Zamba) and it was little wonder that he feared for his toes.

Sylvia, however, was always surprised when a man was unmoved by her profession. In her experience, the vast majority of men would sneer at the discovery of her whoring or shake their heads slowly like disappointed parents. About half of these would then offer to pay her for sex and maybe she would accept and maybe she would not. The other half would not offer to pay her for sex but she knew that they wanted to. Or consider it at least.

Sylvia often thought about the effects of prostitution on a woman's state of mind. Superficially prostitutes adopted various attitudes to their sexuality, their profession and men (not 'their punters', mind, but 'men' in general). There were feeble young things who constantly dreamed of redemption and curled up in each other's arms in any break in the trade. There were knackered old whores whose cynicism creased their faces more surely than the cigarettes they chain-smoked. There were brazen bitches who claimed to be empowered by their knowledge of the opposite sex but secretly wept into their heart-shaped pillows and clutched their satin sheets to their cheeks. But beneath these surface differences, certain constants protruded like predictable erections straining different styles of underwear.

'On the game.' Sylvia found that she despised and enjoyed the accuracy of that phrase in equal measures. Prostitution reduced *both* genders (not just the men) to their most basic selves and, in such a state, they were merely unconscious participants in the oldest game in the world. Sylvia thought of young women going to job interviews for high-flying positions in the City (which city? No matter). She imagined them choosing their skirt, maybe a little shorter than usual. And maybe their lipstick was a bit redder too and they wore that top that was a shade tight around the chest and they weren't too disappointed if the interviewer was a middle-aged man with a menopausal wife and lascivious eyes. Of course Sylvia knew that not all young female interviewees went to such flirtatious lengths. But then not all of them could get the job, could they?

Sylvia then thought of the way prostitutes dress and she remembered a conversation she'd once had with an academic who'd been a regular punter some twenty years before. Lipstick, he had told her, was first worn by Roman prostitutes as a sign of their willingness for oral sex. And Sylvia realized that whores were forever dressing for interview (and they were so much *better* at it than their City counterparts) and every man was a potential boss and there was no industrial tribunal to turn to when that 'boss' decided to slide his hand between your thighs. The power dynamics of prostitution were simply fucked up. Hookers found humiliation in the ultimate expression of their womanly power while their punters found masculine strength in their basest, weakest needs. It was for this reason that Sylvia felt that she had a bit of every kind of prostitute

323

in her; she was brazen and powerful, knackered and cynical, and she still dreamed of redemption. Of course she did.

She had met four men in her life who cared nothing about her profession. There was Dalton, the solemn-faced Jamaican boy who'd taken her virginity and her heart (before her father grabbed it back and crushed it between his fat Italian fingers). Of course she wasn't a prostitute when she met Dalton; not in *fact*. But she often thought she was 'born to whore', and when she thought that, she cherished the fantasy that maybe Dalton would have forgiven her. It was just a fantasy.

There was the alcoholic, Flynn, with whom she'd lived for a decade in the eighties. He had always said she was 'a singer' and, before his addiction precluded any sex, he made love to her with tender incompetence no matter how many men she'd been with that day. But over time Sylvia came to realize that booze was Flynn's prostitute and he paid this bitch handsomely and she accompanied him wherever he went, and it was her cool glass form that he liked to sleep with best of all.

Then there was Jim. Jim! Sylvia couldn't help but smile when she thought of him; his stringy white body, his downy beard, his ineffectual efforts at adulthood, his bullshit stories that turned out to be true and a heart so big it was a mystery how it could fit into such a puny chest. She had considered him as a potential partner in idle, drunken or (mostly) lonesome moments. And there'd been more of those than she cared to admit . . . The transatlantic flight, the Manhattan apartment, the Chicago hotel room when she'd awoken from her dreams of Dalton. But he was just a boy, a lost soul reaching into space like someone falling from a cliff. How could she inflict all that she was on him? And surely he only accepted her brackets-and-all status – prostitute (retired) – because he knew no better.

And now Musa. She had known the *zakulu* for what? Three days? But already she felt an attachment for him that seemed to tug at her gut like an umbilicus. Sylvia had known few Africans in her life

– only strange Nigerian businessmen who liked hard, eager sex and showed remarkable pride in their run-of-the-mill bodies – but Musa had an exoticism about him that filled her every sense. *Exoticism!* How ironic! The very word that she once used to describe her coffee-coloured self in a dozen advertisements in a dozen local newspapers in London: 'exotic massage in intimate surroundings'. For all the mysteries of her background, next to Musa Sylvia felt about as exotic as a boiled egg.

But there was more to Musa's attraction than his Africanness; certainly more than the appeal of his sunken, melancholy eyes, his profound tone (even when he appeared to be speaking gibberish) and the sinewy body that she imagined beneath his threadbare clothes. Musa offered her answers and she was more than ready to believe him. Sylvia knew it would take a special man to accept her past. But it required somebody extraordinary to fill the blanks in her personality that yawned wider with every passing day (because 'prostitute (retired)' just wasn't a satisfactory label). And Musa was certainly extraordinary; he was literally 'out of the ordinary', even defying comparison with any of her former punters. A *zakulu*, a witchdoctor, a medicine man, a magical man . . . He was *magical*. And if it took a knight on a white charger to save a princess, Sylvia reasoned, then it surely took a magician to save a whore.

Sylvia recalled her first meeting with Musa in the seeming dead end of Professor Pink's office at Northwestern University in Chicago. 'I was a friend of your great-great-great-great-grandfather,' he'd said. 'I am here to pay a debt.' And he spoke with that ring of confidence that assumed she would nod and reply, 'Oh, of course.'

Since that moment, they had barely left each other's company, although Sylvia's efforts to press the *zakulu* for more information were met with bewildering replies. Musa spoke in a mixture of riddles and quotations, stories and aphorisms, he answered questions with questions and asked questions with answers; and all in a tone as solemn as Solomon.

'Who was my great-great-great-great-grandfather?' Sylvia asked.

'Ah!' Musa exclaimed and he shook his heavy locks from side to side and seemed to count backwards on his fingers. 'He was your mother's mother's mother's mother's father,' he said and he beamed as if proud of such precision.

'What's this debt you have to repay?'

'A debt whose interest increases exponentially into the future,' Musa said.

'Where do I come from?'

'Chicago.'

'No. Originally.'

'England.'

'*Originally!*'

'Where are you going?'

Sylvia stared at him and pinched the bridge of her nose between thumb and forefinger. But curiously she wasn't frustrated; just confused. And she was used to confusion.

'Why am I black?'

'You are black,' Musa said. With the depth of his voice, Sylvia couldn't figure out whether a question mark was tagged to the end of his sentence and she didn't reply. Instead she remembered something Jim had told her; something told to him by the curious Reverend Boomer Jackson. 'It ain't where you're from, it's where you're at.'

Yesterday Musa had sat her down at the kitchen table in their apartment on Chartres. Jim was out exploring (on his own as usual – had he lost interest in her journey?) and the *zakulu* said he wanted to tell her a story. Sylvia waited expectantly but Musa seemed more interested in peeling the yellow paint that flaked from the damp walls and examining it between his fingers until she felt she had to say something: 'You were going to tell me a story?'

It took Musa a full minute to speak. 'When was this room last painted?' he said testily. 'In a climate such as this, a room must be painted at least every two years or else the colour cracks and peels and the effect of cleanliness is replaced by one of squalor. For goodness' sake! In Zambawi our walls are bare brick or mud brick. We are people of few pretensions (apart from Tongo, of course, and look where his pretensions got him).'

Musa looked at her then and his eyes – perversely – seemed to be laughing and he pulled a joint from behind his ear and sparked it with a flourish and said, 'I want to tell you a story.'

He then told her an extraordinary fairy tale; something about a love triangle between a young *zakulu*, a boy with a voice as heavenly as Tuloko himself (whoever he might be) and the chief's beautiful daughter who wore a seashell head-dress. But Sylvia found it hard to follow the plot with all the gaps and leaps and random associations that gave it the texture of a dream.

When Musa was finished he said, 'You see?'

'What is that?' Sylvia asked.

'It is a traditional Zamba folk song.' Musa shut his eyes and his head lolled back and swung in a gentle parabola around his shoulders and he began to sing: '*Sikoko kuvizva sopi vadela, zvumisa vabe pi kupe zvade. Sikadzi kuzvizvi, kadzi dacheke, putela makadi nade.*' His singing voice was utterly unexpected – hardly beautiful but high-pitched and tremulous like the cry of a sick animal – and Sylvia felt droplets of sweat bead at her temples and she stared at him in dismay.

'What does it mean?' she asked.

Musa offered her the joint, which she declined. Then he sucked smoke deep into his lungs and, as he exhaled, he whispered, '"The boy with the voice sounding over cold water sings meanings that no person hears. And the girl wearing seashells, the greatest chief's daughter, has drowned in a lake of her tears." Something like that.'

There was a moment of silence and unconsciously Sylvia reached for the reefer. One drag left her dizzy.

'That's beautiful,' she said. 'You have a beautiful voice.'

Musa smiled shyly. 'Me? I have a voice like an angry jackal. It is you, Sylvia, who has the beautiful voice.'

'I'm just a retired prostitute.'

'Indeed. *Machekamadzi*. A most noble profession.'

After that they'd walked out into the New Orleans night with its atmosphere like melting wax. Sylvia hung from Musa's arm like a teenage lover (which he didn't object to) and she pressed him with more questions (which he did).

'Be patient, *machekamadzi!*' he said. 'You're so busy asking questions that, if you're not careful, you won't hear the answers that your ancestors whisper in your ear.'

'But I don't even know who my ancestors are!' Sylvia protested.

'Precisely. You must listen all the more attentively for the voices you do not recognize.'

They met Jim at a peculiar bar on Decatur, a faux-Irish establishment frequented by all manner of curious locals who could smile with the saddest eyes and frown while the corners of their mouths twitched in a giggle (and these contradictions certainly fitted with Sylvia's perception of black Americans). Most curiously of all, Sylvia realized that pasty-faced Jim seemed to blend into the strange atmosphere just fine. But then that was something she had noticed before: how Jim could fit in everywhere and nowhere, a cultural chameleon – but a chameleon none the less and ever-vulnerable to a sharp-eyed bird of prey. Sometimes Sylvia felt like his mother. Sometimes she felt other things that she couldn't (or didn't want to) explain.

Of course Musa was soon at the centre of a crowding group of Jim's new friends with his witchdoctor's stories and his feeble jokes and tricks. And Sylvia loved him for it – this charismatic man who'd crossed the globe for her! – and she kneaded his thigh with her hand and she rested her head on his shoulder. But Musa didn't seem to notice.

Jim, on the other hand, never took his eyes off her. But his expression was bitter and scornful and later, alone in bed, as she kicked off her sheet in sweaty frustration, she wondered what she could have done wrong. What the hell was his problem?

Today Musa was up early and he opened the shutters of the

apartment and gulped on the air like it was honey waiting to set, and he was sure he could taste the expectation crystallizing on his tongue and smell it on the breeze and it lifted his spirits. He shook Jim awake and he was told to 'fuck off'. He touched Sylvia's bare shoulder and she blinked her eyes as slowly and coyly as a cat waiting for a saucer of milk. She was, Musa thought, a fine-looking woman (unusual for a *machekamadzi*, who generally look as worn as a traveller's boot) and he was certainly pleased to glimpse her future even if her past remained smoky. He brewed some fresh coffee, grilled back bacon and lit a chubby reefer. The unmistakable scent of expectation deserved the most succulent accompaniments!

When Jim and Sylvia finally surfaced, Musa announced that he wanted to visit the voodoo museum just behind Louis Armstrong Memorial Park.

'Who will accompany me on such an excursion?' he asked.

Sylvia was enthusiastic but Jim said he'd rather be on his own. Musa was briefly perplexed. Why did his friend so steadfastly refuse to confront the destiny he'd chosen? A typical *musungu* to ignore the rationality of metaphysics and the mysteries of logic!

At the voodoo museum, the swell of expectancy that Musa had been surfing all but disappeared (as grandiose expectation is often the first casualty of minor disappointment). There were a number of reasons why Musa felt let down. But most of them stemmed from the artefacts on display. A voodoo museum? Surely he could have chosen no finer place to hear the dissonant notes of fate overlaying time's simple melodies. However, as he walked through the exhibits that included desiccated bats' wings, grotesque pottery figurines and even a mummified hand (all accompanied by lurid descriptions, diagrams and anecdotes), he started muttering under his breath and ended up cursing aloud.

'It is as if the famous London dungeon claimed to be a monument to the pathologist's art!' Musa protested. 'I have never seen such shameless exploitation!'

He turned to Sylvia, who looked utterly nonplussed.

'Have you ever heard of bats' wings being used to ward off a curse? For goodness' sake! Only a *zakulu* has such power! And that hand is not a charm but a curio! As genuine as a papal indulgence! And they sensationalize their explanations of arcane mysteries that no layman could possibly hope to understand. *Eesh kabeesh!* I should have expected such nonsense! The arrogance of American culture is matched only by that of the Brits! The people have a right to know!'

With that, Musa stormed from the building and began to harangue the tourist queues at the entrance, his deep voice booming with no need for a megaphone. Sylvia lurked in the background, her expression lurching between bemused and awestruck, between embarrassment and hilarity.

'Do not darken the door of such an institution!' Musa pronounced to the line of tubby Japanese and florid Germans. 'It is a veritable freak show! Fake enough to make a cubic zirconia look like a precious gem; as disrespectful as a flag burning; as pernicious as the rape of Africa that already darkens your souls (with apologies to you, Japonica jellies)! I can see in your faces that you perceive me as a madman. But listen to what I say for I am a genuine *n'anga, sangoma, sabuku zakulu*. I am Musa! The witchdoctor! From Zambawi!'

Unfortunately Musa's polemicizing had precisely the opposite effect to that he intended. As his voice rose and his gestures expanded, the tourists saw a unique photo opportunity and produced all manner of automatic snappers and hand-held digital camcorders from their knapsacks and bumbags. Musa's face darkened in fury and he began to rant in that archaic Zamba dialect that only the *zakulu* understand (and even they don't understand it too well). But such a display only provoked the tourists into a further bout of snapping and one Japanese couple insisted on being photographed either side of the witchdoctor ('For the sake of Tuloko!' Musa exclaimed), the picture taken by a giggling Sylvia. Worst of all, however, was when the museum's curator appeared at the door (as slimy as the Clapham estate agent, Sylvia thought). At first Musa thought that he had at least ruffled the establishment's feathers. But the curator was all smiles and he congratulated the *zakulu* on drumming up so much business and he vainly tried to offer him a permanent position as Musa strode off up the pavement with Sylvia in hot pursuit.

'Where are you going?' Sylvia called.

'We must meet Jim,' Musa replied over his shoulder. 'How could I have been so stupid? This is clearly not the spot.'

Sylvia finally caught up with him only as they turned into Decatur, for, despite his easy stride, he seemed to walk at the pace of a brisk jog. She tugged at his elbow and Musa span round and his eyes were still wide with irritation.

'A corruption! A corruption of voodoo tradition, which itself corrupts the African beliefs that are as old as the oldest continent! Such liberties! Such arrogance! Like the bastard mixed-race offspring of a bastard child of Africa!'

Musa's face was contorted in contempt and Sylvia was taken aback. His venom stung her very self (whoever that might be).

'You could be talking about me,' Sylvia said quietly.

'You?' Now it was Musa's turn to appear shaken. He grasped Sylvia by the shoulders and his face twisted in the agonies of a new misunderstanding. 'How can you say such a thing? Don't you understand, Sylvia? Have I not explained myself adequately? Even my great-great-great-great-grandfather – that blind fucker who was great only in evil! – would be ashamed of me. Listen. You are the destiny that creeps up behind me like infidelity behind a married man! You are the past that stretches in front of me like the road through the Kaprivi strip! You are the key! You are the untold story! You are as ancient as the Zamba and as young as the present moment! You are the collision of my choices and my fate, my guilt and my redemption!'

Musa was panting heavily as if exhausted by such an admission. Sylvia stared up into his face and she felt the weight of his hands on her shoulders and she did what she'd wanted to do since the first moment she'd seen him. The middle-aged ex-prostitute with her penned eyebrows, false nails and God knows what else besides, raised herself to her painted toe-tips and kissed the dishevelled, dreadlocked *zakulu* with a sincerity she hadn't felt for three decades. She kissed him as she'd once kissed a solemn-faced Jamaican boy while Louis Armstrong sang of all the time in the world. She kissed him as her grandmother'd first kissed her grandfather in some shadowed alleyway no more than twenty miles north (in a small town long since subsumed into the New Orleans sprawl). She kissed him as her very great-grandfather once kissed his one true love by a small water hole in a small country in a big big continent. And she felt? Nothing.

And even as Musa responded (in spite of his better nature), she knew it was a mistake and she put her hands against his chest to push him away. But before she could bring the thought to action, Musa himself broke off with an agonized yelp. He stumbled back from the stunned Sylvia saying, 'For the love of Tuloko!' and he tripped over his heels and landed on his arse with a painful bump.

'My toe!' he cried. 'My fucking toe!'

He pointed at the knackered trainer on his right foot and Sylvia saw a bloodstain expand across the dirty canvas like an ink spot on blotting paper. She tried to help him to his feet but Musa brushed off her attentions.

'Why did you have to kiss me?'

'I . . .' she began. But Musa was already hobbling up the street, muttering a vitriolic cocktail of prayers (addressed mainly to the gods) and opinions (addressed mainly to Sylvia) and curses (addressed to both).

'OK, Cousin Moon! So you have taken my toe. Are you happy now? And I beg your forgiveness for the constant twitching of my divining rod! Who ever heard of a *zakulu* with nine toes? Such a shameful state of affairs. What about you, *machekamadzi*? We must find Jim Tulloh forthwith for destiny will not be derailed so easily. Have you learned nothing in your forty-five years? Never kiss a man unless he loves you or you are so toped that only *gulu gulu* will sober you up. That's the trouble with you prostitutes, no sense of romance!'

Musa now stopped at the entrance to Malone's bar and looked back at his companion. She seemed utterly confused.

'Loves you?' he said. 'Of course he does. I know I have the all-seeing eye (albeit somewhat myopic, since eye problems run in my family) but surely you can't be so blind.'

Sylvia meant to say something but her mouth just opened and closed. Musa tutted and shook his head from side to side.

'That's the trouble with you two; too busy finding and losing yourselves to acknowledge what stands in front of you like a confrontational *gudo*. So what happens? I have to go and lose a toe, that's what. *Eesh!*'

Before Sylvia had time to engage her brain, the *zakulu* had ducked into the bar. She followed.

It took Musa's eyes a moment or two to accustomize to the murky atmosphere. But when they did he was struck dumb, rooted to the spot. It could have been the sight of Jim improvising poor (and abusive) white-boy blues that stopped him in his tracks. But it wasn't. Nor was it the ensuing commotion as Sylvia stormed back out of the bar with her destiny in hot pursuit. Nor was it the painful throb of his missing digit whose wound chafed agonizingly against the pinching material of his shoe. No. Musa was stock-stilled by the sight of the old musician by the name of Fortnightly who watched the comings and goings with a placid seen-it-all expression. And when Jim and Sylvia had stormed out and the rest of the bar – Molly, Chillidog, Tompy and the others – turned their attention back to their drinks, the *zakulu* limped over to the blues man and looked him up and down with eyes that didn't believe what they were seeing. Fortnightly met this curiosity with a gaze as steady as his fret hand.

'You're Fortis Holden Junior,' Musa said quietly and Fortnightly's passive expression didn't flutter for an instant.

'Ain't nobody called me that in a long, long time,' he said.

V: *Squeezing the lemon dry*

(Mount Marter, Louisiana, USA. 1920)

Fortis Holden senior didn't see Sylvie (his sister who wasn't no blood relation) again until 1920 was just about ready to be cut loose. But after that meeting behind the Montmorency Hotel, he knew it was only a matter of time. And he was prepared to wait. After all, he'd waited nine years, for landsakes! He knew that Sylvie would find him because he'd felt it in her kiss like a mother saying good night. And the way Lick had it figured, there'd been a whole lot else in that kiss besides. Why else did he run out of Jones that night at the speed of those negroes who race white boys a buck a time? Why else did his heart beat upon his ribcage with the ferocious intensity of Baby Dodds on drums? Why else did Naps greet him out front of his Cooltown tonk like he'd been waiting there at least an hour?

Naps said, 'You found her?' immediately, before Lick had time to catch his breath. Lick nodded and gulped the air like a greedy shooter with ripe fruit.

'What happened?'

'I guess I won't be playin' with Gage Absalom no more.'

'What happened?'

'Another time,' Lick said.

And that was the answer Lick gave every time Naps asked thereafter (much to his best friend's irritation). 'Another time,' Lick said because he wasn't sure what had happened himself. But he knew that 'another time' was coming as surely as he now played jazz music with his whole goddam body.

It was some time between Christmas and New Year and Toothless Naps's tonk was kind of empty since most folk were still sleeping

335

off heavy food and the sweet wine they saved for special. Besides, this was the time when even pee-eyes and husbands went to church and at least one of these were prone to attacks of the guilts (or at least the attacks of their women).

Lick had celebrated Christmas with Corissa and Bubble at the Canal Street apartment; not that there was a whole lot of celebrating to be done. Bubble had some bad infection on his chest that gave him a hack like tuberculosis. The union surgeon said it came from the dust down at the dockyards but Corissa knew better than to trust no white doctor – a stiff collar whose face smacked of revulsion and contempt – so she asked Ma Cooper to take a look at her man. The old woman packed a poultice of menthol and Lord knows what to Bubble's chest and wrapped him in blankets and told him to sweat it out. That poultice reeked worse than old age and was quite enough to put the whole household off their food (though Bubble barely touched a scrap anyways). Corissa said that Bubble would be better for the New Year and she looked to Lick for confirmation and he gave it. But in his heart Lick knew that Bubble was fading fast and he worried for his sister because, once again, her cheeks were pinching in fear and her hips dropping away.

Naps joined them for their Christmas meal because Big Annie (a real God-fearing churchwoman) didn't want much to do with her pee-eye son who was neck-deep in the mack game and a whole lot else besides. And Naps, with his way with words, surely brought a brief lightness to the occasion. But when Naps left at sunset, Lick accompanied him back to the tonk because he couldn't bear to hear no more of Bubble's retching, nor the smell of the poultice, nor the sight of Corissa worrying herself to an early grave.

As the running buddies mooched back to the tonk with their hands deep in their pockets and their shoulders hunched like two Portuguese, Naps said, 'It's gonna be all right, Lick boy. You hear me?'

'That's what I tells Corissa,' Lick said and he couldn't even bring the grimmest smile to his chops.

336

A couple of nights later and there was nobody in Toothless Naps's but real dope fiends and cleeks. Even the band was kind of decimated since Jig was home with his new wife and Popskull, the clarinettist with a hunger for dime hooch, was down in the Crescent City visiting his momma. But that didn't stop Lick blowing so hard that Ash Hansen (with his sweet trombone) struggled to keep time.

'You *tryin'* to crack my jibs?' he asked between songs, laughing through a mouthful of Vaseline.

But Lick shrugged and didn't reply. Because he was blowing to drown out the sound of Bubble's cough and the future he saw for Corissa that no poultice could do damn for. Most of all, he was blowing for Sylvie and he had to play loud, because who knew where she was? And hadn't she told him, 'I always hear you, Fortis. I always hear you'? Hadn't she told him that?

By 3 a.m. Naps surely wanted to shut up shop for the night. Business was slow – nobody left but drunks and drop kicks – and his girls were yawning and getting catty with each other and robbing alcohol from the bar. But, whatever Naps said, Lick showed no sign of letting up.

'Why you have to get dicty on my ass, Lick boy?' Naps asked. 'You know you my personal fuckin' nigger.'

'You pay me to play till folk go home.'

'An' they don't go home till you stop playin'.'

'T'ain't my problem.'

Lick was playing like a man possessed; the 'real African shit', as Naps liked to call it. He chops were good and supple and the emptiness of the tonk gave the place accoustics he rarely enjoyed. Was it his problem that Naps couldn't hear good music above the silence of the register? Lick played all his favourite joints: recent compositions that slammed the hot style so flavoursome up in Chicago; technical masterpieces that he'd figured out with Dipper Armstrong in idle moments in Henry Ponce's tonk; and desperate blues that had the bugaboo niggers gazing mournfully into their empties. But most of all Lick enjoyed playing those old church songs that reminded him of Momma Lucy, Kayenne and his dead brother and his dead sisters and his sister who was surely to die and his sister who was more alive for him than she'd been for the best part of his twenty-one years.

'Sweet Jesus,
On the far bank of the Jordan,
Sweet Jesus is a-beckonin'
Me.'

Lick played with his eyes tight shut. He played until his head was full of joy and sadness, his chops hummed with anger and sympathy, his heart pumped with love and hate, and his groin ached with lust and revulsion. He took that simple melody and he twisted its hope inside out until it wailed a warning to the faithful from his brass mouth. He upturned its melancholy until the clarity of the minor key sang hope to the desperate. And his brow was sweating buckets and his lungs burst with exertion and his prayer joints shook with emotion until he didn't know where he was or who he was or when he was no more. Lick felt his music transcend his person and he wasn't sure what he felt but he knew that he was more than a disempowered, dislocated, disrespected third-generation slave nigger! Or maybe that's exactly what he was but he claimed such identity as his own!

He held that final top C so long that his lips buzzed like a hornet. He held it so loud that Naps took time out from slapping one of the prostitutes and stood with his mouth gaping like a fool and his peepers pricking sore. He held it so tender that Sylvie, who was standing in the doorway, felt it whisper about her soul like wind in a cave.

When he opened his eyes Lick found Ash Hansen standing in front of him, head bowed, like a priest before a crucifix. Ash slowly shook his head from side to side and then, self-consciously, he reached for Lick's cornet and rubbed his hand over the shining metal like it might give him a touch of the magic to keep for himself.

'Lick Holden!' he exclaimed. 'One day they gonna tell stories about you, man. One day they gonna tell stories about your music.'

Lick laughed. He was embarrassed. 'Nobody tell no stories about no third-generation slave nigger.'

'One day,' Ash said and then he too was embarrassed by the reverence in his tone and he too began to laugh. He could feel unmanly tears of appreciation welling in his eyes and he shyly turned away and swung his gaze around the room.

'Look at that high-yellow boogerlee,' he said, nodding towards the door, just to make conversation. 'Damn! She an ice-cream dream!'

Lick's breath caught in his throat and his fingers depressed every valve on his cornet, a reflex action. 'Sylvie,' he muttered.

He was off the stage in one bound and over to Sylvie in five. But when he reached her, he found that she was looking so nervous and so ladylike (in that white cotton dress and those lace gloves and the clutch purse she cradled in her elbow) that he just didn't know what to do. He wanted to hug her into his chest and swing her off her feet in his arms. But she just seemed so goddam *white* that a respectful handshake and a nod and a 'yessum' felt a lot more appropriate. So Lick just twitched from foot to foot and his bold features formed all kinds of uncertain expressions.

'Fortis,' Sylvie said quietly.

As for her, when she saw Lick approach, her innards knotted tighter than corn rows. It was a real long time since she'd been back in Cooltown and it had taken her two days to muster the courage to visit (while Johnny Frederick spent Christmas with his family on the plantation). Somehow, on his home ground, Lick looked so much bigger than that night outside the Montmorency, and older too and just so goddam *black* that part of her wanted to cling to him like a barnacle and part of her wanted to plain run away. Instead she found she couldn't move while her eyes devoured his person: the easy movements of his long limbs, his heaving chest like a steamship in chop, the exposed patch of blue-black skin at his navel where his crumpled white shirt rucked behind his suspenders. Was this really the same little boy who'd followed her down Canal Street like a dog behind the butcher? Who'd listened to her sing the blues when she'd taken a wupping from Kayenne? Whom she'd called her 'negro servant'?

'Fortis,' Sylvie said again and this time the sound was almost a moan upon her lips and she couldn't help herself but reached her arms around Lick's neck and hung there like a little girl from the white daddy she'd never known. And when Lick pulled her to him and whispered 'Sylvie' in her ear, she was lost in his musk and the touch of his strong fingertips that caressed her back as gently as the elegant curves of a cornet.

They must have stood like that for a minute or two, rocking gently to the sounds of their personal music, before Naps interrupted their embrace.

'Ain't nobody gonna introduce the owner of this establishment?' he said.

Sylvie broke away and stared at the gap-toothed, scar-faced negro who was dressed so spic and span, with his teeth biting on a fat cigar, and her glistening brown eyes widened in surprise.

'Isaiah?' she exclaimed and Naps's face creased into a wide grin.

'Isaiah? Now that's a name I ain't heard in time; not since I was a shooter. These days folk calls me Naps.'

This time it was Sylvie's turn to smile.

'So that nickname stuck, huh? Oddnaps. 'Cos you'd sho' sleep any place when Big Annie was on the war path!'

'Bible name never suit me anyways,' Naps said and he shrugged.

'So I heard.'

'So you's Lick's . . .' Naps began. But Lick caught his eye with a warning that stopped him from forming a sentence and the word 'sister' froze on the pee-eye's lips.

'Sylvie,' Sylvie said.

Naps nodded. 'Sylvie. Way I remember it we used to call you the Queen of Sheba, what with all your airin' and gracin'.'

'Nobody call me that no more. Not since I be workin' up in Jones.'

'So I heard,' Naps said and his smile twisted wickedly. 'Course I could find you work down in Cooltown for sho'. Come and work for Toothless Naps, the man with the masterplan! 'Cos the Queen of Sheba surely still *talk* like us po' niggers!'

'Naps!' Lick exclaimed. But Sylvie was laughing as hearty as the dope-fiend hookers on a hit.

'S'OK, Fortis,' she giggled. 'I knows a compliment when I hears one.'

By now the tonk was emptying for lack of music. Ash Hansen looked quizzically at Lick and then began to pack his trombone away and the rest of the depleted band followed suit. The prostitutes skulked out of the door or blank-faced under the arm of some drunkard or other. The gamblers counted their losses at Georgia skin and cotch and the cleeks heaved deep sighs and swilled their last drop around their teeth and the dope fiends bounded home with the sound of Lick's horn in their step. Naps beckoned them to a table by the bar and he popped a bottle of whisky – not the cheap jick, mind – and poured them each a generous measure. He lifted his glass.

'To reunions!' he announced. ''Cos you two seen each other for the first time since time!'

'But we already seen each other a few months back,' Lick said.

'Then to the future! 'Cos you two ain't never gonna be apart so long again!'

Sylvie lit a cigarette that was almost as long as a drum stick and twice as thin.

'I can't make no promises to the future,' she said and she exhaled blue-grey smoke that dissipated in the air.

'Well, ain't you two a sorry pair?' Naps said.

He tried to laugh but it caught in his throat and they sat for a moment or two in silence until Lick spoke up as confident as an oath.

'To us!' Lick announced. 'Right here, right now. 'Cos any wise nigger tell you he don't know nothin' about the past and he can't make no plans for no future.'

'To us!' Naps agreed, downing his drink with a flourish and a wince.

'To us!' Sylvie whispered and she felt Lick's coal-black eyes burning holes in her pretty cotton dress.

The three of them must have sat there until Old Hannah began to stretch her limbs behind the horizon to the east, jabbering all kinds of chatter about music and dancing and family and such. Naps said how much he missed Storyville since its closing, with its round-the-clock vibe and atmosphere you could bottle and sell (although he'd never actually visited New Orleans, let alone the Tenderloin, in his life). Sylvie said how much she missed her family and the Canal Street apartment (although she'd never made the effort to visit Corissa and had never met her husband Bubble). But, truth be told, Lick didn't join in any and he didn't say nothing because he didn't know no words for what he was feeling, only notes. Instead Lick just stared at his beautiful pale-skinned sister (who wasn't no blood relation) and printed every detail of her sweet self on the ready canvas of his mind's eye. Because he knew she couldn't make no promises to the future.

Eventually, when the first cock cleared his throat for morning, Naps yawned expansively. 'I's going to bed,' he said. But he didn't move.

'I should . . .' Sylvie began. But she had no intention of finishing that sentence; just threw the words high in the air like a shooter playing ball.

'Stay!' Lick said. He hadn't spoken for so long that his voice came rasping and over-eager. 'Stay! I gots a room out back. Ain't much but the bed sho' is comfortable.'

'For sho',' Sylvie said and she blinked as slowly as dreaming.

342

Lick stood up then and he offered her his hand and she wound her delicate fingers through his own and he led her from that smoky tonk. And as he watched them leave, Naps sparked his cigar and tried to ignore the pain in his middle that was for the past and the future and for the right here and right now. He knew there were surely all kinds of reasons for that pain. But he had no desire to confront none of them.

That first time, Sylvie stayed at Toothless Naps's tonk for a whole five days and she and Lick barely surfaced from his rooms and they squeezed the lemon so dry that walking came kind of awkward for both of them and their eyes were misted with the sharpness of it all. Sylvie only left for her apartment in Jones when 1921 began to cry for its momma and she had to wrench herself free from Lick's grasp and planted a kiss that was tender and firm all at once on his bristling black cheek (because he'd had no time for shaving).

'We been together two years, Fortis.'

'We been together *in* two years,' Lick corrected her. '1920 and '21.'

'We been together a lifetime and you knows it.'

'Why you gots to go?'

'Johnny Frederick back any day now an' you know I gotta be there when he calls.'

Lick winced. He hated to think of that no-good pink sharing any kind of affection with his . . . his what?

'Besides,' Sylvie continued, 'what you want me to do? Share your rooms out back of a low-down tonk? I got dreams, Fortis, an' plans big enough for two. An' anyways, nobody leave them white boys but a woman who likes the sting of a whip or worse. 'Cos you know they take it kinda personal.'

'But you my woman now,' Lick said. And he ducked his head when he saw the darkness cross Sylvie's face. Because she had a black woman's temper and a white woman's tongue, a lethal combination!

'I ain't nobody's woman,' Sylvie spat. 'An' what you gonna do when them good-time boys come lookin' for you? Blow your sweet horn at them? You know you my destiny, Fortis Holden. But destiny don't make no promises an' if that ain't enough for you, then you sho' don't love me like I thought!'

With that Sylvie Black strode out on to Canal Street and left Lick's heart squirming like a mongoose in a sack. And for the next three weeks, until she returned, Lick's blues took on a spiciness that had even the hookers (for whom tears were surely a luxury) weeping for a love they'd never known. And Lick hit the tonk's good whisky so hard that Naps began to pass him the cheap jick and he was too damn melancholy to notice. But, truth be told, the next four years – sure it must've been about that time – were the closest that Lick Holden ever came to happiness (outside of his music anyways).

It didn't take long for Lick and Sylvie's relationship to slip into some kind of pattern. It wasn't no pattern that could be described as 'typical' but it worked well enough for them.

Lucky for Sylvie that Johnny Frederick wasn't one of those white boys who treated the *plaçage* apartments like a second home. No. Johnny was one of those shame-faced daddies who, most times, liked to be in and out of Sylvie's apartment in under an hour (and that included time for talking and maybe even a hot coffee). So, generally speaking, even if he'd taken Sylvie dancing and shown her off on his arm, she'd be on her own by 2 a.m. (even earlier if she could bring herself to really turn it on for him). Of course, sometimes Johnny would be so drunk and so spent that he'd fall asleep on her bed, flat on his face like a dead man in the Mississippi. But you can bet Sylvie learned a few tricks to keep Johnny awake. A caress here, a pinch there and a gentle nudging towards the door that made him feel like he was leaving of his own accord.

Then Sylvie would take a bath. And what an operation that was! She'd be in and out of that tub in ten minutes but it was surely a painful experience. She wet herself all over, soaped up and then scrubbed herself raw with the rough stone meant only for feet. Sometimes she even drew blood because she couldn't bear to have one drop of Johnny's fetid funk on her body! Sylvie dressed in a hurry – real pretty for her brother (who wasn't no blood relation) – and she headed down to Toothless Naps's tonk for, say, 3 a.m.

In the first months of this arrangement, Sylvie liked to make straight for one of the tables at the back of the joint, furthest from the small stage, and she'd sit on her own or with Naps and drink some alcohol and allow her life in Jones to be carried away on Lick's music. How she loved to listen to her man play! His tone was the same as their sex, passionate and tender and clean and dirty and happy and goddam tragic all at once! And Sylvie sat with her drink for the two hours until Lick finished and, by the time he came over to her table, she almost felt herself again (whoever that might be). Naps used to call this her 'blackanized time', the time when she'd be blackanized by a real negro environment. Because Naps had a way with words.

Lick and Sylvie retired to bed around half past five every night and they made love until the heat of the mid-morning sun had them both panting and coming up for air. But they still wouldn't go to sleep. Sylvie wound herself around Lick's wholesome body like a creeper and she nestled her head in his neck and they discussed their favourite dreams.

'We's goin' to Chicago,' Lick said. 'I goin' to make a stack of money with King Oliver or some other crackerjack band an' then we buy some land an' raise a real happy family of our own.'

'How many kids?'

'At least four,' he said definitely. 'Named for Jacob, Lucy, Sister and Ruby Lee.'

'An' they be all colours of the rainbow.'

Lick laughed. 'An' they all be negroes.'

'What about me, Fortis? What if folk take me for a white lady?'

'A white lady? Folk see you with a blue-black negro like me an' a bunch of negro kids an' they sho' you a nigger like the rest of us. Damn straight!'

And Sylvie felt reassured by such a thought.

Some time around the middle of 1921, Lick was woken by Sylvie singing in the bath. It was a sound that eased him out of slumber like an old-timer helped from a rocker. Surely he hadn't forgotten how good she sounded? He lay back with his hands behind his head and he listened as silent as prayer for close on two hours. Even when Sylvie got out of the tub, she kept singing as she oiled her body and slipped into one of Lick's baggy shirts that she liked to wear for the scent. Even when she busied herself around the bedroom, Lick half-closed his eyes and pretended to sleep so that he could take his turn to bathe in the lather of her voice, so rich and smooth and soft and sensual. He listened to her sing and he felt the hot sun through his one window rise from his toes to his groin as it lifted to its midday zenith. Eventually Sylvie was silent and Lick opened his eyes and he found her standing above the bed looking down at him with an expression sweet enough to make him hungry.

'Sylvie,' he said slowly. 'You gotta sing with the band.'

She smiled and shook her head lazily from side to side until Lick was sure she'd turn him down. But instead she said, 'I wondered how long it take you to ask.'

Now before Sylvie Black joined Lick Holden's band they were a run-of-the-mill Louisiana outfit that just happened to boast a top-notch trombone and a lost genius on horn. Real jazz heads certainly came from New Orleans to hear Lick play but the majority of business was still the flotsam and jetsam of urban life. But when Sylvie's voice, like a fallen angel, was thrown into the mix? Well! The reputation of the orchestra at Toothless Naps's tonk spread around the state like wildfire and the joint was packed to busting every night. When Sylvie took the stage there was a barely controlled sense of expectancy and when she hit her first note the men began to holler all kinds of praise and lust and such, like they were in the last throes of straining their greens. 'Sweet honey! She so good!' and 'Work it, baby!' and 'Sing it loud, momma!' and other nonsense like that. Because if Lick played his horn with four parts of his body

346

then, in the main, Sylvie sang with only one part of hers, and there still isn't no decent word for it.

But if Sylvie became known for the guttural rasp of her hot numbers, then that tells more about men than it does about her singing. Because Sylvie could also sing a style of blues (with only Lick's horn for accompaniment) that told the American negro experience more truthfully than any so-called 'black history' and she sang love songs that had pimps come over romantic, and melancholy laments – 'the real African shit', as Naps used to say – that had folk remembering a time they'd never known.

Of course Lick Holden's band played a few of the day's standards to please the crowd; but the majority of their songs were their own compositions (Lick and Sylvie's), which flowed on the hot mornings after sex as naturally as breathing. And some of these songs – like the 'Quatrain Blues', for example – are now standards of their own. But you can be sure that there isn't no credit given to Fortis Holden nor Sylvie Black.

'My grandma was a negro,
My grandpappy, he was white,
My pappy was a white man too,
No shakes that I's so light.'

One time, after his chops were blown out for the night, Lick was beckoned to a group of good-time boys who'd taken a table in the furthest corner of the tonk. Generally it was a gambling table, out of the way of the dancing and bustle, where steam men lost their earnings to nimble-fingered experts with 'Who, me?' faces, but not when small-eyed white folk decided that was their chosen position for the night. No, sir! Now Lick knew most of Toothless Naps's white clientele by name and the rest by sight and he was used to passing the time of day with them and pulling house-nigger expressions when required. But Lick hadn't never seen this bunch before and there was something in their manner that made his fingers clench and flex.

'You want a drink, boy?' one asked; he was a skinny blond kid with pallid eyes and crooked teeth that protruded when he spoke.

'For sho',' Lick said and he shrugged. He was playing it cool. Nobody called him 'boy' these days; leastways not in a negro honkytonk in a negro part of Mount Marter. But Lick surely had no taste for no white folk trouble.

Crooked teeth poured Lick a tumbler of whisky and shoved it across the table. 'Take a seat.'

'Thank you, sir.'

Lick sat down. One of the other kids – a real fat fucker, Lick thought – was giggling nervously, like he hadn't never shared a table with no nigger before.

'Lick? That what they call you? Lick?'

'Yessir.'

'You play that horn real pretty and the girl sho' can sing.'

Lick nodded and took a deep draft of the whisky. He was damned if he was going to waste a free drink from these fool-ass pinks!

'An' that top note,' the man continued. 'Damn, boy! How you hit that top note so hard? You got magic in those big negro jibs of yours?'

Jibs? Lick almost laughed aloud because there wasn't nothing so funny as a white boy trying to talk jive! But instead he bit his lip and gave his pat reply. ''Cos I fed on powerful stuff as a shooter, sir. Made my lungs powerful strong.'

'What were you eating?'

'Cheese,' Lick said and he enjoyed the confused expressions as much as ever.

After a moment or two, Crooked Teeth said, 'Well, you'd better keep eating that cheese, boy.' And Lick said 'Yessir' and stood up from the table because he recognized the dismissal.

'Thanks for the drink.'

'No problem,' the kid said and he smiled wide enough to show his crooked teeth to worst effect. Lick smiled too and he turned away and walked back towards Sylvie at the bar and his breathing came easy because that confrontation wasn't nearly so bad as he'd expected.

As Lick walked away, the fat giggler caught the kid with crooked teeth by the arm and pointed across the tonk. His companion raised his eyebrows but he didn't make no effort to lean forward and the giggler had to raise his voice above the arguments and laughter and clatter and chatter.

'Henry! Don't that singer look like Johnny Frederick's quadroon?' he shouted and Henry with the crooked teeth narrowed his eyes.

But Lick had reached the bar and he was way out of earshot.

V: *The last time*

(Mount Marter, Louisiana, USA. 1924)

Truth be told, it was September 1924 before things began to get complicated in one of those surprising collisions of moment that come about real sudden and bear all the hallmarks of fate's clumsiest intervention. And it started with Bubble's death.

Corissa's husband had been sick for the majority of four years and he hadn't worked in all that time, just faded slowly away until he couldn't do nothing for himself and there was nothing that Ma Cooper or no white doctor could do about it. At first the sickness in his lungs took grip until his breathing came like a train rattling through a tunnel. Soon he struggled to climb the stairs to the Canal Street apartment (let alone lift a heavy bale on to a pallet). Then came the apoplexy, when Corissa found him fallen from his chair with eyes like two mirrors and saliva frothing from his mouth. And after that she had to bathe him like a baby and she fed him smooth porridge with a spoon. But still Corissa wouldn't admit no reality.

She confided in Lick. 'Taking longer than I hoped but he'll be back at work for Easter,' she'd say. Or 'back at work for cotton'. Or 'back at work for Christmas'. But Lick knew that Bubble wasn't going back to no place but the house of the God that made him. Of course Lick, who made better money than most at Toothless Naps's, ensured that his sister never went short. But money didn't improve the situation any better than dime hooch quenches a thirst.

Fact was that Corissa simply couldn't handle Bubble's decline. This was the little girl who'd been beaten by all manner of no-good pimps and johns as she clung to her momma's skirts. This was the girl who'd lain on the bed and not eaten a morsel of food for two weeks after Kayenne died. This was the girl with no appetite for the harsh truths of life in Mount Marter (and a black woman in particular needed a strong stomach for such a fight). And Bubble may have been a sickly dock worker with a brain so slow folk said he lived in a bubble, but he was Corissa's husband and he treated her like a lady and she loved him as well as any man ever was.

When Bubble finally let go, Lick worried for his sister. She'd already been dropping weight for a long time and now she looked like she was about ready to let go too. He sat up with her the night of Bubble's passing and she didn't speak a word. Occasionally he made soothing noises and he said things like 'He in a better place, for sho''. But Lick didn't sound very convincing and, truth was, he wasn't very convinced. When he looked at his sister's face, taut and drawn like a shirt for pressing, he didn't see no evidence of God's presence. And as for paradise? You really think they'd let a nigger into a high-class establishment like that? Way Lick saw it, the only negroes would be playing in the band and they'd get in by the service entrance!

Corissa was but twenty-nine years old and she looked just about as tired of life as a person could be.

The next night Lick told Sylvie of Bubble's death as soon as she arrived at Toothless Naps's. Sylvie had never met Bubble (matter of fact, she hadn't seen Corissa for near on ten years) but she shook her head slowly and heaved a deep sigh and said, 'I'm real sorry to hear that, Fortis. Real sorry.'

'Corissa in deep trouble for sho',' Lick said. 'Maybe you go visit her. What you think? We all the family she got now.'

'I'm real sorry,' she said again and, for all the right noises, Lick knew that her mind was elsewhere.

'It sho' is sad,' he said and he bent his head and tried to look Sylvie in the face. But she wouldn't meet his eye. 'Course you don't have to sing tonight if you don't wanna.'

Sylvie looked up sharply and her reply came hard and fast. 'Why I not gonna sing?'

'It's a sad time.'

'So you think I not gonna sing? Damn, Fortis! Course I gonna sing. I gonna sing so hard an' so hot that you think I the happiest African outside of Africa an' you know why? 'Cos I's a nigger jus' like you. An' we sing when we's happy an' we sing when we's sad 'cos tha's all us po' fuckin' niggers can do!'

There was a pause. Lick didn't know what to say so he returned to his original tack: 'You gonna see Corissa?'

'Why?' Sylvie said and she turned away as if her attention had been caught by something unmissable.

'We her family.'

'So what?'

'So we all she got.'

'She ain't *got* me,' Sylvie said and Lick noticed that her lip was quivering. But he was beginning to feel so angry himself (or confused anyways) that he didn't much care.

'She ain't *my* family, Fortis,' Sylvie continued. And now her voice was as soft as shame. 'Not blood-wise. We jus' brought up by the same po' woman who died before her time with a bunch of other shooters who mostly already dirt-nappin' before theirs. What you want me to do? You think I can provide a little comfort for Corissa? Damn! You think that an' you a fuckin' jigaboo nigger to your boots! There ain't no comfort for no black folk in this shit-hole town. We got . . .' she paused. She took a deep breath. '*I* got enough problems of my own, Fortis. I got problems for two.'

'But I love you!' Lick said with a voice that sounded a whole lot more irritable than loving.

'An' I love you too,' Sylvie whispered. 'An' that's the point.'

She looked at him then, straight in the face with firing eyes that he didn't understand, and she stalked off to the bar, where she downed a shot of whisky to make her nostrils flare. Lick had never heard his sister (who wasn't no blood relation) speak like that and he was shocked to hear cuss words fall so easy from her tongue. As Naps had said, the Queen of Sheba who looked down on all her brothers and sisters (to the point of denial) surely still talked like a nigger.

In the week leading up to the funeral, they didn't discuss Corissa again. Fact was that Sylvie seemed just about as cold as winter wind and Lick was so damn pissed that he wasn't sure what he might say if his mouth got started. During that week, Sylvie stayed at the tonk four nights out of seven (which was just about average). But they didn't make love. Lick tried a couple of times but Sylvie just turned her back and whispered into her pillow, 'I's not in the mood.' And Lick knew hisself that there was a gap between them that he couldn't figure and he knew hisself that sex wouldn't help any. But since when did that ever stop a red-blooded man from trying?

In fact, the preparations for the funeral gave Corissa a sense of focus that kept the dark shadows temporarily at bay. She made pots of coffee for the reverend and planned the service just right; she cooked a stack of food thanks to the generosity of her neighbours; she accepted Naps's offer (at Big Annie's prompting) of the tonk as a receiving venue for the mourners; and she sent word to the few folk down in New Orleans who might want to attend (and, unknown to Lick, to one couple in Chicago too).

Corissa asked Lick if Sylvie would be coming and Lick was taken aback.

'What do I know about Sylvie?' he asked, all innocent-like, and his sister looked at him with a sharp intelligence he'd never seen on her face before.

'A lot more than you's sayin', that's for sho',' Corissa said and she smiled a weak smile that conveyed nothing but deep sadness. 'You livin' in a small town, Lick, and don't you forget it. Jus' 'cos I's a married woman – a widow now – don't mean I don't know what been goin' on down in Naps's tonk ever since my husband got sick.'

'What you mean?'

'I hears things, Lick! I know that Sylvie been singin' with your band; course I do.' Corissa's eyes blinked sleepily. 'An' else besides, I shouldn't wonder.'

Lick tried to say something but he couldn't think of no useful words. Corissa wasn't finished in any case.

'T'ain't none of my business, brother-mine,' she said. 'I ain't your momma an' I ain't much of a sister (four years older or not) an' I knows you watch out for me 'fore you even watch out for yourself. But I hope you don't forget the way Sylvie looked down on us dark-skinned negroes when we were shooters in this very apartment. I hope you remember that.'

Lick didn't reply. He just looked at his boots.

'So, brother-mine, you think Sylvie gonna come to Bubble's funeral?'

'I guess not,' Lick said.

'An' that's what I figured.'

The day of the funeral itself was a strange one, no doubt. The weather had a brooding feel to it, like it might just be building to some kind of spectacular cataclysm, like if the world ended on such a day nobody would be so surprised. At sun-up the sky was pallid and the light eerie; wind whistled down alleyways and screamed up the streets. It span eddies of leaves and tugged at oversized black hats with elaborate beading and lace and veils and such. Later the high clouds collapsed and pressed in upon Mount Marter, swirling like the water pot of a clerk cleaning his nib. By the time the mourners began to file into the church, raindrops spat in the dust like bullets and the children made their mothers stumble as they clung to their legs and the men ignored their women's complaints and buried their hands deep in their pockets.

Lick stood in the doorway next to Corissa and he shook folk by the hand and said, 'Your consolation is appreciated.' Some of the men looked to the sky and shook their heads and Lick nodded agreement, saying, 'Sho' God shows his sympathies too.' When women asked, 'An' how your sister holdin' up?', Lick shrugged his shoulders and said, 'We's copin'. Thank you for your kindness.' Then he looked at Corissa and he knew he was telling lies for sure. She was dressed immaculately in polished shoes and a pretty black shawl (many sizes too large) that she'd borrowed from Big Annie. But she seemed as small as a shooter girl with her thin, hunched back and Lick figured that if he hugged her into his broad chest he'd most likely break her in two. Only when she turned her head did you get a real conception of Corissa's plight; her face was already as tired as an old widow who's waiting for the grave.

So many folk showed up to Bubble's funeral (because funerals were always an 'occasion' in Cooltown) that Lick must have shaken at least a hundred hands. There was folk he knew, folk he'd known and folk he swore he'd never seen before. Even Toothless Naps's was represented by more than just the proprietor himself. Jig (who was friend to everyone) arrived with his chin on his chest and his eyes ready to burst. Ash Hansen accompanied him and he fingered the brim of his smart hat nervously and he squirmed against the starch of his suit. Popskull came too but he was, of course, already so slooped that Lick had to lead him away from the church and park the stumbling clarinettist under the cover of a nearby tree. There were round-the-way folk and dock workers and Bubble's sour-faced sister from New Orleans who'd already been sniffing around for money where there was none; like a dog around a cooking pot that's already been licked clean.

You couldn't say Bubble was a popular man. But he was a good man, no doubt, and folk respected such a simple fact. Because, generally speaking, life in Cooltown was too hard to leave a whole lot of room for goodness.

Just before the service was due to start, an automobile – a dilapidated Ford with rusty wheel arches and an ill-fitting side panel – pulled up outside the church pursued by the usual throng of shooters yelping and giggling. Out of it stepped a tall middle-aged negro in a black frock-coat and half-moon spectacles. His woman appeared from the other side, a handsome-looking lady with a proud neck and chin and kind eyes that reminded Lick of his mother. Corissa hurried towards these late arrivals through the quickening rain that was beginning to puddle on the church path and she greeted the woman like family, throwing her arms around her neck and unable to suppress her sobbing. Lick was astonished. He'd never seen no negro driving an automobile before; leastways not without a white man pecking his ear from the back seat.

As the newcomers approached the church, Lick saw the elegant lady's face widen in recognition and she lifted a hand to cover her gaping mouth. Then she spread her arms wide towards him and he began to feel a little embarrassed.

'Fortis Holden?' she said. 'You Fortis Holden?'

'For sho'. Do I . . .'

'What? You don't have no hug for your sister?'

Lick stared at her for a second and then he said, 'Sina?' and the woman nodded, touched by the apparent recognition, and she pulled him towards her and held him for so long that he had to manoeuvre her into the church porch from out of the rain. He hadn't actually recognized his sister from Chicago at all. After all, she'd left Mount Marter near twenty years before and he hadn't peeped her since. But, with most of Kayenne's kids dead, it wasn't so hard to hit upon her name.

'This my husband,' Thomasina was saying. 'The Reverend Isaiah Pink, pastor of the Apostolic Church of All Saints, one of the largest black churches in the whole of Chicago.'

'I sho' pleased to meet you,' Lick said and offered the older man his hand. The Reverend Pink accepted it and shook it curtly.

'Likewise,' he said and his voice showed no sign of meaning it.

The service itself was a disaster. Afterwards Lick could remember little about it but the furious weather and the look of resignation on Corissa's face as she sat nestling into Sina's shoulder. The reverend, an ineffectual little man with the inappropriate name of Strong, was clearly threatened by the presence of another preacher (and such a proud-looking one at that!) and his words were stuttered out with the clarity of a straining steam engine. And he surely wasn't helped by the storm that broke over the church with the first notes of the opening hymn. Lick had just raised his cornet to his chops when the thunder cracked and the whole congregation visibly shook in their seats. Thereafter, the entire service was conducted above the insistent rhythm of a downpour on the corrugated roof. And folk looked at one another just as dolefully as could be.

Afterwards, the intention had been to lead the procession down to the docks as always and Lick fancied that maybe Sylvie would show up there as she had for Kayenne's funeral. But who was going to march in such rain that softened you up for the wind to cut you in two? As Naps said later, 'Negroes got enough trouble in their lives without fighting God's own nature.' So instead they headed straight down to the tonk, where Big Annie and Lil' Annie dished out generous helpings of soul food to all the guests and a number of 'sooners' besides (who knew that nobody would complain or be disrespectful at a funeral, for landsakes!).

Lick was quickly taken up talking to Sina, who was soon asking him questions he didn't feel too comfortable to answer. And truth was, he didn't figure he owed no explanations to a sister who'd returned after twenty years with her Jim Crow attitude, respectable husband and bragging of the big-city life. Worst of all, she chastised him for his life in the tonk as 'ungodly' and 'disrespectful'. Like she'd heard him play! The horn was his prayer voice and there was more God in his music than in no handshake from her husband, that was for sure! And at least his music respected his people more than some preacher's wife who 'yessum'd' to a white-folk sense of propriety!

Eventually Lick – generous-hearted soul that he was – got so dicty that he snuck away to his room with Naps and complained to his jig and they damaged a bottle of jick until folk went home.

'Way I see it, Lick boy,' Naps said, 'if you ashamed to be a negro, then you a dumb nigger, no doubt. An' if you proud to be a negro, then you a dumb nigger too. Me? I's jus' a negro an' I ain't gonna brag about it an' I ain't gonna apologize neither.'

'What about me, Naps?'

'You?' Naps drank long and hard and then started to laugh so hard that he spluttered the jick over his shirt and out of his nose. 'How many times I gotta tell you, Lick boy? You my own personal fuckin' nigger!' He got to his feet, inebriated, and stumbled over to where Lick was sitting. He gripped his hands to the back of his head and bent down until they were eye to eye. Naps was struggling to focus and he pushed his forehead against Lick's. 'My personal fuckin' nigger,' Naps whispered and he held Lick there for a moment before backing away, laughing and weaving his way towards the door. 'I's goin' to bed.'

Left on his own with nothing but alcohol for company, Lick tried some straight-thinking. He tried thinking about Corissa as he feared for her future. He tried thinking about Thomasina and her uppity husband and those images of a big city like Chicago where King Oliver – wasn't he almost an acquaintance? – had his band. He tried thinking about Sylvie who he loved like music, but didn't she have some attitude that he couldn't figure? But Lick couldn't straight-think about anything because that jick spirit addled his brain better than the scent of a fine whore, and it took all his effort just to undress himself to sleep. Thing was, those three subjects – Corissa, Sina and Sylvie – surely merited some kind of analysis, but their questions were answered the next day anyways and, when all's said and done, Lick needed sleep a whole lot more than destiny needed a cornet player's explanations. Even if he was, leastways for argument's sake, the greatest damn horn man that was ever lost to history.

Now there's a saying down in Lousiana that 'a man supports his woman from on top' and it's a flexible kind of truth that can mean just about anything you choose. But one interpretation sets out why nobody but Lick was surprised when Corissa was found dead in the Canal Street apartment the very next morning. When Bubble was carried away from Corissa's deceptively strong shoulders, the weightlessness of his departure crushed her like a beetle beneath a shooter's thoughtless foot.

Naps woke Lick with the news when Old Hannah was high in

the sky and the day was already half gone. But Lick, whose head throbbed like the chorus of crickets on a balmy night, didn't wait to listen. He sprinted out of the tonk and up Canal Street and he three-timed the steps like a man possessed. Corissa was lain on Kayenne's old bed with Big Annie and Ma Cooper standing over (the Reverend and Mrs Pink were already gone to Chicago). Lick was out of breath. His big heart strained and his ears popped and he didn't even hear their words of sympathy. Lick had seen death and plenty of it; more than any young man has reason to expect. But Corissa's passing hit him harder than any. For hadn't they lived almost like husband and wife on his release from the Double M? Lick remembered what he'd said to Professor Hoop one day as they stood opposite Echo Hill: 'God put me 'pon this earth to care for Momma Lucy, Kayenne and my sisters.' And now Momma Lucy, Kayenne and all his sisters (excepting Sina and Sylvie) were dead. And worst of all, Corissa – the only sister he'd ever had the chance to really look after any – was dead too.

Lick stumbled from the apartment as numb as a bantam girl sent for a scrap of coal in winter and he didn't hear Big Annie speaking to Ma Cooper. 'That family sho' so unlucky they make the rest of us negroes feel like God's own people,' she said. And this was the woman who once said Lick 'sho' lucky to be alive'.

Sylvie was waiting for Lick when he returned to Toothless Naps's. But he wasn't surprised to see her any despite the fact that she was generally in Jones around the middle part of the day. She looked, he thought, kind of sad and he wondered if she'd already heard about Corissa herself. He opened his arms wide to pull her into his chest but Sylvie wouldn't come and wasn't that typical of her recent attitude? She just shifted from foot to foot and inverted her lips like she was embarrassed.

'You heard about Corissa?' Lick said.

Sylvie shook her head.

'She dead.'

Sylvie didn't seem surprised and she couldn't even feign sorrow.

She just kept sucking on those lips of hers like a kid with a comforter. He stared at her. He saw now, with some surprise, that Naps was standing behind her and his expression was just as awkward-like. Lick hadn't noticed him there before.

'Yo, Naps,' Lick said. 'Any way you fix me a drink?'

'Sho', Lick boy. But Sylvie got somethin' to tell you.'

'Yeah?' He raised his eyebrows at Sylvie and she was just about to open her mouth. But Lick was suddenly distracted by another thought. 'Ain't nothin' to keep me in Cooltown no more. Damn! Ain't nothin' to keep me in this whole goddam state, Sylvie. Nothin' but you.'

There was a pause that weighed just as heavy as Lick's heart, like the counterbalance to one of those winches at the docks. Sylvie licked her lips and she made fists of her hands to try and moisten them a little. Her throat was so dry it felt like there might be a spider playing there.

'Fortis,' she said. 'I's pregnant.'

He was silent, like maybe he didn't even speak English no more.

'It's definitely yours, Fortis,' Sylvie continued quickly. ''Cos you know that white boy ain't never gonna have no kids. 'Sides, it musta been two months ago when Johnny was outta town.'

Lick shook his head like he was trying to judder some sense back into it. The news surely explained why Sylvie been acting so peculiar!

'Well,' he said finally. 'Now we's definitely leavin' this shit-hole town, Sylvie! 'Cos no child of mine gonna be brought up as no Cooltown nigger like his father, an' that's the truth!'

Lord alone knows how Sylvie figured Lick might respond to the news of impending fatherhood, but she certainly didn't get the reaction she expected. She was smart enough to know that bringing another negro child into the Louisiana mix was a burden at the best of times. And her situation with Johnny Frederick? It surely meant nothing but trouble. But she knew that Lick was one surprising smokestack! Like the support he gave to the family from the age of seven with his work on Old Man Stekel's ice cart; like the time she'd heard him blow at Kayenne's funeral; like the way he'd touched her on their first night together, just as firm and just as gentle as the matinee idols in the New Orleans picture house. And now? Now Lick surprised her better than ever before.

Lick took in her news with a maturity that Sylvie didn't generally associate with men. He sat her down that afternoon in the tonk and they made a plan of action that gave her a buzz of excitement and a confident glow. The main thing, they agreed, was to ensure Sylvie was as far away from Cooltown as quickly as possible. Who could tell how Johnny Frederick would react when he found 'his girl' had gone missing? But you could guarantee it would sure be ugly.

Sylvie was to return to the *plaçage* apartment that evening and pick up her meagre savings and pack a few clothes. If Johnny came round, she'd plead the curse, and she'd try to be back in the tonk to spend one last night with her man. Then she'd be on the first train to the Crescent City in the morning and straight on to Chicago and her sister Sina.

Sylvie didn't like this part of the plan. She hadn't seen her sister for so long *and* she was married to a preacher *and* Sylvie dreamed of New York, which folk said was now the capital of hot jazz. But Lick had to stay in Cooltown to fix arrangements for Corissa's funeral and he didn't want Sylvie to be in the East Coast metropolis on her own. Of course, New York *was* the final destination. So he arranged to meet her at Grand Central Station, beneath the clock tower, at midday in one month's time. Or the day after that or the day after that or as soon as he could make it.

Sylvie returned to the *plaçage* apartments in Jones and she was in luck. By 9 p.m., there was still no sign of Johnny. In fact, there was no sign of anybody much except the ditzy girl Sweet Elly who could have passed if she chose. She banged on Sylvie's door and entered without waiting for an answer. Sylvie pushed her half-packed case under the bed, like a shooter caught with a finger in the cake mix.

'What you doin', Sylvie? I ain't seen you for days an' days an' days!'

'Nothin'. I jus' sortin' a few things.'

'You goin' somewhere?'

Sylvie stared at Sweet Elly – a jaw-blocking jasper if ever there was one! – and she couldn't help herself. She was just so excited that she had to tell somebody because she felt fit to bust.

'I's leavin',' Sylvie said. 'I's goin' east, outta this shit-hole town! Way out!'

Sweet Elly was dumbstruck. She didn't know what to say. Way she saw it, how could Sylvie want to leave Jones and her arrangement with a white 'boyfriend' like Johnny Frederick? More to the point, how could she leave such a stack of the prettiest clothing you ever did see?

'What 'bout your dresses, Sylvie?'

'It his money, honey!'

'An' that's the truth, Ruth! Can I look through?'

'Help your sweet self. Anythin' you's wantin'.'

'You's bad, Sylvie!' Elly whispered. 'What you gonna tell Johnny?'

Sylvie frowned. 'I ain't gonna tell him nothin' and neither is you. I's leavin' town with Fortis an' that's that; an' it's a secret between you and me and Jesus. OK?'

'Who's Fortis?'

'My man,' Sylvie said. And she realized she'd never said that before and she liked the way it sounded.

'You can trust me,' Sweet Elly said and Sylvie wondered whether she'd come to regret her confidence any. Of course she never did. But then she never knew the facts.

The last time Sylvie walked back into Cooltown, down the back alleys so's to avoid being seen, didn't she appreciate the smell of Mount Marter? A good honest smell of hard work and hard lives. The only other place Sylvie had ever been at that time was New Orleans. And these days, of course, that old rambling city has gobbled up its smaller neighbour like one of those greedy kids that eats half the menu at some fast-food joint or other. Lord alone knows what stands over those back alleyways now. Probably warehouses or shopping malls or perhaps even the expressway.

The last time Sylvie Black sang with her brother (who wasn't no blood relation) . . . Well! Imagine how it must have sounded! This was a woman who went on to grace Fletcher Henderson's orchestra (at least once anyways) with a voice as sweet and as soothing as honey in hot lemon. And how she would have hit the notes that night! With a future stretching out in front of her like a path to the promised land: a path out of Jones, a path out of prostitution, a path that led all the way to New York. Perhaps it's possible to picture her looking at Fortis with his big heart pump-pump-pumping in his chest and his strong hands caressing that cornet and his honest eyes wide with the exertion of it all. Best guess is she felt a happy pin-prick to her eye and maybe that blurred her vision to the go-wrongs fate surely had in store.

The last time Fortis Holden played with his sister (who wasn't no blood relation), how he must have blown so loud that his past stuck its fingers in its ears like a grandpops and his future wailed like a baby picking up on a mood! This was a man who once played with Louis Armstrong (for a month anyways) with a horn that told a story that has never been heard since. There's no doubt that Lick blew that night with a joyful head, a sympathetic mouth, a loving heart and a lustful groin. But it's hard not to wonder whether there wasn't no foreboding hidden in those emotions somewhere, like a runaway slave in the bayou shallows.

The last time Lick and Sylvie made love is surely a private affair and that's the way it should be. But can anyone resist a little prurience, if only in the mind's eye? Fact is that folks' bodies – their limbs that entwine and their lips that meet with insistence – sometimes speak a language of unknowns that words can never match and minds never acknowledge. So imagine that couple (and the little one growing in Sylvie's belly), a family in waiting who deserved gentle destiny more than can be said of most. When lovers know they won't see each other a stretch, they tend to squeeze the lemon dry like it will be the last time. And then one day it is. Because fate is surely a restless suitor who won't be distracted when he's got his eye on the main story.

And nobody can do anything about that.

I: *Her past sneaked right up in front of her*

(New Orleans, Louisiana, USA. 1998)

The old man was certainly fond of digression. That's what Sylvia figured.

'Y'all don't know me,' he was saying and his voice was kind of defensive. 'Y'all don't know nothin' 'bout me 'cept I'm the one gonna finish this story and you 'spect it to sound as clear as the music from this ol' horn.'

Get on with it! Sylvia thought. But she wasn't angry, just as tired as she could remember. She stared fondly at Fortnightly – what was he? Her step-uncle or some such (about as related as that pervert great-uncle Fabrizio). But she loved the way he fingered her grand-father's cornet, like the old brass might give him a touch of inspir-ation. She loved the way he told Lick's story, like it had been waiting to burst out of him for more than half a century. She loved the way he spoke, engaging her eyes, or Jim's, or Musa's, to ensure they were listening. And he could talk, all right! And now she was tired.

The story had been going on for most of two days and it was her fault. Because she could have accepted 'Your grandfather was Lick Holden (an unknown jazz musician). Your grandmother was Sylvie Black (a prostitute and sometime singer – doesn't that sound familiar?).' She could have left it at that. But names or backgrounds or races were never going to give Sylvia (named for her grandmother, who swapped the 'e' for an 'a' because it sounded more Italian to her ear) the sense of identity she craved. Because only the whole story would tell who she was and she needed to know everything. How else was she to make sense of it?

In any case, she wasn't tired from listening. She was tired because of the feeling in her gut that was growing with every passing hour.

Despite her best hopes, she sensed an anticlimax around the corner as certain as London's February rain. But how could it be an anticlimax if she saw it coming? And it wasn't like her feelings of prescience had done her much good up to now.

For all Fortnightly's appeal, Sylvia realized she was no longer listening but staring at Jim and Musa, who were sitting at the old man's feet like children around a teacher, their faces still as eager as ever. They looked so comical that she had to catch herself not to laugh. Musa's foot was swathed in an elaborate parcel of self-applied bandages, concealing the stump of his lost digit. Sylvia had offered to help bathe and treat the wound but Musa was sulking and would not let her near it. How the hell had he lost a toe? She had a hard time accepting his explanations of metaphysical intervention. Of course it was a grotesque injury but Sylvia couldn't believe 'the gods' (whoever they might be) would take such blackly humorous retribution. Besides, if promiscuity was a crime, then she would surely be toeless and probably fingerless too. But maybe describing a prostitute as 'promiscuous' was like describing a surgeon as 'bloodthirsty'; because even deities must understand that everyone has to make a living.

Unsurprisingly Musa found little humour in his missing toe (the fourth on his right foot, again an apparently random selection). This was partly because of the unignorable pain of his injury, partly because of the shameful ignominy of its cause, but mainly because its loss seemed so undeniably metaphorical (as most things do to a quick-witted *zakulu* – the restoration of a bride's virginity, a gossip's cold sores, rain at a funeral). For the previous two days, Musa had stumbled around New Orleans, only able to walk with the aid of a stick.

'You see, Sylvia,' he'd said, 'I am missing but a single toe and yet my balance is troublesome. In all meaningful ways I am a complete man and yet I cannot walk unaided. Such an apparently minor ailment for such a treacherous consequence!' The *zakulu* then looked at Sylvia significantly. 'I am sure you catch my drift.'

Frankly, Sylvia had no idea what he was talking about. Although later, when she thought about it, she almost understood.

As for Jim, he was so shamefaced that he couldn't meet her gaze. Of course his injuries didn't help. His right eye was still half-closed with the bruising and his left was so bloodshot there was barely any white visible. At least she hadn't broken his nose. Sylvia felt suddenly guilty at the sight of his swollen nose, which looked so painful. She'd caught him with a good shot, all right. That would teach him to cross a prostitute (retired). That would teach him to cross a *machekamadzi*!

In spite of herself, she was smiling. For a moment Jim looked up at her and then immediately dipped his head again. She realized he was scared of her. Good.

After Musa had lost a toe with her kiss, after they'd walked into Malone's bar and witnessed Jim's drunken karaoke, after she'd smashed him in the face, Sylvia had stalked off through the New Orleans streets, her mind jumbled with all kinds of different images and ideas. She'd walked for most of the night, stopping in bars here and there, listening to good and bad music, dipping her knuckles in ice buckets (to try and ease the swelling), and enduring lazy propositions from drunken men who liked the elegant sway of her hips and figured she was too old to be choosy. She couldn't remember much of that night, her emotions were so fierce. But she remembered the questions she'd asked herself. And they were so fucking obvious she found it hard to believe she hadn't asked them before.

What was she doing in New Orleans? What was she doing in New Orleans with a crazy African witchdoctor and a well-meaning white kid (but a kid none the less)? What did she hope to gain? Was her ancestry – or rather her blackness – really so important to her? Would the answers to her questions – these and the other big ones: the whos, wheres and whys – really help her at all?

Sylvia only knew one thing for sure: she wanted to go back to London. Of course there was nothing for her there: no home, no family, no waiting partner with broad shoulders and a generous ear.

But at least it was a nothing she knew and she was used to knowing nothing; she knew it like a well-practised excuse.

By the time Sylvia got back to the apartment on Chartres, the sky was beginning to glow with the first pink of morning. She let herself in quietly. She had half a mind to pack up and leave then and there without so much as a goodbye. But as it turned out, Musa and Jim were awake and sitting in silence in the small kitchen. The *zakulu* was smoking a therapeutic joint with his feet on the table while Jim morosely nursed a bourbon, occasionally snorting a blood clot from his tender nose. They both started when she came in, like they'd hardly expected her to return at all. Jim jumped up and began, 'Where have you been?' But Sylvia soon sat him down with a look that could have withered spring.

'I've decided to go back to London,' Sylvia said.

Musa sucked on his reefer and looked at her through the haze of smoke. He coolly lowered his legs and then failed to suppress a wince as the blood rushed into his painful foot.

'I've found it,' Musa announced quietly. And for all his laid-back demeanour, there was more than a hint of pride in his voice.

'Found what?'

'Your history,' Jim proclaimed.

But Musa shook his head. 'Your destiny,' he said.

'Oh,' Sylvia said feebly. She knew she was supposed to be excited but she'd quite forgotten why. 'I'm going to bed.'

She lay down on the bed in her clothes, her powder muddying the pillow. She shut her eyes and her mind was blank but she wasn't asleep when Jim entered the room. She heard the creak of the door and, when he squatted down beside her, she smelled the whisky on his breath.

'I'm sorry,' he said.

'It's fine.'

He was silent for a moment and his cheeks seemed to swell a little. She wasn't sure if the pause was supposed to be dramatic or if he was merely suppressing a belch.

'I've fallen in love with you.'

Sylvia looked at him and her eyes were ironic and her heart was so full of self-pity that she had no room for anything else but contempt (a notoriously compact feeling). 'So fucking what?' she said.

The following morning Musa had woken her early. She'd considered telling him to leave her alone, that she didn't care any more. But she knew that she had to buy a plane ticket to New York and she figured it would take a day or two, so what did she have to lose? Besides, she was still enough in awe of the *zakulu* to recognize his expression brooked no argument.

What a bizarre sight they made, the three of them, as they walked out into the French Quarter! Musa was up front, hobbling awkwardly and using a baseball bat as a makeshift walking stick to maintain his precarious balance. Then came Sylvia, as beautifully made up and immaculately dressed as ever. Her long coat swished as she walked and her glossy lips seemed set in a permanent pout. Jim trudged behind, like a little boy sulking, and his face was enough of a mess to provoke the odd sympathetic glance.

Fortis Holden Junior was waiting for them at the bar. Malone's was morning empty and it smelled of a curious combination of coffee and detergent. Musa introduced Sylvia to her long-lost relation and she took to him at once. There was something sprightly in his manner. When he spoke to her, his tongue flicked over his tired lips and it was pink and wet, like he hadn't used it in years.

They settled at a corner table and ordered coffee and orange juice. Fortnightly wanted nothing but a glass of water and he sipped on it periodically throughout the morning before switching to whisky as the shadows began to stretch across the floor. At first Jim was trying to catch Sylvia's attention like he had something more to say for himself (another apology or declaration, no doubt). But she steadfastly ignored him and he soon gave up. Instead he chain-smoked and swilled coffee around his teeth until he, too, was so wrapped up in Fortnightly's tales that he barely noticed when the day had reached a respectable hour for drinking to start.

'So you Sylvie Black's little girl?' the old man began.

'Granddaughter.' It was Musa who corrected him.

'Granddaughter, eh?' Fortnightly leaned forward. A ray of sun was illuminating a myriad of dirt particles above the table and he pushed his head right in among them to get a better look at Sylvia. 'I sho' wonder if you looks like her any. Course I never met Sylvie Black but I figure she musta looked jus' like you. Lighter skin, though. An' I guess I always pictures her round the age of twenty-one.'

It took the old man almost two hours to outline Sylvia's family tree in enough particularity for her satisfaction. Occasionally he repeated himself or got stuck on a name – a slip of age rather than memory; then Musa would jump in with the missing fact. Sometimes the witchdoctor added details of his own, as if he wanted to relate the whole story himself. He told her, for example, that her slave ancestor's name was Ezekiel Black, known to everyone as Zike (pronounced 'Zee-kay'). When Musa said this, for some reason Jim muttered the words 'sacrificial gift' and Sylvia had to shut him up with that look again.

She wondered how an African *zakulu* could know so much about her past. Maybe he'd already heard the whole story from Fortnightly (although that didn't seem so likely judging by the old man's surprised expression). Or maybe it was just some weird Zambawian juju of the kind that could amputate a toe. Frankly, Sylvia didn't much care.

When Fortnightly finished the family tree with Sylvie's flight to Chicago with Lick's baby in her belly (Bernadette Di Napoli, would you believe), Jim stood up with an air of finality and he shouted an order to Molly for a pint of Nigerian Guinness. But Sylvia wasn't nearly done.

'How do you know all this?' she asked.

''Cos I made it my business to know. See, Lick Holden was the greatest horn man ever lost to history. 'Sides' – the old man shrugged

– 'he was my pappy an' jus' 'cos I never met him don't change that.'

'How come you never met him?'

Fortnightly stared at her seriously. His eyes that must have seen most things seemed to glaze a little and he sighed deeply enough to turn back time.

'My momma . . . Bea Holden, you remember?' he began slowly. 'She was a crazy prostitute an' I don't remember her with much in the way of 'fection. Now don't mistake me none. Ain't nothin' wrong with bein' a prostitute nor with bein' crazy neither. But I jus' sho' that the two don't mix so good.

'Fact is, jus' about the kindest memory I have of that woman is when I came into our apartment – over the way there, on Basin Street – an' she was surely cryin' like a baby. "Forty!" she says to me (because that was the pet name she called me, after her favourite liquor). "Forty! Yo pappy's dead!" Figure I musta been 'bout seven years old. Figure musta been 'bout 1925.'

For a moment or two Sylvia and Fortnightly gazed at one another intently in silence, like they were trying to see deep into their innards like only family can. Musa, who was watching, wondered if maybe their eyes had a similar look to them; the eyes of Lick Holden perhaps, or a young African songster by the name of Zike.

Eventually Sylvia blinked and she said, 'Please. I want to know everything.'

So Fortis Holden Junior told her just about all he knew about Lick, information collected a lifetime ago (in the late thirties perhaps) from characters with names that sounded larger than life: Lil' Annie and Jig and Popskull and the like – characters who lived in Cooltown before the second world war, when Mount Marter was still a boundaried place worthy of its own name. He started with Lick's breech birth in Kayenne's Canal Street apartment, he told her about his incarceration in the Double M and he lingered for almost three hours – naturally enough – upon anecdotes from Lick's two years in New Orleans: stories about Buster Buster, Black Benny and, of course, his own mother, Bea Holden. Fortnightly told Sylvia with melancholy pride about his father's brief associations with Fate Marable, Kid Ory and King Oliver and she was suitably impressed (though Musa and Jim were largely nonplussed). And when Sylvia questioned, disbelieving, the old man's claim that Lick played with the great Louis Armstrong, Fortnightly shook his head and said, 'You know what Dipper wrote in his memoirs? "That boy Lick taught me the meanin' of the word 'hot', all right. He blew that horn so hard you could see the brass sweatin'." That's what Dipper wrote an' you can sure find it for yourself if you don't believe me any.'

Fortnightly talked all day, concluding with the incident at the Montmorency Hotel when Lick saw Sylvie for the first time in years. Then he just stopped, suddenly, and sighed and he eased himself gingerly to his feet. It was around nine o'clock.

'Where are you going?' Sylvia asked.

'Home. I'm tired.'

'Now? You can't go now. You've got to finish! You've got to tell me everything!'

'Tomorrow. Damn, cousin of mine! You sho' got your grand-mother's temperament! I been waiting eighty years to tell this story; another day ain't gonna make no difference.'

'But . . .'

'Tomorrow. I'll see y'all tomorrow. I wanna take you some place.'

With that, Fortnightly tottered out of the bar and Sylvia was left avoiding her companions' eyes that were inquisitive, apologetic and just so fucking intrusive. The three of them walked back to their apartment in silence and she went to bed straight away. She could hear Musa and Jim talking. They must have been talking about her because their voices were low and secretive. But she didn't care what they were saying anyway. After a while Musa knocked on her door and stood in the doorway. Sylvia's eyes were open but she didn't turn them towards him.

372

'We have a saying in Zambawi,' he said. *'Kumuru ku mastike chi bhundu sazvopuro kanaka loro o zvakola kupi gudo.'*

Sylvia didn't reply.

'It means, "Anger that storms into the bush returns the way it came or sleeps with the baboons."'

'What's that supposed to mean?' Sylvia asked.

But Musa shrugged. 'Jim is a good boy. Don't be too hard on him.'

'I'm not,' Sylvia said. And she closed her eyes until the *zakulu* got the message and left her alone.

The truth was, she wasn't angry with Jim. Not really. Of course his impromptu singing had been embarrassing and his black-eyed, simpering penance was more so. But Sylvia had been described as a lot worse (and less accurate) things than a past-it whore in her time. When she thought about it, she remembered Musa's words in the angry aftermath of their brief kiss, just before they'd entered the bar. 'We must find Jim Tulloh forthwith,' the *zakulu* had said, 'for destiny will not be derailed so easily.' It was this phrase that stuck so obstinately in her throat. *Who the hell does he think he is?* Sylvia thought. And she went to sleep wondering whether Musa or destiny itself was the object of her frustration.

The next morning they again met Fortis Holden Junior early and the three of them were still hardly talking. It was as though, Sylvia thought, they accepted this apparent conclusion to their respective journeys as the end of their forced mutuality. Certainly Fortnightly recognized the discomfort because he pulled a wry smile and shook his head with that assumed, wordless wisdom that only very old people carry off with any degree of authenticity.

They didn't even go into Malone's bar this time. Fortnightly had his battered Chevy parked outside and they got in unquestioningly and the old man pulled out into the brisk morning traffic. Musa sat up front (because of his sore toe) and Jim and Sylvia shared the back seat. Sylvia was sure that Jim was watching her but she didn't acknowledge his attention. She was too busy trying to control her racing heart because Fortnightly was a menace behind the wheel, driving with a serene carelessness, like he knew his time was about up.

After around half an hour crowded with near-death experiences, they turned into a long street leading up a gentle hill. On either side, functional warehouses (where whorehouses had once stood) rose mightily from the curb like sentinels at the gate of progress and there wasn't a pedestrian in sight, nor even a car; just the occasional forklift that serviced one of these monoliths like a worker bee around the queen. Fortnightly was tutting. 'Mount Marter, what's left of it,' he said. 'Lost to history.' Sylvia had noticed this was the old man's favourite phrase.

They pulled up outside a very different building, nestled amid this industrial sprawl. It was the trunk of an old house – Sylvia didn't even try to guess its date – and its wings had clearly been amputated to accommodate the buildings on either side so that it looked like a float bobbing helplessly in a strong tide. On the tall barbed-wire fence, a condemned notice hung like a pre-emptive tombstone. Fortnightly switched off his engine.

'This was the Mount Marter Correctional School for Negro Boys,' he said. 'Jus' figured you folk might wanna see it.'

Inside Fortnightly sat down at the bottom of a collapsed staircase on an upright chair that might have been put there for the purpose. The others arranged themselves on the dusty floorboards that creaked menacingly. Sylvia was irritated to have to dirty her clothes. As the old man collected his thoughts, Jim seemed overexcited. 'I can really picture Lick here,' he said. 'Can't you?' And Sylvia nodded passively, although she didn't agree. She tried to conjure the shade of her grandfather in the corner of her eye: a small boy lurking in a corner, hiding from the teachers or – what had Fortnightly called them? – the Knuckles, with a cornet in his hand. But she couldn't picture anything. She realized that Jim was assembling a plot from the building blocks of his imagination – films and novels and articles in Sunday magazines (i.e. other stories) – but she was trying to construct a history that was true for her, something relevant and contemporary, and that was a lot trickier. Besides, the nagging sensation in her innards was growing by the second and it was hard to think about anything else.

Fortnightly continued Lick's story and he wove it with such finesse that Musa and Jim were totally enwrapped. He told them about Jim and Sylvie's collaborations at Toothless Naps's honkytonk. He even sang a snatch of 'Quatrain Blues' in a voice that had once been tuneful and Sylvia had to admit that she recognized the melody. He told them about Bubble's funeral and the arrival from Chicago of the Reverend and Mrs Pink ('Professor Pink's grand-parents,' Musa remarked sagely). He told them about Corissa's death and Sylvie's pregnancy and Lick's plan for New York. But his words barely penetrated Sylvia's person, surrounding her with a cold meaning that couldn't even make her shiver, like mist coalescing on a waterproof. She felt airy, lightweight, floating perhaps. And it was an anchorless, uncomfortable feeling that left her clinging to the uncertainty in her gut for some kind of grounding.

But now Sylvia just wanted the old man to get on with it, like a car speeding through that mist with no idea what lies on the other side. But now Fortnightly was digressing again like a breath before climax (or anticlimax, Sylvia thought). But now she found her mind wandering over the past couple of days and her very being ached for an end (and any end would do). But now she forced herself to concentrate on his words, to hear what she needed to know.

'Let me tell it like it is to all you young folk,' the old man was saying and he stared directly at Sylvia. 'An', cousin of mine, you still young even though you don't think so. Let me tell it like it is. The mouldy figs come to this ol' town and analyse the jazz music like that's gonna make them understand it any. Truth be told, jazz has its patterns and its predictabilities. But, trust me, any time you think you got it figured, it gonna play a trick on you. Because in jazz music the future, the past and the present are all happenin' right now. You think jazz facin' one way an' it turn right round on you like a nigger bein' chased 'cross the bayou. An' that's true of the simplest story and the simplest jazz. Damn! That shit's even true of the simplest twelve bar blues. An' don't you forget it.'

Fortnightly slowly turned his eyes to each of his listeners in turn. But Sylvia was shaking her head spasmodically.

'Please,' she said, 'I just need to know what happened.'

The old man saw her suffering (though he didn't understand it) and he drew a deep enough breath to finish the story. Jim saw her suffering (though he misunderstood it) and he leaned across to lay a comforting hand on her knee and she didn't object. Musa adjusted his position. He was suffering pins and needles in his missing toe, which, he thought, was the strangest sensation he'd never had.

'So Lick sent word to his sister in Chicago,' Fortnightly began. 'An' Sylvie boarded that train jus' as soon as she could. I guess Lick musta kissed her on the lips an' said, "I see you at Grand Central Station, my sweetheart. At midday in one month's time." Somethin' like that. An' I guess he musta believed it too.

'With the help of Big Annie and Naps, Lick arranged Corissa's funeral an' it passed off a week later without no problems. It was a quiet kind of affair, most appropriate for Lick's grievin', 'cos after a while any folk who sees as much death as he done is all grieved out. Only thing I ever heard about that service was from Ash Hansen. He tells me, "I didn't never hear Lick play like that before." "What you mean?" I asks. An' he says, "Well, that day Lick played good for sho'. But the music was real hollow like the sound of an empty cooking pot on the grate." Like the sound of an empty cooking pot on the grate is what he said! I always figured that 'cos Lick jus' about done with Cooltown by then an' that service musta been some kinda conclusion.'

The old man looked at Sylvia for acknowledgement but she was still shaking her head and he hurried on.

'Anyways, with the funeral done, Lick was 'bout ready to head for New York an' you can bet he felt good. Course he had no idea of the stink that was risin' in Jones like a warnin' from a skunk, else he been on the first train. But I guess Lick figured that he had plenty of time, since he didn't have to meet his pregnant sister (who wasn't no blood relation) for the best part of three weeks. Well! Ain't it a shame how folk see time like money in the bank when it's more like a loan that might jus' fall due any second?

'I guess it musta been round 1946 before I figured what went on in Jones in that week. 'Cos that was when I finally tracked down Sylvie's friend from the *plaçage* apartments, the girl by the name of Sweet Elly (though, by the time I found her, she weren't a girl no more and she'd surely dropped 'Sweet' from her name). She was livin' in El Dorado, Arksansas, and hadn't she sho' 'nuff found her pot of gold? She was passin' as a white woman (wouldn't Sylvie have laughed?) an' married to an old Dutch gentleman by the name of Hoekema who worshipped her like she was Mother Mary her own self. So you can bet she weren't none too pleased when a blue-black negro like me turns up at her door, all eager to talk about the past! But I as stubborn as a nigger when I wanna be an' she chose to talk in the end.

'Apparently, when Sylvie Black left, Johnny Frederick an' some of his good-time boys too, they tore through the *plaçage* apartments like a twister through a rundown barn, throwin' kids down the stairs an' slappin' those women for fun an' causin' all kinds of mayhem besides. Way Sweet Elly understood, Johnny Frederick musta loved Sylvie more than she ever knew ('cos didn't he buy her jus' the prettiest clothes?). But I figure that no white man ever like to be made to look like a fool. An' by a nigger from a family you once owned? That shit surely smarts and no mistake!

'Course, when the good-time boys found Sweet Elly all dressed up in Sylvie's clothes that Johnny had bought . . . Well! You can bet they had somethin' to say about that! Sweet Elly told me she feared for her life when they beat her but she still made that no-good white dog sound more like a hero than no villain ('cos, for some folk, even a beatin' don't convince them of the truth). So you can imagine the scene: a dumb-ass bantam girl what wishes she was white, you think she gonna take much punishment for her colour? Guess she musta said somethin' like, "Sylvie Black run away with a negro called Fortis." Somethin' like that. An' Lick Holden's celebrity was surely known to one or two of those white good-time boys who liked to drink in a black tonk once in a while.'

Again the old man paused. Sylvia knew that he was watching her – probably Jim and Musa too – but she didn't look up. She heard a match strike as Jim lit a cigarette and the sound was somehow elongated as though time was stretching.

'I figure, standin' on Elly Hoekema's doorstep in El Dorado, she surely saw my thinkin' diggin' into my face as sho' as a plough in soft earth. Either that or she been carryin' guilt for more than twenty years. "What's I s'posed to do?" she snaps. "Way I sees it, Sylvie Black musta been crazy to walk out on Johnny Frederick for some negro!" I remember she spat that word "negro" like it a mouthful of gristle. "Anyways, I didn't do no wrong. Jus' told the truth an' the truth don't never harm nobody." I swear that's what she said to me! "The truth don't never harm nobody!" Damn! Some folk so goddam ignorant you wonder how they even manage to wash their own bodies!'

Sylvia heard Jim interrupt. His voice was eager. 'What did you tell her?'

'What did I tell her? What you want me to tell her? You think I told her what Johnny Frederick gone and done? What for? I didn't tell her nothin'! Black folk got enough misery in their lives, boy. Even black folk what imagine theirselves white.'

More silence. The pain in Sylvia's gut was unbearable and she crossed her arms across her belly and rocked a little. She could feel her eyes begin to needle and sting. She sneaked a look at Fortis Holden Junior and his lips were quivering and he dabbed at the corner of his eyes with a pristine white handkerchief.

'I don't know much 'bout what happened, anyways. Ash Hansen was in Toothless Naps's that night but he was still haunted, all right, an' he didn't wanna talk. Everythin' I know I heard from Popskull 'cos he was drunk when it happened and drunk when he was tellin' me an' I guess the liquor brought him some comfort.

'Seems that Johnny Frederick and his boys went down the tonk jus' before sun-up. It was the night before Lick gonna leave. Can you believe that? Ain't fate one sorry-ass bitch! Course they weren't plannin' no worse than to hand out a hidin' that no negro could forget. 'Cos those boys weren't no killers. But that ain't what happened. Way Popskull told it, they tied hisself an' Jig an' Ash Hansen an' Naps to the bar an' you can bet that Naps was cussin' them white boys so good he was lucky to live. Then they beat Lick with his own cornet, knocking that instrument out of shape on his arms, ribs an' skull. They even jammed the bell into his chops, again an' again, until he was spitting his teeth and his jibs were sho' ruined. Imagine that! A set of lips sweet enough to talk to God with no go-between!

'"Stay down!" That's what Popskull was shoutin'. An' even Naps too. "Stay down, Lick boy! Sweet Jesus! Stay down!" But Lick didn't hear them; leastways he didn't pay them no mind. 'Cos every time his prayer bones buckled, he got back to his feet for more punishment an' didn't that provoke Johnny Frederick all the more. That white boy screamed like a madman an' he battered Lick again an' again until Popskull and the rest couldn't see for tears. Then they heard someone say, "He ain't movin', Johnny! Shit! He ain't movin'!" An' those good-time boys tore out of the tonk, their good time all over.

'It took Naps 'bout half an hour to free himself from those boys' clumsy knots and by then the poppa I never met was already good as dead. Naps held Lick as he died an' he kept sayin' the same thing over an' over: "You my personal fuckin' nigger, Lick boy. My personal fuckin' nigger." Shit! Popskull say that Naps loved Lick like a brother. More than that, even.

'If Lick'd stayed down, maybe he'd've made it. But he didn't and Popskull couldn't explain that any. I dunno. Maybe with his chops busted, Lick figured he had nothin' left to live for. But what about Sylvie Black and his baby? Or maybe he remembered Johnny

Frederick dancin' with his love at the Montmorency Hotel; an' he remembered the whole set-up with the white boys an' the light-skinned sisters an' no black men allowed but the Uncle Toms in the band. I figure he remembered the way he faked to pass out an' he thought, I ain't gonna go down for no white fools again. Who knows? Only thing I know for sho' is that everybody say my poppa had a heart big enough for Louisiana, so maybe that what got him killed. Damn!'

The old man's voice faltered and a sob shook his tired chest, catching him by surprise. Sylvia wanted to look at him but her own eyes were streaming with tears that the others wouldn't understand. She pushed her knuckles into her sockets and they came away black with eyeliner. I must look like a clown, she thought.

'Look at me,' Fortnightly said, 'weepin' for a man I never met. Ain't no fool like an old fool.'

'What happened to Naps?' Jim asked quietly.

'After Lick put in the ground – Shit! Three funerals in a month! Don't that say somethin'? – he had business to see to in Mount Marter, if you know what I'm sayin'. A couple of years later Naps did go to New York to look for Sylvie. But I guess he didn't find her. Anyways, I heard from Lil' Annie that she got word of his murder. He died a grifter, they said, but I dunno much 'bout that. I figure that smart smokestack plain ran out of words.'

Sylvia wiped her eyes on her sleeve and raised her head for the first time. Musa and Jim and Fortnightly, they were all staring at her, all with different questions lighting their faces. She swallowed hard and hugged herself tight, like she was trying to keep her guts from spilling out. 'What happened to Sylvie?'

'Sylvie? What you mean? You know what happened. She married a rich I-talian by the name of Tony Berlone an' they raised Lick's daughter (your momma) as their own.'

'Did you ever try to find her?' she asked and she saw Fortnightly's expression harden, almost imperceptibly, the kind of subtle shift that only family will ever notice.

'What business I got with her?'

Again Sylvia swallowed. Her head buzzed and her every joint was aching. The anticlimax in her stomach was nauseating. So this was how completion felt! But she didn't feel complete so much as finished.

'Why didn't she come back to find Lick?' she asked and the old man almost seemed to snarl.

'Let me tell you somethin', cousin of mine. Love don't live beyond the grave. Sometimes it don't live beyond no city limits.'

'How do you know?'

'All I know is it's a man's fate to die and a woman's to survive, but don't ask me which is harder.'

Those words cut Sylvia deeper than a blade, almost as deeply as a tragic blues, and she got to her feet with her whole body shaking and she stumbled out of the door of the derelict building and into the bright sunlight that blinded her. This was to be her fate and her conclusion! She was the product not of love but survival, still the guilty secret that her parents had done their best to ignore. She knew now what the anticlimax was. She was a throwback! Nothing more! And how could a throwback ever hope to move on? Gulping in that hot Mount Marter air, her sobbing came as heavy and as suffocated as history. There were footsteps behind her and Sylvia turned and her face was screwed up tighter than the first page of a book that can't be written.

Jim was reaching for her and, weakly, she tried to push him away. 'Oh fuck!' she spluttered. 'I . . .' But, in spite of herself, she fell into fate's arms and she let Jim wrap her up in an embrace that held a passion she hadn't felt since God knows when. And she heard the beat against his ribcage and she wondered, not for the first time, how a heart so big – a man-sized heart – could fit into such a skinny white boy's chest.

I: *Sylvia and the coffee-coloured woman*

(Heathrow, London, England. 1999)
The coffee-coloured woman was sitting in the faux-Italian sandwich shop in the food court at Heathrow Airport. Her face was bare and her hair was scraped back in a simple bunch. Passers-by who took the trouble to check her out would have found it hard to believe this was a woman who'd spent half a lifetime beneath a make-up mask, false lashes and nails. But few passers-by took such trouble and those that did were too busy enjoying the rewards of their attention to think of much else. Because the coffee-coloured woman was simply elegant. Sure she was getting on, but she had that kind of beauty that seduces young men and has husbands' minds wandering. Best of all, her every movement encapsulated that secure poise and confidence that makes boys feel like men and men like boys. Exotic? No. That's not right. Elegant will do fine.

One man stopped to stare at her, a grey-suited, grey-haired, grey-skinned businessman wearing a club tie. He vaguely reminded the coffee-coloured woman of someone, a former client perhaps. But she chose not to remember those times any more.

Nobody who saw her would have believed she was nervous. But she was. Because she was waiting for a cousin she'd never met. What's more, her two ancient American step-uncles (if that's what they were), who were as different as black and white, had died within days of each other a month earlier (which must have been the closest they ever came to sharing an opinion about anything). So the cousin she'd never met was her last living relative.

The coffee-coloured woman craned her graceful neck to look for her boyfriend. Can a 46-year-old woman ever have a 'boyfriend'?

Only if he is actually a 'boy', she thought. And it brought an involuntary smile to her face. But he was nowhere in sight.

To calm her nerves, she lit a cigarette (although she rarely smoked) and she tried to think about something other than the cousin she'd never met. Of course she ended up thinking about love because that is all the recently smitten can think about. But at least her thoughts were less boring than most.

She thought about how lovers liked to describe their meeting as 'fate', as if that were somehow the most romantic notion in the world. 'We were meant to be together,' pimpled youths said to their hipless partners, as though that helplessness marked some kind of strength. 'You are my destiny,' a celluloid goddess breathed into a prominent pectoral and she spoke so huskily that it sounded like the highest form of flattery when, in fact, her real meaning was that she no more chose him than she chose to allow time to pass. And what was so romantic about that?

The coffee-coloured woman knew a thing or two about love because desperate and not-so-desperate people learn any skill for money. She'd loved numerous taxi drivers, businessmen and pot-bellied businessmen (a genre in their own right); she'd loved the odd priest, rock star and academic; she'd loved a serious Jamaican boy, an alcoholic pianist and a scrawny, big-hearted drifter. Or fucked them all at least. And the coffee-coloured woman still wasn't convinced of a difference. You could choose to love . . . to lose your innocence or to find it, to ingratiate or annoy, to be scared or feel safe. Or you could choose to love for hard cash. And the only kind of love that was better to choose than that? Well! The coffee-coloured woman chose a love that had a future and she was happy with that and fuck romance! Because what did a prostitute (retired) know about romance anyway? Maybe Jim Tulloh was her fate and maybe he wasn't but only time would tell and it would render the question pointless in the telling. After all, as Louis Armstrong sang it, they had all the time in the world. Whatever an old man had told her, the story of fate was as simple as an elementary twelve bar blues. But you still can't sing a song if you don't know the tune.

She thought about an African witchdoctor then. She remembered a conversation they'd shared almost a year ago in an Irish bar in the French Quarter of New Orleans. Musa the *zakulu* was about to leave for Zambawi (via New York, London and Lilongwe) and he held her earnestly by the hands and he told her what his ego thought she wanted to hear (although his id may have known better).

'Do not give our encounter another thought,' he entreated her. 'You have found your fate, so you must not make the wrong choice.'

He was feeling self-righteous (as *zakulu* generally do), so he decided to have a shot at some pop psychology.

'Human relationships are naturally triangular,' he continued. 'For a woman has a relationship with her partner and then an imagined relationship with what she would like him to be. Of course that was where I came in and it is understandable that you found me irresistible. But, *machekamadzi*, I suppress my desires for the sake of your destiny and you must do the same!'

The coffee-coloured woman nodded seriously as if impressed with this theory and she gave the *zakulu*'s hands a thankful squeeze. He looked pleased with himself and stood up decisively. 'You will come and see me soon, no doubt!' he announced and then he kissed her on both cheeks and counted his toes on his fingers, stopping at nine with evident relief. He nodded formally and headed for the door. The coffee-coloured woman watched his back impassively. She thought about what he'd said and she realized that she hadn't replied because she didn't want to hurt his feelings. But she knew that her love was not triangular because, when you've loved countless strangers, a triangle represents an unappealingly dull development. But a one-on-one relationship (be it fated or chosen)? Now that sounded exciting.

Of course the *zakulu* didn't know that his hypothesizing had fallen on such deaf ears and he walked away with a spring in his lame step and resolved to develop his theory further. As far as he was concerned, he had tried it out on Tongo Kalulu and Sylvia Di Napoli with considerable success. But he knew that chiefs and prostitutes had too much in common to represent any kind of cross-section.

In the doorway Musa turned back and waved at the coffee-coloured woman and he shouted across the teeming bar. 'You are Sylvia!' he yelled. 'Be happy!' And she waved back and she thought, at least he's right about that. And, all things considered, for the most part, she was.

Sylvia Di Napoli tugged on her bitter cigarette and her thoughts lingered on her dear friend Musa, who had shown her her destiny with more chance than design. With a little luck and a little planning, she'd see him again tomorrow. He'd said he had some places to show her – a dried-out lake, a *musasa* that looked like an old man's face – and some dreams she needed to share. As usual, Sylvia hadn't known what he was talking about but he'd seemed pretty definite. As usual.

She shook her head and looked at her watch. Professor Coretta Pink (the cousin she'd never met who chose to go by the name Bunmi Durowoju because a name tells a story) was late and Sylvia's own flight was due for departure in less than two hours. What was she meeting her cousin for? It wasn't a family reunion. Sylvia and Jim were supposed to collect the documentation for some special package that was to be transferred at Heathrow; a package so precious that Professor Pink had accompanied it herself from Chicago. Musa had arranged it. Sylvia had asked Jim what it was but he didn't know either, which was just about typical of a boy who was frantic with curiosity one moment and lazily blithesome the next.

She wondered where Jim had got to. She knew he was trying to secure an upgrade but it rarely took this long. She had seen him in action at a check-in desk before (in New Orleans International) and his tactic, he said, had around a 50 per cent success rate. He would look at the desk official and attempt an upper-class English accent. 'Don't *you* know who I am?' Jim said, as though he were a dignitary travelling incognito. But his intonation was always flawed with that peculiar accent on the 'you' that gave the question an almost imploring, unfinished quality. It sounded like it should be succeeded by something like ' . . . because if you do, please tell me!' Then half the desk officials (typically women of a certain age) would bump him to business class while the rest would dump him in economy (usually the worst seats: bang in the middle, right at the back). At New Orleans International, Jim's technique had worked and Sylvia was impressed, which was important. Because they hadn't been together long at the time.

That was the best part of a year ago.

'Sylvia Di Napoli?'

Sylvia jumped to her feet and stubbed her cigarette. In front of her stood a tall and strikingly beautiful black woman wearing a sloppy sweatshirt and jeans. She had a knapsack thrown over her shoulder and carried what looked like a small cooling box in her arms. Her hair was knotted into short, tight dreadlocks and her eyes held that attractive mixture of confidence and melancholy that so suits the terminally disappointed. She placed the cooler delicately on the floor and dropped her knapsack next to it.

'Professor Pink?' Sylvia asked.

'I call myself Durowoju. Olurunbunmi Durowoju. I don't use the name Pink. That was my slave name.'

'I'm sorry,' Sylvia said and she felt awkward. There was an uncomfortable blip of silence. 'Di Napoli was my father's name,' she said. More silence. 'I don't like it much either. He was an arsehole.'

Bunmi smiled then and Sylvia smiled too and any thorniness disappeared, as you would hope with long-lost family (but it rarely happens).

'So you're my cousin, then,' Bunmi said.

'And you're mine.'

And the two women embraced and Bunmi sat down at the table like an old friend and she lit one of Sylvia's cigarettes without asking (although she rarely smoked) because that's what family do.

386

'How did you recognize me?' Sylvia asked.

'Pastor Boomer told me what you look like.'

'How is he?'

'He's cool. Still just as crazy as ever. The Reverend Boomer Jackson driving around the South Side in that Lexus of his like he's the first mack priest!' Bunmi's expression flickered with amusement and she pulled hard on her cigarette. 'He took quite a shine to you, cousin Sylvia. There're quite a few ladies in his congregation who'd hate you for that!'

'I've got a boyfriend,' Sylvia said and she smiled. 'What about you? You married?'

'He left me.'

'Your husband?'

'Somebody else's,' Bunmi said. And she laughed like she didn't care.

'There'll be someone else,' Sylvia said because it sounded like the right kind of thing to say. And her cousin pulled an ironic face, her eyebrows rising to meet in the middle.

'I'm an archaeologist. I work with archaeologists.'

'So?'

'So I'm not much of a one for beards,' she said and this time she laughed for real. 'So what about you, Cousin Sylvia? What do you do?'

Sylvia thought for a moment, weighing up her answer. 'I'm taking singing lessons. Jazz.'

'That's right! Pastor Boomer told me all about you. He said you had quite a voice. So you're keeping up the family tradition of Great-Aunt Sylvie and Great-Uncle Lick. Now wasn't that some story? He told me . . .'

Sylvia interrupted: 'Did you know I was a hooker?'

'Yeah. I knew that,' Bunmi said without pause. Their steady eyes met over the table. Bunmi's twinkled naughtily. 'Way I figure it, you're just keeping the family tradition. Like I said.'

She puffed out her cheeks and stubbed her cigarette. She was pleased to meet this long-lost cousin but she had no energy to reassure an ageing ex-whore; she had insecurities of her own. Besides, Sylvia didn't look like she was in much need of reassurance.

Bunmi lifted her knapsack from the floor and pulled out some official-looking documents and a pen. She smoothed the papers on to the table and looked at her watch. 'Better get on with it. I'm boarding back to the US in twenty minutes.'

'Twenty minutes?'

'The jetset lifestyle of the international archaeologist,' Bumni said drily. She turned the documents and handed Sylvia a pen. 'You just need to sign receipt and then deliver the artefact to Dr Moso at the University of Queenstown. I don't know what they're going to do with it. For all I know, they might send it down to Zimindo with you. Thanks for doing this; saves me some time and my department a plane ticket.'

'What is it?' Sylvia asked, scrawling her name.

'What's what?'

'The artefact. What is it?'

'You mean that *zakulu* friend of yours didn't tell you?' Bunmi was surprised. She reached for her cousin's cigarettes again. 'You mind?'

'Help yourself.'

'He didn't tell you?'

Sylvia shook her head. She felt a little stupid. 'Maybe Jim knows.'

'It's a traditional Zamba head-dress from Zimindo Province,' Bunmi said. 'We've had it at Northwestern for dating. We thought . . . *I* thought it was from around 1800. I thought it was going to back up a theory I've been working on. About pre-colonial sub-Saharan trade routes.'

'But it doesn't?'

'Uh-uh,' Bunmi shook her head. 'Judging by the vegetative record, we're talking 1920 earliest.'

'So?'

Bunmi puffed morosely on her cigarette. 'So how could I have

388

been so stupid? So the facts don't fit the story. So two years' work goes right down the drain.'

Sylvia looked at her cousin closely. She didn't understand but she assumed she was the one being dumb. 'What have the facts got to do with a story?' she asked. 'Who's to say you're wrong? Who's to say there isn't another head-dress out there? Truth doesn't prove anything but itself. Stories are about people.'

Bunmi was shaking her head. Then she stopped and her face lit up a little. 'I guess so,' she said. 'Anyway, since when did an archaeologist let the facts get in the way of a good story?' She began to laugh and Sylvia tried to join in although she didn't know what she was laughing at. Clearly it was an archaeologist's joke.

Bunmi stood up then and Sylvia stood up too.

'I'd better go,' Bunmi said and she patted the cooler at her feet affectionately. 'Look after this for me, won't you?'

'Of course.'

The cousins looked at one another awkwardly, neither sure how to end this first meeting. Bunmi extended her hand just as Sylvia leaned over the table with her lips pursed and they exchanged a clumsy farewell.

'Be in touch,' Bunmi said, slipping her knapsack on to her shoulder and backing away.

'I will. You too.'

'What you going to Zambawi for, anyway?'

Sylvia shrugged. 'I'm going with my boyfriend. We're visiting the *zakulu*. You know, maybe find a few roots.'

Bunmi paused for a second. A sadness fluttered her expression like a breeze across hanging linen but nobody would have noticed it but family. And then her face was placid again. Maybe even a little mischievous.

'In Zimindo,' she said, 'I know the chief down there. Nice guy. Tongo. Watch out for his wife, though. She's a real traditionalist. How's your Zamba?'

'I don't speak a word.'

Bunmi put her hands together, fingers pointing upwards. 'When you meet her, you need to clap like this. And you say "*Uribo hoore*". It's a greeting. She'll be real impressed.'

'*Uribo hoore?*'

'That's it. *Uribo hoore*. And you can tell Tongo I taught you.'

With that, Bunmi smiled pleasantly and headed for Immigration.

Left on her own, Sylvia sat down again and tried out her new phrase for size. She sparked another cigarette. There was an announcement over the public address: 'Flight BA212 for Queenstown is now boarding at Gate 23.' She looked around for Jim but there was still no sign of him. She pocketed Bunmi's documents and slid the cooler between her feet. On the top was written 'Dr Joshua Moso. Queenstown University'. Around this label were numerous stickers saying 'Fragile Cargo!' in bright red. Sylvia couldn't help herself; she flicked the latches on the front and opened the lid, furtively, like a smuggler checking her contraband. She looked inside.

A polythene seal covered the padded interior. Beneath it was a tatty grey object that looked like an ancient string vest or desiccated seaweed. Sylvia peered closer. She could make out various tiny dull seashells and a scrap or two of purplish pigment. She was bemused and disappointed. This constituted an 'artefact'? This constituted a 'fact'? Certainly it would take a considerable imagination to conjure a story from *this*.

Sylvia sat back in her chair and puffed on her cigarette. From the corner of her eye, she saw Jim making his way towards her. She spotted him by his haphazard path, stumbling over toddlers and trolleys with a succession of 'oops' and 'excuse mes', like a polite hedgehog in traffic. She began to giggle. He was still wearing the same ridiculous pair of sunglasses he'd adopted ever since developing a taste for jazz. She'd have to have another word with him about those.

'Hi, Mum!' Jim said and he kissed her on the forehead. Jim'd taken to addressing her as 'Mum' ever since she'd chastised him for being so publicly affectionate. 'People will think I'm your mother,' she said. Jim roared with laughter. 'Your coffee-coloured self?' he said. 'I doubt it.' 'Anything's possible,' she replied.

Jim sat down opposite her proudly brandishing two first-class boarding passes.

'First class?' Sylvia said. 'Your tactic worked?'

'Better than ever,' he enthused. '"Don't *you* know who I am?" I asked. And guess what? The woman at check-in gave me a lecture on the importance of self-definition. Turns out she's reading some self-help book. It took half an hour and bored me to tears. In the end, she felt so guilty she bumped us right past business straight up to first class.'

Sylvia stared at her partner, her other half, her *boyfriend* . . . whatever . . . and she thought he looked just like a kid, he was so excited. He was out of breath and his scrawny chest was heaving and his pasty cheeks were flushed pink. Sometimes, with Jim, she didn't know whether to laugh or cry. It was the same feeling she got when she sang the blues and her mind backed up to her last lesson. She had complained to her teacher about her difficulties with a particular tune and he sat her down to explain. 'Most melody is about consonance,' he said. 'Notes that go together like apple pie and ice cream. But jazz? Jazz melodies are discordant, sweet and sour. They're harder but so much more spicy. If you want an easy life, sing Lloyd-Webber or Gilbert and Sullivan. But if you want spice, then you need to understand dissonance.' In fact (or story), if not musically, Sylvia knew all about dissonance because her life had been discordant in the extreme. But Jim Tulloh was the spice that gave her notes meaning, better than the sheet music, which only gave them fact.

Sweet and sour, she thought. Sweet and sour.

Sylvia stood up and lifted the cooler on to the table.

'What's that?' Jim asked. 'The artefact?'

'It's a story.'

'A story? Marked "Fragile"?'

'Of course,' Sylvia snapped and before Jim could say another word she planted a professional kiss on his mouth that he'd remember until the next. She loved the smell of him, incongruously manly in a delicate sort of way. She loved the feel of his thin lips that seemed to quiver beneath her own and his nervous tongue that flicked across her teeth. She loved the taste of him; good enough to eat.

When she pulled away Jim was beaming and he wrinkled his face winningly. 'Thanks, Mum!' he said. 'Shall we go?'

'Go where?'

Jim pointed towards the departure gates with a dramatic flourish. 'To Africa!' he exclaimed and his eyes were wide and naive as his sunglasses slipped from the end of his nose.

Sylvia looked at him and her face was blank and she was silent for a moment with that blankness and silence that only comes with emotions that have been suppressed for pushing half a century. Eventually she raised a thin smile and a shrug.

'Sure', she said. 'Why not?'

And as they walked hand in hand beneath the sign that said 'Travellers Only', some people turned their heads to watch this odd couple pass and they wondered who they could be.

Coda: Because stories are untold

(Harlem, New York, USA. 1926)

Harlem in the 1920s? That place was buzzing more hectic than a hive in the honey harvest. Folk arrived in their thousands, from all over, and they blended into the Harlem mix before you had time to say 'Lenox Avenue'. Folk vanished too – running back to Momma or into the churning gutters or sinking to the bottom of the Hudson in a pair of concrete boots – and nobody even noticed. Because if you didn't have the balls for the Big Apple, there was a queue to take your place that stretched right around the corner. Black men called each other 'brother'. White men said this was because the comings and goings among negroes were so speedy that nobody bothered to remember names. Whatever. There hasn't been no district in no city in no country in the whole goddam world, before or since, that compares to Harlem back then. Some say it was a godless place. Others say God was there but he was surely just as confused as the rest of us. So perhaps it's no surprise that the story of Toothless Naps got lost as easily as a droplet in the ocean.

Stories come in all different shapes and sizes and styles – off the peg and made to measure, tight-fitting and loose around the middle, in gaudy colours and sombre shades of grey – and that's why they go in and out of fashion as surely as right and wrong. But the fact is that some stories are more resistant to changes in taste than others. Some stories live on (generally thanks to their descendants rather than any essential quality) while others are recycled and many die out, buried with their protagonists. And, sad to say, it's this last fate that took the story of Naps. Because it's a basic truth that Naps wasn't no musician, he had no friends but Lick and no descendants neither, and he didn't leave no battered horn that sits

393

these days in a small London flat, polished to reflection by a granddaughter he never knew.

Lick Holden? It's a sad tale and no mistake (though you can find redemption there if you're only prepared to take the trouble). But Naps? That story's dead and buried. We exhume and examine the remains and we try to imagine flesh for the bones. But it's an artist's impression at best and it's never going to be accurate enough to help us catch Time, that light-fingered thief who stole the story from us before we knew we wanted it, decades before most of us were born.

Naps arrived in Harlem in late '26. There wasn't nothing for him in Mount Marter after Lick's murder and, in his mind, he had an obligation to find Sylvie, no doubt. Now, fact was that Naps had never had a whole lot of time for Lick's sister (who wasn't no blood relation) but he'd kept such opinion to himself. Naps always figured that Sylvie had the airs and graces that lead to nothing but trouble for a negro. And so it proved (though it gave him no satisfaction). But the 'main man' loved Lick as much as his 'personal fuckin' nigger' loved Sylvie and that was good enough for duty. The way Naps saw it, Lick's love deserved to give Sylvie an explanation – why he never showed up beneath the Grand Central clock tower, why he was never there to be a father to his child, why she was left to marry a white man – even if she didn't deserve it her own self.

Maybe you could figure it was Naps's uncertainties about Sylvie Black that caused him to tarry in Mount Marter for the best part of two years. But there was a more pertinent reason that is surely piquant enough to shorten your breath as quick as a nip of moon-shine. After Lick Holden was murdered? Well! The little we know of Naps, we can be as sure of one consequence as the fact that Old Hannah rises in the east (whatever occurred the night before). Simple truth is, there was no ways that a certain white good-time boy by the name of Johnny Frederick was going to live to old age. He wasn't never going to inherit the family plantation nor raise kids of his own with a sweet girl with a bone-china complexion nor eat butter pancakes on no porch on a bright summer morning. No ways in hell! Naps would see to that.

But Naps, for all the passion that smouldered in him as unseen as the first sparks of a bush fire, wasn't no rash smokestack and it took him close on eighteen months to plan the deed. The 'murder' – though Naps never saw it as such – was reported in the newspapers in Mount Marter and even New Orleans, so we know when it happened (January 1926) and where (an alley in Sinclair). But the details were never explained because of the editors' sense of propriety. And perhaps that's a good thing too. Because, the little we know of Naps, there was a blade involved, no doubt, and we know he learned some cruel tricks from Dogtooth Jones in the Double M and we can be sure that Johnny Frederick didn't die an easy death (if there ever is such a thing).

Lil' Annie (who read her brother a whole lot better than she ever read a book) quickly guessed who'd done the killing and she told Naps to leave town.

'I ain't sayin' you's wrong an' I ain't sayin' you's right,' she protested. 'All I's sayin' is that now you's wanted as sho' as sugar is sweet an' you better leave town 'fore they hang your negro ass.'

Naps pulled a gap-toothed grin which infuriated his sister and no mistakes. 'Well, ain't that somethin'?' he exclaimed. 'Ain't nobody never wanted *me* before.'

But he was still gone the next morning and the law officers never caught the killer. Course that didn't stop Mount Marter's white good-time boys from a little justice of their own. They strung up some poor jigaboo who'd worked for the Frederick family for twenty years without ever answering back. And sure you can grieve for that negro if you want to; but only if your heart's got the capacity for the ache of one more untold story when must ordinary folk, who never left a footprint on a fine carpet, got plenty of aches of their own.

When Naps arrived in New York, he headed straight for Harlem because he'd heard that was where a black man could make a name for himself. Of course the smokestack had nothing behind him but a small-town arrogance, a mouthful of chatter and a dexterous knifehand. And such commodities were a dime a dozen in Harlem back then. But the supply was never going to outweigh the demand in a grifters' neighbourhood like that.

First off, Naps found himself a room on Convent Avenue and asked around for a high yellow girl by the name of Sylvie like a real bush negro who reckons everyone knows everyone else. But it didn't take him long to realize he was going to be staying a while and he set about finding his black ass some work. Now, if you've been paying attention, you'll recall that Naps figured work was something done only by 'niggers an' Jews an' fools'. So his job hunting was made up of street corners and bars and no-good joints until he cracked the rules of the big-city game.

Fact is, in those first six months, Naps got himself in some serious scrapes and no mistake; all kinds of black-folk trouble and white-folk trouble and law trouble too. That's the bare bones of the matter but there's no doubting his state of mind was still buried in the past like a seed in the ground. Because Naps, it ain't too hard to guess that Lick's murder affected him at what you might term a 'psychological level', that the killing of Johnny Frederick released a side of him that his momma was sure lucky she never saw. But it's still guesswork none the less and there's no person's story so false as the one you tell in words of your own. So maybe we'll just say Naps found trouble and we'll leave it at that; with no need to elaborate any.

Point is that, in Harlem, trouble draws attention like shit draws flies and it wasn't so long before Naps had that kind of unenviable reputation that a lot of folk envy (because New York City's an upside-down kind of place). He wasn't attached to no racket but even fools learned to keep their distances from his sharp tongue and sharp blade and it was only a matter of time before he caught the crooked eye of one of Morningside's heavyweight hustlers.

Now in the twenties, a cool breeze Italian known as Jonny

Numbers ran business all the way from the Heights to Tribeca. Of course his main bake was the numbers games, as his name suggests, but he had his fingers in so many pies that even the Catholic church was known to turn to him for help (what with God being so confused and all). Harlem, however, was a neighbourhood blackening all the time and it wasn't so long before the sharp negroes wanted a piece of the action to call their own; and top of that list was a terrifying character by the name of J Smart. Folk called him that because he spoke in a Jamaican accent and he surely was smart. Of course, after his death, acquaintances remembered him only as 'J'. And they didn't remember him for long and that's the truth.

It was J Smart who started a numbers racket of his own and it caused a stir round Harlem because even fool niggers knew that losing dollars to a negro was a whole lot classier way to be broke. And it must've been around the same time that J Smart took notice of a hard-nosed bush motherfucker called Naps.

At the time J Smart decided to have this grifter paid a visit, Naps was living in the Convent Avenue apartment with a six-out-seven young man known as Sweets, Harlem born and bred. But we won't go into that arrangement. Because we all knows how folk likes to give a story their own slant that tends to tell more about theirselves than no facts (and can't a funny guy make the worst joke catch a laugh?).

Simple truth is, when J Smart's heavies broke into Naps's apartment they were confronted by Sweets smoking an opium pipe on the floor as naked as the day he was born. If that stopped these two muscle brains in their tracks, it's nothing compared to the weight of the blows that rained down on them from behind as Naps beat them to shit with a metal chain. They didn't even get the chance to give their boss's greeting and you can bet that J Smart laughed at such a hangdog story from his best men before he gave those ugly booger bears a wupping of his own.

Course Naps's reaction to the surprise visit didn't discourage J Smart any from figuring this bush negro might be worthy of a job.

In fact, his cold thuggery encouraged the hustler better than any résumé and he resolved to pay a call to Naps in person.

J Smart entered the Convent Avenue apartment to find the smokestack sitting on the floor opposite, swigging from a bottle and puffing on a gage butt. In the far corner of the room Sweets was wrapped in a blanket with his eyes wide shut as he surfed an opiate wave. J Smart noticed that the young man had heavy bruising around his eye and he figured that this Naps character didn't reserve his violence for strangers. He stared right at Naps and Naps stared right on back. There was something disconcerting in his expression (even for a real tough guy like J Smart): a cut-loose, freefall kind of look; the kind of look that takes a punch and says, 'That all you got? I want more.'

Who knows? Maybe Naps had lost his mind by now. There's nobody left who can tell you anything about that brother no more. So we say, 'Who knows?' and we shrug it off without too much bother.

'What you want?' Naps asked.

'The name's J Smart.'

'So fuckin' what?'

'So you took care of two friends of mine.'

Naps eyed him creepily and swigged long from the bottle. J Smart took off his hat and smiled calmly. But he was feeling uneasy and he fingered the pistol in the pocket of his long coat.

'I run the numbers now,' J Smart said. 'Figure I could use a jig like you.'

'I won't be stayin' long in New York.'

'Figure you could use a jig like me,' J Smart continued, as if he hadn't heard. 'Figure any newcomer on his own in this big ol' city needs a friend or two, no doubt. An' me? I's a good friend to know. An' a bad enemy, if you catch my drift.'

Naps nodded. He caught J Smart's drift, all right. And, though he didn't much care, he needed to make a buck or two and fast.

'Sho',' Naps said. 'Then I guess I's your man.'

'I guess you are,' J Smart said and his smile widened. He turned to look at Sweets lying in the corner and he couldn't help but say something. 'What you doin' with that pip shooter?'

'Fuck you!' Naps exclaimed.

J Smart turned his head so slowly that Naps thought he must be dreaming. The hustler reached into his pocket and pulled out his pistol and cocked it in an instant. 'I kill niggers for less,' he said. 'So you owe me, Naps, you hear? You owe me.'

Now that he was staring down the barrel of a gun it was Naps's turn to smile, but it was a gritted, grimacing kind of expression: two parts madness to one part anger with a dash of bitterness and life on the rocks. 'I hear you,' he said.

When J Smart was gone, Naps dragged himself to his feet and stumbled over to Sweets's prone body. He buried his foot in the boy's gut and screamed 'motherfucker!' at the top of his voice. Then he tripped backwards on to the floor and lay with his eyes gaping for an hour or more. He was watching his own personal cinema, no doubt: pictures of Lick's final breath and the forlorn pleas of Johnny Frederick and all kinds of other horrors too. But nobody cared about Toothless Naps then any more than they do now. And don't bother arguing any because that's a matter of fact, not opinion.

Naps worked for J Smart as a numbers runner and he was sure good at his job. He may have lost his mind but it still functioned just fine and he could remember upwards of fifty combinations with no need to resort to paper and pencil. What's more, you reckon any debtor's going to spin a line to a crazy-ass grifter like Naps? Think again! There's never been no numbers racket run with such ruthless efficiency. And all the while he searched for Sylvie Black so hard that he could hardly remember the reason why.

Numbers and Sylvie. Sylvie and numbers. 48 – 23 – Sylvie. 56 – Sylvie – 16. Numbers numbers numbers. Sylvie Sylvie Sylvie.

And Naps didn't think about Lick Holden no more; about his dead eyes that arced to the ceiling, his last breath that tasted sweet on the tongue, his dark jibs that played God's own music. And Naps didn't think about Johnny Frederick no more; about his squealing like a pig for slaughter, begging like a weak-willed woman, the tears and the snot and the blood.

Sylvie and numbers. Numbers and Sylvie.

Of course the success of J Smart's racket didn't go unnoticed by the man called Jonny Numbers and you can bet he wasn't none too pleased. He called his most trusted hoods together and they agreed to hit this negro business hard and Naps was on the front line. Now we all remember who was working for Jonny Numbers back then, don't we? A young Italian-American who was supporting his brother's wife and kid after the brother got taken with TB the previous year. This mook didn't care much for his sister-in-law, nor the daughter called Bernadette (a good Catholic name), who surely had the word 'bastard' running through her like the lettering through a stick of rock. But Fabrizio Berlone wasn't going to disappoint his dead brother's memory any more than Naps would let down Lick Holden.

What was it that an old man once told his great-niece? 'It's a man's fate to die and a woman's to survive.'

Now any student of jazz music won't be surprised that it was Fabrizio Berlone that caught up with Toothless Naps. Because even improvisation has rules and, for all its heavy build, fate can improvise like the most nimble-fingered pianist. Sure the only surprise is that New York's finest should ever catch and convict a man for the crime (a testament to the stupidity of Fabrizio who bragged like a newly cured virgin).

The murder took place one dark night behind the cathedral of St John the Divine, in an alleyway where you could rent all manner of humanity for a spare buck. Of course Naps (who once had a way with words but now let his blade do the talking) could have taken Fabrizio with one hand tied behind his back. But that is an unfortunate metaphor considering the sexual indiscretion in which he was caught. And it is a humane rather than a poetic thought that Naps was as high as the Empire State when the knife slit his throat.

As his head hit the wall and the life flowed out of him like the Mississippi to the Gulf of Mexico, what do you figure? His brain counted down from fifty to one. The one called Sylvie. Black.

So fate spins its patterns like a spider spins a web. And a hornet scoffs until he's stuck fast and then he's too busy saying prayers to his maker to be cursing his bad luck. Most likely, a careless duster will take down that web before too long and fate will begin to spin again, in a similar corner of a similar room, a similar pattern but no two webs are ever the same. So we shake our heads at the story of Toothless Naps and we can't help but comment on fate's taste for an ironic twist. But humanity's begging you, though you don't hear it: don't restrict the untold story of a flawed hero to one meagre adjective. Please. Because the tale of Toothless Naps is the coda to the most beautiful twelve bar blues that Lick Holden ever played and it fills our guts with an emptiness to swell souls. And the horn hits that final note and it flattens it blue. And the song is ever incomplete and it leaves us wanting more.

Permissions